From above them, a cry went up. "It burns. The river burns — and the Wraith with them!"

This time, Teyla made no move to stop the Dalerans climbing the trees to witness for themselves. Indeed, she immediately pulled herself aloft and stared across the eastern fields. The sight was mesmerizing and more than satisfying. The entire eastern portion of South Channel was a blazing inferno. Lines of fiery serpents began to appear through the far fields, where the oil had flowed along irrigation channels. From this distance it was not possible to make out individuals, but she could see many smaller flames moving about, like the wicks of a hundred candles. Having stumbled into the oil, some of the Wraith had been set ablaze. The gruesome creatures had extraordinary regenerative properties, but it was doubtful if those caught in the fields of oil could survive such a sustained conflagration. The three vast columns of Wraith began to fall back.

Cries of joy traveled across the treetops, and Teyla felt a measure of relief. The battle to come would not be easy, but the people of Dalera were now empowered by the sight before them.

Ushat touched her arm. She took his Shield from him, and he signaled the warrior below to blow the trumpet. Reply calls from the Citadel told them that the EM fields close to North Bridge and the western end of the wall had also been disabled. Just before the roiling black smoke obscured her vision, she noticed the nearest column of Wraith headed in their direction.

"They come!" cried a lookout. At the speed the Wraith were moving, the first waves would soon be upon them — far sooner than Teyla had planned.

STARGATE
ATLANTIS™

THE CHOSEN

SONNY WHITELAW &
ELIZABETH CHRISTENSEN

FANDEMONIUM BOOKS

An original publication of Fandemonium Ltd, produced under license from MGM Consumer Products.

Fandemonium Books
PO Box 795A
Surbiton
Surrey KT5 8YB
United Kingdom
Visit our website: www.stargatenovels.com

STARGATE
ATLANTIS™

METRO-GOLDWYN-MAYER Presents
STARGATE ATLANTIS
JOE FLANIGAN   TORRI HIGGINSON   RACHEL LUTTRELL
RAINBOW SUN FRANCKS   and DAVID HEWLETT as Dr. McKay
Executive Producers BRAD WRIGHT & ROBERT C. COOPER
Created by BRAD WRIGHT & ROBERT C. COOPER

WWW.MGM.COM

ISBN: 0-9547343-8-6

Printed in the United Kingdom by Bookmarque Ltd, Croydon, Surrey

To Cody and Amber
—SW

To James
—EC

Thanks also to:

The cast and crew of Stargate Atlantis for creating such a fun world in which to play. Special thanks to David Hewlett, David Nykl, Torri Higginson, and Paul McGillion, all of whom took time out of their extraordinarily busy schedules to offer insight into their respective characters, and to my children, who sustained me with unending cuddles and chocolate fish.

—SW

Many, many thanks are due to Sonny, for being willing to take a chance on me, for her invaluable guidance along the way, and for being the most generous coauthor I could have imagined. Thanks also to Sabine, for instantly welcoming me into the fold; Sally and Tom, for trusting Sonny's judgment; my family, for their faith in me now and always; and my husband, for his endless support, understanding, and fantastic cooking.

—EC

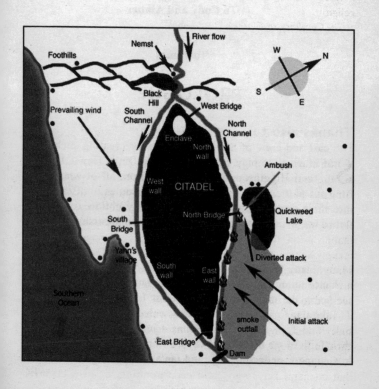

Any sufficiently advanced technology is indistinguishable from religion.
— *Corollary to Clarke's Third Law*

PROLOGUE

Somehow he felt just a little cheated. Sitting on the grass, the mid-afternoon sun warming his face and the breeze ruffling his hair, Major John Sheppard decided that this day was just about perfect in every way. The brilliant blue sky—ideal flying weather, the aviator in him noted idly—was completely inappropriate for the magnitude of the decision he was about to make. Storm clouds would have been more fitting, or at least something with a little less cheer and a little more drama. *Figures.* He allowed a wry grin to twist his lips. Unpredictability seemed to define his life.

Taking the road less traveled was one thing, but he was pretty sure Robert Frost had never considered that it might lead to another galaxy.

God, another *galaxy.* He still hadn't wrapped his mind around that concept. Days ago, he'd been minding his own business at McMurdo Station, secure in his view of the world: namely, that it was far from perfect but at least followed a rational set of rules. It was quiet, he was getting lots of stick time, and the environment, while hostile, didn't come with gun-toting inhabitants determined to blow him out of the sky. At least, that's what he'd thought until that freaky missile had fired at him. Then he'd taken a seat in that equally freaky chair, and everything that he'd thought he understood about the world had gone out the window.

It was an unparalleled opportunity, they'd all told him with the same expression of wide-eyed wonder. Travel instantly to another galaxy, explore the culture and technology of a race far more advanced than our own, and take a stab at defending Earth from a nasty fate. He was a strong natural carrier of the all-important gene. Think what they could do with his help. There was just that one tiny detail about possibly never coming home.

It surprised him that he wasn't more afraid of that prospect. Then again, he wouldn't exactly be leaving behind a stellar career and devoted family, and Antarctica was already about as close to an alien environment as he could imagine.

Still, another *galaxy?*

Leaning back against the hillside, John wondered if the idyllic weather was a sign. He dismissed the thought when he couldn't be certain if it was telling him to stay on Earth, where there were lovely sunny days, or to consider this 'opportunity' a step toward a brighter future. And because he couldn't interpret the potential omen and had no better luck interpreting his own turbulent thoughts, he returned to his original plan.

Years of special-operations flying had instilled in John a deep respect for mission planning. He'd chosen the site and the time of day, selected the unit coin, even checked the wind direction; though that might have just been his inner aviator again, hoping irrationally to get in one last flight before reporting to Cheyenne Mountain. He had planned out every last detail of this life-altering decision—then placed his future squarely in the hands of fate.

Tails meant returning to the status quo at McMurdo, where they got the football games on videotape a week late but at least no one asked him about Afghanistan. Heads meant a potential one-way trip through a big metal ring that would dump him out…somewhere else.

He stared hard at the coin, then flipped it into the air. It spun gracefully, the sunlight glinting off its face, and landed with a satisfying *smack* against his palm.

Tails.

Apparently fate was telling him to stick to his own galaxy.

And yet—what if they really didn't have anyone else with the same knack for operating that weird equipment? What if they somehow needed a pilot? What if, through some thoroughly unnatural confluence of events, that other world ended up giving him the sense of purpose he'd misplaced somewhere along the way?

No. He'd left the decision to fate, and fate had slapped him with tails. End of story.

And yet...

John Sheppard had never been particularly good at blind obedience. He shot the coin a look of contempt, then flipped it again—

CHAPTER ONE

CHAPTER ONE

"Heads!" Aiden Ford announced, his boyish features alight with triumph. "Victory is mine."

Teyla's brow creased. "What have you won, Lieutenant?"

"The last brownie." Pocketing the coin, Ford grabbed the desired treat and plunked it onto his tray. Stackhouse walked away with slumped shoulders.

"We still have brownies?" John Sheppard's eyebrows shot up as he settled into a seat at the nearest table.

"That was the last one."

"Damn."

"Yeah."

"Please tell me the defenders of our fine city aren't spending their time mourning the lack of desserts." Rodney McKay announced his arrival with a characteristic scoff.

After the waking nightmare that had been the storm and the concurrent Genii assault on Atlantis, they'd all gained a new sense of ownership, for lack of a better term, in this place. It *was* their home, damn it. They'd paid for it in every way imaginable. Right now, just being able to sit here and argue about dessert was enough to provoke a sensation of deep relief in John Sheppard. It was normal, and normalcy had been in short supply from day one.

"You're getting on *our* cases about provisions?" Ford looked indignantly across the table at Rodney. "After your little one-man melodrama with the coffee?"

"Do I need to explain the debilitating neurological effects of caffeine withdrawal again?" the scientist fired back.

"No," John cut in, glancing over at their Athosian teammate. "Teyla? A little mystified by this overdose of Earthly idiosyncrasy?"

Teyla looked grateful that someone had brought her back into the conversation. "I am still pondering this 'coin toss' Lieutenant Ford spoke of. It is a contest of some kind?"

Ford withdrew a coin from his pocket. "We generally use them as currency, but sometimes we use them to make a choice by tossing it in the air, and assigning a decision to whichever side lands face up."

"Would it not be more beneficial to weigh the positive and negative aspects of each option, rather than make a choice at random?"

"Well, yeah, but there are times when both options seem equally right, so you leave it to chance, fate."

"I see." Her tone suggested that she didn't. With long fingers, she plucked the medallion from the Lieutenant's hand and studied it. "The design is intricate."

"That's the symbol of my Marine division." Ford pointed to the crest. "There's a tradition that says if someone catches you without your unit coin on you, you have to buy them a drink."

"A drink?" Teyla cast a curious glance at him.

"Of alcohol, preferably," John elaborated, reaching for his glass of water. "But if there are any stills cropping up around here, Lieutenant, I don't want to know, because I'd have to put the responsible parties in my weekly report. And you know I like to keep those as short as humanly possible."

Ford's expression froze somewhere between a knowing grin and feigned innocence. A second or two passed before he opted for a change of subject. "You got a challenge coin, Major?"

"What? You thought it was just a Marine tradition?" John reached into his back pocket, withdrew a scratched silver coin, and handed it to his second in command.

"Special Ops. Cool," said Ford, reading the designator. "Bet you've got some hardcore stories to tell, huh, sir?"

On second thought, maybe that hadn't been such a bright idea. "Stories, yes — stories to tell, not so much."

"Because you can't say? Or because you don't want to?" The young man's expression betrayed his naïveté.

"Little of column A, little of column B." For John, part of the allure of the Pegasus Galaxy had been the fact that, here, his record wasn't nearly as remarkable—and not in a good way, either—as it was on Earth. He'd been happy to let the Marines believe that he was nothing more than a throttle-jockey, rank notwithstanding. His days of relative anonymity on that front were probably over, thanks to his star turn during the Genii attack. Now, there could be no denying his... What was the proper euphemism? Breadth of experience? The trail of dead Genii in his wake during the storm had seen to that.

Then there'd been the unrelenting *thud* of bodies striking the 'gate shield, one after another, until a rational person could no longer keep count.

Deliberately shoving that thought aside, John grabbed something that passed for a French fry off Rodney's tray before redirecting the conversation. "I used that to decide whether to come along on this little road trip."

"To *Atlantis*? You flipped a *coin*?"

John shrugged, choosing not to complicate the issue with details. Rodney, of all people, nodded understanding and pulled something from inside his jacket. "I keep a Loonie around for just such contingencies." He held it out to Teyla, pointing to the bird on the dollar's face. "This is legal currency in my home country, as opposed to whatever those two are carrying around."

Behind a tall glass of Athosian fruit juice, Ford was hiding a smirk.

The Canadian scientist made a great show of turning to him in mock curiosity. "I presume you have some brilliant play on words to share? Because, gosh, I've never heard a Loonie joke before."

"No, nothing." Ford made a valiant attempt to resist the urge to make a wisecrack, but ultimately failed. "It's just... Is that a Loonie in your pocket, or are you just happy—?"

John groaned and lightly smacked the back of the Marine's head. "A wide-open shot like that, and that's the best you can do? Not only are you banned from naming things, you're relieved of mocking duty."

"Yes, hilarious, Lieutenant. Did I miss your thirteenth birthday last week?" Rodney glared across the table at them both, but then his attention was diverted by a minor commotion. A huddle of three engineers, expressions running the gamut from irritatingly determined to determinedly irritated, strode into the mess hall.

"This oughta be good," John muttered to Ford.

As the trio neared the team's table, their back-and-forth chatter became audible. "I'm telling you, it wasn't the power surge. It was—"

"Yes, yes, we know. Something else. Helpful suggestion, that."

"Dr McKay," the female member of the gang began. "We've run into a problem with the life-support systems."

Regarding the three-person squad with mild interest, Rodney seized the last of his fries before John could sneak any more off the plate. "A little clarification goes a long way, people."

"The storm caused a lot of damage."

The remark had fallen casually from the engineer's lips. Damage. That was one way to put it. John cast a surreptitious glance at Rodney.

While the scientist's face didn't overtly change, he tugged unconsciously at the sleeve over his bandaged arm, legacy of a Genii-style interrogation. "As usual, I'm impressed by the collective talent this group has for understatement," he grumbled.

That sounded enough like Rodney's normal self for John's concern to fade somewhat. Normal was good. Hell, even fake normalcy was worth something, because eventually they'd start to believe it.

"Right," replied the engineer. "Well, with the city's help we were able to restore primary life-support power shortly after the storm. Problem is, there are facets of the system that the city doesn't consider crucial. Potable water is critical, for instance, but waste disposal apparently isn't. Hence, a few days' worth of waste, even with a group as small as ours, is beginning to strain the capacity of the storage tanks."

Of all the things that could cause problems on an intergalactic expedition, the possibility of clogged toilets had never entered John's mind. Eat your heart out, Buck Rogers.

"And this relates to me in what way?" Rodney wanted to know.

"Kwesi thinks that —"

"Kwesi thinks that he can speak for himself, thank you," another of the engineers cut in, his gentle Ghanaian accent sharpened by annoyance. "It takes someone with the ATA gene to make much of this technology work, Doctor. We believe that if you could interface with the city systems, you might convince it to rearrange its priorities."

Rodney still looked nonplussed, but John imagined that he could see a glint of something new there. Pride, maybe. Rodney had successfully received the gene therapy, and there was something to be said for being one of the select few to have the magic touch.

"As flattered as I am that you see my potential for a job in sanitation, the city seems to like the Major here better than me."

John's focus snapped fully into the conversation. He got the distinct impression that he'd just been volunteered for something. "Say what?"

"Well put, as always," Rodney muttered dryly.

"But you know the systems better than anyone, Doctor," countered the female engineer, whose name John still hadn't learned but whose skills at buttering up the boss apparently were top-notch.

"I suppose duty calls, then. I should have had overtime pay built into my contract." Rodney rose from the table. Mess hall tray clutched in his hands, he somehow managed to adopt an air of unwavering self-assurance. "Lead on."

The rest of the team followed, picking up their trays and carrying them to the cleanup area. Ford reached down to save his hard-won brownie and discovered it missing. He jerked his head up just in time to see Rodney pop the last bite into his mouth.

"Hey!"

"Don't disparage a man's national symbols or his coffee habits, Lieutenant." The astrophysicist's voice was entirely unapologetic.

John tried not to crack a grin at Ford's crestfallen look. This version of 'normal' felt a little forced. Still, it was a start.

The computer screen stared at her, blank faced and accusing, until Dr Elizabeth Weir gave in and leaned back in her desk chair, massaging her temples. The gritty sensation behind her eyes warned her that she might be coming down with something. She told herself that it was probably just stress brought on by recent events. Nevertheless, she made a mental note to have one of the engineering teams analyze the city's biohazard containment capabilities. While they'd brought HAZMAT gear with them, it would be good to know what facilities the Ancients might have installed in the city. One never knew what new pathogens lurked in this galaxy.

That small seed of data fell into a jumbled pile with all the others she'd collected over the past months. Precious few were finding an appropriate place to take root. There was so much to be done, so much to be learned. It was far more than they could possibly grasp in a lifetime — even if they weren't stumbling into adversaries every other day. What had begun as an expedition to the lost city of Atlantis had almost immediately turned into a continuous battle for survival; against man, beast and nature, often simultaneously.

Had she honestly expected any less? When SG-1 had first stepped through the Stargate years earlier, they had opened the proverbial Pandora's Box. That Atlantis was presenting similarly daunting challenges should have come as no surprise.

During her brief tenure as head of Stargate Command back on Earth, Elizabeth had learned that some enemies were, as Daniel Jackson had pointed out, pure evil. The Wraith might or might not be evil, but they assuredly were vicious predators to whom humans were nothing more than food. How was a person bred for diplomacy meant to face an opponent with whom there could be no negotiation?

A knock on her door interrupted her thoughts. Probably just as well, despite the fact that she hadn't yet managed to write word one of her report on the events of the past week. "Yes?" She looked up, an expectant smile firmly, if artificially, tacked in place, to see the tousled dark hair of Major John Sheppard.

"Hey." His smile was cautious, not quite reaching his eyes. "You busy?"

"No! No. Come in, John." She stood and walked around to the front of the desk. "Actually, you're just who I wanted to see. It occurred to me that I never thanked you for taking down Kolya. I've never had my life saved quite so…directly before."

The Major seemed to shrug off her gratitude. "Had to make sure I didn't get stuck with all your paperwork." He eased into the room and the glass door slid shut behind him. "How're you doing?"

His gaze remained guarded, betraying the weight of the obviously loaded question. Elizabeth didn't take offense at his concern. During her years negotiating peace agreements, she had encountered more than her fair share of moral lepers, people who regarded the lives of others with no more compassion than she gave to the contents of a trashcan. She'd seen that same look in Kolya's eyes, heard that same tone in his voice when he'd held her and Rodney captive. Before, though, she had always seen such things from a distance. With Kolya, she'd been close enough to feel the coldness.

Gesturing for the Major to take a seat, she leaned back against the desk. "I just wish it could have gone another way."

"Listen —"

"I know!" She held up her hand. "I know that the Genii attacked us first. I know they've been deceptive from the start. It's just that they're not Wraith. They're human, and the Wraith are far greater enemies — to both of us. It's such a waste for us to be fighting one another."

"Is that how you think it works?" John asked with a humorless chuckle. "In your experience, have people ever been all that great at setting aside their differences and working together in the face of a common foe?"

Taken aback by his uncharacteristically acerbic tone, Elizabeth examined John more carefully. She'd wanted him on this expedition because he carried the Ancient Technology Activation gene, and more significantly, used it without any apparent effort. Just as importantly, he'd enjoyed working with the highly individualistic people in the confined and hostile environment of McMurdo Station. Military background notwithstanding, Major John Sheppard had proven to be a surprisingly good diplomat; perhaps better than any of them, herself included. If anything, he'd seemed almost too trusting, too friendly—until they'd encountered the Genii.

The surgical precision with which he'd systematically taken out each of the attacking Genii, the way he'd aimed at Kolya and fired without a second thought... She could still feel the hot whine of the bullet as it sped past her ear. Her very next memory was of him offering her a hand and asking her if she was okay. With sudden insight, Elizabeth realized that, despite his professionalism, what set John Sheppard apart from men like Kolya was the way he reacted to killing.

Wondering if he himself could see that distinction, she said, "I'm trying to tell myself that we can't hold ourselves responsible for the Genii's actions. It was their choice to see us as an enemy. Likewise, if you're still rethinking your decision to close the shield, please don't. Yes, a lot of their soldiers died, but you and I both know what they were coming here to do."

He cast a sharp glance in her direction, but a knock at the door cut the metaphorical thread. Peter Grodin was looking through the glass panel. She considered asking him to wait, but his excitement was obvious. Opening the door, Elizabeth stood back for him to enter. "Yes, Peter?"

"Dr Weir!" he declared. "I think I've found one." Peter's eyes darted to Sheppard. "Sorry, Major. Am I interrupting?"

"One what?" said John, standing.

Feeling a surge of anticipation, Elizabeth replied, "I asked Peter to work backward through the database, to locate the worlds most recently visited by the Ancients before the city was placed under siege."

"Before they accepted the possibility that the Wraith might defeat them?" John's interest was obviously tweaked.

"Of course they could still have visited those worlds via the Stargate, even after Atlantis had been submerged," Peter explained as they left the office and crossed the walkway to the control room. "We assumed that, by then, they would have been concentrating their resources on defending Atlantis. If the Ancients were forced to abandon outlying worlds in a hurry, they might have left a ZPM behind, one that's only ten to fifteen thousand years old. Which is exactly what appears to have happened with P3Y-986. Here, come and have a look."

Peter moved in front of the large flat-screen monitor mounted on a panel behind the DHD, and tapped the screen. "The Ancient database indicates that the Stargate is in orbit around the planet."

"We still don't know why they placed certain 'gates in orbit," said Elizabeth.

"Quarantine?" The Major's brow creased, and he rubbed the side of his neck where the *iratus* bug had been attached. "Having a 'gate in orbit would've restricted travel to space ships."

"That's a reasonable assumption." Elizabeth nodded. "We can send a MALP through. That would tell us for certain."

"Why don't I just take a puddle jumper? We can't afford to keep losing MALPs."

"I agree with that," Elizabeth said, looking at him. "But we can less afford to lose you if there's a Wraith ship—or worse—waiting on the other side."

"Fair enough," he said slowly, his smile suggesting a compromise. "How about we get the puddle jumper ready, then send a MALP through ahead of it? If it looks okay, we go, recover the MALP and—"

"How can anyone be so stupid?" demanded a loud, familiar voice.

Elizabeth's enthusiasm was tempered by resigned amusement—which quickly turned to distaste. Leading a delegation of three extremely angry people in her direction was Dr Rodney McKay. At least, it was someone who walked and sounded like him, but it was hard to be certain because he was—

"Having a crappy day, Rodney?" John quipped, keeping his distance but looking remarkably cheerful.

The sight and smell of raw sewage wasn't new to Elizabeth; she'd spent plenty of time in dirt-poor villagers in third world countries. But seeing Rodney literally covered in effluent, stomping across the pristine floor of the control room, was so bizarre that she had to stop herself from laughing.

"Oh, yes, biohazards are a laugh riot, aren't they?" When

it came to sarcasm, Rodney existed on a wholly separate level from anyone else she'd ever known.

"Well, it was your suggestion to try it!" declared one of the equally filthy people accompanying him.

"You could have at least warned me!"

The argument gained volume. From what Elizabeth could make out, it sounded like some sort of explosion was involved, but beyond that, the details seemed to be in the eye of the beholder. "All right, everyone. Calm down," she called. "Now, is anyone hurt?"

"Calm down!" Rodney spluttered. "Calm *down*? It's not enough that I'm probably going to catch pneumonia because some lunatic forced me to work outside in the middle of a hurricane. Do you have any idea of the number of pathogens that inhabit a septic tank? If just one of the billions, *billons*, of bacteria gets inside this cut—" He pointed to his arm. "Rampant septicemia. That's it," he added conclusively. "I'm gone!"

"Why don't you go get cleaned up and have Carson check you over before we discuss what happened?" Elizabeth suggested.

Rodney's expression managed to turn haughty, quite a feat considering the brown sludge on his face. "Because I wanted you to see with your own eyes—"

"Okay, Rodney," she replied in a well-practiced pacifying tone. "I can see."

"And smell," John added, ever helpful.

Behind them, half a dozen people snickered. Elizabeth did her level best to ignore them. "Now, was anyone else…injured in this explosion?"

"No, but that's beside the point. This is just one more example of—"

"Ah!" Elizabeth wrinkled her nose and motioned in the direction of the living quarters.

The arguing group, still led by Rodney, made its way out of the control room, although the noisome smell lingered.

"Well, that ought to make him the butt of a few more jokes," John said.

The sniggers in the control room were louder. Elizabeth shot him a reproachful look. "Try not to aggravate him too much, Major. He's been through a lot lately. We all have."

The Major's expression conceded the point. Turning his attention back to the screen, he gestured toward the symbols on the display. "So, you want us to go take a look?"

"Why don't you wait until tomorrow morning? That'll give Rodney time to get cleaned up and calmed down." At the Major's look of uncertainty, she added, "Do you have a problem with that?"

"No. McKay can be a pain in the ass — and no, I didn't mean that as a joke — but he's got his uses."

Unless she was mistaken, John Sheppard was beginning to like the scientist. "All right. In the meantime, I'll go talk to Rodney, find out what happened."

"The cut is healing well, and it's clean." Carson Beckett, the biologist and chief physician of the expedition, pulled his gloves off. "No sign of infection."

"Regardless, I'm absolutely certain that I'm coming down with the flu." Rodney sniffed theatrically and looked around the rooms that had become the research laboratory and infirmary.

"I very much doubt that," Carson said, giving Elizabeth a long-suffering glance. "Every member of the Atlantis expedition underwent a thorough medical examination before stepping through the Stargate. You can't catch a cold from thin air. It's probably one of your many allergies. I'll give you an antihistamine."

"Now, Rodney," Elizabeth asked. "What happened?"

Rolling down the sleeve of his jacket, Rodney exhaled loudly before launching into a tirade. "Most of Atlantis's systems are either self-regulating or can be operated with the push of a button. Once the Wraith became a serious threat, the Ancients apparently employed gene recognition technology to protect crucial systems like weapons and life-support. So, only those with the ATA gene, or in my case, where the gene therapy has been successful, can access critical life-support operations."

No doubt he assumed that the conclusion he'd drawn from

that to be obvious, but it took Elizabeth a moment before she could even hazard a guess at it. "Are you suggesting that not everyone should be given the gene therapy in case they inadvertently trigger something dangerous?" That didn't feel quite right. Rodney was an intellectual elitist, but he had limits.

"That is in fact the polar opposite of what I'm suggesting," Rodney declared, rearing up off the stool in order to pace the room. "Every time somebody wants an Ancient device activated, or a secure door opened, they come running to me, as if I had nothing better to do with my time. If everyone had the gene therapy, they could open the damned doors themselves. Life-support isn't as crucial as it was when the city was hundreds of feet underwater."

As usual, his theory made a good amount of sense. Turning to Carson, Elizabeth asked, "How's the research on the gene therapy coming?"

The doctor gave a small shrug. "From what I can tell so far, it's going to be effective in a little less than half of everyone who receives it. And we're still not entirely certain of the long term risks."

"All right, then," Elizabeth replied. "We'll work out a roster system so that those with the ATA gene, natural or otherwise, only need make themselves available for a few hours each week. Think of it as being on call."

"How's that going to help if someone decides to wait until it's my turn to, oh, I don't know, open a trapdoor into a recycling plant?" Rodney turned to Carson. "Isn't there something you can do to make the gene therapy more effective? Rain dances? Sacrifices to the DNA gods?"

"I'm working on a way to efficiently produce large quantities of the vaccine, Rodney, but you can't rush these things." Carson's frustration with him was evident.

Exchanging a look with the beleaguered doctor, Elizabeth eased toward the door. "Rodney, Major Sheppard is taking a team to P3Y-986 in the morning."

"If this is another trade delegation—"

"We think it might have at a ZPM. A more recent one."

Rodney suddenly looked interested. "As I was saying, excellent idea."

"And Major Sheppard made a point of asking if you'd be ready to participate." Close enough to the truth, she reasoned.

"He did?" A surprised smile appeared on Rodney's face, masked quickly by confidence. "Well, of course he did. Leaving aside my myriad talents, he's no doubt assumed — correctly, I might add — that he's got some work to do to get back on my good side, what with the mocking and all."

"Just check in with Peter after you're finished here, and we'll get started on the pre-mission planning." Elizabeth ran a hand across the back of her neck as she exited the infirmary. The day's events had already left her drained. Maybe Carson was right about the flu, but she definitely felt like she was coming down with something.

CHAPTER TWO

Lieutenant Aiden Ford studied the planet looming above the jumper's windscreen. Almost three quarters of the blue-green world was in daylight, while the rest was blanketed by a nighttime shadow. Odd angle notwithstanding, he had to admit that P3Y-something-or-other looked pretty from several thousand miles out. Sort of like Earth, except that there was just one landmass.

"Would it be too much to ask if you could keep us upright?" McKay griped.

"We're in space," Major Sheppard replied, maneuvering the jumper behind the MALP with careful precision. "There's no such thing as 'upright'. You're gonna have to get used to that if you want to learn to fly one of these things outside an atmosphere." He allowed the probe to touch the sloped face of the jumper with just enough force to halt its forward momentum. "Okay, dial her up."

The vortex shot out of the orbiting Stargate then snapped reassuringly back into place. "Atlantis, Jumper One," McKay called. "Ready to receive the MALP?"

"Go ahead, Jumper One."

Aiden watched his commanding officer make just the tiniest motion with his hand. The jumper came to a stop, while the MALP continued through the rippling blue event horizon at a slight angle relative to their point of entry.

"MALP received. Good luck, Jumper One." With that send-off, the event horizon vanished.

"That was skillfully done, Major," Teyla said.

Until then, Aiden hadn't realized that he'd been holding his breath. He had every confidence in the Major's ability to pilot the jumper, and in any case a lot of it was automatic. But the 'gate-in-space thing still kind of freaked him out. Getting stuck in one hadn't been a whole lot of fun, and he really didn't want a replay.

Sheppard gave a noncommittal shrug. "I just hope I didn't dent the fender."

"On this thing?" McKay said dismissively. "The jumpers have been demonstrated to be more or less indestructible. Not that I want to give them a stress test."

"I meant the MALP. If it landed hard on the 'gate room floor, you know that'll be coming out of my paycheck." Sheppard stretched his arms up over his head and cracked his knuckles. "You're up, Rodney. Do your thing."

McKay set his hands on the console to manipulate the craft's sensors. "The troposphere extends about twenty-four kilometers above the surface. Let's start at eighteen kilometers up."

"Eleven miles it is," the Major replied amiably. The conversion earned a huff of annoyance from McKay, which Aiden suspected was what Sheppard had intended. "What kind of scanning range have you got?"

"Plenty. We shouldn't have to do too many orbits to cover the majority of the planet. Your role at present is simply to set us on a stable course. Of course, I suppose there's no reason why I can't do that myself—" McKay reached out to touch the panel, only to have his hand knocked aside by a glaring Sheppard.

"Okay," said the Major, with exaggerated patience. "You've tried this once with the training wheels on, so good for you, but you're not getting your mitts on a jumper in space until you've had a proper lesson."

"And what wisdom do you have to impart that I haven't already heard and mastered?" McKay wanted to know. "Straight and level—wasn't that pretty much all there was to it?"

"As we just talked about, Rodney, things work a little differently in space."

"I suppose you were an astronaut before coming to Atlantis?"

"No, but I do know enough about flying to perform a positive exchange of controls." Sheppard fixed him with a stern look that suggested this lesson was non-negotiable. "It goes like this: the pilot in command says 'You have the controls,' and the other pilot repeats 'I have the controls.' Then, and only then, does he touch something. End of lesson."

The scientist's eyes narrowed. "This is yet another way of attempting to make me subservient to your authority, right? Real pilots don't actually go through that rigmarole."

"We sure as hell do—otherwise you can get conflicting control inputs, and that's how bad days get started."

"Fine, fine." McKay retracted his hand. With a quiet grumble that might or might not have included the word 'tyrant,' he turned his full attention to the readouts in front of him. "The 'gate appears to be in a geostationary orbit. I'd imagine that any civilization is located not far beneath us. That is, of course, if you're willing to accept the term 'beneath', given that it's space and all. Not much in the way of higher life forms yet... Hold that thought."

"Have you found a native populace?" Teyla asked.

"Possibly. There's a concentrated group of life signs down that way." McKay pointed to the edge of a large land mass. "Assuming the planet rotates in the same direction as Earth, then it's just after dawn. It's the only reading I'm getting, so I suggest heading in that direction."

"You're the boss."

The jumper's flight path arced toward the indicated heading. McKay hunched over his readouts, his eyes crinkling in concentration. "I'd definitely call that a civilization. Thousands of distinct life signs, organized mostly among a set of structures perched on a basalt outcrop near the coast. In fact—" He fell silent while his fingers skipped over the console to call up a graphic on the head-up display. The screen showed groups of the white dots they'd come to recognize as human life signs hovering in and around a city-sized cluster of buildings. Though mostly contained within a massive encircling wall, other life signs were scattered in groups along the coastline and the countryside.

The sensors' magnification capabilities were impressive, and McKay made good use of them. Except for one leafy area about the size of a football stadium, it looked to Aiden like the city had been carved out of the surrounding black rock. The buttressed walls of buildings were interconnected, with powerful, massive turrets melding it all into an imposing structure.

"Check it out." Sheppard pointed to the monumental stonework and wide, sturdy walls. "This place was designed to take a pounding."

McKay shook his head in undisguised awe. "If whatever society exists here is as archaic as some of that architecture looks, the sheer magnitude of all this is incredible."

"Sorta like a cross between a monastery and a gigantic castle, surrounded by the Great Wall of China," Aiden observed. For once, no one ridiculed his description.

"Complete with outer ramparts and— You gotta be kidding. Is that a moat?" The Major pointed to the display.

"It appears that a river has been diverted to flow around both sides of the hill," McKay replied. "That was a startlingly bright move. Fresh water would be available at all times, even under a prolonged siege."

"There's more here than just the city." Aiden leaned forward in his seat to examine the countryside and coastline now coming into view through the window. The land was dotted with farms and, where life signs were concentrated, villages. He couldn't be certain from this height, but the objects in the harbor looked like they might have been boats. "Think they have much left over from when the Ancients were here?"

"Doesn't look like the kind of thing the Ancients would go for." Sheppard indicated the heavily fortified hill structure. "You'd only build something like this if you're expecting a ground assault on a huge scale. Thing is, if this is the only civilization around, which sure looks likely going by the life signs, who'd be doing the attacking?"

"Everyone battles the Wraith," Teyla said.

"Not like this. So far in our experience, the Wraith don't come knocking on your front door. They strike from the air."

"Maybe there were other civilizations," Aiden ventured. "You know, in the past—"

"Hang on." McKay interrupted, squinting at the screen. "Now

that's interesting."

Aiden wondered if this was the kind of 'interesting' that involved some cool new tech or the kind that involved pissed-off natives taking target practice at them.

McKay, fortunately, wasn't one to leave anything unsaid for long. "I'm getting some strong electromagnetic readings from the city. They just popped up, and they're very patchy. Don't descend any further," he snapped.

"Why not?" Aiden asked.

"Because if we cross paths with one of those EM spikes, it's another M7G-677."

That reference was met with a blank stare from the Major.

"Really, how taxing is it to remember a simple six-digit identifier? The place with the marginally more civilized version of Lord of the Flies."

Aiden was none the wiser. "I don't get it."

McKay shot him an exasperated look. "Children? Bows and arrows? The jumper doing its best impression of a glider? Would you like me to find a nice crayon and draw you a picture, Lieutenant?"

"Okay, kiddies, don't make me turn this car around," Sheppard warned, leveling off at about ten thousand feet. "Where's the EM field originating?"

"There's no central point of origin. They're separate fields. The layout is mostly random, although largely concentrated over the western and southern sides of the city and immediate countryside." McKay looked even more skeptical than usual. "If this is meant to be a protective shield, it's a lousy design."

"Offending your obsessive-compulsive tendencies?"

Poised to retort, McKay didn't see Teyla stiffen, but Aiden did. "Major, Doctor," he broke in, glancing over at his teammate.

Sheppard turned in his seat and frowned. "Teyla, what's up?"

Sitting straight-backed, the Athosian lifted a hand toward the screen. "There is something else."

The sensors showed a separate inorganic item just a few miles from the fortified southern wall. Composed of a different material than the structures, it sat perched in a field not far from one of the larger coastal villages. Its shape struck a familiar discordant note in Aiden's memory. He smothered a curse. "That's a Wraith Dart."

A look of profound sadness crossed Teyla's face. Aiden shot her a questioning glance.

"Each time I travel through the Stargate to a place that I have not yet visited," she explained, "I hold within me a seed of hope that we will find a world, just one, which the Wraith have not touched."

Well, *that* was a shiny, happy thought to start the mission.

"Is it a complete set, or is the Wraith sold separately?" The Major directed the question not to McKay, but to Teyla.

She shook her head. "I sense no life, but then, we are some distance away."

"It's dead," McKay confirmed. "Not even a blip of energy coming off that thing. It must have met up with one of the EM fields."

"It wasn't the only one. Take a look." Aiden tipped his head toward the windscreen. Scattered around the plowed fields were fully a dozen Darts. Each looked to have been the victim of a crash landing.

"I have never seen such a display," Teyla said in surprise. "Is it possible that these people have found a way to defend themselves against a Wraith attack?"

Sheppard surveyed the wreckage and gave a low whistle. "All right, color me impressed. For a lousy design, they're doing all right for themselves."

McKay seemed to be working on convincing the sensor to record the data it was rapidly generating. "This Picasso-inspired checkerboard strategy wouldn't stop everything. The law of averages dictates that a number of the Darts would find the unshielded areas, either through skill or blind luck."

"But it did knock a bunch of them down." The Major's expression conveyed a kind of appreciation. "Once on the ground, the Wraith's advantage would be seriously cut down. Would their stunners even work within the shield?"

"No, of course not, and the shields would repel any blasts fired into it from the outside. As I said, it's like M7G-677."

"And that's where the fortifications come in. I've gotta say, as tactics go, this isn't half bad." Sheppard brought the image of a ruined Dart up on the screen. "I want to get a look inside one of those things. Anything we can learn about their style of offense will help us play better defense."

Judging by the lack of griping about sports metaphors, McKay must not have heard the Major's last comment. "No thanks to those oh-so-adorable little demon children, I discovered that the EM field on M7G-677 harnesses that planet's unique magnetic field. Assuming these considerably smaller shields operate on a similar principle—" He tapped his finger at the patchy network visible on the display. "I can use the differences between the planets' respective magnetic fields to recalibrate a smaller shield to suit any planet. If it could then be scaled up to cover an area the size of, say, Atlantis—"

"It'd take a lot more power than we've got," Aiden finished.

"Yes, obviously. But these people seem to have the power available, so that's all the more reason to find out where they're getting it."

Teyla looked uncomfortable. "We should introduce ourselves before intruding on these people's land. We may mistakenly violate their customs if we act without making our intentions known."

The scientist shifted his gaze to her, as though he hadn't considered the possibility. She explained, "We have more to gain from being open with them at the outset. There is much farmland here and their boats are no doubt employed for fishing. In addition to technology, we may also have the opportunity to trade for food."

"Makes sense to me." The Major called up a topographical map on the display. "All right, McKay, how about finding us an area not protected by the EM fields that's relatively close to both a Dart and one of the villages?"

"As always, your wildly improbable wish is my command." After only a few moments, though, McKay stabbed a finger at a coastal village. "Try there."

"You'll warn me if I'm getting too close to the shield this time, right?"

"Have you always been such a nervous driver?"

"It's just gonna be a little hard going back for a repair kit with the Stargate in orbit." He headed west toward the nearby mountains, cloaking the jumper as they went.

"You're going the wrong way." McKay looked confused.

"Just taking a quick look around. I like to eyeball the landscape on my way in."

It was a subtle euphemism for reconnaissance, and that idea suited Aiden fine. Until last week, he had pegged Major Sheppard to be a decent superior officer with a typical flyboy attitude. No one would mistake him for a Marine, to be sure, and Aiden had heard enough scuttlebutt about his record to understand why Colonel Sumner hadn't been too thrilled about having him on the expedition. But after the damage that Sheppard had inflicted on the Genii, there wasn't a Marine on Atlantis who hadn't gotten the picture and fast. More than anyone, Aiden now understood that the Major's glib remarks camouflaged the mindset of an experienced tactician.

Capped with snow, the mountain range glinted in the early morning sun. "Air's clean," McKay observed, his nose still buried in the sensors. "Pre-industrialized society, at best, although there is a lingering trace of air pollutants. It's likely that they went through a more developed phase between Wraith cullings, which would explain the construction of the city."

The jumper's inertial dampeners took some of the fun out of it, but it was still a rush, zipping between the peaks low and fast. They abruptly exited into a wide valley, and the Major took them down to about five hundred feet. Spread out before them were patchy woodlands. Here and there, narrow roads bisected meadows of wildflowers and fields cultivated with what looked like orchard trees and newly planted crops.

"There's a house." Aiden pointed to a thatched stone bungalow. In a nearby field grazed some animals. He couldn't make out the details, but they looked like large sheep, or maybe goats.

"Place sure seems nice."

"Hmm?" McKay finally looked up from the sensors. Eying another of the farms with suspicion, he added, "Very quaint. If we get dragged into a harvest celebration, so help me, I refuse to be held responsible for whatever reaction I might exhibit."

"I think it's a little early for that. There are still patches of snow in some of the ravines."

"Whoa. That's…imposing," said Sheppard.

They had turned out of the valley onto a long, rolling plain dotted with more farms and woodlands that extended to the nearby coast. But that wasn't what had drawn the Major's attention. When he realized what *had*, Aiden almost gaped.

If it had been impressive from fifty thousand feet, from this angle the hill fortress, city, or whatever, looked awesome. Spread across an area slightly smaller than Manhattan, the hill jutted at least five hundred feet above the surrounding plain. A lot of the buildings had definitely been carved from the rock, with piecemeal additions constructed later from the same material. It was a Frankenstein kind of architecture, but damn if it didn't look sturdy. "Sure wouldn't want to have to lead a ground assault on the place. It'd take some serious ordnance just to make a dent in it."

"Don't go any further than that clump of trees." McKay warned, pointing to an area about a mile away from the wreckage of a Dart.

They got their first view of the natives while on approach to land. "There are many people hurrying along the paths," Teyla said. "They appear to be traveling from several directions."

"Life sign detector is telling me the same thing," McKay verified. "Hundreds of them, all rushing toward a handful of villages."

Aiden pulled his eyes from the Darts and looked around. "Maybe they're late for church?" the Major remarked, slowing the jumper to a halt. "I'm going to park in this gully. Less chance of someone tripping over us."

The moment the jumper settled, Aiden was out of his seat and pulling on his pack. He grabbed his P-90, flicked off the safety and, exchanging a quick look with Sheppard, stood just inside the rear hatch as it opened.

No sign of life, except for a couple of the sheep-type things on the grassy slope of the gully. The animals lifted their heads and stared at him a moment, then went back to grazing.

Once outside, Aiden heard a deep, low noise that rose in pitch, then tapered off. "Wonder what that is?" The same sound echoed in the distance.

"Its sound is similar to the horns that my people use to signal one another when hunting," Teyla said, joining him. She pulled her jacket close against the icy chill carried by the wind. "Perhaps it would explain why the inhabitants are making for the villages."

"Yeah, but what's the hurry?" Aiden wondered.

"Okay," said Sheppard, powering down the jumper and checking its cloaking device. "We head for the village and find out."

Aiden watched with some amusement as McKay struggled with his overloaded pack. "You did say that our powered equipment isn't going to work under the shields, didn't you?"

"Yes, but we won't always *be* under the EM fields, will we?" snapped the scientist. "Be prepared, isn't that the Marine motto?"

"That's the Boy Scouts."

"Ah. Close enough."

Before Aiden could fire off a stinging reply, the Major shot him a warning look. Rank sure had its privileges. McKay's self-importance was generally more entertaining than annoying, but taking a man's hard-won, *real chocolate* brownie was no laughing matter. Neither was disparaging the Corps.

Although the sun was up, they were still in the shadow of the fortress, and the air had that fresh, dewy smell to it — with a tang of salt that Aiden recognized from his time on Atlantis. Crickets or their native equivalent chirped, while a few birds chattered in the branches. In the near distance, he could hear the sound of surf. Everything seemed peaceful enough, except for the periodic, insistent sound of horns. "I think the loudest call is coming from the village," Aiden said.

"How perceptive of you." McKay promptly stepped up to his ankle in what presumably were sheep droppings, except that they had the size and consistency of wet cow patties.

Aiden didn't try to refrain from laughing.

They reached the trail a few minutes later. Too narrow to be a road, the lack of wheel ruts in the sandy soil told Aiden that the path must be a wide foot track. It wound through a few stumpy dune trees and emerged in the outskirts of the village, only a few hundred yards away. From the opposite direction came the sounds of people running through the forest, crying and shouting hysterically. He readied his weapon at precisely the same moment as his commanding officer.

"That doesn't sound good," the Major observed, then jerked back as a figure sprinted past them toward the village. He stepped off the path and motioned for them to take cover behind some bushes.

"Oh, that's fantastic," McKay groused, floundering around in the branches. "I think I've just encountered this world's version of brambles. With my luck, it'll probably be industrial-strength poison ivy."

Dozens of people burst over the top of the rise. Dressed in simple tunics and thick hide boots held in place by leather thongs, they looked like farmers and hunters. Overhead, a flock of startled birds took to wing. The Major turned, and Aiden followed his gaze. Running behind them through the trees, also headed to the village, were still more people. All of them had the same look of dread that Aiden had seen on the Athosians' faces the night the Wraith had struck. The tension in his stomach ratcheted up several more notches.

"They attack!"

Women clutching terrified children and heavily bearded men carrying axes flooded past on either side of the team. They didn't look like the sort of people who'd normally run from much of anything.

"*Who* is attacking?" McKay asked no one in particular. "Not us, right?"

No one replied. Aiden had seen enough frightened mobs in his time to know that this one probably hadn't even noticed them. Just in front of him, someone stumbled, dropping a burlap bag, while another person appeared to go down. A woman stooped to recover the bag, but the man with her shouted, "Leave it. There is no time. They come!"

The horns continued to blow. People pushed past Aiden, knocking him aside in their desperate flight. Unless they went with the flow, the four team members were in serious danger of being trampled. He looked to the Major, who was shouting something and pointing to a rocky outcrop. The crowds, now screaming unintelligibly, seemed to be skirting around it. Following Teyla, Aiden made his way across the growing surge of humanity.

McKay's self-preservation skills had kicked in fast. By the time Aiden reached the rocks, the scientist was already clambering up the side, yelling, "Where the hell did all of these people come from?"

"I'm more worried about what's following them," Sheppard shouted back.

"Of course," McKay declared loudly. "It's these patchy EM fields. The life signs intermittently vanish and reappear once people emerge from the shields' umbrella."

Teyla reached the top of the outcrop ahead of Aiden, and looked down at the living tide. "They are searching the sky."

"Wraith!" Aiden declared, hauling himself up. He looked out across the ocean, half expecting to see a swarm of Darts headed in their direction. Instead, all he noted was a bunch of large wooden boats tied up in the harbor.

Sheppard rounded on the Athosian. "Teyla?"

A slight frown marred her features, but she seemed more puzzled than concerned. "I feel nothing," she declared.

The crowds had tapered off until only stragglers, mostly the elderly, panting and struggling with their few meager possessions, hurried by. A long, keening cry came from a ditch off to one side of the path. Something was alive down there. Without hesitation Aiden jumped off the rock and went to investigate.

A young woman—a girl, really, probably around sixteen—was

desperately trying to bury herself in leaves and twigs. Aiden briefly glanced back to see the rest of his team coming up behind him. Dropping to one knee beside the girl, he said, "Hey, you need help?"

Her pallid features were contorted with pain and abject terror. "My leg." A flash of confusion crossed her face when her eyes took in his clothes, but it didn't distract her from her plea. "They are coming, and I cannot run!"

"Someone probably knocked her down," McKay observed needlessly. "The same thing almost happened to me. Thankfully, I had the presence of mind to — "

Ignoring him, Teyla stepped down into the sandy ditch, quickly brushed aside the leaves, and gently ran her hands along the girl's leg. Unlike the sturdy looking footware of the people who had been running, this child's hide boots were thin and patchy. Teyla quickly unwound the leather bindings. "I believe one of the bones below the knee may have been broken."

Aiden pulled off his pack, intending to take a splint from his med kit. The girl clutched at his sleeve. "Please! We have little time before the Wraith come. We must get to the inn!"

"I still sense nothing." Teyla glanced up at the Major. "If we attempt to move her leg before it is immobilized, the damage will be great."

Stragglers continued to stumble along the path, breathless but doggedly determined. None stopped to offer help, although one or two cast a sympathetic look in their direction.

"Perhaps they have some kind of early warning system?" McKay theorized, looking around nervously.

Sheppard scanned the area. His eyes settled on the village. "If there is protection there, it'd be closer than heading back to the jumper."

"Whoa, hold on a minute!" McKay objected. "If by protection you mean the EM field, let's use some basic common sense here. With or without their energy weapons, I don't really care to enter into yet one more running battle with God knows how many Wraith attacking from every direction."

"If they're even coming," Sheppard retorted, glancing at Teyla.

"Lieutenant? How long before you get that splint in place?"

"Not long, sir." This, at least, was something he was trained to do. Aiden swallowed hard and went to work, ignoring the girl's screams and scrabbling hands. A busted leg hurt like hell.

Teyla was trying to reassure the girl with gentle words. "What is your name?"

"Lisera," she supplied between cries. "Please stop. It hurts so much!"

"Almost done." Aiden tightened the splint. "It's not perfect, but it should do 'till we get back to the jumper."

"The inn," Lisera whimpered. "Not far. Please!" Her face was pale with shock and her eyes were imploring. "We must get there in time."

"Teyla?" said Sheppard again, his gaze on her intense.

Pursing her lips, Teyla hesitated before replying, "Perhaps it is as Dr McKay says. These people may have a distant warning system."

The horn blew again, and several more people ran past. "If we're caught out in the open, we're toast," said the Major. "Even in the jumper I don't like the idea of negotiating a swarm of Darts to get to the 'gate." He gestured toward Lisera. "Ford, can you carry her?"

"No sweat, sir." Aiden pulled his pack on, swung his P-90 to one side and gently scooped Lisera into his arms. The girl cringed with pain, but stoically bit her lip and wrapped her arms around his neck. "Lisera, my name's Aiden Ford. These are my friends Major Sheppard, Dr McKay, and Teyla."

"Meet and greet later. Move now." Sheppard's gaze was focused on the village, where the majority of the mob was beginning to disappear from sight. "Why is everyone going to the inn?"

Seemingly confused, Lisera took a moment to reply, "For the Chosen to lead us to safety, of course."

Ahead of them, Aiden saw McKay shoot Sheppard an inquisitive look and mouth 'Chosen?' The Major gave a quick shake of his head and kept going.

Aiden could feel Lisera's trembling, and her tears were dampening his collar. This kid was beyond terrified and well into the first stages of shock. And she was light as a feather. He'd thought her legs were kind of skinny, but the rest of her was just as bony.

Keeping pace with him, Teyla, asked, "Are these attacks common, Lisera?"

"The Wraith have not come for many years, since long before my birth." She noisily sniffed back her tears. "It was not until recently that the raids began again."

The backs of his two teammates went rigid, and they traded a glance. Aiden knew the Major felt responsible for waking the Wraith, but to his way of thinking, the issue wasn't even worth debating. Leaving Colonel Sumner behind—leaving *anyone* behind—hadn't been an option. Besides, Aiden had taken out plenty of the guards himself. It just didn't make sense that one rescue mission had been enough to start this galaxy's version of the *War of the Worlds*. Then again, for all anyone knew, just landing on the Wraith's godforsaken planet might've been enough.

"Where is the place of safety?" Teyla asked.

"Inside the Citadel. The winged monsters cannot fly over the lands protected by the Chosen, but the Wraith will attack on foot, just as…" A tremor went through Lisera's voice, and she leaned into Aiden's shoulder. "Just as they did two weeks past, when my brother was taken."

The same jolt of sick fury hit Aiden every time he heard something like this. His arms had been getting a little tired, carrying the girl, but he hugged her closer, trying to infuse her with his determination to save her. "Almost there," he said reassuringly.

McKay pulled up short, looking at his now-dark handheld scanner. "We're under the EM field. Everybody stick together, because the radios aren't going to be worth much."

"We're at the village," Aiden said to Lisera.

The girl's head turned in the direction they were traveling.

"So the Chosen come to the inn to help move everyone inside the Citadel?" Sheppard asked over his shoulder.

"There is a transport there," she replied. "But the Chosen

will not wait for long, for fear that the Wraith will discover the transport and use it to penetrate the Citadel." Her eyes turned to the massive wall encircling the city, about three miles away. "We must hurry!"

"Which direction?"

"Pass the well," Lisera said through clenched teeth. "And then go to the left, along the waterfront." Her terror of the Wraith clearly outweighed the pain she had to be feeling.

Walking quickly beside Aiden, Teyla drew her P-90 closer, all senses primed to detect the first sign of attack. He met her eyes, and she shook her head. If the Wraith were coming, they were still out of range of whatever it was she used to perceive them.

Ahead of them, the village streets were deserted. Aiden glanced around, noting possible places of refuge. Most of the single-story structures were made of wood, black stone and some sort of thatching on the roofs. Fishing nets were strung all over the place, and a strong odor drew his attention to racks of drying squid-looking things.

They passed a couple of piles of rubble that might once have been buildings, before they'd become the targets of some artillery-level weapons.

Lisera's voice hitched as she explained, "The second time the Wraith's winged monsters came, they breathed fire on the market stalls. Then the Chosen used their powers to protect the village and the monsters fell from the sky." Her voice dissolved into whimpers. The pain was really getting to her now.

The Major's head snapped back, and he started to say something, but a growing commotion nearby diverted his attention. They reached a stone well featuring an old-fashioned hand pump, and looked left down a cobblestone road that opened out into an expansive square. The area was rapidly filling with people, crowding against each other, some spilling down toward beach. The tension level was skyrocketing. As they drew closer, Aiden began to make out what was being said.

"The Chosen have forsaken us."

"The transport cannot take us to safety!"

"The Wraith will kill us all!" came the increasingly desperate cries.

Lisera stiffened, and her arms tightened around Aiden's neck. He felt her heart pounding and her breathing quicken. Wild-eyed, she began to sob and shake her head, saying, "No, *no*," over and over again.

Red-faced and panting from exhaustion, people ran up behind them, desperate to force their way through, but there was nowhere to go. In order to better see, a few climbed on top of boats that had been hauled up onto the beach.

Jostled by the surging crowds, Lisera cried out in pain. "We're going to die!"

"Hey, it's okay. We'll be safe. I promise." Aiden tried to inject as much reassurance as he could into his tone, but he had to admit, he wasn't feeling too comfortable with the general situation.

"My brother said that," Lisera blurted through her tears. "Then the ghosts came, and...and I ran. My brother came after me. That's when the Wraith took him. And now they will take me!"

"The Wraith are coming," someone cried, pointing to the sky.

Shadows passed across the face of the sun. *"They come!"*

CHAPTER THREE

It was nothing more than a flock of large seabirds. John didn't have to ask Teyla; the look on her face was enough. The Wraith weren't about to start feeding on everyone, but hysteria sure was. Unless these people calmed down, someone else was going to get trampled. Possibly a lot of someones. "Okay, everyone, just hold on a minute!"

Maybe a few villagers heard him, but it was tough to tell. "Well done, very effective," Rodney shouted through the screams. "Any more inspired ideas?"

"As a matter of fact—" John leaped on top of what looked like a market cart full of reddish fruit, and fired a short burst from his P-90 over the heads of the crowd. A few bullets ripped clumps of sod from the roof of the nearest building, and sent bits of timber and an ornate weather vane-looking thing flying. "Yes."

It had been a risky maneuver, potentially triggering the very thing that he was trying to avoid. But the flash and the explosive clamor from his weapon had the desired effect. A few high-pitched screams abruptly cut off when everyone except his teammates fell to the ground. Only the sound of distant horns and surf rolling up the shingled beach penetrated the shocked silence.

"That's better. Now that I have everyone's attention, who's in charge here?"

A big, yellow-bearded guy, dressed in filthy clothes and a generous coating of fish scales, cautiously got to his feet. Before John could address him, Teyla stepped forward and said, "We are sorry to have further alarmed you." She tossed John a slightly disapproving frown.

He replied with a shrug. In this instance, he was okay with the idea of the ends justifying the means. Around the square, more people began getting to their feet, eyes darting nervously between the sky and the newcomers.

"I am Teyla Emmagen, daughter of Tagan. These are my friends, Dr McKay, Lieutenant Ford and—" She glanced up at him. "Major Sheppard. Why is it that you believe the Wraith are coming?"

Several people started to reply, but the fish-scale guy silenced the crowd with a curt gesture, and spoke in a deep voice. "The alarm came from the Chosen within the Citadel. As chief of this village it is my duty to send the warning signal forth." He lifted a half-spiral animal's horn. "From whence do you come that you do not know this?"

Maybe it was time to jump down before he upset the entire applecart. At least, the red things John was crunching under his boots looked like whatever passed for apples on this world. The guy standing by the cart, considerably younger than the chief but just as barrel-chested, appeared none too pleased with him. Apparently even an imminent attack couldn't deter some folks from keeping business foremost in mind.

"What is it with the introductions?" Rodney demanded. "We need to find this transport and get it operating. Where is it exactly?"

This time, there was nothing slight about the disapproving look Teyla sent in Rodney's direction.

John opened his mouth to reply to the chief's question, but Teyla got in first. "I am Athosian. How long before the Wraith appear do the Chosen raise the alarm?"

"They didn't raise any alarm last week," declared someone in the crowd.

"That's because it was night," barked the chief. "And the Shields of Dalera did not awaken the Chosen."

"You mean the Chosen slept while the Wraith stole our children from their beds." The woman's voice was filled with acrimony.

"Now they have not come to the transport, dooming us all to die!" The disgust in the man's voice wasn't exactly subtle, and echoed that of many in the crowd.

"Silence! All of you," demanded the chief. "You bring the

Wraith upon us because of your barbarian ways. Little wonder the Chosen have abandoned you."

"You are more guilty of trading in Wraithcraft than any of us." The young applecart owner spat on the ground. "But now that the Wraith have returned, you have all suddenly reacquired your faith in the divine power of the Chosen."

"Perhaps the Chosen are mistaken," declared the runner who had come close to knocking John off the road.

"The Shields of Dalera are never mistaken," retorted the chief.

"Shields?" piped up Rodney.

Ignoring him, the chief turned to Teyla and John. "My name is Balzar. The Chosen do not always give warning, but when they do the Wraith follow, of that there can be no doubt. Still — " He pulled at his beard. "The Chosen may not come to our village this time because we are protected by the Shields. Perhaps the Wraith have gone in search of easier game."

Lisera whimpered and clutched Ford a little tighter. Easier game. The outlying farms and villages unprotected by the patchy EM fields definitely fit that category.

Teyla looked less certain. "I do not believe the Wraith have yet arrived on this world."

"Which probably means that a hive ship is bearing down on us right now, coming from somewhere in not-so deep space," Rodney snapped. "I won't know for certain until I get a look at their warning system. Either way, the Wraith will have to land outside the EM fields, which means they'll attack on foot. And that brings me back to my earlier point. We came here to see the transport, and while we're on the subject, I'll need to take a look at those shields."

Leave it to Rodney to have such a universal sense of entitlement.

Balzar's expression turned thoughtful, which could only mean that he'd missed Rodney's demands entirely. Addressing John, he said, "Only last week the Wraith attacked as you say. They arrived on foot and stole the lives of many of our people. We were fortunate in that there were only two of the monsters."

"Did the Chosen kill them?" John asked.

"The Chosen wouldn't dare risk their almighty, overfed hides," scoffed the applecart owner. "That is why they have not come and opened the transport — "

"Yann!" Balzar snatched up a wicked looking double-bladed axe and brandished it. John dodged sideways, bumping into Rodney. Most of the men, none of whom were exactly tiny, raised equally deadly-looking swords and axes. Okey-dokey. That answered the question of how they'd managed to kill a Wraith.

"Time, people. We're running out of time here!" Despite the oversized pack on his back, Rodney was all but jumping up and down. "Transport? Shields?"

"Cool it, Rodney."

"Cool it?" he cried, still hopping. "The Wraith are coming, probably in one of those hive ships we've all heard so much about, and you've now broken my toe, which means that even if we leave these good people to their little Stephen King-style Wagnerian opera, the chances of us reaching the jumper and thus the 'gate in time are approaching statistical insignificance!"

"The Shields and transport are forbidden to all but the Chosen," snapped Balzar. Not much doubt how he felt about that.

"Well, can we at least take a look? We may have something similar on our world." The transport sounded to John like those on Atlantis, which meant it might just operate on the same principles.

"What harm can the strangers do, Balzar?" Yann the applecart man cast an appraising eye at John's P-90. "The horn from the Citadel still blows, and the Chosen do not come."

"It is a test of our faith," Balzar replied belligerently.

"More a question of payment," Yann muttered.

Balzar curled one of his ham-sized fists and stared at Yann with narrowed eyes.

"I promise I won't touch anything," John added with a reassuring smile.

Lisera moaned again. Ford was looking more than a little worried. "Sir, I really need to take another look at her leg."

Yann abruptly pushed past Balzar. "If I am to die this day, let me at least die with ale in my belly. Innkeeper!" he called, motioning with his head for John to follow. "Five of your finest, against my coin."

The inside of the tavern smelled of spilled beer laced with the stench of mortal fear. Somewhat better dressed people clutching armfuls of bags reluctantly moved aside to let them through. John nodded and smiled politely as they made their way to the bar, well aware that they might as well be wearing neon signs blazing 'Not from around here.'

It wasn't until he glanced toward the far left side of the inn that he saw the distinctive geometric glass doors. *Aha.* "Oh, Rodney?"

"I see it."

"Thought so. Just...take it easy, all right? We don't want to upset these nice folk."

"What makes you think that I upset people? I'm the epitome of reason and composure at the moment, in spite of what I'd call an increasingly hostile atmosphere. Notice also that I'm not even complaining about my mangled toe, so you're welcome. I would like to state for the record, however, that you're heavier than you look."

Outside, another argument—or maybe it was the same one—got underway. Those in the inn eyed them, silent and suspicious, unwilling to give up their place by the transport doors. Judging by their dress, it seemed merchants and townspeople had first crack at gaining entry to the Citadel. Although John was sorely tempted to push his way past the bar and through the crowd to the transport, Teyla's expression told him that the Wraith were still a ways off. In his experience, giving people a little time to get used to strangers invariably resulted in fewer misunderstandings and lower body counts.

"You risk much, Yann," growled the innkeeper, a wizened old man with a potbelly and arthritic, misshapen fingers. He filled a copper tankard with something that frothed like beer and set it on the wooden bar with a thud, spilling half the contents in the process.

The distant horn sounded again, and the argument outside spread into the tavern. People began muttering among themselves. They'd been primed to expect a Wraith attack, or a rescue, or both, and now nothing was happening except a bunch of out-of-towners dropping in for a surprisingly good beer.

Man, how long had it been since he'd had a beer? And it was *real* this time, which was a bonus. Too bad they were on a tight schedule. John licked the froth off his lips and smiled winningly at the innkeeper. "Mighty fine brew you make here. I'm just gonna go take a look around, okay?" With a meaningful glance at Ford, he tried to edge his way between a couple of farmer types who smelled like the animal dung that Rodney had discovered. They refused to budge, deliberately blocking his path.

Ford tensed, but the young Lieutenant's eyes were resolute. There wasn't a whole lot he could do at the moment with Lisera clinging to him, but if things went to hell, he'd drop the girl. For once, even Rodney seemed to pick up on the tenuous situation, and wisely channeled his energy into observing rather than commenting.

The farmer types glanced past John's shoulder, presumably at Yann, and then, with a surly growl, separated. The rest of the crowd also shuffled back, letting the team through. A buxom, well-dressed woman with apple-pink cheeks and an amazingly hideous hairdo blocked the wall where the control panel was generally mounted. John turned on his most charming grin when Yann, who was now bringing up the rear, said, "The newcomer will not take your place in line. He just wishes to see."

"Love what you've done with the —" John waved his hand in the direction of the woman's tangled braids and added a few more degrees of curvature to his smile.

Uttering something between a simper and a huff, she edged aside. Without a second thought, John brought his hand to the plate. The glass doors opened — and kept opening until the entire side of the inn seemed to fold back.

The effect was instant and profound. The woman visibly paled. Gasps filled the inn, and a cry went up. "He is of the Chosen. They are all of the Chosen!"

Instead of the small, elevator-sized room he'd been expecting, the floor angled down beneath ground level and widened out into a room large enough to take several hundred people.

John was finally getting used to the idea of expecting the unexpected on these missions. And this was mild on the unexpectedness scale, at least so far. Which could only mean that there were a number of proverbial other shoes still waiting to clonk him on the head.

"Whoever these Chosen are, they must have the Ancient gene," Ford reasoned.

McKay rubbed his forehead, grimacing as if that comment had physically caused him pain. "Another brilliant deduction, Lieutenant."

A horde of people surged forward and down the ramp, tripping and sliding as they went. "The Chosen will save us." The call rolled across the mob, bringing with it a palpable wave of relief.

"Whoa! Slow down," John yelled, barely managing to get out of the way.

Everyone froze and stared fearfully at him. Well, that was an improvement over his first couple of attempts.

A florid-faced woman near the inn's doors called, "Forgive us for our doubts."

"We beseech you," implored someone else. "It was only fear that drove us to speak as we did. We beg of you to save us!"

"Oh, please," Rodney said with disdain. "Major Sheppard wasn't 'chosen' for anything besides iceberg duty back home. How many times do I have to explain that the gene doesn't —?"

John slammed the heel of his boot down on Rodney's toe, trying not to take any satisfaction in the affronted yelp that resulted. "I didn't say stop," he called out, directing a threatening glare toward the scientist. "Just take it easy." Ignoring Rodney's theatrics as the scientist grasped hold of the bar and massaged his foot, John turned to Teyla. "Still no Wraith, huh?"

The villagers and fishermen kept pouring past them and down into the transport, although their pace was somewhat less frantic than before. Balzar, and then Yann walked past, ducking as he went, as if trying to hide.

"Hey, Yann?"

The man froze, and then turned a wary head in John's direction, refusing to meet his eyes.

"I owe you a beer, pal."

If anything, Yann looked even more confused, but he nodded and kept walking.

"I still do not sense the Wraith," Teyla said. "Nor do I understand how it is that anyone on this world carries the blood of the Ancestors within them."

"Gene," corrected Rodney through clenched teeth. "And did you absolutely have to injure me? A simple 'shut up, Rodney' would have sufficed. Although why it is — "

"Rodney? Shut up."

"Maybe they're straight-up, no-kidding Ancients, sir," Ford said. "Just think, we might finally get to meet one."

The crowds began to pile up, until it was clear that no one else could fit in the transport. "Looks like we'd better save that thought for later. Ford, go with Rodney and these people into the Citadel. Teyla and I will hang out here and bring up the rear."

An imminent objection was visible in Rodney's eyes even before he voiced it. "What's the rationale behind this division of labor? I'm all for leaving, but we don't have the first clue what we'll stumble into when this thing dumps us out into the Citadel."

John's discomfort with the unstable situation was growing, and his teammate's commentary wasn't helping, so he wasted no time with his rebuttal. "The alternative is for you to stay behind and risk facing one of those Wraith ground assaults you spoke so highly of. We can't be sure that whoever takes the transport will be able to send it back here in time or at all, and one of us with the gene has to go, so you tell me who it's going to be."

Rodney's jaw clicked shut. "Point taken."

It wasn't the scientist's fault that strategic thinking wasn't exactly second nature to him. John let go of the edge in his tone when he added, "Wait inside the Citadel for us. We should be able to move everyone in two trips, three at most."

"All right." Rodney sent him a quick, hard stare. "Don't take long."

"We won't. Go."

Once Ford had taken his place inside the transport with Lisera, Rodney squeezed in behind him, which wasn't easy, considering the girth of his pack. The expression on the scientist's face clearly said that he wasn't enjoying the proximity of so many people. He squinted at what John presumed to be a control panel, then raised his hand to touch it. The wall slammed back into place with a forceful, metallic *clang*. Not exactly the smooth, relatively silent operation of the transport on Atlantis. A locally manufactured copy, maybe?

"Okay, then," John said, exhaling a long breath. "Now we wait for the next train."

Teyla kept a watchful eye on the remainder of the crowd, which was still large by any measure. They were calmer now that a rescue operation was underway, but the undercurrent of fear persisted.

"How long does it usually take between transports?" John asked someone who, based on the smell, was a fisherman. The young man was nearly bent double with the weight of the bag he carried. Apparently he subscribed to the McKay style of packing.

The man stared at him oddly for a moment before replying, "It is only the time needed to unload everyone inside the Citadel. A matter of minutes."

"Minutes that we may not have if the Wraith are upon us!" wailed a woman's voice from somewhere near the inn's front door.

"Well, they're not here yet, so let's try to keep a positive attitude, all right?" Once the words were out, John winced inwardly at how trite they sounded. He wasn't cut out for this reassurance thing. "Hey, Teyla?"

The Athosian turned toward him, eyebrows arched inquiringly.

"I'm sure this is a dumb question, but this connection you have to the Wraith... Is there any way you can describe how it manifests itself? How do you tell the difference between general anxiety and an honest-to-God alert?"

"If I could explain that, Major, we would have already solved more problems than this one."

"I figured as much. Let's check the situation outside."

The jostling and shoving in the square abruptly stopped when the newcomers stepped from the inn. John scanned the sky with a trained gaze. Still no sign of the Wraith. He wanted to be reassured by that, but he knew better. The longer it took those bastards to show up, the better the chances that this would end up less like a fast-food run courtesy of a handful of Darts and more like a major harvest involving hive ships.

A fleet of at least sixty ships was out there somewhere, each filled to the brim with scores of repulsive creatures who wanted nothing more than to make a meal out of them. Every time John thought about it, a sick feeling reached in with icy fingers and twisted his gut. He'd been a military man for a long time and understood that people offered many reasons for killing: for duty, for faith, for mercy, even for sport. The idea of a race that killed for its very existence, though, was still barely fathomable to him. It left him with some serious doubts about the overall state of justice in this galaxy.

Having some kind of sensor equipment available would have made him feel a lot more secure right now. The EM shields were definitely worthwhile, but they left him functionally blind. Possibly in more ways than one, since he couldn't be sure that the shields weren't preventing Teyla from sensing the Wraith's approach.

Something was pressed into his hand, and he glanced down to find a stooped older woman averting her repentant gaze. "I... I did not pay as much as I should have the last time I used the transport," she confessed. "I beg forgiveness."

John glanced inside the badly cured leather bag she'd given him. A handful of rough gold coins glinted in the morning light. Huh. This was a side effect of being Chosen that hadn't occurred to him. He was tempted to make some lighthearted comment to Teyla about flipping her for the loot, but the entire situation was taking on a desperate edge that precluded that kind of levity.

Others began clambering around them, trying to press upon them everything from baskets of shellfish to furs. He started to say something, but Teyla already had it covered. "We have come to trade with you, not take from you," she called into the encroaching throng.

"But you are of the Chosen. We must give payment so that you will transport us into the Citadel and protect us!"

A child tugged at Teyla's hand. Wide-eyed, but more out of curiosity than fear, he asked, "Where is your Shield of Dalera?"

Teyla hesitated, looking to John. Still trying to convince the old woman to take her money back, he could only toss a helpless shrug in his teammate's direction. If Teyla of all people couldn't come up with a smooth answer, did she really expect *him* to be able to pull it off? Before she could attempt a response, the crowd surged forward and into the inn.

Moments later, Rodney's voice cut through the low, anxious conversations. "Excuse me, excuse me, coming through."

A flare of anger erupted in John, overshadowing his relief that the transport had returned. There was a lot that he didn't love about the Air Force, but at least there, people *listened*. Usually. "McKay, what part of 'wait with Ford' wasn't clear to you?"

"He seemed perfectly all right with the others. The chief, what's his name? Balzar? And Yann. Would *you* cross those two? They're gargantuan."

"Dammit, Rodney!" John pushed his way through the villagers toward the unapologetic scientist. "Did you even poke your head out of the transport and look at what they were walking into?"

"I didn't see any point, given that both our options and our time were limited, and I couldn't be sure that the transport would immediately return here without someone to command it. Would you rather I left you out here a while longer to soak up the ambiance?" He pivoted away, already moving on.

There was truth under that layer of perpetual impatience, John realized. For all his overdeveloped tendencies toward self-preservation, Rodney had been concerned enough about the rest of his team to override both his instincts and his instructions. Tough to argue with that.

The sea of people parted to let them pass, recognizing that deliverance was near. Once inside the inn, John shouldered his way through the crowd by the transport entrance and activated the panel. As before, the walls folded back, and as before, the villagers rushed inside.

The room filled to capacity in minutes, and for the first time, all the panicked shoving ceased. "Is that everybody?" John quickly moved through the now-empty inn and ducked out into the square to check. Sure enough, there was no evidence of life remaining in the village or along the beach—which, he noted for future reference, had a nice wave break near the point. He hustled back into the packed transport and scrutinized the control panel. The expected map was absent, and only one light glowed on the plasma screen.

"A single point of egress, apparently," Rodney declared unnecessarily, smacking his hand down on the light.

Just like the transports on Atlantis, all right. The doors opened almost immediately, spilling filtered light into the chamber. Before any other sensations could make themselves known, they were assaulted by a pungent odor. John crinkled his nose in disgust and leaned closer to Rodney, sniffing experimentally.

His teammate jumped away, looking at him like he'd lost his mind. "What is wrong with you?"

"Just checking. You did shower after your little encounter with the waste storage tanks, right?"

Glowering, the scientist chose not to dignify the question with an answer. "Thank you oh so much for that reminder. I certainly couldn't have done without ever thinking of that incident again."

"The smell is...pervasive," Teyla observed, her features carefully schooled against any reaction.

"Maybe they've got a busted pipe somewhere." John stepped

out of the transport and took a look around. They'd been deposited in some kind of huge, enclosed marketplace. The villagers, moving with far less haste now, began to disperse into an already large gathering.

"Merchants," groused one of the new arrivals to another. "There are more of them each time."

"Of all the places in the Citadel to do their peddling, must they take over the one set aside for our shelter?"

"They know this is our place of refuge, but that doesn't put coinage in their hands. It seems to matter not to them that without us, they would have no goods to sell."

So capitalism was alive and well, maybe at the expense of other things. John continued to mentally catalogue the area, filing details away. He wasn't convinced that all was okay just yet.

The market stalls were mobile and arranged in no particular pattern, complicating the flow of foot traffic around them. Most likely it was an every-man-for-himself setup, with each merchant claiming whatever space he or she could find in the vast building. The upper walls of the structure were lined with a venerable display of medieval-style stained glass windows, which explained the dingy, filtered light. Above it all were ornately carved, cross-vaulted cathedral ceilings. Except for the fact that it was just one wide expanse of semi-organized commerce broken up by stone support columns, the whole place had a distinctly church-like feel to it. Completing the effect were massive, crouched gargoyles that were, oddly, positoned over the *inside* entrances at each corner of the building. John did a double take when he realized the larger than life statues weren't gargoyles, but Wraith.

In general, the sellers seemed to be a better-dressed bunch than the villagers, which probably shouldn't have surprised him. Nearby, in a stall featuring what looked like herbs and medicinal items, Balzar stood watching Ford and a middle-aged woman tend to Lisera's leg. Some of the merchants eyed the kid periodically, casting glances of appraisal that tweaked John's nerves. Where he came from, looking at a teenage girl like that typically earned a guy an introduction to her father's shotgun.

Of course, Lisera didn't have a father standing by. She had them instead.

"Begone from here, you village rabble! You're disturbing my customers."

John turned to see an irritated merchant shooing away a pair of village children who'd made the mistake of lingering near his fruit stall. The kids' mother protested hotly. "You have no right to call us such — this is our place of safety. The Chosen have decreed it to be so. We paid to come, and you should have long since departed!"

Similar quarrels had broken out in other areas. All in all, these merchants were a very different crew from the villagers. When one of the farmers gestured toward John in an obvious attempt to explain his Chosen status, the merchants displayed none of the obsequiousness that he'd witnessed at the inn. In fact, he was getting a definite vibe of resentment from them.

"I'm thinking that maybe we don't want to advertise ourselves too loudly around here," he suggested to Rodney, who blinked, unaware of the tension.

"Not quite as impressed by the Chosen as the villagers were?"

"Something like that."

Any further conversation was cut off as the underlying noise level in the marketplace increased sharply. Storming in from all four entrances were men outfitted in leather uniforms, reminiscent of Wraith soldiers. The metal breastplate was an innovative addition, and the animal horns on the men's helmets added a distinctly Norse twist. More attention-grabbing was the fact that each warrior carried a leather bola in one hand and a double-bladed axe with a long handle in the other.

John had three thoughts in response to this dramatic display. The first was that those axes looked damn heavy, and that the men wielding them were even more muscular than the villagers. The second was that unless the Wraith had brought can-openers with them, the chest armor was likely an effective deterrent to snacking. And the third was the vain hope that these guys hadn't shown up because of his team.

Behind them, a sound signaled the reactivation of the transport, and an imperious but oddly pitched voice shouted above the clanking of metal. "Wraithcraft. There are Wraith objects among us!"

The pathways between the stalls cleared rapidly to let the warriors through. John turned back toward the opening doors of the transport and got a look at the person doing the yelling. Despite the gravity of the situation, he had to bite down hard to keep a smirk off his face. The guy, walking out of the transport ahead of an incoming bunch of yet more villagers, was the walking definition of 'overdressed.' The cape of striped fur fastened at his shoulder with an elaborate gold pin contrasted sharply with their generally grimy surroundings. On his head was a winged helmet and around his neck hung a thick gold chain, from which dangled a familiar looking pendant about the size of a child's fist.

"Oh, man," Ford said. "This guy dresses worse than a Goa'uld."

Not having had the pleasure of a Goa'uld encounter, John didn't have much of a basis for comparison, but it sounded good. There was a fair amount of déjà vu involved here. The thing around the guy's neck looked remarkably like the personal shield device that Rodney had discovered their first week in Atlantis. Then, almost as an afterthought, it hit him: the crystal inside the pendant was *glowing*. Not green this time, but the same hue as the 'gate chevrons.

There weren't all that many coincidences in this galaxy, so this was yet another avenue they'd need to investigate. Later, though, for a whole new wave of panic was now sweeping across the marketplace.

"Wraithcraft!" bellowed the robed man, his hands waving furiously in the air. The timbre of his voice carried easily above the murmurs of the crowd, even as they grew in intensity. "Who defiles Dalera's Citadel by bringing Wraith objects here?"

"They tricked us!" That shrill cry came from the same woman who had given John her gold coins only minutes before. The cynical part of his brain knew what was coming even before she stabbed one gaunt finger in his direction. "They are *not* Chosen.

They do not wear the Shields of Dalera."

"They must be Wraith disguised to walk among us," accused another voice. "They have used Wraith trickery to penetrate the Citadel!"

Terrific. Help a few hundred people avoid a culling, and this is the thanks you get.

Ford sprang up from his position near Lisera to join his teammates, and John appreciated his instincts. Getting separated would definitely not help matters. "Hey, hold up a minute," he tried to yell over the din, but that turned out to be a fairly useless effort.

People and voices swarmed accusingly around them. The Valkyrie-helmeted guy advanced, his features distorted into a snarl of rage. His axe-wielding buddies formed a barricade around John and his teammates that effectively pinned them against the nearby wall. Behind the row of axes, the merchants egged the warriors on, joined enthusiastically by some of the villagers.

"Did we or did we not just save those guys' asses?" John demanded, tightening his grip on his weapon.

"Preaching to the converted, Major." Rodney's glib remark was belied by the unrestrained dread in his eyes. "A little on the mercurial side, these folks."

"Kill them!" shouted a fisherman.

"Quarter them!"

Lesson learned, John thought as the axe-men edged closer to his team. *Next time you come upon an Ancient device, assuming there is a next time, keep your hands to yourself.*

CHAPTER FOUR

Comprehension struck, and Rodney fumbled with the switch on his radio. "Turn off everything!" He yanked the sensor from his jacket.

"What?" Sheppard called back, raising his P-90. "Okay, everyone, we don't want any trouble here."

Was it courage or idiocy that allowed the Major to sound so reasonable when they were about to be hacked to pieces by a crazed mob? Had to be the latter, right? "Turn off every piece of technology that you have. Life sign detectors, radios, everything." Rodney cursed under his breath. He should have seen this coming. Hell, he halfway *did* see it coming, but halfway didn't count, and where in blazes was the switch to this thing?

"Take care, Kesun," shouted Balzar, backing away from the prostrate Lisera and the P-90 that Lieutenant Ford was pointing into his face. "Their weapons spit fire that passes through even hardened metal."

"Blasphemy!" cried a cowering merchant. "Kesun is of the Chosen. He will protect us."

Face screwed up in obvious confusion, Ford shot a swift glance at Rodney. "What's the point in turning off our radios? They're not working, anyway."

"Turn off everything or we're dead!" Rodney ripped out the tiny power pack of the sensor, and then, pulling off his backpack, scrambled through the contents. What else had he switched on, and what had possessed him to drag around all this equipment in the first place?

"*Kill them!*" A woman's screeches spurred the warriors on. "Before they kill us as they killed my children."

From the corner of his eye, Rodney could see the armed men advancing. This was not good. In fact, this was very, very bad.

"Do it." Sheppard switched off his radio and the life sign

detector with one hand, the other still aiming his weapon. The shouting increased. "We're not Wraith, but we will defend ourselves," he announced, his tone a deadly matter-of-fact.

Rodney was too busy ripping power packs and batteries from assorted equipment, Ancient and Earth related, to see exactly what happened next, but someone must have decided Teyla appeared the easiest target. *That* was an incredibly big mistake. The next moment, her legs and arms were flailing. An ornate blade passed mere inches above his head to bury itself with a solid 'thunk' into one of the timber columns. Then his ears were being hammered by the staccato noise of a P-90. Muzzle flashes lit the dank interior of the marketplace. He ducked low, crouching protectively over his pack. Maybe the instruments were currently useless, but they were valuable nonetheless. With access to Earth impossible until they found a ZPM, he wouldn't be able to replace them any time soon.

When the firing stopped, Rodney raised his head and chanced a look around. A Wraith carving, doubtless serving the same ridiculously superstitious and utterly pointless function as a medieval gargoyle, smashed down into a market stall, scattering assorted pots and pans.

He welcomed the aroma of spent cordite, even if it failed to mask the obnoxious scent of poorly maintained sewers. In a brief moment of detachment, Rodney realized that he didn't entirely like what that said about him. He'd had a much clearer viewpoint on weapons, and perhaps the military mindset as a whole, up until a few days ago. Kolya's cold-blooded tactics had altered his perspective. Now, he viewed the weapon at his side not as a necessary evil, but as *necessary*.

In any case, the automatic fire had halted the warriors in their tracks, and provoked a mass evacuation of the markets. Not a bad start.

Unlike everyone else, the Hagar type, Kesun, hadn't ducked for cover, but was instead directing troops to run off and do whatever it was that troops like these did. No doubt it would involve reinforcements and considerably more lethal weapons than the Viking-inspired battleaxes and halberds currently being wielded. On the plus side, around the official's neck, the pendant which looked suspiciously like a personal shield device had now faded from its formerly brilliant glowing aquamarine to a flat, somewhat dull turquoise. Hopefully, that would put an end to this absurd situation.

"They're not Wraith, Kesun!" called a newly familiar voice. "They come from a far away land."

"Yann's right," Sheppard replied, not relaxing his weapon's aim. "The Wraith are just as much an enemy to us as they are to you."

"Yet you carry Wraithcraft," Kesun rasped.

"Yes, but we've turned them off," Rodney declared with what he hoped was a reassuring smile. He glanced at Sheppard, and pointed to the bluestone accessory hanging from Kesun's neck. "Those aren't personal shield devices. I'm certain they're the source of the EM fields we saw from the jumper. They must automatically detect and deactivate all electromagnetic devices, except the transport and themselves, of course." Belatedly, he recognized the implications of that idea. "Well, that's not going to make it any easier to figure out how they work. How am I supposed to take any readings when they turn off everything?"

If anything, Kesun's glower deepened.

"What? *Now* what did I say?"

"The penalty for Wraithcraft is death!"

"You mean this?" Rodney lifted his sensor. A dozen warriors immediately raised their axes. He rolled his eyes, getting tired of this game. Dealing with ignorance was complicated enough. Ignorance combined with threats of violence was just plain irritating. "You have got to be kidding me. Not only is this equipment completely unrelated to the Wraith, some of it's not even original to this galaxy."

"I don't think these guys are likely to appreciate the distinction." Sheppard lifted the muzzle of his P-90 higher. "Look, this is not a Wraith weapon. Watch." He fired a single round into the ceiling before Rodney could comment about this being the traditional military solution to everything. A few splintered chips of timber rained down. The bluish crystal around the official's neck remained obligingly dull. "See? Not a blink."

Kesun's gaze was still deeply suspicious. "From whence do you come?" he demanded, edging closer and eyeing their clothes.

"Atlantis," replied the Major.

If discovering that Sheppard could operate the transport had come as a shock to the villagers, that little announcement more or less turned the place on its ear. The troops instantly fell to their knees, while Kesun's face displayed an impressive range of emotions, beginning with horror and ending with delirious happiness. "Dalera!" he breathed, turning to Teyla with his hands upraised. "You have returned to us!"

Good grief. All this vacillation was giving Rodney vertigo. And apparently raising one's hands to give thanks to some mythical being was a universal trait no matter what galaxy one inhabited. He made a note to let the anthropology team know about that, assuming they made it safely off this planet before being classified as hostile yet again.

Teyla had barely worked up a sweat after having dispatched the two warriors who now groveled at her feet. Casting a cautious glance around her, she stepped forward and said, "My name is Teyla."

Dropping his hands, Kesun's eyes fell to Lisera, then returned to the Athosian. "You are not Dalera? And yet you are a healer, and you are from Atlantis." His smile turned curious. "You are a sister to Dalera, perhaps?"

"We come from Atlantis, yes," Teyla replied, apparently going for the simple and honest approach. "However, we are not the Ancestors."

"Then how can this be?" Kesun examined the now-closed transport doors, his face a mask of confusion. "Only the Chosen have the divine power."

And there they went again. Divine? This construct of ATA ability as some kind of holy gift was grating on Rodney's nerves. He considered saying something, but a glance toward Sheppard's heavy boots made his toes throb, and he thought better of it.

Behind his carrot-colored beard, Kesun's face went through another contorted set of emotions. "Which of you operated the transport?" he demanded.

"They used Wraith trickery," called Balzar. "Kill them all!"

"Wraithcraft cannot deceive Dalera," Kesun announced, and from somewhere deep inside of his pelt robe, he pulled out another one of the shield devices and handed it to Sheppard.

"The Shield of Dalera," came the mutters of various villagers and merchants who were slowly lifting their heads above the market stalls. "Kesun is allowing the newcomers to touch one of the Shields!"

Rodney accepted the Shield from the Major and inspected it for similarities to the personal shield device. Superficially, it appeared almost identical, except, of course, for the color.

"Pass it to the others," Kesun ordered him.

Reluctantly handing the device to Ford, Rodney muttered, "Hurry up. I need to take another look at it."

The aquamarine crystal within abruptly changed from a lifeless turquoise to black. In Teyla's hands, it remained black, until she handed it back to Rodney. The color returned, although it did not glow. No surprise there, since the devices had obviously been programmed to work only in the presence of the ATA gene. However, unlike the personal shields, these apparently did not encode themselves to a user's unique DNA. Interesting concept. Activating only in the presence of Wraith Darts and stun weapons was certainly an efficient way to conserve power, but it seemed the things blocked all EM radiation, Ancient and human.

Turning to Rodney and Sheppard, Kesun gave a respectful but no longer ingratiating bow, and said, "As Chosen, you are most welcome to Dalera."

"Dalera?" Rodney said, fingering the device. "I'm confused. Isn't that what you just called Teyla?"

"I believe it is also the name of their world," Teyla ventured.

"Come." Kesun headed to the transport. "I shall take you to meet the other Chosen."

Ford hesitated. "Sir? What about Lisera?"

"You are not of the Chosen." Kesun glanced down at the girl, then up at Teyla and Ford. "You may not enter the Enclave."

Rodney was about to protest, but the Major got in ahead of him. "Okay, well, that doesn't work for us. Splitting up wasn't in our plans."

"The transport will not take us to the Enclave if any but the Chosen step within its doors."

Inhaling sharply through his nose, Rodney blew the breath out slowly, keeping a tight rein on his anger. He could play along up to a point, but the idea that these people were making judgments of worth based on a purely random *gene* was more than he was willing to accept. "'We hold these truths to be self-evident, that all men are created equal,'" he quoted under his breath to Sheppard, who tossed a sideways glance in his direction.

"You do realize that you were channeling my high school history teacher just then, right?"

"I'm just saying that occasionally a good idea does emerge from your country."

"Nice. But since getting inside this Enclave could potentially be a big help in your information-gathering, let's wait a while before shoving the Declaration of Independence down these people's throats, all right?" The Major shifted his gaze. "Teyla, Ford, you comfortable with hanging out here for a while?"

"I believe we will be fine with these people," Teyla said, looking around with a tolerant smile. "There is no longer any misunderstanding."

That might have been true, but Rodney wasn't all that thrilled with the aspects of the situation that he *did* understand.

Kesun nodded to four of the warriors. "See to it that the visitors are known by all to be under my personal protection. And remain here with them until we return."

To Rodney, that sounded more like confinement than protection. "Why can't they take a look around outside?"

Leading him and the Major to the transport, Kesun replied, "If they venture from a protected area and the Wraith come, they will be in mortal danger." The so-called Chosen clasped his hands behind his back, which Rodney took as a sign that either he or Sheppard was supposed to open the door. What was that about? Another test? General apathy? It might have been deference, but that was a more redeeming quality than he was prepared to ascribe to these Chosen types at the moment.

Sheppard stopped walking and faced his second in command. "We'll be back before long," he told Ford. "Until then, enjoy the down time."

The Lieutenant gave a solemn nod. Rodney couldn't help but feel like he'd just missed an entire conversation. Under those laconic instructions, there had been a trace of something else. He suspected that Ford and Teyla had just received covert authorization to act as they saw fit, 'protection' or no.

At the entrance to the transport, he and Sheppard looked at each other. The Major spread his hands in a gesture of accommodation. "Want to do the honors?"

It was petty, but that had never stopped him before. Still clutching the Shield in one hand, Rodney folded his arms. "Not particularly."

Sheppard gave him a withering look and reached for the console. The door slid back, and the oddly matched trio stepped inside.

Rodney was reminded of the opening line to any number of bad jokes. *A soldier, a genius, and a zealot walk into a bar...* Well, hell. Time to think positive. If his suspicions about this Enclave place were confirmed, it would at least be less of an assault on his olfactory senses than the marketplace.

This time, the control panel on the inside of the transport opened out to the full-sized display seen in the transports of Atlantis. On the plasma screen map, Kesun touched a light located at one end, which, if Rodney recalled correctly, was also the highest point of the hill. The door shut with a somewhat less than graceful metallic sound, and for the fourth time that day, he was instantly somewhere else.

When his companions disappeared inside the transport, Lieutenant Aiden Ford relaxed his stance, demonstrating to Dalera's warriors that he had no intention of defying them. Lisera openly stared at him. Weapon poised, he had stood ready to defend her, just as her mother had often described the Ancient hero-warriors of the fabled Atlantis. "Lieutenant Aiden Ford." His name was as exotic as his deep brown eyes and gentle smile.

He turned and moved back toward her. "Call me Aiden." Removing his cap, he smiled and kneeled beside her again. "Morphine kicked in yet?"

"The potion has indeed rid me of much pain." The memory of his strong arms gave her warmth despite the chill in the dank hall. Never in all of Lisera's years had she dreamed that her mother's tales were anything more than children's stories — until the night that the Wraith had come. The hideous nightmare beings were indeed real, but then so too were the legendary warriors who battled them.

"See? I told you the needle would make you feel better." Aiden gently probed her leg.

The striking woman who claimed not to be Dalera, but called herself Teyla, smiled her approval, then turned to the apothecary and said, "Is there a place of healing where we can take Lisera? The bones of her leg must be set properly to ensure that there is no permanent damage."

A look of sympathy crossed the woman's face. She was a merchant, a seller of healing potions capable of fixing many ailments, but her words confirmed what Lisera feared. "Only Dalera could heal such an injury so that the bones are set true. You truly are not her?"

Perhaps Lisera imagined it, but it seemed that Teyla's smile took on an edge of regret. "No, I am not."

Despite her determination to be brave, Lisera's breathing hitched as she battled tears. The pain in her leg was now a dull throb. The pain of grief and fear could not so readily be eased. She would be crippled. To survive the Wraith she would have to remain in the Citadel. With no coin to pay for her food and keep, she had but one option.

Many years ago, her mother had told her, the Citadel had

been a fine place, and the Chosen honored as the protectors of Dalera. Then came the Great Plague. The Chosen had withdrawn to their Enclave, barbarians had taken over, and the Citadel had become a place of evil, the horrors of which could only be guessed at. But when the Wraith had returned, just a few short weeks ago, the Citadel had offered their only protection.

After the first wave of attacks, entire villages had been decimated. Those who had not been taken had lost their homes, their crops and their loved ones, and something more — their souls. The horrors of life in the Citadel had spilled out into the countryside, and now nowhere was free of the pillaging, raping, even killing.

"I know a healer that might help," Balzar replied gruffly.

The flesh on her arms crawled. The chief's look was agonizingly familiar to Lisera, for it was not only strangers who could not be trusted. The day the Wraith had taken her brother, she and her mother had tried to escape to the Citadel. Balzar, a man she had believed to be a friend, had first refused them entry to the transport inn because their only form of payment was no longer acceptable. Lisera had not understood the promise that her mother had then made until Balzar had come to them that night, in the dank shadows of this same Sanctuary Hall. After defiling her mother, he had turned his attentions on Lisera. She had run away, desperately seeking a place to hide in the bowels of the great city. For two days she had roamed the streets, hungry and cold, barely one step ahead of men whose eyes gleamed with a different kind of hunger, one she now recognized in the merchants' eyes.

"This one has no coin or goods to pay a healer," Balzar continued. "Her family is dead, her home burned. Leave her with me and I will see what I can do." He bent down to grip her arm.

Recoiling, Lisera grasped Aiden's leg and clung to him.

"Then we will tend to her ourselves." Teyla placed herself in Balzar's path. Her smile remained in place, but her eyes held a warning.

Balzar was many times Teyla's girth and weight, but Lisera

saw his hesitation. The warriors who had attacked Teyla had both instantly been felled by her swift blows. These same men now exchanged an approving look with one another.

A deep pain drew Lisera's attention back to Aiden. "I'm sorry," he said, gently wrapping her leg again. "The pressure should keep the swelling down, but it needs to be X-rayed and set properly." His words confused her, until he added, "Maybe we should take her back to Atlantis and have this taken care of."

"You would do such a thing for me?" The brief surge of relief that swept through her abruptly fled. She bit her lip and shuddered, aware of the merchants' eyes. Balzar's expression gave her warning. One man or many, the choice was hers. "Balzar speaks true. I have no coin, nor even crops or goods to pay."

"Yes, you do." Teyla pulled a large bag from her shoulders and, reaching inside, withdrew a small packet. Handing it to the apothecary, she added, "This is our payment for your kindness in allowing us to remain here while we wait for our companions. Brew it as a tea to help the pain and bleeding of childbirth."

The apothecary offered a toothless smile. "Such tea is always in great demand."

"That was unwise." Balzar's eyes narrowed and he stepped back. "Such acts rarely go unnoticed." Casting a warning look in Lisera's direction, he pushed past the smirking warriors and stalked off.

"I am curious," Yann said, sidling across to join them. "What sort of payment could a slip of a girl like Lisera have to offer?" He withdrew a red fruit from his pocket and bit into it.

The fruit sounded sweet and crunchy. Since escaping the Citadel and fleeing into the forest, Lisera had eaten nothing more than wild berries, birds' eggs and a few fish she'd managed to trap in tidal pools. It was then that she saw something in Yann's gaze which differed from Balzar's. Yann looked at her as a merchant might appraise goods that he approved of. Then his eyes took in Aiden and Teyla's strange weapons. Not having any understanding of what this meant, but fearful just the same, Lisera blurted, "What payment I can give you, I will."

"Well," said Aiden, packing his medicines away. "Our arrival accidentally set off your alarms. So really, the least we can do is make sure you're okay."

Teyla made herself comfortable on the ground, her back to the apothecary's store of goods, the weapon resting lightly in her fingers. "Lisera, could you tell us of your world? Among my people, stories are believed to be a worthy trade item."

Yann went to speak, but Aiden said, "I'd like to hear it from Lisera." His smile reminded her of her brother, in times when they had shared a secret from their mother.

Shrugging, Yann squatted on the floor beside them. "I will fill in any details that Lisera might miss." He bit into the red-fruit again, and Lisera stared longingly at the juices that flowed down his jaw.

"And your price for this would be?" Teyla inquired.

"A story from Atlantis?" Yann replied, pulling a cloth from his jacket and wiping his mouth. "Two stories, and I would forego the ale promised to me by Major Sheppard."

Teyla's eyes danced with amusement. "It seems a fair trade. Well, then, Lisera, perhaps you might begin by telling us of Dalera."

Looking up to the first of the teaching windows, where Dalera was giving the laws to her people, Lisera swallowed hard. Balzar was right. They had blasphemed, and were now paying with their lives.

CHAPTER FIVE

John wasn't quite sure what he'd expected from the Enclave, but if first impressions were a reasonable indication, it was a temple rather than a place of residence. Stepping out of the transport, they entered a large expanse of polished stone floors and ornately carved pillars. The basic design had all the hallmarks of Ancient architecture, but the actual structure and furnishings were more like the lovechild of a dark Gothic cathedral and a Scandinavian stave church.

Soaring windows lined the walls of the long chamber, with animal skins and battle-axes hung in decorative displays, but what caught his attention was the absolute quiet compared to the marketplace. There wasn't a soul in sight. "Are we here to meet the other Chosen?" His voice echoed along the empty hallway, which added to the temple effect.

Kesun handed John another Shield from within his robe. "As is your birthright."

"Um…thanks." Accepting the artifact, John noticed that Rodney's face was undergoing an amazing set of calisthenics. He felt a momentary flash of sympathy for the scientist. They'd just been given a couple of pieces of potentially vital technology, with a philosophical price-tag that was apparently pushing a bunch of McKay's many buttons.

With a restrained bow of assent, Kesun added, "The arrival of visitors from Atlantis has long been anticipated. You will be most welcome."

So the fact that they weren't Ancients wasn't a big problem. That was good to know. Rodney was fumbling with his pack, attempting to withdraw a notebook while still holding on to his Shield. John didn't envy whichever lab assistant would get the eventual pleasure of transcribing the chief scientist's chicken-scratch handwriting. *Technology — you don't know what you've got 'till it's gone.*

Experimenting, he hooked a loop of the Shield's metal setting through a clip on his belt. It seemed secure enough, so he plucked its companion out of Rodney's awkward grip and fastened it likewise. The other man offered a 'hmpf,' which was as close to a sign of gratitude as John could reasonably expect. "Lead on," he told their guide.

Kesun escorted them into another chamber where there was considerably more activity. Sort of. The half-dozen occupants of the room were—what was the politically correct term for it these days? *Ah, screw it.* These guys were *old*. They looked like contemporaries of Moses. John's initial suspicions about the Chosen being power-hungry despots-in-training were already taking a hit.

"I bring good news, Father," Kesun announced grandly, his arm sweeping out to indicate the visitors. He pulled off his helmet and rested it on the worn wooden table. Its silvery wings glinted in the light cast by a massive log fire at one end of the room. "The Shields did not warn of a coming attack. They instead foretold the arrival of messengers from Atlantis! I believe that they may be able to aid us in our time of need."

Aid them in their time of need? If these Chosen were expecting him and Rodney to somehow help them solidify their position, they were in for a rude awakening. John knew as well as anyone that upsetting whatever balance of power existed here was a recipe for disaster.

The man that Kesun had addressed as 'Father' had to be pushing ninety if he was a day. He sat at an oblong table with the others, his shoulders stooped so far forward that John wondered if the table was holding him upright. Milky blue eyes peered out from underneath a bushy set of snow-white eyebrows, sizing up the newcomers. "Forgive us our surprise," he addressed them in a feeble voice. "It is only because you are not quite what we expected."

Man, if he had a nickel for every time he'd given this explanation. "We do come from Atlantis. However, we're not Ancients... Ancestors." John raised his voice when a few of the

Chosen looked as though they were straining to hear.

"But you are of the Chosen," one of the others pointed out with a slight wheeze.

"We come from a planet called Earth. It's where the Ancients went after they left Atlantis. My name is Major John Sheppard. This is Dr Rodney McKay."

Distracted by the carved inscriptions on the heavy timber walls, Rodney offered a noncommittal nod of greeting.

Kesun's father processed this information, the proverbial wheels in his head clearly working overtime. "You must also be Dalera's children," he declared.

John wasn't entirely confident of that, but contradicting the man would probably be bad form. "That may be true, in a way. In any case, we'd like to learn more about her."

Surprise resulted immediately from that statement. The old man's brows knitted into one solid furry mass. "The smallest child knows the story of Dalera. How can it be that you do not?"

"They come from a different world, Father," Kesun reminded, his expression asking the visitors to be patient. John couldn't blame him. Most of the Chosen looked like escapees from a nursing home. More than one of them were teetering on the brink of senility, and one old codger looked and sounded like he could really use some oxygen therapy. *This* was the cornerstone of the Daleran defense system?

Rodney possessed a better poker face than might be expected, but he rarely bothered to use it. His expression now conveyed a shade of disillusionment that bordered on derision. "I suppose this explains why the coverage of the EM fields is patchy."

Kesun was apparently a quick study, because he looked shrewdly at Rodney and said, "If you refer to the protection given us by the Shields of Dalera —"

"The PENEs, but yes."

"Say what?" John was sure he'd heard that wrong. Must've been the Canadian accent.

Rodney blinked at him, clearly missing a clue. "Personal Electromagnetic Nullification Emitters."

John rubbed at the bridge of his nose, hoping to avoid the onset of a McKay-induced headache. "All right, now *you're* banned from naming things, too. How about we stick to calling them 'Shields'?" He sent the same apologetic look to Kesun that the youngest Chosen had offered him moments earlier. "You were saying?"

"The Wraith left us in peace for generations," Kesun began. "But they returned several weeks ago to bring death once more. As Dalera commanded, the youngest among us left the Enclave and traveled to the Chosen's ancestral homes, which are known by all as Stations, to stand in defense. But the Citadel has grown much since Dalera departed this world, and our protection is no longer sufficient."

Looking unmoved, Rodney wandered off to examine the Ancient lettering that had caught his attention. "This tells of our history," Kesun explained, crossing the room to join him. "As do the teaching windows in the Sanctuary Halls."

John walked with him. The elder Chosen at the table appeared not to notice their departure. "You mean that marketplace we transported into?"

"There are many such Halls scattered throughout the Citadel." Kesun's jaw flexed. "We ordered them cleared of stalls after the Wraith returned." He shook his head in resignation. "We warned Gat and the merchants that their blasphemy would be punished, as generations past have been punished for their lack of reverence. So soon memories fade."

Visibly bristling, Rodney whirled around, his notebook falling to his side. "And how precisely do you define blasphemy?"

"Ahem." John tapped his toe in warning. He wanted to wait as long as possible before they inevitably did something to piss these people off. "Let's get the full story."

Pointing to the Ancient writings on the stone tablets set in the wall, Kesun said, "Five thousand years ago our world was a peaceful place."

That didn't add up. "Five thousand years?" John glanced at Rodney.

"Near as I could tell from our preliminary scan, this planet's orbit around its sun takes twice as long as Earth's. So, their years are—"

"Twice as long. Just checking." He smiled at Kesun and indicated for the man to continue.

"When word of the Wraith reached us, the Ancestors returned to their home in the heavens, Atlantis. One Ancestor, however, remained behind. Her name was Dalera."

"She stayed to protect you?" John ventured.

Kesun shook his head. "The Ancestors banished her to this world for her sins, and cast the great ring into the heavens." His eyes looked skyward.

"What exactly were her sins?"

Smiling sadly, he replied, "Dalera fell in love with a man of this world, and bore his children."

"Hold on a minute," Rodney demanded. "You mean Dalera, an Ancient, was banished for having children with a human?" He spun to face John. "Do you know what this means?"

"It would explain why these people have the ATA gene."

The impatient gesture he received in response hinted to John that he wouldn't have won any money on a Rodney-designed game show with that answer. "Yes, obviously. Try not to strain yourself by looking a little deeper for a change." He waved his pen around like a weapon. "It also means the Ancients viewed themselves as being superior to mere humans, to such an extent that they placed a taboo on mating with them!"

That wasn't a particularly happy thought, but they'd been learning new facets of the Ancients everywhere they went. Not all of it cast the architects of Atlantis in an entirely positive light. "One step at a time, okay?" John tossed another, less certain smile in Kesun's direction.

"When the Wraith came," Kesun continued, "those who remained on the great hill upon which the Enclave was built were protected by an invisible wall that none could penetrate. Our numbers were few, and the land inside this wall, which extended from where the river divides to where it rejoins once more, was sufficient to feed us.

"Generations passed." Kesun's tone had taken on the cadence

of a teaching allegory. "Then came the day when the Wraith attacks ceased. Dalera, whose children by then had grown and had children of their own, devised a set of laws that would protect her people for all time. The invisible barrier was removed and a wall built along the shores of the river. The entire island within became known as the Citadel. The people crossed the channels to sow new pastures and to fish the nearby seas. Dalera and her children fashioned many thousands of Shields—"

"Thousands?" Rodney stopped scribbling in his notebook to massage a cramp out of his hand.

"Yes. For as her children and her children's children went forth and multiplied, each took with them many Shields of Dalera to protect those outside the Citadel should the Wraith return. Dalera also fashioned the transports." Kesun walked across to another wall and, opening a wooden panel, revealed an Ancient-designed ground plan of the Citadel and surrounding countryside.

The strategy was immediately obvious. Set up the Citadel as a highly defendable fortress, and install transport systems in outlying villages. When the Wraith attacked, the Chosen within the Citadel would create an overlapping coverage with the Shields. The EM fields of the Chosen living in the villages would also activate, forcing the attackers out of the sky and giving farmers and fishermen time to evacuate through the transports ahead of any ground assault.

John had to give the long-departed Dalera credit. Whatever else she might have been, her tactical instincts had been damned good.

"The plan must not have been carried to its ultimate conclusion," observed Rodney. "Since there's only one continent, by now the entire planet's landmass should be protected by a series of cities and villages spread at equidistant points. It would completely forestall any Wraith culling whatsoever."

"So what went wrong?" John asked.

"It was as you say. Dalera had meant for our world to one day be protected from the evil of the Wraith." Kesun's expression darkened. "But as time passed, Dalera left us, and many generations without an attack dispelled the people's fear of the Wraith. They betrayed Dalera's memory, breaking her most sacred laws."

Even without looking, John could tell that Rodney had something to say about that. He stepped in to head off the objection. "Exactly what were these laws?"

"That people who ventured forth from the Citadel to till the lands beyond must only do so in places designated by the Chosen."

"Based on this defensive plan," John said, examining the map. "That makes sense."

Kesun inclined his head in agreement. "Few were willing to travel great distances to settle and farm areas selected by the Chosen simply in the name of protection against an enemy whose horrors none could recall. Instead, they turned barbarian. Abandoning their belief in Dalera, they felled forests and tilled the earth in unprotected places."

Without technologically sophisticated means of transportation, John could understand why the farmers wouldn't want to trek for miles to get their goods to the primary market—the Citadel. A sudden thought struck him. "Couldn't they have used the transports built by Dalera to get their crops to the city?"

"This was done, yes. That is why the Sanctuary Halls have traditionally been used as markets during the times when the Wraith leave our world in peace." Kesun closed the panel. "Farmers, hunters and fishermen paid the Chosen for this service."

Rodney shook his head. "Is it me, or does that demonstrate a stunning lack of foresight on the part of a supposedly enlightened being? The system by its very nature creates an imperialistic society with a ruling class based on birth."

Cursing inwardly, and wishing he could install some kind of tact filter on his teammate, John watched Kesun's reaction. The Chosen's once-placid expression had tightened somewhat. He might not have fully understood the terms that Rodney had used, but there was no mistaking the veiled haughtiness in the scientist's body language. With a glare, John flicked his hand in a 'knock it off' gesture.

His bearing more guarded than before, Kesun continued. "The Chosen refused to transport those crops grown in forbidden places. Those who turned their backs on Dalera's laws became outlaws — barbarians — and responded by setting up their own towns and villages. Time passed and these barbarians dabbled in the black arts, developing Wraithcraft — which is also forbidden under Dalera's laws."

"Lovely. Perfect way to ensure the oppression of a society, by inhibiting technological development," Rodney muttered. "They were called the Dark Ages on Earth for a reason."

A moment passed as John just looked at him in disbelief. For an intelligent man, McKay could be incredibly shortsighted. "You're the one who figured out it was our stuff than triggered the alarms," he reminded him. "With Shields going glowy all the time, their early warning system would be useless. Which means the Wraith could simply attack on foot and get the drop on everyone."

"It was as you say," Kesun told them. "For this, the barbarians were banned from the Citadel and the protected lands. But with their Wraithcraft, their numbers multiplied. They settled distant lands until soon there were many more of them than of those who followed the old ways. These barbarians said that Dalera, and indeed Atlantis, was but a myth and the Wraith nothing more than evil lies fostered by the Chosen. They claimed that the Shields were wicked things, meant only to destroy their Wraithcraft, which besotted them."

John had studied enough history to get an idea of where this was headed. It depressed the hell out of him, because it meant that no matter where humans set up shop, they invariably made the same mistakes. Not the kind of thing to give a guy a lot of confidence in the notion of self-determination.

"Dalera is compassionate, but she does not suffer betrayal. For as it is written, the Wraith returned." The regret that marred Kesun's face was genuine. John glanced over at Rodney, but he'd gone off in exasperation and was busying himself with a study of the Ancient texts. "From all across Dalera, people fled to the Citadel and sought the protection of the Chosen. But it was refused."

A mutter that sounded something like 'naturally' drifted from Rodney's direction.

"It was not an easy choice, but it was one that had to be made. With so few followers of Dalera, the Citadel had fallen into disrepair, and the Chosen knew that they could protect only the Enclave."

For an instant, John felt a flicker of the same ire that Rodney had displayed. The last time he'd faced a choice like that, about who could and couldn't be saved, it had started him down a road in Afghanistan that hadn't exactly served him well.

"When the culling was over, those who survived begged our forgiveness. The Chosen emerged from the Enclave, and urged the people to once more follow the righteous ways of Dalera. But through the ages, the sequence of events which led to the tragedy was repeated again and again." Kesun turned and walked out on the balcony.

John followed, and he realized that they weren't in the main part of the city anymore, but on the highest point of the Citadel. While the expanse of sky, picture-perfect mountains and surrounding greenery was striking, he was more interested in focusing on what little he could see of the city below. A massive stone bridge, not unlike a smaller version of London's Tower Bridge, spanned one of the river channels. The square leading onto the bridge seemed alive with activity, as did the cluster of surrounding streets and alleys.

He recalled the semi-controlled chaos that had reigned in some of the garden spots to which he'd been deployed. Earth certainly couldn't point any fingers when it came to coexistence of divergent beliefs. Humans there had been doing a spectacular job of tearing each other apart for such things all by themselves. Throw a savage alien enemy into the mix, and he counted the Dalerans lucky to still have any semblance of a civilization left.

Leaning on the edge of the balcony, Kesun said, "Your friend does not agree with our ways."

Glancing back at Rodney, John replied, "They're foreign to us. Some of us take longer than others to accept the idea that different ways aren't necessarily wrong."

"I understand. Although it is the barbarians who bring the Wraith upon us, Dalera charged us to protect all against this most ancient of foes, showing favor no more or less to one or another." An air of defeat resonated from the Daleran. "Yet we are once more forced to choose, for we are too few to shield all designated villages from attack. Indeed, we are too few to protect even the Citadel."

Eyes clouding, Kesun turned to face him. "The Wraith have also returned sooner than expected. We prayed to Dalera to give us guidance. When you said you had come from Atlantis, I had believed our prayers were answered. Our situation grows increasingly dire. You see, I am the last of the Chosen. Our hope for the future died when my wife died in childbirth just six months ago."

"I'm sorry for your loss." It was a conditioned response, and it wasn't until after he'd given it that John thought about the wider implications of that statement. "I have to be honest with you. I'm not sure how we can help."

"You have come through the ring from the city in the heavens. Your very presence here is evidence that our faith is not misplaced."

Kesun's expression of faltering confidence was almost painful to witness. The survival of his people was at stake, and everything he had ever believed was telling him to place his faith in strangers. John recalled the distrust they'd faced in the marketplace, and it clawed at his insides to realize that Kesun's hopes were built on a very tenuous foundation.

"We didn't come here to prop up your evangelistic little regime." That harsh declaration came from the doorway, where Rodney stood with folded arms and a sour expression.

That did it. John drew on all the patience he possessed and turned to Kesun. "Would it be all right if my teammate and I took a few minutes to discuss some things?"

The Chosen nodded acquiescence. "Of course. I will wait

inside." His spine rigid with tension, he strode past with barely a glance toward Rodney.

The moment Kesun was out of sight, John spun toward the scientist, making no attempt to curb his irritation. "How hard would it be to bite back those superior comments for just a little while? Would it really be beyond your social skills?"

That triggered a flash of something dark in Rodney's gaze. "You really think enabling a whole system of misplaced beliefs is a better idea? You did get filled in on the concept behind the Goa'uld at some point, didn't you?"

John wasn't about to admit it, but that parallel hadn't crossed his mind. Having joined the Atlantis expedition at essentially the last minute, his knowledge of the Stargate program back on Earth had some gaps in it.

On an intellectual level, he knew that his expedition existed to discover technologies that could be used to defend their home galaxy against the enslaving Goa'uld. But that long-term view was hard to keep in focus when the short-term frequently challenged them just to stay alive. "It's not their fault that they don't have the outside knowledge we do," he argued. "From their perspective, this all makes sense. When people stray from Dalera's rules, the Wraith eventually attack, so they naturally connect the two."

"That's all very well and good, but there's a fundamental catch, and it goes like this: correlation does *not* imply causation." Rodney stalked further out onto the balcony. "In other words, just because two events happen in close proximity — "

"I know what it means, McKay. You're not the only one who ever took a lab class." The switch to his last name made an impression, and Rodney closed his mouth, at least temporarily. "The thing is, the two *are* correlated," John continued. "The Wraith can only attack successfully when people settle outside the limits of the shields and transport system that Dalera put in place. We see it as a technological limitation; they see it as a lack of faith. Either way, the end result is the same."

"They only see it that way because they've lost their knowledge of what Dalera really was." Rodney waved the notebook in his hand. "Otherwise they wouldn't have deified her."

"You don't know that. They view the ATA gene as a mark of favored status—"

"Which is undeniably ludicrous!"

His vehemence shocked John and might have even surprised Rodney himself. After a moment of awkward silence, the scientist continued in a more controlled tone, "The humans who lived here at the time of the Ancients must have realized that they weren't infallible, because Dalera's experiments were dismissed as failures."

"Experiments?"

"Some sort of automated neural interface device, probably to do with ascension. There are mentions of her work all over the place—the writing is quite literally on the wall. But since I've currently got no sensors, it's anyone's guess as to whether any of her equipment or data still exists." He waved his hand dismissively. "My point here is that those humans died out. Left behind, Dalera and her offspring did such a bang-up job of running things that everyone got a little too comfortable with the state of affairs. Eventually, if you'll pardon the reference, the Chosen started to drink their own Kool-Aid."

The analogy was disturbing, if not altogether unjustified. "Let's think big picture for a minute," suggested John. "Flat-out attacking a society's belief structure is generally not a good first step. I don't know if you noticed, but there are some very sharp-looking objects on this planet, and this might just get the wrong end pointed at us."

Rodney cocked an eyebrow. "Not fond of telling truth to power, are you?"

"They stationed me in Antarctica. Draw your own conclusions." John trained an unflinching gaze on Rodney until the other man yielded.

"Fine. Let me study the Shields, and I'll bite my tongue. I just— I find it absurd that an entire civilization can act according to fatally flawed reasoning. Especially the kind that segregates power in one place and one place only."

There was more to it than that, John suspected, but this

wasn't the right venue to explore it. "Their backs are against a wall, and they're assuming we're here to help. We need to find out what they're open to and try to stay as open as possible ourselves."

Rodney gave a shrug of indifference and turned toward the balcony door, tossing a last comment over his shoulder. "Incidentally, did our young Lieutenant pick himself up a groupie, or what?"

Smothering a grin, John remembered how Lisera had looked at Ford like he was the 'cute one' in a boy band. Taking one last scanning glance over the Citadel, he tried to gauge where that particular Sanctuary Hall might be located. He hadn't been able to get much of a look at the map inside the transport, something he intended to rectify on the return trip. Teyla and Ford would be getting along famously with their Daleran hosts by now, he was sure. There was no reason to worry or feel guilty about leaving them on their own.

Nope, no reason at all.

Other than the fact that concern and self-recrimination seemed to be built into his job description. There were some distinct downsides to being in charge.

Running a hand through his hair, John sighed and followed Rodney inside.

CHAPTER SIX

Not being an idiot, Rodney knew that Sheppard was right about making nice with these people. Their brief experience in the marketplace had demonstrated that becoming the subject of a witch-hunt would be ridiculously easy, and no one had ever accused him of being careless with his own welfare.

Kesun's expression was carefully neutral as they approached, but he kept his gaze trained on Sheppard, politely ignoring Rodney. Yep, he'd landed himself on probation already.

"Are you agreed?" Kesun asked without preamble. "You will aid us?"

Sheppard's eyes flicked toward Rodney for a second before he answered. "I'm not entirely sure that we can."

"It is a simple truth," Kesun persisted. "One that has been proven time and again for all to see. The blasphemous ways of the barbarians bring the Wraith upon us."

His resigned tone was one that Rodney knew well. It had been heard from any number of Atlantis's scientists when they were unable to make everyone around them see the brilliance of their ideas. Problem was, their ideas were only occasionally brilliant, yet the tone was chronically present.

With the sort of revelation that seemed reserved only for zealots, Kesun added, "Your arrival from Atlantis is undisputable proof of Dalera's existence. I believe it is a sign that only when every barbarian acknowledges Dalera, and abandons their sinful ways for all time can we be saved. A demonstration of your power may encourage this." He glanced at Sheppard. "Perhaps your weapons—?"

You're joking, right?

Before Rodney could decide how best to word his emphatic refusal, Sheppard responded, "We didn't come here either to affirm or question your people's faith in Dalera. In any case, what you've just suggested is not likely to restore your defensive capabilities, especially now that the Wraith have returned." Quickly and, Rodney had to admit, tactfully avoiding the reason why the Wraith were putting in an appearance ahead of schedule, the Major added, "What happened to reduce the numbers of Chosen so drastically?"

No longer able to contain his disdain, Rodney snapped, "That's patently obvious." Creating a genetic hegemony in any society could only lead to one, inevitable outcome, especially when it had been maintained over several thousand years. On that note, senility probably wasn't the only thing plaguing their mental faculties.

Sheppard looked at him expectantly.

"The Chosen don't really, ah, get out much, if you catch my drift." Rodney stashed his notebook in his pack.

Further explanation didn't appear to be required. The Major's forehead creased thoughtfully. "Kesun?" he said, offering up a polite smile. "Have any of you taken husbands or wives outside the Chosen?"

Kesun shook his head. "It is forbidden."

"One of Dalera's laws?"

"Once, every child born to this world was touched with a Shield. If the Shield's color came alive, such children were considered Chosen. Alas, during the times of the barbarians, these children were put to death, along with their mothers. When the Chosen emerged to defend against the Wraith, we banned this ritual so that no child should ever again suffer at the hands of the hateful and ignorant."

The idea that there might have been a legitimate reason for their isolation took Rodney by surprise. He'd expected something more pompous. Unfortunately, the validity of the practice wasn't the issue.

"When I was a child," Kesun continued, "the Great Plague befell us. While it killed many, it struck most deeply at the Chosen until only a few remained."

Nothing like several dozen generations of inbreeding to genetically predispose a population to disease. The only surprise was that the population of self-styled Chosen hadn't crashed centuries earlier. Realizing that the only way they were going to get out of here in any kind of hurry was by offering up a solution, Rodney said, "If you want to restore your numbers, then you'll have to rescind this moratorium. On marriage as well as touching the Shields. You need some sort of nationwide testing. And you need it now." That had come out sounding a lot like an ultimatum, he realized belatedly as the Major shot an exasperated glance in his direction.

Kesun looked at him curiously. "It is different among your people? There are no divisions between Chosen and others?"

Launching into a detailed civil rights lecture wasn't high on Rodney's to-do list, and neither was explaining the fact that almost no one on Earth knew or cared about the ATA gene. Therefore, he went for a simple if incomplete answer. "None. And I might add that the Chosen here owe their very existence to the fact that Dalera herself had offspring to someone outside of her kind." This time, he was rethinking the wisdom of the glib reply almost before it was out.

Beside him, Sheppard coughed. If the Major didn't read him the riot act on the ride home, Elizabeth certainly would during the debriefing. Tough. They'd wanted help. He'd given them the only viable answer. Besides, Kesun didn't appear to have taken offense. If anything, his interest seemed tweaked. "As you say," he replied. "These are things to consider."

"Fine, fine. Well, now that's settled," Rodney muttered, easing toward the transport.

Unfortunately, Sheppard didn't appear to be in any hurry to leave. "Something I don't get," he said. "Since the Chosen are now so few in number, don't the villagers know that they can't depend on you showing up in the transports?"

Brows furrowing in alarm, Kesun replied, "Even the most righteous among them blaspheme, which is what brought the Great Plague *and* the Wraith upon us all. Their faith *must* be restored before the Chosen can protect them."

Oh, this was just fantastic. "They don't know that most of the Chosen are dead, do they?" Rodney snapped.

"It is a question of faith!" Kesun almost hissed between his teeth. Visibly taking control of himself, he lifted his chin haughtily and added, "Your arrival will give them that faith."

Before Rodney could launch into another tirade, Sheppard stepped in with a healthy dose of reality. "Unfortunately, that won't resolve the immediate problem."

True. The old geezers could each grab themselves a dozen wives tomorrow, but even supposing the act alone didn't give most of them a massive coronary, the Wraith weren't likely to postpone their culling until the Chosen offspring arrived to save the day. As a scientist, he was trained to investigate all possible avenues. Realistically, that only left one solution. "The gene therapy."

Sheppard rounded on him, his eyebrows reaching up into his hairline. "You want to run that by me again?"

"It's an immediate solution." Rodney didn't add that it would effectively eliminate this hierarchical mess they'd gotten themselves into. "I don't see a downside to it."

"Other than the near-certainty of Dr Weir kicking our asses for offering something like this without consulting her?"

"I'm not offering it to them. I'm simply pointing out the only viable way out of their predicament. And presumably the reason that we're still standing here having this discussion is that you'd rather not leave them to be Wraith chow."

"Of what do you speak?" Kesun wanted to know.

Rodney turned toward him, but once again, the Major beat him to the punch, which was becoming more than annoying. "We have a way of giving a person a...medicine," Sheppard said, caution evident in his tone. "It would allow more people to operate the Shields."

Since Sheppard had insisted on dragging him into this otherwise futile discussion, he'd be damned if he'd see any proposed solution only shift their grand pecking order somewhat. "Many more," Rodney added purposefully.

If they'd been looking for a way to finally crack the Chosen's seemingly infinite patience, this might have been the silver bullet. Kesun's eyes grew huge, and he opened and closed his mouth several times before finding his voice. "This cannot be," he sputtered. "The Chosen are granted favor by Dalera herself. We cannot interfere with her will!"

"Genetics don't depend on anyone's will," Rodney argued. "That's the whole point of the term 'random selection.'"

Sheppard had been leaning against the wall, but now pushed himself off from it to stand upright. "Listen, Kesun, as Dr McKay said, we're just pointing out the options. The...medicine doesn't work on everyone, so maybe Dalera's still having her say that way." A glance in Rodney's direction dared him to protest at his own risk.

Doubt verging on panic was written clearly across Kesun's features. "Barbarians have no respect for Dalera's ways. What would become of us if they were made Chosen?"

"You could try working for a living." And that was a bad idea, too, because the man's once-pale skin now turned an entertaining shade of reddish-purple.

"Your lack of reverence is greatly disturbing to me, Dr McKay," he admonished. "I had expected better from the citizens of Atlantis."

"I apologize," Sheppard said immediately, adjusting his stance to something approximating attention. "This is my team. I should have better control of it."

What the *hell*? Rodney had never seen the Major even attempt to pull rank on him before. What was the point, since he didn't even *have* a rank? He turned an indignant gape on Sheppard, only to be met with a coldly imperious stare.

The melodrama had an effect on Kesun, though. He nodded, albeit stiffly. "I must confer with the others."

"We understand," Sheppard replied. "Should we wait here?"

"Please." With a final, scornful look in Rodney's direction, the Chosen turned on his heel and strode back into the main chamber.

Sheppard crossed his arms and regarded Rodney, the fierce demeanor fading into annoyance. "Rodney," he said dryly. "I can't tell you how warm and fuzzy it feels to know how highly you value my opinion."

Well and truly incensed by the way he'd just been treated, Rodney snapped, "Your opinion?"

"That whole 'work and play well with others' pep talk from the balcony? Ring any bells?"

"I appreciate the complexity of the situation, but since you insist on wanting to help out here, there's a limit to how much of this divine-will crap I can swallow. These people will be sitting ducks for the Wraith if someone in this place doesn't open up their mind just a fraction." Rodney could accept a certain amount of that nonsense from the others, but from a trusted colleague? He didn't see the need to go quietly. "And while we're on the subject of working and playing well with others, what precisely was that little display about? You should have better control of *your* team? If your goal was to sound just as superior as they do, fantastic job!"

"Thank you," Sheppard replied amiably.

Rodney halted, confused. Then he got it. He'd only paid the barest amount of attention in his intro sociology class in college, but the old 'When in Rome' axiom seemed to apply here. He blew out a long breath. "You can't honestly think I'm wrong about this."

"I didn't say that." Sheppard's gaze was hard to decipher. Not that Rodney had ever been an expert at reading people, but this man seemed to have a singular talent for inscrutability. "We're already crossing about six different lines that probably shouldn't be crossed, but we're here now, so let's see how they respond."

A less-than-comfortable silence fell in the corridor as they waited for a signal from inside the main chamber. Sheppard eventually offered up a neutral token of conversation. "So, no ZPM, huh?"

"I doubt it." Rodney pulled his Shield off the belt clip and examined it. "They appear to be modeled on the personal shields, drawing just enough energy from the bearer to activate the crystal inside, hence the change in color from black to aquamarine. Primary power likely comes from the very EM fields and any incoming energy weapons' fire that they're blocking, which in turn causes the crystals to illuminate, thereby serving as a warning to the bearers. Similar to the way I used lightning to power the shield generators on Atlantis. Rather imaginative, really." Ignoring the Major's rolled eyes, he examined the casing. Something was buried inside one end of it. "Probably also has some sort of capacitor—"

"The others will speak to you." Kesun addressed Sheppard. "Come." With a soft hiss of fur across the polished floor, he led them back into the main chamber.

Rodney hung back a step. If they respected Sheppard more for whatever reason, then let him handle it.

Kesun's father regarded them coolly. "The scourge of the Wraith has remained constant for thousands of years," he said. "Barbarians have seen to that. Now that their wickedness has poisoned even the righteous with their Wraithcraft, Dalera has turned her back upon us all."

Oh, yes, another hugely profound surprise. Divine self-righteousness taken to its ultimate conclusion. The Wraith would get more sustenance from a used toothpick than they would from these Chosen, so let the masses burn—or in this case, have the life sucked from them—as punishment for their evil ways. "Anyone spell Armageddon?" Rodney muttered. He probably could have shouted it because no one except Sheppard seemed to hear.

"The arrival of our guests from Atlantis could also be a sign that Dalera is giving us a final chance, Father," Kesun suggested.

An emphysemic wheeze erupted from one of the others. "You encourage us to interfere with Dalera's design for her people?" A second wheeze followed before he added, "How are we to know that this potion you offer is not Wraithcraft by another name?" A crackle of falling logs and a shower of sparks in the fireplace seemed to add weight to his point.

Kesun looked mildly appalled at that. "An offer was made and declined. There is no cause for accusation. I am merely suggesting that if the Chosen were also to return to the old ways, of taking unto them wives from the people, and testing each child at birth—"

"I will hear no more of this!" Kesun's father decreed with a weak pounding of his fist on the table. The helmet wobbled dangerously close to the edge, and Kesun snatched it up. "Dalera has deemed that the wicked shall be punished."

The warning look that both Sheppard and Kesun shot Rodney wasn't necessary. He was so far beyond irate that he could focus only on the thing they'd come for. And since it was obvious that even if there was a ZPM someplace, there was no possible way he could locate it, he clutched firmly onto his Shield. At least they'd gained something from this otherwise utterly wasted excursion.

"I will accompany our visitors back to the Sanctuary Hall," Kesun said, giving a polite bow in the general direction of the table.

They made an awkward attempt at bidding farewell to the Chosen and left the room, trailing in Kesun's wake.

The drink that Yann had purchased from a nearby stall was sweet and warm, with a trace of an unfamiliar spice. Teyla smiled her thanks, clasping the mug in both hands.

Lieutenant Ford made a surprised sound. "It's like hot cider!" he said happily, passing his cup to Lisera.

The girl's answering smile was genuine, if a bit blank. Seeing the Lieutenant pleased, it seemed, was enough to please her. She took a measured sip of the steaming drink, as if afraid to offend by indulging too much, then shyly handed it back to Ford, and pointed up to the last of the teaching windows. "Entire families of Chosen once lived in the protected villages, along with garrisons of warriors. But then barbarians broke Dalera's laws, settled in forbidden lands and, having invaded the Citadel, forced the Chosen to live inside their Enclave." She cast her gaze downward. "The lack of faith by some punishes all."

Soot and grime smudged the once brightly colored windows. When Teyla pulled her gaze from them, Yann's hard-faced expression caught her attention. "Is there more to tell?" she asked him.

Yann hesitated, casting a glance at Lisera. "The girl is not wrong," he allowed. "But she speaks with the voice of a child. Farming lands outside the Chosen's decree was not done to give insult to Dalera. It was a necessity. The prescribed lands are far from the Citadel and heavily forested. While we have blackpowder that can be used to remove tree stumps from some lands, the problem of distance cannot be remedied, and the Chosen have long neglected the task of transporting the crops to market. We have been forced to use beasts of burden to pull our goods by cart, but the distance is too great. Unless the nearer lands are tilled, the crops spoil before reaching the Citadel." He stood and shook the stiffness from his legs.

"Perhaps the Chosen would come to the transports more readily if people paid what was asked of them." Lisera's reply was given in a timid voice, but its point was blunt.

With a quick glance at the guards, who were out of earshot, Yann retorted, "A full payment for a half-measure of protection?"

A brief light display interrupted his words, and signaled the arrival of a transport. Kesun stepped out, with Major Sheppard and Dr McKay beside him. The scientist looked more irked than usual, while the Major, behind his usual mask of nonchalance, was pensive. "Ford, Teyla," Sheppard said to them in greeting. "Making friends?"

"We have learned much," Teyla responded.

"Same here. And now I think it's time we headed home." The Major's hooded expression told Teyla that there was a great deal to discuss.

"Sir," Ford asked, picking up his pack, "what about Lisera?"

"Her injury is beyond the medical capabilities of this world," Teyla explained. "If left here, she would not regain the use of her leg."

The Major glanced at Kesun. "Would it be acceptable for us to take Lisera back to Atlantis? Just for a couple of days."

A range of expressions that Teyla could not fully interpret crossed the face of the Chosen. "Dalera was the greatest healer our kind has ever known." With a sly edge to his voice, he added, "If the girl were to return from Atlantis with her leg mended, I believe it would help to convince *all* of our people of the righteousness of Dalera's ways — including a return to the traditions of which we spoke. Very well. Take her to Atlantis, so that she may come back to us with knowledge of its wonders."

The joy that lit Lisera's delicate features was indescribable. The young woman turned shining eyes to Lieutenant Ford. "You have saved me once more," she whispered.

Taken aback, the Lieutenant could only offer an embarrassed smile. "I don't know about that," he began, but Sheppard and Kesun were already discussing specifics.

"If our doctor — our healer — can treat Lisera easily, we'll return with her in two days," the Major explained. "In the event that she requires more time, we'll report back to you."

In response, the Chosen gave a small bow. Teyla noted that he faced Major Sheppard directly, not acknowledging McKay.

Having seen the return of the rest of the team, many of the villagers milled about in the vicinity of the transport. "Guess these folks could use a ride home," Ford said. He went to pick up Lisera, but Yann had already done so.

"Yeah. What's a few hundred hitchhikers?" The Major opened the doors with a swipe of his hand across the touchpad, and the villagers shuffled into the transport. "Rodney, you want to take this group or the next?"

"What am I, a bus driver now?" Dr McKay muttered, stepping into the transport.

While they waited, Teyla noticed that the villagers Kesun had transported into the Sanctuary Hall were pressing payment into his hand. That left her to wonder about the eventual fate of those, like Lisera, who had nothing to give. Would they be left outside the Citadel when the Wraith sought a full harvest from this world?

Teyla waited for the transport to fill once more before stepping in behind Sheppard. When they emerged into the same inn that they'd left hours earlier, the villagers streamed out of the building with murmured and somewhat begrudging thanks. The Major, however, lingered until everyone had left. With a quick glance around the inn to make certain that no one was observing him, he returned to the transport and bent to examine the panel inside.

"What is it?" she inquired, watching from the door.

"Aha. Found it," Sheppard replied. "Teyla, would you step back in here a minute?"

When she did so, he touched a second, cunningly concealed panel, and a row of three colored buttons appeared. Pressing the first caused the doors of a larger wall panel within the transport to slide back, revealing the same style of map and grid of lights as seen inside the transports on Atlantis.

"That's interesting. Unless you've suddenly acquired the ATA gene, Kesun wasn't being entirely honest about who could and who couldn't access the Enclave. It's just about knowing where to look. Okay—" Giving her a quick grin, the Major closed the panel again and gestured for her to step outside with him. "Try closing the transport doors."

She did as he asked, but the exterior panel remained unresponsive to her touch. "It appears that in this, at least, he spoke true. Only a Chosen may operate the transport."

"There you are," McKay called impatiently from the entrance of the inn. "Do you think we could leave now?" Teyla watched as McKay followed Sheppard's gaze in the direction of the bar. The air of tension between the two men was made even more apparent when the scientist grumbled, "Don't tell me you're thinking about having one for the road."

"Nah. This isn't the time to test any kind of bottle-to-throttle rule." The Major smiled longingly. "Can't blame a guy for wishing, though."

The humor in his voice did little to mollify Dr McKay, who was evidently impatient to return to Atlantis.

Just outside the inn, Yann, with Lieutenant Ford and the innkeeper's assistance, was fashioning a makeshift stretcher. Once Lisera was on the stretcher, they made their way out into the square and then down the path that led out of town. "So what's your grand plan?" McKay took rapid steps to keep pace with the Major's long strides. "Bring the girl back here with a neatly packaged plaster cast, pat everyone on the head and say 'good luck'?"

"I didn't think you much cared," Sheppard replied mildly, glancing down at the Shield that Dr McKay was clutching.

Rolling his eyes in frustration, McKay retorted, "The question of 'caring' is superfluous — this is about the principle of the situation. They need the gene therapy, and I'm not going to waste any more time trying to convince you because you already know that I'm right."

"I also know that they refused the gene therapy, so let's not treat this like a foregone conclusion, okay?" The Major offered him a tight smile.

"Of *course* they refused it! They're the almighty Chosen." McKay threw a disgruntled hand in the air. "They can't stand the idea of their happy hierarchy being imploded, when that's exactly what needs to happen, because it's disenfranchising the vast majority of the population."

Dismayed by his attitude, Teyla now understood what had provoked Kesun's barely civil farewell. In her travels, she'd learned that each society viewed the Wraith through whatever lens their culture provided them. The Dalerans' belief in a divine influence to protect them from attack was no doubt more comprehensible than Dr McKay's curt lectures on electromagnetic field theory. "Have you made any attempt to take their view?" she asked, prompting McKay to look back at her. "Kesun is working within his own knowledge and experience, just as you work within yours. You should not fault him because the two are not the same."

"And he's a realist," Sheppard added, not slowing his pace. "I didn't get the feeling he'd sacrifice his people just to keep a grip on power."

"Oh, no? It sure felt like that to me." McKay's foot caught on a root and he stumbled. He leveled a muted curse at the offending tree. At that moment Teyla realized that the scientist always seemed at odds with whatever world he inhabited. Every misfortune that he encountered was always due to the shortcomings of others, be they objects or people. "Kesun may be the most visible of the Chosen," McKay finished, "but what about the rest of those old relics?"

"They have had many centuries to develop their understanding of the Wraith," Teyla said. "Such things do not immediately change based on the claims of a few strangers."

"There's a typically provincial mindset," McKay muttered. "A little perspective adjustment didn't hurt the Athosians any, did it?"

A wave of molten anger flowed through her veins. How *dare* he? She'd known him to condescend before but never like this.

Before she could respond, the Major spun around, halting their motion. "That's enough," he warned, his voice low and dangerous. "Nobody's all-knowing. Least of all us." That last part was uttered with a hard stare at McKay. "Let's just get home and work things out there."

Still simmering with resentment, Teyla held her tongue, even as the scientist blithely continued. "And if you really think the Chosen's viewpoint is worth saving, you might want to ask them why nothing changed after the plague hit them, and *only* them, so hard. Do they really expect to be able to maintain their status now that they're down to about twenty?"

So few? That did come as a surprise to Teyla. Recalling the display in the puddle jumper, she now realized that no more than twenty EM fields had been scattered about the Citadel.

Beside her, Yann fumbled the stretcher and ceased walking. Teyla saw a look of fear cross his eyes and was about to castigate McKay for his unchecked words when the merchant blurted, "Wraithcraft!"

She followed his gaze to where the puddle jumper had suddenly appeared. Remembering her first encounter with the vessel, Teyla smiled in understanding. "Ancient craft," she corrected, walking down into the shallow gully. "This is how we traveled to Dalera from Atlantis."

McKay's reaction was less docile. "Uh oh." He yanked the glowing Shield from his belt. "These must've deactivated the jumper's cloak."

Sheppard pulled his own Shield free, and the two men shoved

them into Teyla's hands. The Shields, cool to the touch, went obligingly black, and the jumper vanished from sight again until the Major deactivated the cloaking device.

"Truly wondrous," Yann murmured, eyes wide with unashamed awe. He and Ford maneuvered Lisera inside and onto a bench, while Sheppard slid into the pilot's seat and laid a hand on the control panel. The answering hum of power and array of lights to which they'd become accustomed never came.

"Already used up your allotment of brain power for the day?" McKay guessed.

The Major shot him a dirty look. "If yours is so limitless, you try it."

McKay shrugged and put his hand down on the controls. No response. Lines of concentration appeared on his brow. "If this is what it looks like, I'm about to reach unprecedented levels of frustration," he commented brusquely. "It's possible that even though they're currently unpowered, the capacitors in the Shields are still having some residual effect based on proximity."

Comprehending, Teyla kept her hold on the Shields and, indicating that Yann should follow, stepped out of the jumper. The craft promptly came to life. Even from outside, she could see McKay's eyes blaze. "Son of a *bitch*."

"Calm down, would you?" Sheppard told him.

"If it's all the same to you, I'd rather fume for a moment, thanks very much! There were two and only two leads on this backwater planet. One was Dalera's supposed research on neural interfaces, which I'll never be able to even locate, let alone study properly, without powered equipment. The other is the Shields, and if we can't even take one of them back for research, this excursion just went from marginally pointless to completely pointless!" Lips compressed in anger, he stood and stormed out of the jumper.

Some nasty corner of Teyla's mind was starting to wish that Dr McKay would show up for one of her training sessions in the gym. She would not injure him, but she would make him think twice about dismissing everything that didn't fit his point of view.

Joining them outside, Sheppard said, "I'm not all that wild about the idea myself, Rodney, but seeing as we don't have a whole lot of choices, we're going to have to leave the Shields behind."

With an exasperated sigh, Rodney thrust his Shield at Yann — who promptly stepped back, a look of shock on his face.

"Is it not forbidden for any but the Chosen to touch the Shields?" Teyla pointed out. Fully aware that she herself was currently holding them, she still felt the need to remind McKay of the culture he seemed to be giving thought to deconstructing.

"It's not one of Dalera's laws." McKay's fists curled in frustration. "Just another one of those guidelines that's so helpful in marginalizing commoners."

Sheppard looked thoughtful. "Well, Kesun did imply that when Lisera returned, he could probably rescind that particular ruling."

Along with the revelation that the Chosen were few in number, his words left Teyla in no doubt about what discussions must have taken place in the Enclave.

"Perhaps you can hide the Shields." Yann pointed to the outcrop of rocks on the edge of the gully. "I will tell no one of them."

Although she sensed no overt deception, she nevertheless felt that something was amiss. Hesitating a moment, Teyla walked to the rocks and found a suitable crevice. She hid the Shields within and carefully covered the opening with a thorn-covered sod.

"In two days' time, I shall return to this place," Yann continued.

"We'll see you then," Sheppard replied with a smile that failed to mask the uncertainty in his eyes. It was apparent that he, too, was not comfortable with the situation. But to return to Atlantis, it seemed that they must indeed leave the Shields behind, and it would be both foolish and wasteful to simply cast them aside.

Yann moved away from the jumper, while Teyla and the others went back inside and took their seats. The hatch slowly rose and locked into place with a metallic *clang*. When the jumper ascended, Lisera's eyes widened and her hand scrabbled for Ford's sleeve. The Lieutenant looked embarrassed, but gave her a reassuring smile, closing his fingers around the girl's.

"It is beyond futile to drag me along on these outings to provide solutions to problems, and then refuse to accept the *only* practical solution because it offends your moral sensibilities." McKay sullenly stared out at the sky, which quickly darkened to the speckled blackness of space. "I can't believe you'd be willing to condemn those people to death just to avoid stepping on a few toes."

Teyla's anger flared again, but the remark seemed to be directed at the Major, who responded without delay. "And I can't believe you think that's all this is. Didn't we already learn the hard way that, once a society has its mind made up about something, it's damn near impossible to change anything? Weren't the Hoffans pretty much a case in point on that subject?"

There was a brief pause, and Teyla recalled the Hoffans' single-minded willingness to sacrifice half their people in order to protect the remainder against the Wraith. McKay, however, wasn't dissuaded. "This is not even remotely close to the same thing," he replied dismissively. "The Hoffans took a *vote*, for Pete's sake. If the Dalerans had a fraction of those same democratic rights, this would be different. But it's not, and you can't tell me that they're exercising their own free will to rely on the Chosen when they've been fed a bunch of crap about what makes them Chosen in the first place."

"Quit putting words in my mouth," Sheppard said tightly. "I'm no more satisfied with this setup than you are. But if you're going to insist on dismantling their entire religion, could you at least keep your voice down about it?"

"Oh, as if the concept of gene therapy could have made any sense to Yann or anyone else. It's so far beyond their scientific understanding, assuming there is such a thing as science on their planet—"

Teyla had heard enough. She allowed a short bark of derisive laughter to escape, causing both men to turn in her direction.

"There is a word your people use," she said. "I have forgotten it, but it means a person who criticizes others for the very traits that he or she displays."

Sheppard's gaze shifted cautiously toward McKay. "Hypocrite," he told her.

"Yes." She faced the scientist with no mask for her contempt. "You, Doctor, are demonstrating yourself to be the worst kind of hypocrite."

"Me?" McKay's eyes bulged. "I was perfectly happy to leave these people alone until the Major here decided to play hero. Yet the moment I suggest a way to help, you dismiss it because it undermines their privileged class!"

"Because your 'help' is shortsighted and shows no respect for them. You say you want to end the elitism of the Chosen, but you look down on them simply because they do not see their world through the same eyes that you do. How is your elitism any better than theirs?"

"Hey! Excuse me for not displaying the politically correct level of deference to their belief system, but it's those beliefs that are going to destroy them!"

Teyla heard his indignant tone and understood that she would get no further. His arrogance was well entrenched. She held few remaining illusions about the fallibility of her human companions, but every reminder held a fresh pinprick of sadness. They were not the Ancestors, to be sure. "How fortunate for you," she replied with icy civility, "that your perspective is the only one required to explain the universe."

A painful silence fell in the cabin of the jumper. McKay's eyes narrowed but he turned to face forward without comment, while Sheppard looked surprised by her use of sarcasm. Teyla glanced back at Lisera, but the Lieutenant had been speaking quietly to the girl, and she seemed too enthralled by her surroundings to have noticed the disagreement.

When the Stargate appeared, Sheppard pressed the coordinates on the DHD and the 'gate obediently activated. "Atlantis, Jumper One reporting in."

Dr Weir's voice answered within seconds. "This is Atlantis.

How was your trip, Major?"

"Oh, you know, the usual. The drinks were overpriced and the lines were too long for the rides." A typical response from the Major, but it sounded forced. "We're coming in with one extra passenger. A local needs a broken leg set. Think Dr Beckett can spare a few minutes?"

"We'll give him a heads-up. Can I assume from this that you're planning on returning to the planet?"

Sheppard's gaze swept over his brooding teammates. "We do intend to go back. What we do once we're there is still up for debate."

"All right. Come on home."

CHAPTER SEVEN

"Historically," John finished, "during an attack, in order to maximize coverage of the EM fields until everyone made it in from outlying settlements, some Chosen manned the transports while the others spread out with the warriors around the villages."

"Sounds like an effective system," Elizabeth said, dabbing her nose with a tissue. Carson had given her something to fight the worst effects of the head cold, but the medication hadn't dulled the gritty sensation at the back of her eyes and throat.

"Oh, absolutely," scoffed Rodney. "As long as no one's bothered by the fine print that forbids any use of technology."

Elizabeth regarded him without speaking for a moment. It was difficult to determine what had their chief scientist more riled up: the fact that they'd found nothing on the planet that would aid them, or the existence of this theocratic culture.

If the mission had been merely unsuccessful, that would have been one thing. The tension radiating from the members of her flagship team, however, made it clear that there were other issues to be confronted. When she'd seen them in the jumper bay upon their return, John had been the only one to meet her gaze. Ford had been busy with their injured ward, while Teyla and Rodney had avoided looking at her or each other. There was a distinct frost over the group, and Elizabeth was troubled by the idea that she couldn't yet understand it, much less resolve it.

Aloud, however, she simply said, "While I can see your point, Rodney, I think it's best under circumstances like these to consider our primary mandate."

"Oh? And which one would that be? The need to acquire the technology to save Earth from the Goa'uld? Locate ZPMs in order to reestablish contact with Earth? Or, and this is my personal favorite, find some way to defend ourselves from the all-but-inevitable Wraith attack?"

"I thought your personal favorite was locating a planet with a stash of coffee beans," muttered Lieutenant Ford.

Despite herself, and the strain in the briefing room, Elizabeth was unable to choke back a laugh. It abruptly turned into a wracking cough. Not that that was enough to faze Rodney. The scientist immediately clutched his lidded coffee mug and pulled it close.

"Don't panic, Rodney," John smirked. "No one's about to steal your precious—"

"And now we're back to the insults, which are both mean-spirited and immaterial to the issue at hand." Rodney spun his chair to face Elizabeth. "By standing idly by and allowing this religious elitist farce to continue, we're washing our hands of an entire civilization. This bunch of self-styled fanatics will continue to subjugate the masses until they've led the whole planet into their own version of the Apocalypse. Maybe I'm fuzzy on the details, but didn't we used to be champions of the downtrodden?"

He'd said 'we', but Elizabeth knew the remark had been directed at her. Although she was accustomed to hearing that tone from him, the object of his ire was a surprise. Overpowering concern for the well-being of strangers seemed uncharacteristic for the Rodney McKay that she thought she knew. Then she remembered the way he'd stepped between her and Kolya's gun just days ago and revised her opinion. The storm had brought to light hidden attributes in all of them. Still, there was no getting around the facts of the current situation. They were hardly in a position to help themselves, much less others.

"Dr McKay," Teyla said in cool tones, "did not Kesun say that Lisera's return will encourage all Dalerans to embrace their ancient traditions?"

"Including testing the general population for the gene, and marrying outside of the Chosen," John finished.

"Oh, and we're meant to believe that exclusive club of octogenarian zealots is really going to let him shake everything up?"

"Kesun's only one of a handful of Chosen who are even capable of leaving their Enclave," said John. "It's not exactly like they have radios, television, or even servants to inform their retirees of what's going on out in the real world."

"From what we saw it was pretty low tech," Ford added. "But then so are a lot of other places we've visited. Most of the people looked to be in reasonable shape. Except Lisera. But she'd been on the run since her family was culled."

"The markets were filled with many, many items for trade," Teyla added. "More than I have seen on most planets. And their apothecary was well-stocked."

"So their economy is operating well," mused Elizabeth. "That's always a good sign."

John wrinkled his nose. "Something doesn't smell right, though."

"Boring," snapped Rodney. "Joke's worn thin."

"Not you. I meant the setup as well as the sewerage. It was more of a deep, ingrained stench than your average busted sewer pipe and musty ancient stone smell."

"You're missing the point entirely — all of you!" Rodney sat forward. "These people are in a unique position. With the Shields, they have the capacity to defend against the Wraith — if they're administered gene therapy. Without it, they're as good as dead. Given how rare the gene is on Earth, testing everyone in Dalera is unlikely to turn up more than one or two in the entire population. To properly defend the Citadel and even a fraction of those villages beyond, they're going to need at least a hundred."

Elizabeth frowned at Rodney. She wasn't pleased that he'd offered the gene therapy to their new acquaintances in the first place. What should have been a moot point following the Dalerans' refusal, however, was rapidly turning into a kind of crusade for the scientist. She just wasn't certain what had triggered it. His not finding a ZPM on the planet was likely contributing to his overall frustration. Or perhaps it was simply that he needed to believe that the Wraith could be thwarted. If that were the case, she could hardly blame him.

"I understand your feelings on this, Rodney, but Atlantis is simply not in a position to go barging in and impose our system of values on other cultures. I agree with you that the situation is not ideal, and I agree with the idea of introducing low-tech items in order for people to get to the transports or directly to the Citadel faster. Bicycles, for example."

"Personally, I'd vote for skateboards." John slouched low in his chair and flashed a grin, briefly resembling a teenager.

"Brilliant." Rodney had apparently redirected his irritation into dismantling the ideas of others. "And exactly how would they go about using a skateboard in the middle of a plowed field or forest?"

John feigned pondering the question and quirked an eyebrow. "Mountain skateboards?"

It was an obvious attempt to lighten the tension in the room, and Elizabeth appreciated it, but Rodney had gone beyond seeing the humor in anything. Snapping his mouth shut into a thin, bitter line, he crossed his arms and stared at some fascinating point on the ceiling, impatiently waiting for the meeting to end.

"All right," she said, choosing to cut her losses. "For the moment let's focus on a trade deal, food in exchange for improving the Dalerans' method of transport. It'll give some of the engineers a break from making repairs to the city. Let's see what we can come up with before your next arranged meeting time on the planet."

Rodney was the first to exit the briefing room, brushing past the swiveling wall panels while they were still in motion. Elizabeth stayed in place as the others streamed out, reaching for the box of tissues she'd taken to carrying around.

Whatever unglamorous sound she made with the tissue must have caught her military advisor's attention, because he remained behind. "You're looking pretty far under the weather," he observed, concern shading his features. "Somebody bring some Pegasus germs back through the 'gate?"

"That's Carson's best guess. If I ever find out who it was, I'll put him or her on mess hall duty indefinitely." She attempted a faint smile.

It didn't fool him. John folded his arms and half-leaned, half-sat on the edge of the table near her. "If there's stuff you need to hash out, I'd like to think I could be a reasonable sounding board."

The offer would have felt less awkward had he not been studying the floor when he made it. Even so, Elizabeth was grateful. Moreover, he was right. There weren't many people on Atlantis with whom she could engage in any kind of personal conversation. John Sheppard, whether by position or character, was one of the few.

"I'm not indifferent to the Dalerans' situation," she began, swiping at her reddened eyes with a second tissue.

John's brow creased. "I never thought you were. Neither will Rodney, once he snaps out of his funk about having to leave the Shields behind."

"I suspected something of that nature." Her quick smile faded. "It's just that this is an incredibly difficult issue on which to take a stance. As usual, it's all shades of gray, which is something that Rodney has never been very good at dealing with." She gave a soft sigh, resting her elbows on the table. "I seem to spend a lot of time lately second-guessing my decisions, wondering if some small difference might have led to a better result. You have to admit that this expedition can't exactly be called a smashing success at the moment."

"Based on the original mission parameters, I'd agree with that. But here's the thing." John fixed a serious gaze on her. "The mission was designed in another galaxy, before anyone had the first clue what we'd find out here. No one back on Earth could have predicted the choices we'd have to make, and the really tough ones tend to fall on you more than anyone else. So you can't try to hold any of this up to Earth standards. They don't apply."

Elizabeth was mildly surprised by how much sence that viewpoint made. Then again, she'd immersed herself in all things Ancient for months leading up to the expedition, which might have given her a false expectation of familiarity. John, by contrast, had joined them much later and viewed every last detail as foreign. Reality probably lay somewhere in between. "I guess we are making up our own rules, to a certain extent. Still, there are times when I worry about overstepping our bounds, and I hate feeling like I'm working without a net." For a moment, her thoughts turned to Simon. Safe, gentle Simon. He'd always provided that support. If — *when* they found a way to get back to Earth, well, the prospect of seeing Simon again was something to hold on to. Meanwhile— "If I make a wrong move, will you tell me?"

His eyes flared wide for a moment, as if the trust inherent in that question had startled him. "Elizabeth, if I think you're making a wrong move, you'll know it." He offered a wry smile that concealed far more than it showed. "I try not to act like a caricature of my service record, but the fact remains that I'm not known for unquestioning obedience."

She knew that, of course, having seen his file back in Antarctica, and having received a warning from General O'Neill and a sharper one from Colonel Sumner about what it meant to take on an officer with that kind of reputation. At the time, she had dismissed their concerns. As O'Neill himself had demonstrated on countless occasions, independent thinking was not necessarily an undesirable trait in an officer. She hadn't found any cause to revisit the issue thus far.

"Anyway, you're doing fine," he continued, dispelling the brief unsettledness. "For what it's worth, I think you're right about what we should and shouldn't do regarding the Dalerans. Kesun's not being completely honest with us, at least when it comes to who can access the Enclave."

When he elaborated, she nodded. "Okay, that helps me. I'm fairly confident in this one. In my experience, sudden, forced cultural changes generally leave a vacuum that makes things far worse before they can get better."

"Mine, too." John's response was unassuming, but once again, it was what he didn't say that spoke louder.

"You must have seen a lot in places like Afghanistan."

"Enough to know that, to mess around with issues of faith,

we'd need an airtight plan for the fallout. And I've yet to run across any of those."

Elizabeth replied with a contemplative smile. "True enough. Thank you, John."

"Any time. Feel better, all right?" He moved toward the door, but glanced back with a glint of humor in his eye. "I'll ask the mess hall sergeants if they've got any chicken soup."

It had been a terrifying yet wondrous dream. No. More than that, for Lisera could never have envisioned such things as she had beheld this past day. She had flown as high as a bird until the Citadel appeared as nothing more than a patch in a blanket of many patterns across the land. Then the sky above had swiftly grown dark, as if night had fallen, and she had looked down upon Dalera and seen it as she saw the twin worlds that crossed the sky at night. She was in the heavens, on her way to a land that many, including her mother, had held as nothing more than a child's tale, a myth. Home of the Ancestors, home of Dalera; Atlantis!

When the ring of magic appeared, she had gasped and looked upon it in awe. Parts of it had glowed the same color as the Shields. She'd cried out in amazement when water shot through the ring, and Aiden had clasped her hand. Plunging into the bright, rippling pool, the glowing tunnel beyond had dazzled her. Then abruptly, it was over, and they were inside a beautiful and light-filled room.

So much to see, so many smiling people, welcoming her to Atlantis! She was nothing, just a girl of no consequence, and yet she was made to feel as important as a Chosen. After she had been taken to a smaller room where people were dressed in white cloaks, Aiden had left her with the promise that he would later return.

Someone had given her yet more medicine. This time, the needle remained in her arm and a strange, transparent rope connected it to an equally transparent bag of water. They told her that the water would make her better. A great tiredness had overcome her, and she had slept.

When Lisera awoke, her leg was encased in a thin white rock. Oddly, the worst of her hunger and thirst had gone. More, she felt clean, and was garbed in a soft robe. Time passed. She met each new visitor with a hopeful smile. Aiden would come soon. He had promised.

One such visitor had brought a platter of marvelous tasting foods. So much food! Biting back tears of gratitude, she had eaten every last crumb. Then night had fallen, and she had slept for a time. But the strangeness and comfort of such a wonderful bed could not be wasted on sleep. Her time here would be short. A night, perhaps two, was all she would be allowed on this world in the heavens.

Sitting in the darkness, running her hands across cloth of such quality, breathing in air tainted only with a sweet, salty tang, Lisera's happiness slowly receded. She could walk, they assured her, but what they called a cast must remain upon her leg for fifty days. Once back in Dalera, like so many others who had lost all, she would still have to fend for herself. With her pace slowed, she would not be able to outrun the Wraith. This left her with no other option. She must remain in the Citadel rather than return to living off the land. The images of what Balzar had done to her mother, the foul smell of his breath and the gleam in his eyes, returned to haunt her, and she began to cry.

Soft footfalls came from behind her. Turning, she looked into the darkness. "Aiden?" A light appeared by her bed, and with it came more disappointment. It was the one called Dr Beckett.

"Hello, lassie. What's this? Tears?"

Sniffing and rubbing a hand across her cheeks, Lisera said, "I am sorry to have woken you."

His smile was kind, as were his eyes. "Hardly. I was just examining your blood work. Hadn't eaten in a wee while, had you?"

Unbidden, her tears fell in full measure. Perhaps it was the gentle manner in which he spoke, or his kindness, but she was reminded of her brother, and all that she had lost.

"Are you in any pain?" Dr Beckett asked, examining the bag of healing water.

She shook her head.

Sighing softly, he pulled a white cloth from a nearby box and handed it to her. It was obviously intended for her to blow her nose, but the material felt too precious to spoil. Unwilling to offend, she reluctantly used it.

"There are different kinds of pain, Lisera, some of them no medicine can cure," he continued.

Lisera looked into his eyes, and saw in them a faraway sadness. "You have lost those you loved to the Wraith?"

His mouth lowered in regret. "Let's just say that I know what it's like to lose people you care for. You're young yet, and so it's very hard to fathom, but the pain will fade in time." When she said nothing, he added, "Do you want to tell me about it?"

If she spoke the truth, would they punish her? Her mother had always taught her that a lie was like theft, for it took from others as surely as stealing. She had given the payment of storytelling to Teyla for bringing her to this marvelous place. No matter the consequence, she must give truth to those who had treated her with such kindness. Truly, no punishment they could mete out could be as bad as what she would face upon her return to Dalera.

They circled each other slowly, warriors of different worlds, each taking the other's measure in full before committing to the attack. Normally it was Major Sheppard who struck first, but this time it was Teyla, sensing an opportunity and swinging her staffs simultaneously toward his midsection.

Sheppard blocked the first move easily, the second less easily. After a few moments he tired of being on the defensive and spun, crouching low and sweeping one staff out to catch her in the legs. It knocked her off-balance for only a second, but it was enough to shift the momentum of the match in his direction.

That was acceptable. For the moment. Teyla continued to deflect his blows, even as their speed increased and he drove her backward in a wide arc. It would take time, but Teyla was both patient and observant, two traits that she had found useful when facing off against the Major. While he was in good condition, he tended to pour all of his energy into the fight from the start. Eventually he would tire, and his focus would slip, just enough for her to take advantage.

It wasn't obvious. A flick of his eyes — which had previously been trained on hers. She had faced him sufficient times to recognize it. The moment was coming. There —

Lying on the floor with her foot placed carefully but firmly on his chest, Sheppard cursed under his breath. "*Damn* it."

From his observation post on the bench, where he'd been sprawled since his own defeat a few minutes ago, Lieutenant Ford whistled. "That was one slick move."

Teyla sensed that the Major was caught somewhere between irritation and bemusement at ending up in this position yet again. "Your skills are steadily improving," she told him, dropping to the floor to sit beside him.

His eyebrow arched in a manner that she had found common to the men of Earth. They often tended to think they were being patronized, regardless of whether or not they indeed were. Despite his knowledge in many things, Dr McKay in particular seemed most susceptible to this.

"Because it took you fifteen minutes to have me flat on my back instead of ten?"

"You expend too much effort too soon." Teyla smiled. "It inevitably dulls your focus."

"Holding you off generally requires that much effort," Sheppard replied in defense. He sent his staffs skittering toward the bench against the wall.

Recognizing his frustration, she folded her legs beneath her, and said, "You like to run along the piers, do you not?"

"I wouldn't say I like it, but it keeps me in shape." He pushed himself up on his elbows, watching her. "You're telling me this is a distance run and not a dash."

"I am."

"All right, message received." There was a note of grudging acceptance in his voice, and she knew he would not disregard her advice.

Teyla enjoyed instructing the members of the Atlantis expedition. Fostering a bridge between their peoples seemed to her a noble pursuit, and many of the Marines had shown real aptitude for the fighting style. In truth, she looked forward to sparring against Major Sheppard the most. He listened and learned on a deeper level, and on occasion his resolve and unpredictability would challenge her in refreshing ways. It was another of his many contradictions.

The Major pushed himself upright, climbed to his feet, and offered her a hand up. "Penny for your thoughts?" he said. Perplexed, Teyla went to speak, but his soft laugh stopped her. "A penny is another form of currency."

The assigning of a token to the value of goods or services was not new to Teyla. Using such tokens to decide one's fate was, however, a novel concept. "Is it also used for making decisions?"

If the Major had not been wiping sweat from his brow, she suspected she would have seen his smile. "Not exactly," he replied, accepting a water bottle from Lieutenant Ford. "You're still bugged by McKay's wanting to make the world — well, one world, at least — a better place for all?"

Teyla, too, had accepted a bottle from the Lieutenant. Taking several mouthfuls of water gave her time to consider her reply. "Until the Wraith come."

"That does kinda have a leveling effect."

"The Athosians have traded with many worlds. We see no purpose in imposing our ways upon others." She turned to him. "Is it common for your people to differ widely in their beliefs?"

Sheppard's lips twisted ruefully. "On Earth there are very few completely unified beliefs about anything. It's part of our charm."

"That's one way to put it," Ford said quietly. His tone warned Teyla that the Major's sardonic streak had crept through into his last comment.

"At first, I understood that it was as Dr McKay reminded us in the meeting. Your people came to Atlantis hoping to find ways to defeat an enemy to your world, the Goa'uld."

"Well, that's part of it."

"I had assumed that you had developed a warrior class in order to fight this enemy, but I have since come to understand that few on your planet have knowledge of the Goa'uld. Your battle skills were developed to defend against peoples — nations — on Earth who would impose their will upon one other. Yet you, who are of this warrior class, take the view that it is better to leave the Dalerans to their ways, while Dr McKay, who is not a warrior, believes otherwise."

Sheppard tilted his head in a restrained shrug. "Rodney's a theoretical scientist, not an historian."

"Does your history teach you to respect the ways of others?"

"Not exactly. It records the consequences when people don't. Studying the history of conflict is required in our military. I've also had a couple of chances to see the results of changing regimes firsthand, and I know it's not pretty. I'm more of a live and let live kinda guy."

She found that self-assessment fitting. "I have wondered if the Ancestors would approve of such an evolution of their ideas. They would not have desired to be represented as all-powerful, as the Dalerans have come to believe."

"I wouldn't bet money on that."

Disturbed by his remark, Teyla said, "I do not understand."

The Major hesitated, as if weighing a choice, then charged ahead. "I'm not convinced that the Ancients were wholly benevolent. For one thing, they bailed out on several occasions, either abandoning one galaxy for another, or ascending. And Ascended or unascended, they weren't exactly concerned about the welfare of those they left behind. They had no problem with trapping and studying that shadow energy being that Jinto found. I mean, that's tantamount to abandoning a caged animal. And they set up a Stargate on that foggy James Herbert world with no regard for the thousands, possibly millions of the misty little inhabitants the 'gate killed every time someone used it."

"Perhaps the Ancestors were unaware — "

His look forestalled her. It seemed most unlikely that the Ancestors had no knowledge of the nature of the life form on

M5S-224. Indeed, for what other purpose could the Stargate have existed on that world unless to study the energy beings?

"Based on the reports I've read, the Ancients were researching non-corporeal life-forms long before they left our galaxy. After they ascended, they made some cardinal rule about not helping others."

"That seems…" Her voice trailed off.

"Selfish? Didn't we just agree that it wasn't a good idea to go interfering with people's beliefs?"

Less certain now, she said, "Helping is not interfering."

"Depends on your point of view. Rodney thinks he's helping."

"I've read some of those reports, too," Ford put in. "Any Ascended who helped anyone on the lower plane, or whatever it's called, got themselves banished."

Sheppard grimaced. "Harsh. Isn't that what happened with that guy from SG-1? You know — archeologist, glasses, briefly dead for a while?" He shifted self-consciously at Ford's look of disbelief. "What?"

"Dr Jackson," the Lieutenant supplied with a smile. "I thought you said you'd read some of SG-1's reports."

"The military reports, sure. You ever try reading Jackson's? My book is faster going. Anyway, he managed to get himself demoted to human form for helping."

"As Dalera was banished for loving a human." Teyla frowned. "It seems that even amongst themselves the Ancestors did not always agree."

The Major nodded. "I'd buy that explanation. They could easily have had a wide range of beliefs and conflicting opinions, just as we do."

His radio signaled then, and Ford picked it up from the bench and tossed it to him. "Sheppard." Listening for a moment, he nodded. "All right, we're on our way." Turning to them he explained, "Beckett wants us in the infirmary. Something about Lisera."

Gathering her belongings, Teyla followed the two officers out of the room. She was not sure how well she concealed her feelings, but this conversation had unnerved her in a way she could not quite name.

CHAPTER EIGHT

"Lisera thinks of herself and her entire family, as barbarians," explained Carson Beckett. His voice held a mixture of sadness and anger. "She's utterly convinced that she's somehow responsible for the Wraith attacks."

Aiden stared at him. "How?" He didn't have lot of faith in Beckett's analysis of the situation. The doctor might be some sort of super-smart biologist, but he was generally too busy blabbing about what he didn't know or why something wasn't his fault to pay a lot of attention to what was going on around him. "We're the ones who woke the Wraith."

Together with the Major, Teyla and McKay, Aiden was standing with Beckett in the room next to where Lisera was resting. Through the glass door, he could see Dr Weir sitting on the bed, holding her hand. Aiden had planned on visiting Lisera earlier in the evening, but by the time they'd finished debriefing and getting something to eat, he'd been due for his scheduled workout with Teyla.

Leaning toward the Major, McKay wrinkled his nose theatrically. Sheppard shot him an odd look. "What?"

"Nothing." McKay's expression said otherwise.

"Many of those boats you saw were not used for fishing," Beckett continued, "but to explore distant towns that, while now deserted, were once inhabited by people that the Chosen also viewed as barbarians. The crews would scavenge items they could sell in the markets. Things more advanced than they themselves could create."

"How could this be possible?" Teyla frowned. "What they call Wraithcraft causes the Shields to glow, alerting the Chosen."

"Yes, but the *products* of technology wouldn't necessarily do so," McKay said. "It would account for those quality steel axes everyone was carrying around. Most of that stuff was cast, not wrought, and you can't get that kind of temperature in a blacksmith's wood-burning forge." He inched toward Aiden and sniffed experimentally.

Teyla sucked in a deep breath. "It would also explain the many fine goods in the markets."

"Without warriors patrolling outside the Citadel, no one's policing their laws." The Major looked thoughtful.

"The apothecary told us that with the Chosen no longer operating the transports as they once did, many now cart goods into the city across the bridges." Teyla's frown deepened.

Nodding in understanding, the Major added, "Contraband has probably been finding its way into the markets for decades."

"And Lisera's family," said Carson, "was involved in the transport of such goods. When the Wraith first put in an appearance, those dealing in Wraithcraft were blamed for having attracted their attentions."

McKay's face screwed up. "What *is* that smell?"

Slowly turning to face him, Sheppard replied, "The result of working out, Rodney, something apparently unfamiliar to you."

"I would be most pleased if you would care to join us next time." Teyla's smile was more predatory than anticipatory. Aiden winced. If McKay ever took her up on the offer, the only thing that would be getting a workout was his backside—as it hit the floor.

Glancing at her sharply, McKay remarked, "What a shock. My assessment was, oh, let's see, *completely* accurate. Their idealistic aboriginal culture is—"

"Rodney," interrupted the Major. "Let's hear what Lisera has to say before jumping to any conclusions."

Beckett shook his head. "She became quite distraught, so I gave her a sedative. I have no doubt she's told Elizabeth the rest of it." His eyebrows lowered into a deep frown. "Things a girl wouldn't want to share with a man, if you get my drift. Bloody monarchists by the sounds of it. Sitting in their high and mighty palace, extorting payment for protecting people from the Wraith, but doing naught else while the city turns into a squalid den of murderers and thieves."

Aiden followed Beckett into the room. On the bed, Lisera was curled up as much as the plaster cast would allow, arms wrapped around herself. When he saw the tear stains on her cheeks, he smiled reassuringly. Despite the sedative, she glanced fearfully at the others. McKay's lips did that thing that Aiden supposed was meant to be a smile but came off like a bad case of indigestion.

Dr Weir stood from the bed. "Get some rest now, Lisera. We'll talk again in the morning."

"As I said," McKay continued. There was no mistaking the satisfaction in his smirk this time. "Me. Right. So it was, and so it ever shall be."

"Let's take this discussion elsewhere." Dr Weir's warning glance was directed at McKay.

"I'll be along in a few minutes," Beckett said. "I want to check the results of Lisera's blood work."

Lisera's eyelids began to droop. "Aiden?"

Leaning down, he took her hand. "I'll bring you some breakfast."

"Do you promise?"

"Sure. Haven't broken my word yet, have I?"

Aiden didn't fail to notice Dr Weir's concerned look as the five of them went to the briefing room. Neither did he fail to notice McKay's smugness, and Teyla's troubled expression.

When the ornate doors closed behind them, Dr Weir took a seat, rested her elbows on the table and briefly ran her hands across her face. Her eyes were red and puffy and her voice sounded thick with a cold. "What did you say was the name of the chief?"

"Balzar." Sheppard pulled a chair out and sat down. "Why?"

"He threatened to tell the Chosen that Lisera's family brought the Wraith upon them by trading in Wraithcraft."

"Yes, we got that," McKay said impatiently.

Taking a deep breath, Dr Weir added, "What you didn't get was what Balzar demanded of her mother, and then Lisera, in return for saying nothing and allowing them to enter the transport to the Citadel."

A swift silence fell over the room. No one needed her to explain further.

"What?" McKay was incredulous. Unfolding his arms, he sat forward in indignation and blurted, "She's just a kid!"

The look in Teyla's eyes was nothing short of murderous. Not that Aiden was feeling any less inclined to rip Balzar limb from limb, but even he was surprised at her vehemence when she spat, "Such creatures as Balzar are not fit to be called human. They do not feed from hunger, as the Wraith do, but gorge themselves on fear."

Well, at least McKay and Teyla had found something on which they could agree.

Lips pinched in barely controlled anger, Dr Weir continued, "Lisera ran away from him and tried to take refuge in the city. Faced with starvation, she returned to find her mother had been taken by the Wraith. The Chosen have apparently made it clear that they will protect only those who truly believe in Dalera — which Lisera's mother had not. Lisera left the Citadel and has been living in the forest near the ocean ever since. So the Chosen's system isn't functioning as well as it may have seemed."

Dr Weir pulled a tissue from a box she'd placed on the table. "Did any of you see anything outside the marketplace?"

"I believe," McKay said, sitting back with his arms folded, "the term 'mortal danger' was bandied about, so no."

Apologizing, Dr Weir blew her nose. "Still, leaders generally aren't as important in a society as they'd like to think they are. What about their bureaucracy?"

"We didn't get much of a feel for their infrastructure," replied the Major. "We need to take a look around the place."

McKay was practically preening. If the issue at hand had been any less grim, Aiden suspected that they would have been treated to some kind of victory dance. "If anyone would care to recall my varied and eloquent comments throughout the mission, warning of precisely this circumstance, I'll be accepting apologies in the form of coffee rations."

"You've made your point," Sheppard muttered, turning his chair to face Dr Weir. "So what's the game plan for our next visit? Offering the Dalerans better transportation won't fix the corruption that's probably running wild."

"For right now, caution is the operative word. We don't fully know what we're dealing with yet."

Without forethought, Aiden spoke up. "Ma'am, what about Lisera? We can't just take her back and leave her there."

Dr Weir's expression made him apprehensive even before she answered. "As much as I despise the situation, we can't afford to take in any more refugees. I'm sure we can work out something so that Lisera won't be left to fend for herself. Perhaps Kesun would accept payment of some sort to make sure she's taken care of until she can walk again."

His protest would have been impassioned, but McKay's was faster and, for better or worse, sharper. "That strategy could be compared to upgrading her steerage ticket on the *Titanic*."

Before McKay could add anything, the leader of the Atlantis expedition captured them all with an iron-willed gaze that was undiminished by her cold. Aiden hadn't known what to make of Dr Elizabeth Weir at first. But back when she'd led Stargate Command he'd learned that, while her standard demeanor was gracious, she had the capacity for nearly limitless resolve. "Understand me," she said, her words deliberate. "I have been in more refugee camps than I can count, and each time I've wished that I could save every person there. Major, Lieutenant, I know you've had similar experiences. There's always an exception, one child that you become personally involved with on some level, one you feel you have to find a way to save. But you've been trained to recognize that choices have to be made."

Aiden glanced across the table at the Major and saw that his assessment reluctantly matched Dr Weir's. That, and his own admittedly limited experience in such situations, didn't make it any easier to stomach.

"Right now," she continued, "the best thing that we can do to help these people, and all of the people in this galaxy, is to find a way to defeat the Wraith. As much as it tears us up, we have to accept our limitations and do the best we can within them. We're hard pressed just keeping ourselves alive here, and if the Wraith are coming, Lisera will be in as much danger on Atlantis as on her home world."

It was a painfully rational standpoint. McKay breezed past it without missing a beat. "Which brings us back around to the original argument, because the only thing that has any chance of protecting the Dalerans from the Wraith in the short term is the gene therapy."

"And how will that help restore their society?" Teyla asked pointedly.

The scientist swiveled his seat toward her. "Now I'm getting whiplash. Are we in favor of the *laissez faire* approach, or aren't we?"

"We're still weighing options, Rodney, so have some patience." Dr Weir brushed her hair back with a weary hand. "The social implications are not the only potential consequences here."

The doors slid open to admit Dr Beckett, who hovered in the back rather than take a seat at the table. "Carson, your timing's impeccable," McKay greeted him brusquely. "Elizabeth was just about to raise a concern that the gene therapy might pose some kind of health hazard to the Dalerans."

That seemed like a big leap to Aiden, but Dr Weir gave a slight nod of admission. "Isn't it possible that their biology might differ from ours in some minor respect?"

"Aye, but right now it's not the differences that trouble me so much as the similarities." Beckett twisted a pen in his hands, looking uncertain. "I've run a number of tests on Lisera, both for the purposes of treating her and of learning whatever we can about the other inhabitants of this galaxy. The results were a bit of shock, to say the least, but it's been confirmed. Lisera has the ATA gene."

The energy in the room abruptly changed, as five heads swung toward the doctor. Their collective shock reigned in silence until Sheppard leaned forward. "Okay, I'll be the one to say it. What the—?"

"How is that possible?" Dr Weir demanded.

"The ATA gene, although rare, exists in the human population on Earth, doubtless for the same reasons." Beckett pulled out a chair and sat at the table. "As I understand it, there were times throughout Daleran history when children born with the gene were put to death, along with their mothers."

Nodding in comprehension, Dr Weir said, "Parents would then have gone to great lengths to avoid having their children tested, until a culture of fear became ingrained in the entire population."

Sheppard shook his head. "If there are enough others out there with the gene, they've got a perfectly capable defense against the Wraith hiding in plain sight. Unbelievable."

"What do we do now?" Aiden had to ask.

"We test them. As many as possible." McKay cut off Teyla's objection before she could respond to Dr Weir's immediate look of doubt. "Their society is unsustainable without ATA-capable people, and the only way to bring those with the gene to light is to test them. You can continue to shake your head at me, but only if futility is your thing, because I can assure you that I'm very practiced at tuning out misguided opposition."

"And if there are only a handful of others besides Lisera?" Dr Weir asked.

"Then gene therapy is still an option." That statement came from Beckett, not McKay, and caught the rest of the group off-guard. "I realize that we're not comfortable with the idea of forcing change on these people," he added, pouring himself a glass of water. "But if it comes down to a choice between defying their beliefs and leaving them as victims of a corrupted oligarchy and eventual prey for the Wraith, I'm afraid I have to agree with Rodney."

"Try not to sound so enthusiastic about that," McKay muttered.

"You know, this could work for us," the Major commented thoughtfully. When both women pinioned him with stares, he raised his hands in surrender. "Hey, none of this was *my* brilliant idea. And I'm not suggesting we dive right into the gene therapy. All I'm saying is that Lisera being a Chosen might be useful in changing some attitudes. She's been brainwashed into thinking she's responsible for the Wraith. The simple fact that she's been to Atlantis should undermine that and simultaneously elevate her position. It might give Kesun an edge to convince everyone to convert."

McKay's eyes grew huge. "So you'd just use her to continue propagating this insanity?"

"Tone down the indignation, would you?" Sheppard glared at him. "I'm trying to back you up, if you hadn't noticed."

"And thanks ever so much for that, but it's a near-certainty that I've thought this through farther than you have, so kindly stop helping." Still facing a less than receptive audience, McKay continued. "We can tell Kesun the truth. Since we don't have taboos on touching Ancient objects, we discovered Lisera's gene when she came to Atlantis. In Kesun's mind, this will just confirm what he already believes, that there may be others who have the gene naturally. He'd have a good reason to test a lot more people."

McKay hadn't been kidding about thinking this through, but Dr Weir didn't look convinced. "Touching the Shields would require them to overcome a deeply entrenched cultural taboo."

"Which Kesun is already in favor of rescinding." Sheppard drummed long fingers against the table top, considering. "He was also happy for Lisera to come here, citing the fact that Atlantis is a place where healers come from."

"All of which fits in with our vaunted goal of not disturbing their delicate belief structure." McKay looked at Teyla as if challenging her to disagree. "And if the Chosen do object, we'll know for certain that they're not the idealists they claim to be."

The team members traded glances, weighing each other's reactions. At last, Aiden spoke up. "I gotta say, Doc, you're sneakier than you look."

"No argument on that," the Major agreed.

"Thank you. I try."

Teyla still seemed uneasy, possibly more so than before. Dr

Weir picked up on her discomfort immediately. "Teyla, don't be afraid to say what you're thinking. This may not have started out as the most democratic effort — " She leveled a stern look at McKay. " — but I want us all on the same chapter at least before we proceed."

McKay spread his hands wide. "Yes, if you have a more palatable method of protecting these people from the Wraith, by all means."

The Athosian continued to hesitate, her features set, but her eyes were turbulent. "I do not feel confident in this," she said at last. "It is difficult for me to see the point at which an act of this kind ceases to be mere assistance and becomes interference. But I cannot disagree with the goal — to protect them from the Wraith." She directed a pointed gaze at Rodney. "And while I do not agree with the manner in which the Chosen offer or deny protection from the Wraith, I do not believe we should blindly attempt to change these people's way of life."

"Then we proceed with caution. Let's see how many undiscovered Chosen are out there before we make any bolder plans." Dr Weir pulled another tissue from the box. "When you return to Dalera, demonstrate Lisera's ability and approach Kesun with the offer to help test the populace. But that's as far as we go for now."

From his vantage point in the doorway, Carson Beckett watched his young patient devour her breakfast. Lieutenant Ford sat nearby, munching on an energy bar.

"Do you think there is food of this kind in the Enclave?" Lisera asked between bites. "Or such fine clothing?"

Ford offered a shrug, and Carson could tell he was marveling at the notion of infirmary scrubs being thought of as 'fine.' "I don't know. I guess it's probably pretty nice in there."

"And I will see it with my own eyes." The girl's face glowed. "To think that I have lived eight seasons and never knew until now that I was of the Chosen! I know not how I have found favor with Dalera, but I give thanks for it."

"Yeah, it's a miracle." Ford forced a smile. Lisera appeared too excited to notice his hesitation.

"You will visit me, won't you, Aiden? I must find a way to show you the Enclave. Surely Dalera would not turn away a warrior of Atlantis."

Carson decided to step in and rescue the Marine. "Looks as though you're ready to go home, lass," he said, moving into the room. "I've got you a pair of crutches—sticks to use if you have to walk. In fifty days that cast can come off, and you'll soon be ready for dancing."

Lisera bowed her head toward him. "I thank you, Doctor. All of you have given me so much."

Perhaps he was imagining it, but her bearing seemed to have changed somewhat. Armed with the knowledge of her supposed birthright, Lisera drew herself taller in the bed. There was a spark of pride in the lass for the first time since she'd arrived.

Ford took the chance to stand up. "Lisera, I have to talk to Dr Beckett for a minute. We'll be just over there, all right?"

When she nodded, he ushered Carson to an empty corner of the infirmary.

"What's bothering you, Lieutenant?"

"It's like she's forgotten about how bad things were for her up until a couple of days ago." Ford gestured uncertainly. "How can she really want to go back?"

"Lisera's got reason to think things will be different now, at least for her." Carson gave a wistful smile. "And no matter how extraordinary a place this is, there's no substitute for home."

The Lieutenant conceded that point, and the two men stood in uneasy silence for a moment. They hadn't worked all that well together during the storm; both would confess to that, the doctor was sure. Somehow, though, they'd hammered out a truce even before the sun had broken through the clouds.

"You get homesick, Doc?" Ford asked.

"Aye, that I do," Carson answered readily. "Terribly so, sometimes. Don't you?"

"Sure. It's just that you're the only senior member I've ever heard admit to it."

"They've all got their reasons, I suspect. Dr Weir won't show it because of her position. Rodney won't show it because of his personality."

"What about the Major?"

"Most likely a bit of both." As head physician, Carson had seen Sheppard's personnel file, but it wasn't his place to explain that the man hardly had a home to miss.

Ford nodded, glancing back at Lisera. "We're doing the right thing, aren't we?"

Carson sighed. "I hope so. I don't much like the idea of allowing any kind of divine-right imperialistic nonsense to continue, I'll admit. Part of my heritage. But they don't pay me to make those kinds of decisions."

"That would be the difference between you and me, Carson," said Rodney, entering the infirmary with his mission gear. "I see no reason to let my job description dictate when I can and can't point out the error of someone's ways."

"Packing lighter this time?" Ford asked him with a vague smirk.

"Is my hearing impaired, or am I getting a lecture on adaptability from a Marine?"

"Marines are the most adaptable people you'll ever meet."

"Ah, yes, of course. You're equally capable of using either the big gun or the small gun." Rodney cemented his last-word status by turning to Carson. "Is Lisera ready?"

"She is. Have a good trip."

Carson gave Lisera a winning smile as the Lieutenant and Rodney wheeled her out of the room and toward the jumper bay. He didn't feel he knew enough about the planet to hope for a specific outcome, so as usual, he'd settle for his comrades coming home without need of his attention. In the meantime, he had some genes to replicate.

CHAPTER NINE

As soon as the jumper exited the Stargate, John glanced over his shoulder. The expression on Lisera's face was very different to the one she'd worn leaving Dalera just two days earlier. Clean, well fed, and sporting a leg cast decorated with good wishes in nine different languages, she looked and sounded like a normal teenager, which was a very welcome change.

Beside him, Rodney was practically glowing with pride. Not only had the man been proven correct yet again, he was performing surprisingly well in his first-ever spaceflight lesson in the jumper. It was an impressive sight, he had to admit. There was a thin, almost transparent blue ring of dust surrounding the planet, contrasting sharply with the stark blackness beyond. And the stars — God, the stars. He'd never realized before his first jumper ride how many stars the sky could hold. Maybe there were a few pilots back on Earth who didn't dream of exactly this opportunity, but John didn't know any. The best perk by far of this galactic boondoggle was the chance to fly what, though might not be the sexiest looking thing in the air, sure as hell had to be the coolest.

The only one on his team who seemed to be sitting silent and pensive was Teyla. Just as evident as Rodney's excitement was the Athosian's troubled countenance. On one level, John was glad that he was sensitized to each of his team members' moods, but on another he couldn't afford to let the current tensions continue unchecked. They were all on a sharp learning curve, having to accommodate unprecedented situations without so much as an out-of-date guidebook. Even Teyla, who had started out as their roving ambassador, had had to deal both with their alien Earth culture and with having some deep holes punched into her preconceived ideas about everyone from the Genii to the Ancients.

Right now, he was just hoping that everything went smoothly on this second visit to Dalera. Rodney might have had the right idea—although John would be damned if he said *that* out loud, seeing as McKay was already saying it enough for everyone—but John also had enough personal experiences stashed away in the recesses of his memory to suspect that Teyla wasn't altogether wrong.

"Okay" he said to Rodney. "I have the controls."

"Oh, c'mon!" his teammate whined. "At least let me fly it down through the atmosphere."

John smirked at the lack of eloquence. He'd long suspected that their chief scientist had never been a child—or at least not a normal one—but that display had just proved otherwise. "Next lesson. Meanwhile, you can bring up the HUD."

That request seemed to pacify Rodney somewhat. Coming in much higher this time, John noted that none of the EM fields activated before he parked the jumper on the outskirts of the village. That was a good sign.

Although Lisera had grasped the fundamentals of using crutches, she wasn't entirely mobile yet. However, Yann was as good as his word, and was waiting with another couple of muscle-bound fishermen holding the stretcher. After making certain that everything they were carrying was switched off, and that they were well clear of the jumper, Teyla withdrew the Shields from where she'd hidden them between the rocks. Surprised that they were still there, John felt a stab of guilt for not entirely trusting the merchant. The return of the Wraith must have rekindled faith in Dalera's Shields, even if those who currently wielded them afforded less respect.

"Zelenka may actually have come up with a useful suggestion," Rodney ventured, accepting his Shield. "There may be a way to disable the capacitor." He continued to mumble vague hypotheses during the short trek to the village.

Walking along the cobbled road to the inn, they encountered a mixed reaction. It beat their first visit hands-down, but it was still somewhat unsettling. While a number of kids ran up to Lisera, begging her to tell them of the magical things she'd seen, just as many adults looked on with unconcealed resentment. He'd already warned Lisera to say nothing of her 'Chosen' status until presenting the fact to Kesun, but that hadn't kept her from describing Atlantis with a rapid string of slightly embellished adjectives.

When they reached the square, a bunch of people loaded down with goods obviously destined for market were parked outside the inn. None of them looked happy. Check that. One of them, Balzar, had a smug smile on his face. "Market day in the Citadel, huh?" John inquired to Yann.

The merchant's face darkened. "No. Since your arrival, a change has come. We must now double what we once paid before we are allowed entry into the transport. Additionally, we must pay in advance."

"What?" One word was enough to summarize Rodney's disbelief, but naturally he didn't leave it at that. "What can the Chosen possibly need with all that food when there are so few —"

"Dr McKay," Teyla all but hissed. "Had we not agreed to return Lisera to the Citadel first?"

"After you, Rodney." John pushed open the door of the inn and gave the scientist a not-quite-gentle prod in the back. Offering a smile in Yann's direction, and raising his voice so that the waiting villagers could hear, he added, "Let's hold off until we discuss a few things with the Chosen."

"And if the Wraith return?" someone called.

"Then I'll come back here," John replied, lifting his Shield. "That's a promise."

Mutters of grudging acceptance followed him into the inn. The old guy behind the bar was standing in the exact same spot where John had left him, still looking surly, although his expression shifted somewhat when Yann entered with Lisera and the other merchants.

That was yet another thing that had John's self-preservation skills screaming. Something wasn't adding up. He might have chalked it up to the heightened fear and resentment in the village, except Teyla seemed equally tense and watchful. She returned his glance with a subtle shake of her head. No Wraith, then, but *something*.

The fishermen carrying Lisera walked down into the transport ahead of Ford, who was also looking around, alert for anything amiss. Rodney was already inside, practically bouncing on his toes. "I'm looking forward to this."

"Did I mention that I've added a spiked metal plate to the heel of my boots?" John remarked, stepping in beside him and placing his palm on the single light.

"Oh, you won't have to worry about me speaking out of turn," Rodney replied. "I'll be quite happy just to observe and feel utterly vindicated."

The doors opened on a familiar feculent odor, and the scientist's smile slipped a few notches. The Sanctuary Hall was still as grubby and crowded and noisy as it had been two days earlier, although the area around the entrance to the transport seemed marginally less cluttered. In fact, it looked as if—

Too late, John saw thick rope nets fly across them. Before he'd even had a chance to raise his weapon, he felt himself jerked off his feet. Teyla's warning cry had likewise come too late. Rodney yelped an objection moments later, when John found himself directly on top of the scientist, on the floor, twisted up inside the greasy net. Then he became aware of the smell and feel of a dozen bodies crowded around them.

"We will not harm you," Yann called above their cries, "if you cease struggling, and release your weapons to us."

Someone near him—Teyla, by the feel of it—continued to twist around inside the net, no doubt trying to free at least one of her arms. John tried to reach for his knife, but the mesh pulled tighter and Yann called out again, "We promise you no harm, but you must listen!"

Damn it, damn it, *damn* it. And people wondered why he seemed to live by gut instinct rather than set plans. It wasn't out of any deep desire to rock the boat. It was because when he ignored that instinct, crap like *this* tended to happen.

"Is my arm still attached to my shoulder?" Rodney inquired in a plaintive voice. "It's hard to tell at the moment, what with the pain and the awkward angle and the grown man lying on top of me."

"Believe me when I say it isn't by choice, Rodney."

Ford's, "Sir?" was muffled, but John knew what the Lieutenant was asking.

Heaving a sigh, he made the all but inevitable decision. "All right. We're listening."

The net slackened, and they untangled themselves. Their weapons were pulled away, disappearing into the throng of people, and their wrists were bound with thick ropes. Outmaneuvered by a bunch of guys with a net. They were never going to live this one down.

"We have no wish to make enemies of you," Yann began, his expression so earnest that John almost believed him. "On the contrary, we hope you will find us to be worthy allies."

"You'll have to forgive me for not shaking your hand." John gave a sarcastic tug on his bindings.

"I regret that this was necessary, but we were desperate. There is much you should see before returning to the Enclave." The merchant spoke in a measured, even tone. "When the Great Plague visited us two generations past, countless Dalerans, perhaps as many as three quarters of our number, were stuck down."

Rodney's head snapped up at that, but Yann ignored him and continued. "In the years hence, fewer and fewer Chosen ventured beyond the Enclave to operate the village transports. Today, when the Shields glow and the alarm is raised, Kesun alone evacuates but a handful of villages.

"Many of us have long suspected that the Plague struck the Chosen even harder, and as a result, they are now few in number. It is the only explanation for the way they failed in fulfilling their duty to the people of Dalera. The teaching windows tell us that these last weeks have been but a small taste of the great culling to come. And yet with so few Chosen, even the Citadel cannot provide safe haven."

"So you're not overly enchanted with the Chosen right now," John summed up. "We can empathize with that. But —"

A young voice full of idealistic determination broke in.

"Release them. The Chosen command it!"

The assembled merchants turned to where Lisera stood, leaning unsteadily on one of the crutches. John shut his eyes with a wince. Although he appreciated the effort, it probably wasn't the best idea.

"Lisera, we can handle this." Ford attempted to dissuade her.

Ignoring the chuckles and jeers from the crowd, the girl reached for Rodney's Shield and yanked it free.

"What? You couldn't possibly have taken *his* instead?" Rodney jerked his restrained hands in John's direction. Being unable to gesture was definitely putting a crimp in the scientist's style.

No one was listening to him, though, because all eyes were on the Shield that had changed from black to a dull turquoise in Lisera's hand. Through the murmurs, Yann remained unmoved. He cocked an eyebrow at Rodney. John wasn't sure if it was a good poker face, or if they were about to be even more screwed than they already were.

"I knew you when you could not yet speak, Lisera," the merchant said. "When your mother first moved from the Citadel to the village."

Alarmed by the look on Rodney's face, which was beginning to adopt a 'eureka' expression, John was about to explain, but Yann added, "You were not of the Chosen." He turned a calculating eye to his captives. "What has changed between then and now?" John opened his mouth to reply, but again, Yann beat him to the punch. Staring wide-eyed at Lisera, he added, "You were made Chosen in Atlantis!"

That revelation was met with gasps of wonder and loud mutters that spread across the nearby crowd like a tidal wave. "The medicine of which you spoke." Yann pointed an accusing finger at Rodney. "*You* gave her the *genetherapy*!"

"What? Me?" Rodney retorted in a voice that was just short of a squeal. "Don't be ridiculous, I hate needles — Wait, you were actually listening to me about all that?"

While the word *genetherapy* was whispered from person to person, Yann merely met Rodney's gaze with sage understanding. "You are of the Chosen, yet you do not approve of their laws. You have made no secret of it."

"That may well be, but I'd be the last person to administer the gene therapy to anyone. Besides, there was no need. Lisera is a natural carrier."

Or maybe they'd just go with the truth and see how that went.

"Dr McKay!" Teyla hissed.

"What?" Rodney snapped indignantly. "I'm just clarifying the situation. And I'm getting incredibly tired of having to repeat myself. The gene doesn't make anyone *Chosen*. It simply allows them to operate the same technology as the Chosen, which we're going to have to rename because I think we've effectively proven the term 'Chosen' to be inaccurate."

The sour feeling in John's stomach abruptly turned into fullblown heartburn. He whipped around to glare at Rodney while the muttering in the crowd swelled in volume. Rodney blinked back at him. "What? Did you have a better story to tell? Something about magic fairy dust?"

It was a reasonable point, but John was getting tired of McKay's bull-in-a-china-shop diplomacy. "So help me, Rodney, if I could move my hands right now…"

With confusion and a hint of betrayal, Lisera stared at them. Yann quieted the murmurs, took the Shield from her hand and reattached it to Rodney's belt. "This potion you have, this *genetherapy* can make anyone Chosen?"

"The evidence speaks for itself, doesn't it?" Rodney looked somewhat mollified that his Shield had been returned. "I'm a textbook case."

Although Yann might not have entirely understood McKay's explanation, he must have gotten the drift, because his eyes narrowed and he turned to John. "You also received this potion?"

Not much point in hiding the truth now. Still glaring at McKay, John replied, "No, like Lisera, I'm a natural carrier."

If this gang of rebels-in-waiting had a leader, Yann had to be it, because everyone seemed to be looking to him for guidance. "What say you of the Chosen?" he asked, his gaze fixing on

John. "Do you believe their rule is just?"

This time there was no way in hell John was going to let Rodney speak for them. "We don't take sides," he said firmly. "How you choose to live is your business. We just don't want to see the Wraith come in and tear the place apart."

Yann regarded him with cold eyes. "You do not 'take sides,'" he repeated, his voice filled with enough contempt to make John wince. "Come." He gave a sharp gesture to the quartet of merchants who had taken their weapons. The men took up positions around the team and prodded them forward.

"Now what?" Rodney said under his breath.

They were led out of the Sanctuary Hall and through a series of alleys. Within moments, John realized that they'd been painfully ignorant of the truth of this place, and he wanted his ignorance back.

In the backstreets, they found a degree of poverty and destitution that rivaled any on Earth. Beggars staked out their territory, shoving off emaciated children with festering eyes and open sores. He'd been involved in humanitarian missions in Africa, and had seen some truly appalling conditions, but this was far beyond anything he'd ever witnessed.

Holy— He jerked back in shock as the analytical part of his mind identified a lump lying on top of a garbage heap as a corpse, obviously a victim of gross malnutrition. The gasp that came from somewhere behind him sounded like Teyla.

"It is the same in much of the Citadel," Yann said. He kept his gaze trained on the cobblestone path, deftly navigating his way through the worst of the filth. "Those who rule have no interest in anything but taking payment in return for protection that they cannot provide." He didn't need to explain how hunger, squalid living conditions, and the resultant explosion of infectious diseases had created fertile ground for social anarchy.

Ford jumped when a beggar clawed at his arm. One of their guards swiftly pushed the babbling old woman aside. John flinched at the sight, but understood that the guards were acting out of necessity rather than a lack of compassion. If they stopped moving, anything they had of value, up to and including the clothes on their back, would be stripped in seconds. Probably not gently, either.

Yann continued to lead them deeper into the Citadel, cautioning them to watch their feet when he stepped over a nearly overflowing gutter. One whiff of its contents had John silently vowing never again to complain about the plumbing on Atlantis.

"There is no way to be sure, but we believe that dozens perish each day—far more than have yet been taken by the Wraith." Yann wordlessly sidestepped a load of garbage being tossed from a third-floor window, and pointed to an even narrower side-alley. "The entrance is near."

They walked down a set of uneven steps made all the more treacherous by a slick coating that John had no desire to identify. Fortunately, the stairs soon ended, depositing them in a winding tunnel lit by torches. Yann moved decisively, apparently familiar with the route.

A solid *thud* sounded in the dim light, and Rodney stumbled into John's shoulder. "Sorry," he muttered. "There's something on the floor—oh."

There was some*one* on the floor, actually. At least, that limp bundle of rags had been a someone not so long ago. A pair of rodents, roused by the commotion, scurried out from under the body to disappear into the darkness.

"Can I assume," Rodney asked the team at large, "that none of us are clinging to the fantasy of the Chosen as enlightened despots anymore? I don't require any kind of apology, but let's make sure we're all finally on the same page here."

"Not helpful right now," John told him shortly, glancing back at Teyla. The Athosian had remained silent throughout this tour from Hell, but despite her outward control, he was fairly certain he'd never seen her so shaken. Having been more or less on her side when it came to not getting involved in the Dalerans' business, he wasn't feeling too great at the moment, either.

"Be silent," Yann ordered. He guided them into another tunnel, this one outfitted with a thick iron door and several armed men acting as guards.

The men greeted him with relief. "It is well that you have

returned," one guard said. "I do not know for how much longer we can keep word from spreading."

"Word of what?" Rodney demanded.

Rather than reply, Yann led them further into the tunnel. The passage got progressively smaller until everyone but Teyla had to duck low to continue. They soon came upon a small section of rock that had fallen away to reveal a cavern beyond the tunnel wall. The smell of salted fish and something more wafted out from the hole. "What is this?" he asked in a low voice.

Yann gestured. "Look for yourself." His tone was edged with bitterness.

Through the hole, John saw a bunch of flickering torches illuminating a huge chamber. He counted five double doors, presumably leading into other rooms, but that wasn't what caught his attention. As he watched, men carrying square baskets of dried meat walked down a set of narrow steps and carefully stacked them along wooden racks. Then it hit him. Why was so much food being squirreled away, when the Citadel's residents were starving? He moved away so that Rodney could see.

Yann explained, "There are many such places containing dried fish and fruits, cheeses and preserves, all of it payment demanded from us for use of the transport."

"Who are these people?" Rodney demanded in a voice John wished was a few decibels short of a holler.

"We believe they are servants bonded to the Chosen at birth," Yann said. "Until recently, their existence has only been guessed at."

"Oh, come on," Rodney declared, moving aside so that Teyla could see. "That's not servitude, it's slavery. Which explains why the Enclave and the Chosen still have their upscale look. Without this subculture running around looking after them, that temple would be buried under a layer of dust."

"What's it for?" Ford asked, taking his turn at the hole.

"Provisions," John answered before Yann could speak. "The Chosen knew they couldn't protect everyone, so they're stashing as much away as they can in preparation for the next culling."

"Only those who can pay the most have been offered a place inside the Enclave," spat Yann. "It is the one location that has never been breached by the Wraith."

John looked around at the faces of his teammates. Ford's held shock, while Rodney was obviously disgusted. Teyla stared back at him, her features shadowed by anger and a hint of betrayal. "It is unconscionable," she said, the words laced with venom. "Food is stored in these secret halls while children starve in the streets. This deception..." Unable to continue, she fell silent.

The return trip through the tunnels was subdued. John recalled Kesun's seemingly earnest claims with a sick feeling. Even if the man truly believed that the Chosen were following Dalera's will, there was no conceivable justification for such an atrocity.

Once they were back outside, Yann stood with folded arms, impassive. "So," he said simply. "Now you have seen."

Trying to get a handle on the implications, John could only nod. "We've seen," he agreed. "And we recognize that this can't go on. I'm just not sure what the best course of action is yet."

"The Sanctuary Halls are filled with fresh foodstuffs," Teyla said, recovering her composure. "Why do you not share them with the poor?"

"It's not that simple," John found himself answering. He understood the complex and conflicting economic and sociopolitical aspects of the situation. "With a regime this powerful and the corruption so widespread, even the best intentions can get hijacked." He looked at Yann, who nodded once, satisfied that they understood each other.

"The potion you possess," the merchant said. "If it could be given to sufficient people, I believe we would have the capacity to both defend the Citadel and operate the transports. We could achieve that which Dalera commanded, to protect all against the Wraith, showing favor no more or less to one or another."

"Without meaning to say I told you so," Rodney piped up, "I believe this is exactly what I suggested at the outset."

John shot him a glare. "Hadn't we established that since Lisera has the gene, so might a lot of other people? The gene therapy probably isn't necessary."

Eyes narrowing suspiciously, Yann said, "You would refuse us this potion when you know it will save us?"

Behind him, two of the guards looked at one another, and their scowls deepened.

"I didn't say that. I just think it'd save everyone a lot of time and trouble if you tested everyone first."

"And what if only people the likes of Balzar have this gene? Will they use it as Dalera intended? I think not."

"To whom would you give the genetherapy?" Teyla inquired.

"The poorest among us, so that their lives are made precious to all."

It wasn't a bad idea, but John was still hearing more warning bells even as he mentally raced through the possibilities. "I don't know how much of this...*potion* we have to spare," he pointed out. "Besides, I can't promise you anything until we talk to our leader."

"You are not the leader of your people?"

He clamped down on the automatic *Hell, no,* that came to his lips. Already he had far more responsibility than he'd bargained for. "No. So it's not my decision to make."

Yann nodded. "Then two of you may return to Atlantis in your Ancient craft, to confer with your leader. The other two must remain here until you bring us the potion."

"That sounds a lot like—" Rodney tensed as his fisherman buddies took up positions around them, this time clutching their axes with more serious intent. "Taking hostages," he finished, his annoyance colored by a twinge of worry.

John instinctively took a step forward and found himself blocked by a heavy staff across the chest. "This is not the best way to get cooperation from us," he warned.

"I regret once again that it has become necessary. But our people are desperate, in all ways." There was no malice in Yann's expression, but his earnestness almost seemed more dangerous. "Two will remain. They will not be harmed, but they cannot leave."

"*One* stays," John countered. "Me. The rest go back."

A snort came from Rodney. "Think it through before you fall on your proverbial sword, Major. Thanks to your reluctance to let me take the controls on the way down, you're the only one with any experience navigating the jumper in space."

Damn it. This was one decision he was *not* going to make for them. "Where we come from, our warriors have a code: leave no one behind."

"Then you will return for them. With the potion."

Frustration boiling just under the surface, John knew he was in no position to intimidate these people. The fact that he half-way sympathized with them didn't help matters.

"I will stay," Teyla offered, her dark eyes hooded. "I spoke before of appreciating all viewpoints. Clearly there is more left to understand."

"I'll stay too, sir," Ford volunteered. "I mean, I should keep an eye on Lisera."

John hated this with a ferocity that physically burned. He didn't want Teyla punishing herself for her misjudgment, and although he preferred having a military person stick around, leaving a subordinate in a hostile situation while he himself slunk home with his tail between his legs was intolerable.

Some sign of the conflict must have shown on his face, because Teyla stepped closer and forced him to look at her. "We will be all right," she told him. "They have no wish to harm us, and they are in need of help we can provide."

He set his jaw and nodded. "All right. We'll back by morning at the latest." Every ounce of conviction he possessed was funneled into that vow, in the hope that his teammates would take some assurance in it.

They were separated almost immediately, Ford and Teyla pulled toward a soot-stained doorway while he and Rodney were escorted back to the Sanctuary Hall. At the entrance to the transport, their Shields were confiscated and given to a confused and upset Lisera. The ropes were untied, and then they were on their own.

After negotiating their way through an increasingly surly bunch of villagers on the way back to the clearing where they'd parked the jumper, John was ready to snap. No matter which way he spun the situation, there were very few options available, and exactly none that would let him sleep at night. To make matters worse, Rodney hadn't uttered a word since this hideous 'deal' had been struck. Somehow that was worse than the crowing he'd come to expect from the scientist.

At last, the conversational void got the better of him, and he growled, "What, no victory march? Or did you run out of creative ways to say 'I told you so'?"

To his dismay, Rodney looked hurt for a split-second, before his expression hardened. "What kind of sociopath do you take me for, to think I'd be *happy* about what we just saw?"

John instantly felt like a complete and total ass. "You're right—I'm sorry. That was a low blow."

After an uncomfortable pause, Rodney spoke up again. "That said, I hope we've all learned a valuable lesson about listening to each other, or more specifically listening to *me*."

"On second thought, let's go back to brooding in silence."

"Fine by me."

Unfortunately, the renewed quiet only served to magnify John's frustration and sense of failure. Now he'd have to face Dr Weir and explain why he'd returned without two of his people. There weren't many things that felt worse than that.

The room had clearly not been intended for detention, which lent weight to Yann's assertions that they did not wish to harm their...*visitors*. It was relatively well-lit, it had chairs—such as they were—and a small opening high in the wall served as a window. There even was a plate with a loaf of hard bread and some fruit sitting on the table.

Nonetheless, Lieutenant Ford was sitting in a chair, his spine rigid and his expression blank. If Yann and his rebels did not view him as a prisoner, the young Marine certainly behaved as one.

Teyla stood underneath the crude window and stared out at the evening sky, trying vainly to give order to her thoughts. A great many of her convictions had been tested of late, forcing her to question herself more strongly each time.

It had seemed simpler, once. The peoples she had encountered were fellow traders, willing and often eager to assist each other. Perhaps the shared menace of the Wraith had colored her viewpoint, but she had considered almost all of her acquaintances to be kindred. Only when she began to journey with the Earth Atlantis team had she come to recognize greater differences between worlds.

The deception practiced so expertly by Sora still troubled Teyla. Was her trust so easily manipulated? When had the Genii traded compassion for self-preservation? What of the Hoffans, who had abandoned their morality with respect even to their own kind? No one could deny that the Wraith ignited desperation in their victims. But rather than bond together to face a common foe, so many seemed prone to battle among themselves. In that way, the people of this planet were no different from many others.

The Dalerans' plight touched her, more so perhaps because of her earlier misjudgment. Still, the providing them with the gene therapy alone would not offer a solution to their social inequities.

That, of course, presupposed that she and Lieutenant Ford would be freed according to the rebels' demands. Her faith in her teammates ran deep. Major Sheppard would sooner cut off his own arm than leave his comrades at risk, and while Dr McKay was decidedly less intrepid, his intellect could very well prove useful. She only hoped that in resolving the situation, they would also, somehow, find a way to free these people from their current fate.

Clearly sharing her thoughts, Ford finally spoke up. "Think Dr Weir will agree to give these guys what they want?"

"I believe you to be better qualified than me to answer that."

He chewed on his lip. "If we were on Earth, I'd say no way. That's not how we do things. But sometimes, even though it's obvious, I have to remind myself to stop thinking like I'm back there. We're a long way from Earth, in more ways than one."

They lapsed into silence again, and Teyla wondered if the Lieutenant's home could possibly feel as distant to him as Athos now did to her.

"Absolutely not."

Predictably, Rodney didn't react all that well to her answer. "I see. What a relief it is to know that all matters get such careful consideration. That took you all of three seconds to decide."

A flare of white-hot anger surged up, and Elizabeth pinned him in place with her stare. "After your unilateral decision to tell the Dalerans about the gene therapy, you have the nerve to accuse *me* of going off half-cocked?"

They faced each other down across her desk. Off to the side, Carson and John wisely kept their mouths shut.

"I didn't exactly have the opportunity to form a committee to discuss it," Rodney argued. "Also — and you may think this a minor point — this further proves my previous assertion about the utility of the gene therapy."

Elizabeth rubbed her temple wearily. The moment the jumper had returned carrying only half her team, she'd felt an all-too-familiar sense of dread. Somehow, no matter what they did in this galaxy, nothing came without a price. Could they — could *she* — have done something to prevent this? Had they failed yet again under noble intentions? "I understand your point, Rodney, and I agree that genetic inequality is at the heart of the problem. But the circumstances are shifting quickly right now. If we give in to terror tactics, we're setting ourselves up to be continually manipulated. I won't allow that."

The scientist scowled. "Like so many things, it's a matter of perspective," he said. "One man's terrorist is another man's revolutionary. How *did* your country come by its independence, by the way?"

"It's hardly the same — "

"It's *exactly* the same. And not only is the 'we don't negotiate with terrorists' mantra both trite and unreasonably inflexible, it also happens to be counterproductive in this situation. They're asking us for something we intended to give them already."

Rodney stalked across the office. "Let's also bear in mind our diminishing options here. Aside from leaving Ford and Teyla to their aromatic paradise, what else do you suggest we do?"

Elizabeth slid her gaze over to her military advisor. John's expression told her that he didn't like the situation any more than she did. "A six-man team," he replied to the unspoken question. "Can't go in completely covert, since they'll know we're coming, but a second jumper could go in cloaked, and the team could move out after I head-fake Yann and his buddies into thinking I'm complying with their demands. Smoke grenades should help keep the casualties low. But without confirmation of their exact location and the number of unfriendlies around, there's no way to guarantee a clean fight. On either side."

As the scenario was outlined in cool, almost clinical terms, apprehension was becoming increasingly visible on Rodney's face. "They haven't directly threatened our people," he said quietly. "Unlike the Genii, it was clear that they have no intentions of hurting anyone."

John's response was a short bark of humorless laughter. "Not unless we refuse their ultimatum, no. But what happens if we do? They just give up and let Ford and Teyla go? The 'or else' was kind of implied."

Expecting Rodney to snap back at the Major, Elizabeth was surprised when he instead dropped his gaze. John looked deadly serious, though, and she wouldn't have wanted to cross him just then, either. Losing people tended to do that to an officer. "I'd like your opinion, Major," she said, turning fully toward him. "Is a rescue really practical, and if so, what happens next?"

Arms folded across his chest, John exhaled a long breath. "I don't like having this many unknowns," he replied. "And it'll only get murkier once the shooting starts. Our Marines are trained for urban combat, but this wouldn't be anything I'd call standard."

"Then there's the matter of the Shields. I never did get a chance to test Zelenka's theory about disabling the capacitor," Rodney put in, his fire returning. "If we do this, we'll lose any chance of learning something useful from this whole mess. Let's also be clear that a military rescue mission implies leaving the Dalerans to their fate. All of them. There's no way we can go back to help anyone if we've just busted in and out of there with guns blazing."

"Believe it or not, that did occur to me," John informed him with exaggerated patience. "Look, I hate the precedent we'd be setting by caving in to a threat, and I *really* hate the idea of rewarding someone for jumping my team. But in a messed-up way, we can still achieve our objective. We can introduce the gene therapy—first to Yann's group, then to others once things have calmed down and we have our team back. Like Rodney said, that gets us to where we'd planned to be all along."

Elizabeth glanced at Carson, who'd stayed on the periphery of the discussion. "On a logistical level, do we have the reserves to provide enough of the gene therapy to satisfy these rebels?"

The doctor gave a small shrug. "Synthesizing the stuff hasn't posed much of a problem," he answered. "After our talk a few days ago, about giving the treatment to more of the expedition members, I started increasing our reserves. We have a stock of about a hundred doses, but I'd want to keep twenty until we replenish that. I'll need until morning to prepare a proper vaccination kit for the rest."

"The only way they can test whether it's effective or not," John put in, "is to handle one of the Shields. And since they're going to have to overcome that cultural taboo anyway—"

Elizabeth was already nodding. "You can simultaneously test people for the gene. In other words, the gene therapy may not prove to be necessary."

"With Lieutenant Ford and Teyla's lives possibly at stake, I wouldn't recommend giving them a placebo," Carson said.

Was she really that easy to read? "How did you know I was going to suggest that?"

Shrugging, Carson replied, "It was a logical option, and one that I'd considered when I realized how prevalent the gene might be."

"I think we should consider contingency plans in case Yann and his group don't hold up their end of the bargain." Elizabeth turned back to John, who didn't hesitate in his response.

"Assuming they'll want to see if the vaccine is effective, it could take a few days to distribute it and simultaneously test the right people. Tomorrow is Wednesday. If you don't hear from us before Friday, wait until dark, then send in the cavalry."

"I guess we have our plan of action, then." Elizabeth heard and despised the tinge of defeat in her voice. "Give them the gene. Get our people back."

CHAPTER TEN

Yann and his fishermen buddies were waiting at the clearing that had more or less become their official landing site. No sooner had the Major shut down the engines than the whole group came tromping up to the hatch.

"Here goes nothing," Sheppard muttered.

Rodney hitched the medical pack on his shoulder and stepped out of the jumper.

"You have brought the potion?" Yann asked in lieu of any greeting.

"It's right here." Rodney patted the pack.

Immediately, the pair of fishermen moved to take it from him, but Sheppard stepped in to block them. "We'll hold onto it until we see our friends, all right?"

Their faces twisted in identical scowls. "And how are we to know that the potion truly works?"

Sheppard didn't bat an eye. "This is not negotiable."

The men either didn't recognize the word or didn't care. Even though he was pretty sure the Major had stashed an additional weapon somewhere on his person, Rodney didn't like these odds. "You need us to show you how to administer the gene therapy," he said hurriedly, at last halting the men's advance.

Cocking a thumb over his shoulder at his teammate, Sheppard added, "What he said."

Yann raised his voice above the resentful grumbles. "It is a fair bargain. Come."

After retrieving their Shields, they were led back through the village and into the transport, a route Rodney was beginning to think he could now travel in his sleep. When the transport doors began to open, however, the dynamics of the situation once more abruptly shifted. A hard shove from behind propelled him out into the Sanctuary Hall. An even harder shove sent Yann sprawling out across the grubby floor, which, given the size of the merchant, was an indication of the aggression of the person doing the pushing.

Rodney suspected that the only reason why he'd been treated to less force was that he was carrying the medical pack — which he would no doubt be divested of in short order, because it seemed that Yann wasn't the only one who wanted it. Great. Things had just gone from extremely bad to incalculably worse.

"What are you doing?" The merchant rolled over and shouted at his erstwhile fishermen buddies. "What is this?"

The Sanctuary Hall was deserted except for some overfed official types who dressed more outrageously than Kesun, backed up by a bunch of goons armed with long daggers — or maybe they were short swords. For a brief moment, Rodney wondered if he and Sheppard had not somehow been transported into an entirely different city, perhaps even a different planet — until he noted that two of the goons were carrying their P-90s in such a way that suggested they'd figured out how to use them. Then Rodney spotted Balzar's smirking face. "The genetherapy," commanded the chief, stepping menacingly toward them. "The potion of which you spoke to Yann. Give it to us. And the small weapon you carry." His eyes fell to the holster strapped to the Major's leg.

"Now, is that any way to ask?" Sheppard replied.

"You wish to see your friends again?"

Rodney could have sworn that, despite a moment's hesitation, Sheppard handed over his handgun nicely, but the goons felt inspired to show them who was boss. While two of them held the Major's arms behind his back, one sent a punch into his stomach that doubled him over. A second fist to Sheppard's face jerked him out of the arms of the men and threw him against the wall of the transport. It didn't knock the Major out, but as he pulled himself to his feet, spitting out a mouthful of blood, the cut on Rodney's arm began a sympathetic ache.

"What the hell did that prove?" The goons who had been doing the punching turned their attention to Rodney, and his brief burst of outrage evaporated. Backing away, he muttered,

"Maybe I should just shut up."

"Good idea, Rodney."

Sheppard's belated advice was lost, however, because Yann was now shouting at his ex-fishing buddies, "You...treacherous barbarian scum. You agreed that the potion should go to the poor!"

"The poor have no knowledge of how to govern," scoffed Balzar. He swung the handle of an axe against the young merchant's legs, forcing him to his knees, and demanded of Rodney again, "The *genetherapy*?"

Rodney saw no point in being beaten into submission. But as he pulled the pack from his shoulders, he was compelled to ask the other chiefly looking types, "Who *are* you people?"

"Who are we?" snarled the largest of the overdressed officials. "You come to our city and conspire with village rabble like this — " He directed a ruthless kick at Yann's left kidney, which sent the young merchant sprawling again. " — to overthrow our rule, and you demand to know who *we* are?"

"*Your* rule," choked Rodney. "But I thought..." It was then that he realized that none of the officials wore Shields. They weren't Chosen. Given the air of absolute authority being wielded, the awful truth struck him with a force that was almost as crippling as the blows that had been rained on Sheppard and Yann.

Balzar snatched the bag from his hands and handed it to the official doing the talking. The man wrestled with the unfamiliar pack for a moment before taking a step forward and shoving it in Rodney's face. "I am Gat, the high chief of all of Dalera, and you will open this and show me this potion." The coldness in his eyes was several degrees closer to absolute zero than Kolya's had been. "Then finally," he added with a glance back at his entourage, "we can slaughter the last of those decrepit old priests who hide in their Enclave praying to a long dead exile from a forgotten world."

The men with him nodded agreement and voiced their approval.

Rodney was certain that the groan coming from the Major's direction wasn't entirely due to physical pain. The degree of his own monumental blunder had only just begun to sink in when, naturally, someone felt it necessary to state the obvious.

"You… You *lied* to us," Yann blurted to Balzar. "You lied to everyone! You told us that it was the Chosen who demanded payment for transport into the Citadel."

"That fool Kesun is run off his feet all day in exchange for a few tokens of appreciation. But while he might have the power to operate the transports, it is we who control the inns and Sanctuary Halls. And once we have this *genetherapy*, we can finally be rid of the Chosen and anyone else adhering to that pathetic cult of theirs."

"You led us to think… You knew the truth all along, why the Chosen rarely came to our village, yet you deceived us with lies twisted to suit your purpose!" The look of betrayal on Yann's face was almost pitiful. He turned to Rodney and added in a plaintive voice, "I believed it was the Chosen who were secretly storing food!"

Balzar's laugh was a short, ugly bark of disdain.

"You stole from us and turned our hearts against the Chosen," Yann spluttered, barely able to get the words out past his outrage. "For what? To stuff your own bellies?" Eyes wild with panic, he added, "You cannot do this, Balzar. The Chosen have warned us countless times. Those who defy the will of Dalera will bring the Wraith upon us all!"

"You young fool. Anyone with eyes to read the teaching windows knows that the Wraith come, no matter what 'laws' those witless priests invoke. There is no way to fight the Wraith. Only those with foresight to plan for the great cullings will survive. There is sufficient room in the bowels of the Enclave to hide several hundred, and this—" He snatched one of the P-90s from the goon's hand. "—and others like it that we took from your friends, will aid us in making certain that only those that *we* choose may enter."

"Enough!" Gat's attention shifted from Balzar to Rodney. "The potion."

Still reeling from the impact of this revelation, Rodney fell back on the streak of stubbornness that he'd employed with

Kolya. "Fine," he snapped. "Whatever you want. But it's like I told Yann." He pulled out the box of prepared syringes and opened it so that they could all see. "Only Lieutenant Ford knows how to administer it."

Nothing would have given Rodney more pleasure than shoving one of the needles deep into Balzar's arm, preferably with a few embolism-triggering bubbles in the mix. But getting Teyla and Ford back might in some way mitigate this unbelievably disastrous turn of events.

Gat motioned to one of the thugs and said, "Bring the other two that you found. Then round up the priests' warriors. Once we become Chosen, they must obey *our* orders." A vengeful smile distorted his features. "When the Wraith come, we will transport the 'warriors' out to the villages, to stand in defense as they claim their ancestors once did. That will provide the Wraith a suitable diversion while we evacuate those loyal to us."

"Well," Sheppard said to Rodney as they were marched to the end of the Sanctuary Hall and shoved into a rank-smelling corner. "That's another fine mess you've gotten us into."

"Me? I wasn't the only one who assumed the Chosen were running things around here." He wished his words didn't carry such an obvious lack of conviction. "Kesun could've said something to clue us in!" Even as he spoke, he realized that was exactly what Kesun had done. The cycle continued as the priest had explained — but the power currently rested with the barbarians. The problem was that Rodney's disgust at the idea of an advanced technology being regarded as a religion had instantly lured him into his assumptions about the Chosen. Teyla could now add 'blind bigot' to 'hypocrite'.

Before he could further ponder the depth of his flawed judgment, he was surprised to see Teyla and Ford being led in their direction by a squad of goons. Sadly, two of these men also carried P-90s.

"Good to see you guys," Sheppard told the rest of their team when they neared. "They treat you all right?"

Teyla glared at the smirking bully boys and then eyed the growing bruise on the Major's cheek. "Better, I believe, than you. The Chosen are not the leaders of these people."

"Yeah, we got that."

Their guards motioned for Ford and Teyla to also sit on the floor. Rodney waited for the inevitable stream of recriminations from his Athosian teammate, but then Balzar tossed the box containing the gene therapy in his general direction.

"Careful!" Rodney just managed to catch it. "That stuff is fragile, and since our welfare would appear to be directly tied to a positive outcome of this experiment—"

"Enough of your mindless chatter. The potion!" Gat's eyes blazed. Unlike Kolya, the Daleran leader could never be reasoned with.

"All right, fine. Anyone ever tell you that patience is a virtue?" Rodney withdrew the requisite supplies, and handed them to Ford. The reaction was instantaneous. Gat, Balzar and what were presumably the other chiefs—or more accurately, extortionists—inched closer on all sides. As if he hadn't had enough reminders lately that crowds weren't really his thing.

With a glance at Sheppard, who reluctantly signaled his permission, Ford stood, and demonstrated the syringe. "Who's going first?"

Balzar's anticipatory smile vanished when Gat pointed at him. The village chief stared suspiciously at the Lieutenant when the needle was inserted into his arm. A moment's silence followed before Balzar complained, "I feel nothing."

"Well, what did you expect?" Rodney rolled his eyes and got to his feet. "It's gene therapy, not a can of Popeye's spinach! Besides, it takes several hours to come into effect, and not everyone will successfully receive it." As he spoke, he noticed Sheppard and Teyla were also standing and exchanging brief looks with Ford.

It then occurred to Rodney that Yann had gone missing. So, for that matter, had most of their heavies, which meant that Teyla, Ford and Sheppard could conceivably take out this lot and—

A bunch of grubby rags and desperate, hungry faces suddenly spewed into the Sanctuary Hall from the nearby entrances.

Before Rodney's teammates could make a move, the Citadel's desperate poor were climbing all over Gat and the other chiefs. Yann appeared from somewhere in the middle, and with the help of three or four wild-eyed cavemen types, wrested the syringe from Ford.

Yann's wide, ruddy face was almost reverent as he thrust his hand high, holding the now empty syringe up for all to see. "Here is the end of our oppression!" he shouted. "Here is our salvation from the Wraith!"

A disorganized cheer went up. "Oh, brother," Rodney said under his breath. Sure enough, just to keep things interesting, the transport doors opened, and Kesun began muscling his way through the crowds — with his warriors in tow. In addition, even more of the impoverished Citadel's residents were pouring into the place from the other entrances, insane with desperation.

There were eighty doses of the gene therapy, and there were a lot more than eighty people here. Rodney jumped when hands grabbed at the pack, snatching it out of view.

"McKay! Let's go." Sheppard gripped him by the arm and started hauling him through the chaos in the direction of the closest exit.

"Kesun would steal your chance to become Chosen!" he heard Gat bellow. "Kill the Chosen. *Kill them all!*"

The mob seemed to change direction, but before Rodney could make out what was going on, Balzar's voice added to the fray. "The Chosen from Atlantis are no better than the others. Let them be an example of the fate earned by all Chosen!"

There was no way *that* could go well. His heart rate spiking, Rodney stuck close to his team as they attempted to evade the subset of Dalerans who seemed to be on Balzar's side. The Major started to reach into his pocket, only to be tackled from the side and shoved toward Teyla.

Rodney glanced around at the burly men moving to surround them. Just beyond them, someone cried out, "Warriors, defend the Chosen!" An axe swinging through the crowd resulted in a bloodcurdling cry from Gat. The other chiefs also began to fall beneath the avalanche of warriors. Surging against them, a sea of ragged humanity was howling for *everyone's* heads.

Rough hands clamped down on Rodney's biceps and dragged him out of a crowd too caught up in the frenzy to notice. Sheppard was pulled alongside him, while Ford and Teyla were yanked in the opposite direction. Maybe Yann and his army of destitutes hadn't intended to hurt them, but Rodney didn't feel nearly as confident about their prospects at the hands of Balzar and his crew.

A burst of P-90 fire prompted him to look back between the flailing arms and swinging axes. Kesun had somehow been separated from his warriors. In the brief moment before he vanished beneath the blades of the enraged horde, Kesun returned Rodney's gaze. The full weight of the man's desperate plight for his people struck an even more powerful blow than Rodney's earlier realization of his flawed judgment.

Sheppard yelled something at him. Rodney could only stare in reply. He knew he was telegraphing his anguish loud and clear but couldn't find the energy to give a damn. Never before had an action—okay, maybe not an action, but a statement—of his generated such catastrophic consequences. He filed away a mental memo: *exhibiting any kind of humanity only ever ends badly.*

CHAPTER ELEVEN

It hadn't been a bad plan, but the execution had been some-what lacking. Or maybe it had just been an unforeseen complication that had doomed him to fail, something he couldn't possibly have predicted. Yeah, that had to be it: the Pegasus corollary to Murphy's Law.

In any case, John's theoretical jailbreak hadn't gone so well. When he and Rodney had been dragged from the Sanctuary Hall and down a dank hallway lined with prison cells, he'd grabbed a hold of the rough iron bars that formed a cell's door and swung it into one captor's face, knocking the goon to the floor. He'd intended to fell the other with the pocketknife no one had noticed when he'd handed over his sidearm. Somehow he hadn't factored in the possibility of a third goon showing up until a brick-hard arm stinking of fish had constricted around his throat.

When the spots cleared from John's vision, Rodney was still standing there like a deer caught in headlights, and two irked-looking Dalerans were shoving them into the cell. Oh, and the pocketknife definitely got confiscated the second time around. John inwardly cursed himself out. He'd had that knife since survival training.

Unwilling to suffer any further antics, or maybe just out of spite, the goons had bound his wrists to the cell bars with a thick strap of leather. That wouldn't have been so bad, but they'd done it beneath a set of crossbars, low enough that sitting was hell on the spine and standing was right out. Eventually he gave up and lay down on the cold, uneven stone floor, trying to tell himself that the unwashed urinal smell was coming from someplace other than the damp ground.

Rodney's wrists were similarly bound, but since *he* hadn't tried to beat anyone up lately, they'd allowed him the freedom to pace the cell…all twelve feet of it. John looked up at the scientist. He took seven measured steps, pivoted, and took seven steps back. The pattern repeated, and repeated again. One-two-three-four-five-six-seven-turn.

"I'll give you this much," John commented. "Your sense of rhythm's flawless."

"I did have that going for me, if nothing else." Rodney's focus didn't waver. "Never needed a metronome. Standard andante at eighty beats per minute, allegro at one-twenty."

"Um, okay." John assumed that if he needed to understand that comment, it would be explained. "Meanwhile, could you knock that off? Watching you bounce back and forth from down here could give a trapeze artist vertigo."

"So don't watch." The pacing continued for several seconds, until Rodney changed course and flopped down on a rough bench that presumably passed for a bed. "If you were going to try something as monumentally stupid as that escape attempt, you could have at least warned me."

"Not without arousing suspicion." John wriggled his arms experimentally. Shifting the strap might not be impossible, but his wrists would be shredded before he could get anywhere.

"You didn't actually expect that maneuver with the cell door to work, right?" Rodney leaned his head back against the wall.

"I figured we had a better shot out there than we do in here."

"I suppose, but only if, like Yann's rebels, you're going for that whole 'better to die on one's feet than live on one's knees' thing."

John didn't bother to mask his irritation. "Right now I'm thinking I might die flat on my ass, so let me know if there's a cliché for that."

"I'm working on it. And by 'it,' I mean a better plan for not dying, rather than an appropriate cliché for your predicament." As he'd proved on numerous occasions, Rodney could think and talk at the same time. "I guess all this makes sense from their perspective. They've been led to believe that their mistreatment and marginalization has been the fault of the Chosen for so long that trusting us would be a tough sell."

Rolling his eyes toward the ceiling, John muttered, "Ten minutes in here and already you're going Patty Hearst on me."

"Don't be a jackass. I'm decidedly opposed to getting quartered, which I suspect is what awaits us if we hang around here. What I don't understand is why they bothered to lock us up first rather than just get it over with."

"Maybe their schedule was booked up for the day." It was the best explanation John had, which wasn't saying much. "That's of course assuming that your 'they' is the same 'they' that I'm thinking put us in here."

"It has become somewhat difficult to distinguish who's who in the revolutionary scheme of things." Rodney looked as though he saw some merit in John's suggestion, though. "Everyone's probably either fighting to get their hands on some of the gene therapy or fighting the ones who've already gotten it."

As if to bear that theory out, scattered sounds reached them from some distance away. It all ran together, making it difficult to piece together what was happening, but it sure wasn't anything orderly. "Not to mention killing the Chosen," John added. Rodney winced at that. "Or the guys who were actually running this place."

"Whom, if memory serves correctly, Kesun labeled as barbarians," Rodney supplied. "In short, it's complete and utter anarchy." He snorted. "I've never been known to do anything by halves."

John fixed his gaze on his teammate again. Rodney was staring off into space, but this didn't appear to be a 'solving the mysteries of the universe' trance. It looked more like he was wondering how everything had fallen to pieces so damned fast. "I can hear the wheels in your head turning from here."

Shaking himself, Rodney glanced down at him. "Devising a brilliant plan of escape will go a lot faster without interruptions."

So he didn't want to chat. That was new. "Whatever you say."

After a moment, the scientist seemed to slump a little. "No, it

— won't," he admitted quietly. "It won't go faster, because there's nothing to work with and nowhere to go."

"Hey, we're still alive. I'll take that for the moment."

A guttural yell from somewhere far beyond the cell's walls cut into the discussion, mixing in with other rising voices and the occasional clash of metal. It didn't take an advanced degree to realize what was going on outside. Rodney had a few of those anyway and, from his expression, that hyper-critical brain of his was obviously cranking out some nasty answers. John sighed. "Look—"

"What?" The harsh tone surprised them both, and Rodney went back to staring at the wall, this time looking more sullen. "Excuse me if I'm having a little trouble accepting this whole mess. I'm just now learning that in dismantling the social construct of this world, something I championed rather enthusiastically based on a set of completely false assumptions, we may have gotten people killed. I have the right to take a moment, don't I?"

John shook his head, a cold sensation creeping into his thoughts. "Join the club. I'm considering printing up T-shirts."

That seemed to throw Rodney off. They looked at each other for a few seconds. At last, he asked hesitantly, "How do you—?"

"I woke the damn Wraith, Rodney. Responsibility doesn't come much heavier than that."

"It wasn't just you. And it wasn't…" He abandoned the sentiment, doubtless recognizing that they'd both heard it all before, and that it would always ring a little hollow. "What I meant was, knowing that, how do you manage to keep from losing it?"

"By repeatedly telling myself that having no way of knowing the consequences counts as a satisfactory excuse."

"How's that working out?" The interest on Rodney's face contained a slightly desperate edge, as if he were hoping to glean some enlightening crumb from the reply.

"Not that great so far." John forcibly shifted his thoughts into another direction. "Listen, there's stuff we can control and stuff we can't. All we can do is deal with what's in front of us."

"Yeah." The scientist dropped his gaze to the floor, visibly deflated. "Good pep talk."

"Now who's being a jackass?"

Rodney ignored the comment. "Friday, huh? You couldn't have suggested to Elizabeth that we'd be back, oh, maybe tonight?"

"I said we'd check in sooner, but to wait until dark on Friday before sending in the troops."

"And by troops, you meant…?"

"Two jumpers and twelve Marines."

"Comforting numbers, but the odds of these nouveaux Jacobins, or whoever ends up pulling the strings around here, waiting until Saturday morning to execute us are…well, not good."

"I know. I'm hoping that this uprising burns itself out before Markham and Stackhouse show up." His teammate looked skeptical, so John explained. "We weren't sure how all this was going to go down, and I didn't like the idea of our guys walking into the middle of a full-scale revolution, so I asked Dr Weir to give us some time. Now that things have gone pretty well south, there could be any number of newly invested Chosen running around outside the Citadel with Shields, and any one of them could disable our jumper or the others without too much trouble."

"While that makes sense, it doesn't provide us with a way to avoid our respective death sentences."

"Not really, no. But if it comes to that, I'd rather the four of us die here than lose twelve more trying to bust us out."

"Except, of course, that our failure to return will in fact prompt a rescue, in which case —"

"We're back to trying to figure out how to save ourselves before that happens."

Rodney said nothing, but picked up the tattered blanket lying on the bench, and stood. Fingers fumbling due to his bound wrists, he managed to fold the fabric and lay it on the floor beside his teammate. John looked up at him, not comprehending. The scientist gave an impatient tap of his foot. "The floor's cold and wet. You do realize that the single most common form of death that resulted from prolonged incarceration in assorted species of dungeons was pneumonia? At least if you lay on that you won't go hypothermic."

Although he was hardly in any real danger, John couldn't repress a small smile. "Thanks." He awkwardly shuffled his way onto the blanket. "Did I mention that I feel ridiculous down here?"

"You don't want to know how you look, then."

Aiden let out a stream of invectives and, snatching up some loose pebbles in his bound hands, tossed them at the rat. He supposed it was a rat, although it was more the size of a small housecat, and there was green fur on its back and tail. The animal disappeared through the bars into the cell opposite theirs, where it began scratching around in some unidentifiable sludge that might once have been clothing.

"I would not be so hasty," Teyla commented. "We might need the animal for food if we are incarcerated in here for any length of time."

One thing about being stuck in prison with Teyla: she wasn't exactly wimpish. He wondered how the Major was faring with Dr McKay as a cellmate. "Yeah. Maybe we could tame it or something. Get it to gnaw through these." He lifted his hands and smiled ruefully.

"No need." The Athosian had managed to loosen her bindings and now pulled her hands free.

"Hey! How'd you do that?"

Outside, a loud explosion abruptly overwhelmed the sounds of fighting. They both instinctually ducked, but the damp stones that made up the tiny cell only shuddered. It was frustrating as all hell not to be able to see what was going on, but this time around their room didn't exactly come with a view. "They must've figured out how to use the C-4. Wonder what they blew up?" Just as the words were out of his mouth, a series of increasingly loud rumbles warned him that something big was collapsing.

Teyla quickly untied the rope around his wrists. "It is likely that some of those who now rebel against the leaders of this Citadel already had the means of destruction at their disposal."

"Wraithcraft?"

Nodding, Teyla began exploring the damp walls for some means of escape. "Remember when we were in the marketplace, Yann spoke of blackpowder to remove unwanted tree stumps from their fields."

"Same deal wherever you go." He examined the way the set of bars opened and closed. The locking mechanism was about three yards away, along the wall. Even with their bindings tied together to form a lasso, there was no way they'd get enough leverage going to force it open. And digging the bars out from the floor was not an option, given the hardness of the black stone.

"What do you mean?" Teyla was feeling beneath the wooden bench.

"No matter what religion people follow, someone always figures out a way to bend the rules to fit whatever it is that they want to do."

She stood and frowned at the bench. "How then can one discern what is truly right and what is indeed wrong?"

Shrugging, Aiden replied, "My grandparents always taught me that you know the difference in your own heart." He looked up at the ceiling, thick with mold and something more rancid. If anything, this place actually reeked worse than the open sewers outside.

"You were fortunate to have had such people to care for you."

He smiled in fond memory, and felt a stab of guilt for not being able to let them know where he was. "Yeah. Yeah, I was."

A movement outside had Teyla snatching up her bonds and wrapping them loosely around her wrists. Aiden did the same. The next person to open their cell door would be in for a painful surprise.

"Aiden?" Lisera's tearful face appeared around the corner of the cell.

Dropping the rope, Aiden grabbed the bars. "Lisera! How did you get here?"

The girl's face was streaked with grime and blood from a cut on her cheek. Her eyes were filled with the same terror that Aiden had seen when he'd found her in the ditch. Most of the clothes she'd worn from Atlantis were now gone, replaced by rags even more filthy than her original rough burlap covering. She also sported a pair of oversized pants that covered the cast on her leg. "It is the only safe place to hide. Outside..." She swallowed and met Teyla's eyes. Even in the dim light of the cell, he could see her face pale further. "Those elder Chosen who had taken up residence in their ancestral homes, the Stations, to protect us from the Wraith, were pulled out into the streets and...and quartered."

"Yann's group of rebels did this?" Teyla's voice was stiff with shock.

"No." Lisera shook her head vehemently. "Gat's men, the ones who control the Citadel, first killed Kesun. Then many others took up the cry. Yann tried to stop them, for he knows that without the Chosen there will be no protection against the Wraith."

"Where is your Shield?"

Eyes darting between them, Lisera replied, "I threw it aside. Any who are seen with a blue Shield are torn apart. The alleys of the Citadel run red with the blood of not only the Chosen, but those who are now accused of conspiring to become Chosen."

"Oh, great," Aiden muttered. "Sounds like everyone's turning on one another."

Tears silently fell down Lisera's face, and she whispered, "It is as if the entire world has become stricken with a madness that sets brother against brother. I fear that if it does not soon cease, the Wraith need not bother with their culling, for none will be left alive."

Aiden figured it probably wasn't quite as bad as that, but, to a girl like Lisera, the sort of anarchy she was describing would seem that way. "Listen, see that sliding bar down there? Can you open it and let us out?"

Eyes wide with alarm, she vehemently shook her head. "If you go outside, you will be killed as they have slaughtered the

Chosen, for others are seeking you, claiming that your presence will bring the Wraith down upon us."

"If we remain here," Teyla explained, "those who imprisoned us will return and kill us anyway."

"No." Lisera said determinedly. "Not you, for you are not of the Chosen."

"Perhaps not, but they will kill Major Sheppard and Dr McKay."

Torn with indecision, Lisera bit her lip. "But you will be spared. I am sorry for the others, but I do not want you to die, Aiden."

He stared at her. "They're our friends. If they die, we can't help save your world from the Wraith."

"In which case, we will *all* die," Teyla added. The tone in her voice left no room for doubt. "I have seen what the Wraith do to worlds like yours. When they come — and in this both Gat and the Chosen are correct in stating that they most assuredly will come with their great ships — they will leave little behind."

Still uncertain, Lisera cringed when the sounds of more fighting penetrated their confines.

"Do you know where Major Sheppard and Dr McKay are being held?" Aiden asked.

Lisera glanced over her shoulder. "Two levels below this one, in a cell near where some of your bags are being kept."

"Which means someone will definitely be coming back," Aiden said. He suspected it was more likely their packs than the case with the gene therapy. "Lisera, if you release us, and we can get our things back, we'll be able to help you." The desperate look in her eyes demanded an affirmation of his sincerity. "I promise. Okay? Hey—" He offered her a grin. "I'm a warrior from Atlantis, right?"

"Lisera," Teyla said when the girl continued to hesitate. "Releasing us is the only way we can help both you and your people."

Something in the Athosian's expression bothered Aiden. He shot her a questioning look, but she dismissed it. Lisera gave a jerky nod, and said to Aiden, "You promise." Then she hobbled back and opened the locking mechanism to their cell.

The smell of burned timber and metallic compounds assaulted Rodney's olfactory nerves. Less pungent than the eye-watering stench of the dungeon they'd until recently had the pleasure of inhabiting, the odor was terrifying familiar. He glanced back at Ford and Teyla, who were assisting Lisera up the last of the stone steps. "Do you think we should be rushing outside?"

Sheppard, who was ahead of him, suddenly let loose with a surprisingly colorful string of curses. Urged on by Teyla's expression, Rodney followed the Major out into the square, and squinting against the late afternoon sunlight, looked around the streets.

Any momentary relief that Rodney had felt at their freedom was immediately overcome by shocked outrage. Staring up at the twisted, smoking ruin that had once been the Enclave, he burst out, "Are they insane?" The desperation in his voice was tinged with denial. Even the trees that had surrounded the once-elegant structure now looked like a bunch of spent match heads. "What would possess them to destroy the very thing that they most need?"

"They are driven by the madness of hatred."

In the back of his mind, he recognized that Teyla's words were the product of sorrow and not indifference. Nonetheless, her calm tone danced on his last nerve. Rodney whirled on her, snapping off a reply. "This isn't what was supposed to happen! The Chosen might not have been responsible for the way these people were forced to live, but the fact remains that this entire situation would never have come about if they hadn't regarded the gene as providing them with some sort of divine power!"

"How does that make any difference now?" Ford asked, staring up at the smoldering remains perched on top of the rocky hill.

"You agreed with me!" He loathed the way his voice betrayed his faltering control.

Teyla reached out to grasp his arm, her expression gentle but unyielding. "You are not to blame for what has come to pass," she said firmly.

A nice sentiment, to be sure, but an empty one. And Teyla would know, because she'd vilified his stand from the outset. Rodney swallowed hard against a surge of nausea.

"If anyone's at fault, Rodney, it's me." The bitter edge to Sheppard's voice was unmistakable. "I should've seen this coming."

Damn him. The man wasted no opportunity to martyr himself, justified or not.

"How?" Teyla said, turning to the Major. "You were not to know that Yann would be waiting in ambush for us, nor that he in turn would be betrayed by those who hunger for even greater power."

"Because history has a bad habit of repeating itself. Here or Earth, seems it makes no damned difference."

"We should take the transport back to the jumper and get out of here while we can," Ford asserted. He was holding Lisera by the arm. When her eyes widened, he added, "All of us."

"But you promised to help save everyone. You *promised*!" the girl cried hysterically.

The anger in Rodney's belly turned into a tight, sour ball. His childhood had been defined by belittlement and an utter lack of compassion. To escape that, he'd had to become the best, at everything. Yet somewhere in his pursuit of this goal, he had in turn become equally dispassionate; indeed, some would argue, lacking in humanity. It wasn't until meeting Samantha Carter that he'd understood that truly great science was inspired, and that his own suppressed but deeply powerful emotions had been channeled into arrogance. "No!" he declared, whirling around to face his teammates. "I won't accept that we can't stop this and make them see reason."

"And exactly how do you suggest we accomplish that?" Sheppard demanded. "We're four unarmed people in a city the size of downtown LA. You want to try and make peace amongst God knows how many fanatics on... I'm not even sure how many sides? This place was a powder keg before we arrived. We may have lit the fuse, but sooner or later it was gonna blow, just like it has dozens, probably hundreds of times in the past."

"So... What? We just let them destroy themselves and high-tail it out of here?"

"I believe it may be too late for that." Teyla's face stiffened as she spoke. "The Wraith have come."

CHAPTER TWELVE

Well, that answered one question. The EM fields couldn't block Teyla's sensitivity to the Wraith. Of course, if the Chosen had mostly been hunted down and killed — which was entirely possible now that they couldn't sequester themselves in the Enclave — there was no telling how many of the Shields were still in use.

In the near distance, John could hear the sounds of pitched hand-to-hand combat drawing closer. The heavy clomp of boots pounding the cobblestones rounded the corner of a narrow lane, and six people spilled out into the square. There was a momentary pause before the wild-eyed front-runner pointed to the team and screamed, "Kill them! They are of the Chosen!"

"What?" Rodney squealed. "No! We're not Chosen. See?" He pulled his now filthy jacket aside to show that he wasn't wearing a Shield.

The rabble, insane with bloodlust, weren't about to enter into a discussion. Fortunately, some of them were armed with the team's P-90s and sidearms. Since they brandished the weapons like clubs, John could only conclude that Gat and Balzar's goon squad had been overrun, and, having taken the guns as spoils of the infighting, their new owners apparently had no idea how to use them.

One of the men, an overweight and bulbous-nosed guy who looked like he'd spent most of his life propped up against some bar, made the by-now common mistake of thinking that Teyla was easy game. As he bent low to tackle her, she dispatched him with a sickening kick to his head, and wrenched the P-90 from his grasp before he'd even hit the ground. John took out a further two in quick succession, while Ford disarmed a fourth, breaking the guy's arm in the process.

During the scuffle, the last two had managed to herd Rodney

and Lisera to the far side of the square. Hampered by her leg cast, Lisera fell. Rodney dove on top of her, screaming something unintelligible, trying to protect her and drag her out of the way at the same time.

Breaking into a run, John raised his now reacquired P-90—and cursed. The magazine was empty. Ford must have been having the same problem, because he was pulling off his pack, scrambling for a new magazine. Neither of them was going to reload in time, and it was doubtful that John would reach Rodney before the men, but he had to try.

A ghostly image caught the edge of his vision, along with that creeped-out sensation that the Wraith used to confuse their prey. "No, Major!" With the reflexes of a cat, Teyla knocked him to the ground—just out of the path of a Wraith beam, which scooped up McKay's axe-wielding attackers.

"God! That was close." Half carrying Lisera, Rodney staggered upright and stared up at the sky. "The Darts can only mean that nobody's deploying the defensive fields."

Accepting Teyla's outstretched hand, John swung to his feet, caught the spare magazine that Ford tossed him, and reloaded his weapon. "Which means the Chosen are probably all dead."

"What about Yann's rebels, and Balzar, and whoever-the-hell else received the gene therapy?" asked Rodney, his eyes wide in desperation.

A good question, with a not-so-good answer. "Anyone carrying around one of those activated Shields is painting a bulls-eye on his chest."

Rodney's face scrunched in disbelief. "You mean *nobody's* protecting this place?"

"Not quite no one." Teyla pointed to the east, where a Dart plummeted into the ground. They couldn't see where it hit, but the explosion was more than satisfactory.

"We need to find—" John's words were cut off when more people ran screaming through the square, trying, and failing, to outpace another Wraith beam. In the distance, he heard several more explosions as Darts encountered EM fields. The once blue sky was filled with plumes of smoke. "More Shields," he finished, shouting above the noise.

Dozens, possibly hundreds of people were now streaming into the square. From the opposite direction, a smaller band of warriors emerged and met them head-on in a furious assault. After a moment, John realized that the warriors were not actually attacking, but instead were determinedly heading in the team's direction, defending themselves as they came. Defensive tactics or not, the disciplined warriors, better armed and better protected, were methodically cutting the disorganized rabble to pieces when another Wraith Dart sped overhead. The emerging blue beam carved a path through both groups alike, sucking up bodies like an airborne harvester.

"This is insane!" Rodney yelled as the team backed into what looked like a blacksmith's shop. "Absolutely, unquestionably *nuts*!"

"Welcome to the wonderful world of urban warfare," John called back. "Lisera, do you know where there are any Shields?"

White-faced with terror, Lisera nodded jerkily, and pointed to the mangled and limbless torsos now scattered about the square. Battle-axes made for decisive work in close combat. "When the Enclave was destroyed and the cache of Shields ransacked, many claimed the Shields for themselves, and wear them as proof that they are not of the Chosen."

That kind of ass-backward reasoning was another thing he probably should have expected. "Okay. Rodney, stay here with Lisera. Ford, Teyla?"

"On it, sir." Ford was already outside, turning over the first body.

"Major?" Teyla found a Shield on her first attempt, and tossed it to him just as another Dart came bearing down on them. With all the grace of a grand piano—which was surprising, given its aerodynamic shape—the Dart abruptly lost altitude and clipped the edge of a tall building. It tumbled end over end through a narrow street, mowing down a dozen rebels—or maybe they were Gat's bully boys, it was hard to be sure from this angle—and came to a halt in a spectacular heap against the stone fountain in the middle of the square.

The crash seemed to have quenched the rabble's desire for fighting. Like cockroaches, they vanished back into the dark, narrow-gutted alleyways. The warriors reformed into ranks, while the tallest of them, sporting a large blue chevron on his breastplate, pointed to John and called, "The Chosen from Atlantis!"

Muttering in relief and surprise, the warriors ran across the square to join them. The guy with the chevron removed his horned helmet, tucked it under one arm, and, stepping over a smoking chunk of the crashed Dart, slapped a bloodied fist across his chest. Presumably it was some sort of salute, because he dropped to one knee before John, and added, "By your will, Chosen one. We heard you were here and, praying to Dalera that you had been spared, came to release you."

Great, now he had an army. "Okay, well, where I come from a salute is enough. We're not into the kneeling thing. What's your name?"

"Ushat," he replied, standing and replacing his helmet. "I am the leader of Dalera's warriors."

"I'm Major John Sheppard." He pointed to Ford and Teyla, and introduced them.

One of the warriors abruptly cried out. Jumping back like he'd been scalded, the man swung his axe down onto the ground, again and again, scattering pieces of wreckage. His companions laughed uneasily at him, until Ushat called out, "Enough."

Poking his head from the blacksmith's door, Rodney called, "Did you find —?"

Ford tossed him another Shield. An expression of disgust on his face, Rodney gingerly held the device between his fingers. "What is this stuff all over..." His voice trailed off.

John followed Ushat across to where a few chunks of Wraith arm still twitched on the ground. The warrior who'd been doing the chopping was still looking around nervously.

"Search the wreckage," Ushat ordered his men.

"Good thinking." John readied his weapon while the warriors began clambering over the twisted hunks of metal. "A little thing like a missing arm isn't going to stop a Wraith." How anything could have survived that crash was beyond him, but underestimating the general stubbornness of the Wraith always was a losing proposition.

"Here," a warrior called out. He was standing behind the canopy. "The monster lives!" He raised his axe.

"No!" John yelled, running around the remains of the fountain. "Maybe he can tell us something."

With the raised axe paused above his head, the warrior looked past John's shoulder.

Ushat, who was right on John's six, replied, "Major Sheppard speaks true. Stand aside."

John had seen a lot of less-than-pleasant sights in his time. Hell, the entire square was littered with bodies and unattached pieces. The horror here was that the Dart's pilot was still alive. That is, what was left of him. With both of his arms severed, the Wraith had been unable to reach the self-destruct device on his chest. And he wasn't exactly able to wander off anywhere, what with having no legs, and not much of a pelvis to speak of. Despite his loathing of the things, John's instinct was to put it out of its misery with a bullet to the head.

Seemingly oblivious to its injuries, the Wraith, still strapped to the remains of the seat, hissed at him. "Come closer and let me feed upon you."

"Maybe you hadn't noticed, but you're kind of missing a few vital parts. Or are those big teeth for something more than show?"

Snarling in disgust, the Wraith flung his head from side to side, trying to dislodge himself. "Your puny defenses will not stop us."

"Stopped you, didn't it? Darts are pretty much falling out of the sky all over the place."

Abruptly, his thrashing ceased, and his head slumped forward onto his chest.

"Remove its head," said Ushat, nodding to the warrior.

"Looks dead to me, sir," Ford said, wincing.

"Can't say as I blame them for wanting to make certain." John turned aside before the axe slammed down. The absence of Darts now flying around the city didn't reassure him nearly as much it should have. With that thought, he turned back and crouched down to stare at the inside of the Dart's canopy.

"Sir?" Ford squatted next to him.

Something like a HUD flickered intermittently, almost as if it was stuck on a recycle mode. John was about to call Rodney to come check it out when the display sputtered and died—but not before he'd caught sight of a gut-wrenching image.

Beside him, he heard Ford inhale sharply. "Was that what I think it was?"

"What is it that you saw?" Ushat demanded.

"Unless I'm mistaken," John replied, standing and stepping down off the wreckage, "there are two hive ships inbound."

"That bodes ill, but it is no surprise." Ushat turned and looked around at the scattered bodies of rebels and Gat's minions. Spitting in disgust, or maybe to get the bitter taste of defeat out of his mouth, he added, "Kesun told me that when this day came, the Wraith would feed upon the souls of the damned at night, and then, having acquired the strength of their life, attack the Citadel at dawn."

Rodney, still supporting Lisera, had joined Teyla, whose face was drawn and thoughtful. "Okay. All right," said Rodney. "We should rethink our escape plan."

John slowly turned to face him. "Five minutes ago, you wanted to stay and broker a peace deal between everyone."

"Yes, well, I think it's fairly obvious by now that my ideals can easily be swayed when faced with a vanishingly small probability of survival."

Teyla exhaled heavily. "I doubt that escape is now possible. Frustrated by their inability to cull those within the Citadel, the Wraith will most likely spend the night scouring the areas unprotected by the Shields."

"The villages," Ford said.

"I think the jumper option's off the table. Even assuming we could negotiate our way through a city in the throes of anarchy—" John gestured toward what sounded like more street fighting headed their way. "—and fight through the Wraith to get to the jumper, we can't fly it while we're carrying the Shields."

Rodney's face slumped in resigned frustration. "And the chances of surviving a gauntlet of Dart sweeps are next to non-existent."

Clearly troubled by the conversation, Ushat asked, "You wish to leave us?"

Offering up what he hoped was a reassuring smile, John replied. "Just figuring out if we could go for help."

"From Atlantis?" Ushat's eyes turned hopeful.

"Unfortunately, that's not going to be possible." John addressed his team. "The only way through this is to help these people defend the Citadel against the Wraith. And we're going to have to hope we can do that before Dr Weir sends in the backup teams, or they'll be getting our first look at a hive ship — and probably not live long enough to tell anyone about it."

The sounds of street fighting drew closer. John glanced at the ruined Enclave. "Is there anything — any*one* left?"

Ushat's lips curled in regret. John recognized the look in the man's eyes. The Daleran had seen a lot of people die in the last few hours, people he'd been charged to protect. "Knowing that the Wraith would strike in large numbers," Ushat explained, "Kesun this morning ordered every one of Dalera's warriors to assist with repairs to our weakest point, the old eastern wall. Gat and the other barbarian chiefs chose that moment to make their move against the Chosen, whom they have besmirched." His face hardened in anger. "Gat has long demanded payment from villagers before allowing them to enter the transports. Many times I told Kesun that we must stamp out this abhorrent practice, for Dalera charged her warriors and priests to accept only gifts and to never demand payment. But…" He paused and looked at his men. "It was our most sacred law, never to turn our hands against the people. Only against the Wraith."

John was certain he could see the big man's lips tremble behind his blond beard. "Until now, fear of the Wraith had checked their hands," Ushat continued. "But somehow, Gat's followers managed to penetrate the Enclave. They butchered most of the Chosen in their sleep, after which they set the rooms ablaze, fueling the flames with blackwater. Ah!" He slammed the head of his axe into the ground in frustrated rage. "How they could have done this only Dalera knows, for none but the Chosen have the divine power to enter the Enclave."

Rodney's face had adopted that 'guilty-as-charged' look that he was so good at. It was a moot point, though. The servants — or slaves — that they'd seen stashing the food away had obviously belonged to Gat, but Rodney had been right about the condition of the temple. Someone had been doing the cleaning and polishing. Then there was the little matter of that additional control panel in the transport.

Examining the Enclave, John noted that while it was mounted on a plateau, there were probably countless ways in. This wasn't the time or the place to get into a philosophical discussion about divinity, so he opted for the less problematic suggestion. "Even if they couldn't use the transports, couldn't Gat's men have just walked in the front doors?"

As if the thought had never occurred to him, Ushat blinked rapidly. "It is forbidden. Dalera would not allow it." But his words had lost the conviction they might have had, oh, say, twenty-four hours ago.

Teyla had found a third Shield, and after wiping off most of the gore, handed it to Lisera.

Ushat's eyes widened, and John followed his gaze to the now glowing Shield in the girl's hand. "Then it *is* true!" An expression of hope broke across the warrior's face. "Some amongst the people do indeed carry the divine power. Kesun spoke of this after you departed."

"Of what else did he speak?" Teyla asked with a speculative look at Rodney.

"That it was not only the barbarian rulers and the people who must return to Dalera's teachings, but also the Chosen. Kesun was certain that many Chosen would be found among the people. The children's children of Chosen, born in secret during the times when barbarians ruled, as they did until this day. He had intended to test his beliefs as soon as you returned with Lisera."

Glancing up at the still-smoking remains of the Enclave, Ushat's expression crumpled. "Now it is too late, for the mindless horde knows only revenge. By killing Gat and ordering my men to defend themselves against the rabble, I too have broken our most sacred law, that we should never turn our hand against Dalerans."

John clamped his jaw shut. Rodney's face was also crumpling. The scientist's depressive funk while they'd been imprisoned was descending to a new level of self-recrimination. But remorse was an indulgence they didn't have time for. It was getting dark. Assuming Kesun was right about a Wraith ground assault, they had until morning to implement a defensive strategy.

A bloody-faced man with torn clothing ran into the square. The warriors turned and raised their weapons. Panicked, the man took one look at the warriors, pulled a glowing Shield from his pocket, and held it aloft with a scream. "Save me. I am of the Chosen!"

The mob on his heels was brandishing torches, howling for his blood. "Quarter him. Quarter the Chosen and take off his head!"

Ushat snarled and pointed his halberd at the man that John barely recognized in the fading light. "*You.*"

"Yann!" Lisera cried.

"My, how the tables have turned," Rodney remarked, his features stony.

Yann stumbled to a stop, his face screwed up against his appalling choices. Behind him, a mob wanted to hack him to pieces—literally. In front, warriors were already spreading out, cutting off any chance of his escaping down some rat hole. "I...didn't mean for this to happen. This is not what I planned!" he cried.

"Oh, spare me the echo," Rodney snapped. He rounded on Ushat. "If you kill him—"

"I know," Ushat growled. "Protect the murderous rebel. Do not harm him—yet."

Despite the warriors' obvious anger, they were too well disciplined to disobey an order, and they formed a protective phalanx around Yann. ÒI went back to the village, to try and save everyone, as is the Chosen's duty,Ó the merchant babbled. ÒBut none remained. The village is overrun with Wraith!Ó

Which meant the jumper option was definitely out. They were left with only one choice: stand with the Dalerans to repel the Wraith, preferably before the Marines arrived in — John glanced at his watch — less then forty hours.

Confronted by the business end of fifty or more halberds, the crowd hesitated. Someone from behind cried out, "The Chosen and the warriors have failed to protect us. Kill them all!"

More shouts followed, grim cries from people who had lost wives, husbands, children, their homes and livelihoods. With nothing left to lose, these people wanted vengeance, and they wanted it in spades.

Someone must have spotted the glowing Shields in John and Rodney's hands, because the mob's attention suddenly deflected to them. John was getting awfully tired of fickle villagers. He was about to yell something, when Ushat announced, "They are not Chosen. They are from Atlantis!"

That took the wind out of the mob's sails long enough for a loud voice at the rear to cry, "This way. I have heard there are more Chosen hiding in their Stations in the north."

Rodney shook his head. "Somebody had better explain to them that unless they stop killing Chosen —"

"I think we get the picture, doc," Ford muttered.

"Wait!" called a decently dressed guy from the front of the pack. "What if the Atlanteans have come to help us?"

"Risk your own neck to find out, but you will not risk mine."

Scuffles began to break out. As darkness fell, the smoke that curled around the city had been replaced by the angry glow of fires. John recognized the signs. For some, the blood lust was fading and reality was beginning to set in. Their leaders had slaughtered the only people who could protect them from the Wraith and then had themselves been slaughtered. The city was in flames, and now the Wraith were on top of them. It had to have been the worst timed revolution in the history of *any* world.

In an aside to John, Ushat said quietly, "Can you help us?"

"Maybe. First, I need to find a map, preferably like the one Kesun showed me."

"Excuse me?" Rodney demanded, having bounced out of depression into indignation. "You want to go sightseeing?"

"If I'm gonna have to defend this city from a Wraith attack in—" He glanced at two large planets rising over the eastern horizon. "How long until dawn?"

"Twelve hours," Ushat replied.

"For that, I need a map." John glanced at the squabbling crowd. "And a lot of cooperation."

Ushat's eyes narrowed, and he focused on someone in the rabble. "That man is one of the Citadel's engineers. He has access to maps and plans."

A movement caught John's attention. He looked up to see Teyla climbing over the wreckage of the Dart. "With your help," she called down to everyone, "we might yet defend the Citadel against the Wraith. Their winged beasts fall from the sky even though the Chosen are all dead. But you must do as Dalera intended, and work together, for having vanquished this Wraith just moments ago—" She gestured at the wreckage. A sudden hush fell over the square. "We now know that a great cull will take place at dawn. The choice is yours. Surrender to the madness of the Wraith, or work through the night to save what we can."

It seemed to Rodney that no place in the Citadel provided an escape from the eye-watering odors. Currently his senses were battling against the stench of charred... Actually, it was something that he didn't want to consider all that carefully. Unfortunately the public works building to which they'd been led was directly downwind from the ruined Enclave. A dank chamber with little open space and even less light, he had to admit that the building's ambiance was a considerable improvement over their prior lodgings.

Spread out before them on a worktable was a detailed map, hand drawn on some massive animal's skin. Against his will, Rodney's mind catalogued the unknown smell as rancid, oily, and possibly related to aforementioned hide. Oh, for the salt-laden air of a balconied room in Atlantis.

Sheppard was talking tactics and strategies with Ushat, along with a handful of men whom the warrior had identified as city engineers.

When he'd first met the Major, Rodney had assumed the man's ever-present composure to be a sign that not much was going on upstairs, so to speak. He'd long since learned better. In a situation such as this, a calm Major was a very good thing.

After a moment of studying the map, Sheppard said to Ushat, "Do you have any way of signaling the rest of your men inside the Citadel?"

"We have a system of signals using the Wraith horn," replied the warrior leader.

"Assuming that most, if not all of the Chosen are dead, our first priority is to locate and protect everyone who has the ATA gene, or who's received the gene therapy."

The Dalerans' faces blanked. Rodney suddenly had the urge to be ill. If Ushat learned that it had been Rodney's idea to introduce the gene to all and sundry, he was a dead man. Of course, given their current situation, he was a dead man anyway. On the bright side, decapitation by axe would likely be less prolonged than having his life sucked out slowly by a Wraith. "Major," Rodney uttered a warning through clenched teeth.

Chewing the inside of his lip, Sheppard glanced expectantly at Teyla. Great, now he was *definitely* a dead man.

"Kesun was correct," Teyla explained. "Many of your people have inside of them what is called a gene, a small part of Dalera carried down through the generations. We brought with us from Atlantis a potion that when given to all would allow those who carry the gene to activate the Shields and the transport where once they could not."

Could that woman talk, or what? The Dalerans crowded in the room murmured among themselves, greeting Teyla's words with a sense of renewed purpose. Rodney was just about ready to kiss the Athosian's graceful feet in gratitude — until Ushat's gaze turned deadly. Fortunately, the warrior's anger was directed elsewhere. "You stole this potion?" he snapped at Yann.

"Gat and Balzar decided that they deserved a place amidst the Chosen, and took it from us before we could use it," Yann spat back.

Were they *trying* to give him a coronary? "How many times do I have to tell you? They're *not* Chosen!"

"Rodney?" John fixed him with a murderous stare. "Shut up."

"No! There's a principle here. It's a gene, not some divine gift that confers them with special privileges. The very name 'Chosen' inspires exactly the sort of pogroms that have pretty much guaranteed that everyone here is a dead — "

"We shall call ourselves Genes," Yann announced.

He didn't even know how to react to that. Genes? They were going to call themselves Genes? The men around him were nodding in agreement, muttering things like, "'Tis a good name." Rodney opened his mouth to object, when Sheppard shot him a warning look. Well, he supposed it was better than Chosen.

"Now that's settled," said Sheppard. "Can we focus on saving everyone?"

"How many were given this potion?" Ushat asked.

"We carried enough for eighty," replied Teyla.

"The gene therapy only works on forty-eight percent of the recipients," Rodney began. "That's — "

"Thirty-eight point four people," Sheppard replied. "Unlike the Wraith, people need most of their body parts to operate, so let's be conservative and say thirty-five."

"Funny."

"It will be less," Ushat declared. "For I and my men killed Gat and many of the ruling chiefs." He tossed an appraising eye at Yann. "If you did not receive this potion, how is it that the Shield glows for you?"

Meeting the warrior's gaze, he replied, "When Kesun was struck down, his body fell atop mine. When I pushed him aside,

I brushed the Shield, and it began to glow."

The look in Ushat's eyes changed. "Then you are indeed of the Chosen."

A small smile crossed Yann's lips. "Gene."

"Okay, fine," Rodney said impatiently, "now that we've all bonded, can we *please* get on with the plan?"

His head nodding in sage acquiescence, Ushat turned his attention back to the Major.

"See where these Stations are located?" Sheppard pointed to the specially marked buildings around the Citadel. "I'm betting that their height would extend the range of the EM fields." He glanced at Rodney for confirmation.

"That would be true up to a point."

"The Chosen once lived in all of the Stations," Ushat said. "But it has not been that way since the time of the Great Plague."

Well, that confirmed it. "If we can get people with Shields up in, say, these fifteen Stations—" Sheppard pointed to the marked buildings on the map. "I think we'd have a darned good coverage. It won't be perfect, but given the low-level flight performance of those Darts, once they hit an EM field, they drop out of the sky fast. I don't know that it would take too many crashes before they get the picture and back off entirely."

"I could go to a Station," Lisera offered. "There is one close by and I know the way."

Ford went to object, but Rodney got in first. "The girl's right. Those in the Stations don't have to do anything except keep hold of the Shields and stay put."

"I believe I know where most of the other Genes are hiding," Yann said.

"In those areas where the Wraith Darts crashed?" Ford suggested.

"Not necessarily." The Major shook his head. "Anyone holding an activated Shield is more or less marked for death, right?"

Yann nodded curtly and pointed to the map. "Here, inside the transports around the city, is the only place where the Genes are safe."

Sheppard's lips pursed thoughtfully. "We need eight Chosen—" He cast a quick, apologetic smile at Rodney. "Genes, to man the tallest, outer Stations first. That will cover a good portion of the perimeter."

"The five transports near each of the bridges are somewhat smaller, and open to the market squares," Yann added.

"To facilitate movement of goods coming into the Citadel by foot." Teyla nodded in understanding.

"I believe it is where the other Genes have hidden."

"Okay." John turned to Lisera. "Let's have you man this Station here, and as Yann locates more Genes, they can take the others. Next, and before we man these inner Stations, we need to deploy Genes to the outlying towns and villages, to evacuate everyone—and I do mean everyone—into the Citadel."

"What?" One of the engineer's faces hardened. "We do not have time to concern ourselves with the lives of those outside."

"Particularly barbarians," growled Yann in agreement.

"Well, you better start making time," snapped the Major.

"He's right," added Rodney. "You lose all your farmers and fishermen, what are you going to eat once this is over?"

Sheppard waved his hand dismissively. "That's the least of their problems. It's like Kesun told Ushat. For every person you leave outside the Citadel, that's one more meal for a Wraith. That's why Dalera didn't want anyone farming or settling outside of the protected areas. The people who live in unprotected lands, the ones you call barbarians, endanger everyone, because they become sustenance for the enemy. And it's for that very reason that you can't leave them behind. I'm betting that in the days when warriors lived outside the Citadel, the whole purpose of this—" He gently rapped a knuckle against Ushat's chest armor. "—was designed to prevent a little Wraith snacking on the run. The more people we leave outside for the Wraith to harvest during the night, the more we're potentially aiding the enemy. That could make a difference when the main assault force hits us at dawn.

"Now." Sheppard turned to Yann. "I know Gat set up those food storage areas purely for himself and his cronies, but we can still use them. Depending on how long this siege is likely to last, we'll also need to bring as much fresh food as possible, including livestock, inside the Citadel."

"We will also need water from the village of Nemst." Another engineer type pointed to a village sitting on the river northwest of the Citadel.

"Why?" Rodney demanded. "Unless I'm mistaken, you're surrounded by two perfectly good river channels."

The man's fingers moved across the map to the western mountains. "During the spring melt, which is upon us now, the waters rise, bringing with them a sheen of colored rainbow lights. The fish die in great numbers. We cannot drink from the rivers when the lights appear."

"Rainbow lights?" What the hell was that supposed to indicate?

"It lasts but a short time. The children are fascinated by the colors, but when they look close, they, too, see that the rainbows hide black clouds in the water. Where it rests in the rocks and hollows by the shore, the destitute collect every drop of this blackwater and sell it in the markets. The quality is poor, for the people of Nemst also collect blackwater from the vast pools within Black Hill."

Yann's humorless laugh was laced with scorn. "Nemst thrives not because of its iron, but because Gat led us to believe the Chosen demanded blackwater to keep their lights and ovens burning in winter."

That was the second time someone had mentioned blackwater. Rodney was struck with a flash of comprehension. "Oil!"

"I do not know this word," said the engineer.

"Nor do I," Ushat added.

"A black liquid that floats on water and burns when you light it?"

The Dalerans exchanged looks, the animosity between them apparently forgotten. "It is as you describe," Yann said.

Rodney's mind was racing ten steps ahead of his ability to articulate his ideas. This answered the question of why most of the fountains he'd seen around the city looked well used, but were currently dry. Once again, Ford decided to contribute the obvious. "The high water level during spring floods must wash over an exposed oilfield."

"Another astounding observation by the Lieutenant. Give the man a brownie." Rodney ignored Ford's indignant expression and turned to the engineer. "Where's this Black Hill?"

The man's finger barely moved. "It lies between the Citadel and Nemst."

There was nothing even vaguely like a scale on the map. Impatiently, Rodney snapped, "Yes, of course it lies between them, otherwise Nemst wouldn't have untainted water. But how far away? One mile? Ten? A hundred?"

"What does it matter?" Yann shrugged. "A transport will bring us there within moments."

"So that's your grand plan?" Ford's eyebrows lifted in disbelief. "Pour boiling oil on the Wraith when they storm the battlements?"

"How stunningly medieval of you." Rodney began pacing. Rapid thinking was always easier when he was active. So was scoffing at unhelpful teammates. "They teach you that in field training? Of course we're not going to just pour boiling oil on them. If, on the other hand, we can release enough oil to cover the rive

Suddenly, Sheppard's interest was tweaked. "We can set it on fire."

As soon as the plan was verbalized, a potential roadblock occurred to Rodney. He let out a frustrated bark. "No, no, that's not good. Assuming this 'blackwater' is crude oil, up to half of it would evaporate."

"So?"

"We'd blanket the entire Citadel with a host of volatiles even more toxic than the polyaromatic hydrocarbons and assorted carcinogenic particulates that would erupt even before we set a match to it. And once ignited, the smoke would make the Citadel and probably the surrounding area completely uninhabitable. The ecological consequences would make the *Exxon Valdez* incident look like a bottle of spilled ink. I'd probably suffocate. Then you'd have no one to save your over-coiffed ass."

Sheppard's eyes narrowed at the concept rather than the jibe. "What about just part of the river?"

Running a hand across his jaw, Rodney examined the map. "What direction does the wind normally blow?"

"From the mountains," replied Ushat.

"The west," Rodney affirmed.

"I thought a compass was useless in an EM field?" remarked Ford.

"It's purely a point of geographical reference."

Looking at the engineer, Sheppard asked, "What's the weakest part of the Citadel's walls?"

The Daleran pointed to the wall on the opposite side of the Citadel, the east. "With enough men, if we work through the night, we could strengthen the fortifications."

"No, that's the perfect location," said Sheppard. "The weaker, the better."

Teyla frowned. "I do not understand."

"The Wraith pilot said that the main force was coming at dawn," explained the Major, his gaze focused on a point far distant. "Since it has to be a ground attack — they won't risk Darts after the first few crashes — they'd go for the weakest point, preferably with the sun behind them. That's the eastern side. If we could set fire to just that quadrant of the river, the prevailing westerly winds will drive the smoke directly back over the attacking forces."

The Dalerans' enthusiasm for the idea was obvious, and mutters of approval circulated the room.

"The transport in Nemst is close to Black Hill," said Yann. "For the barrels of blackwater are heavy."

"We're going to need considerably more than a few barrels for a sustained blaze," Rodney warned, trying not to be irritated by the fact that no one seemed to be locking on to the plan. "The entire point of my original question was to establish how long it would take for a large quantity of oil to travel down the length of the channels either side of the Citadel."

A second engineer slapped Rodney's back with enough force

to herniate several discs. "Of course! An ambitious but achievable strategy. From Black Hill, you can see the river's divide. The North Channel travels at a fast walking pace — four hours to reach the far end of the Citadel, and rejoin the South Channel."

Yann scratched a bloody scab on his cheek. "I have seen myself the great pools of blackwater."

"You have?" Rodney's head shot up. "How big are they?"

"It is hard to say, for they are underground, but they are not nearly as large as Quickweed Lake."

"Lake?" Sheppard said. "I didn't see any lake, black or otherwise, when we flew over. Just farms and meadows."

"Quickweed Lake lies close to the northeast face of the Citadel," said Ushat with an understanding nod. "Strange mosses grow across its surface, giving it the appearance of a pasture. When the unwary tread upon its surface, they do not progress far before they begin to sink within a sticky black mud."

"Mud?"

"It is used in our boats and buildings. Many a farmer's animal has been lost to Quickweed Lake, and not a few wayfarers, for the ground appears solid until it is too late."

All but dancing in excitement, Rodney shouted, "Tar pits!" He ignored the Major's raised eyebrows, and demanded, "Where?"

"Here." The warrior pointed to a long, inverted C-shaped patch not far from the northern bridge leading into the Citadel. It extended down past the area that would be blanketed in smoke.

"With the prevailing wind, once the river is burning," Sheppard said, "the Wraith will either fall back the way they came." His finger pointed east. "Or they'll be forced to head north —"

"Directly into Quickweed Lake!" Ushat gave an approving nod to Sheppard and Rodney.

"I can't see them going home hungry," Ford declared.

Rodney nodded. "On that point we agree, Lieutenant."

"Which is why we concentrate our forces right here, in this narrow section between the tip of Quickweed Lake and the North Channel." Sheppard tapped the location on the map.

"You wish us to confront the Wraith outside the Citadel?" Ushat looked at him in horror.

Yann's expression turned sour, and he took a step toward the other Daleran. "We have been forced to confront them in our homes and our villages, while your warriors remained hiding behind these walls—"

"Okay, okay," the Major interrupted. "I thought we'd agreed to get past the finger-pointing stage. This is not going to be an unplanned confrontation. Even better, we'll entice them in that direction by deliberately keeping this side of the Citadel free of the EM fields and leaving the bridge unprotected. They probably won't risk using their Darts this close to the walls, but they'll assume they can use their stun weapons to capture people."

The look in Ushat's eyes did not exactly reflect boundless enthusiasm.

"Listen," Sheppard added, making short, firm gestures for emphasis. "The Wraith have absolutely no intention of killing anyone—at least not at the outset. They're interested only in harvesting live food, preferably in good condition."

"Still, to go unprotected—"

"Not unprotected. This is where we concentrate all the war-riors, and anyone else who can: A, fit into that chest armor; B, wield those nets and bolas your men carry around; and," he added, glancing around at the Dalerans, "C, take orders. The idea is not to engage in hand-to-hand combat, but to set up a trap. The Wraith will see a bunch of people, presumably villag-ers, running around trying to get to the undefended bridge near Quickweed Lake. They'll also see that the EM fields aren't cov-ering much of the wall, especially in the area of North Bridge."

Ford was nodding, warming to the plan. "When the Wraith get close enough, we activate an EM field to disable their stun rifles, and then counterattack with nets, driving them either into the flames or the lake."

"This is a good strategy," Teyla said, placing a gentle hand on Ushat's arm. "I will go with you and stand by your side as we fight the Wraith."

Rodney was watching Ushat's eyes. The engineers were crowding in behind, pointing to the map and suggesting refinements to the plan. They were buying it. He had to admit, it wasn't a bad idea, even if he did so say himself.

"If we have to withdraw, we retreat to this village." Sheppard's fingers moved to a small hamlet about half a mile northwest. "From there we can use a transport to escape back into the Citadel. Then the rest of the North Channel can be set on fire. The winds will still blow most of the smoke away from the Citadel. Again, the Wraith will be unable to see. Hopefully a few more will end up in Quickweed Lake."

"How can one set an entire river ablaze?" Teyla wondered.

"It's been done before—not deliberately, but it happened several times to the Cuyahoga River," Rodney said.

"Then how is it that you intend to contain the blaze to this section, between North Bridge and the eastern end of the Citadel, and not have it spread back up the entire length of North Channel and thence to the river?"

"We can do that with little difficulty," another engineer said, stepping forward. "The stone bridges that span the channels into the Citadel also have weirs. When blackwater flows in the spring melt, we raise the weirs. This allows only clean water to travel down the channels through submerged tunnels, which can be opened or closed at will."

"While the oil pools on the surface behind it. Excellent!" Rodney was a little surprised at the engineering skills demonstrated by such an archaic society. Still, he mused, the principles of weirs and canal locks had been used throughout Europe for hundreds, if not thousands of years.

"The system is not perfect," the engineer continued. "Especially now, at the peak of the spring melt, some blackwater finds its way through. This is why we cut the flow of water to public fountains, and why Nemst must supply us with drinking water at this time of year."

"I believe we can achieve more," another man said. "Past the Citadel, where the North and South Channels rejoin, there is a dam. The southwestern bank of the river is a high cliff at this point, while the northeastern shore is low. We sometimes force the level of the water to greater heights, flooding the eastern fields, in order to grow certain crops. My men can control the flow so that the fields can be flooded with blackwater, while the freshwater is allowed to drain through the pipes beneath the dam."

The Dalerans gripped each other's arms in a fraternal gesture, their murmurs growing stronger and more confident. For the first time, Rodney was certain they'd hit upon a plan that could work. "If the fire jumps upstream, the smoke coming off it will still be driven away from the city."

"Either way," Sheppard reasoned, "the Wraith are going to be stumbling around blind. They'll have to withdraw and regroup in order to attack from another direction, presumably with a number of their comrades doing a good impression of a woolly mammoth."

"I doubt they would reattack, Major," said Teyla. "The Wraith are unaccustomed to defeat. Once they see that they will not have such easy access to the Citadel as they assume, I believe they will withdraw entirely. There are other worlds out there whose inhabitants will be easier to cull."

"If we timed it just right," he replied with a dark grin, "we could wait until they're climbing the walls and toast a few."

Rodney closed his eyes. As if he hadn't already seen enough trauma-inducing things to last a lifetime. "Thank you, Major. I really needed the image of a greenish marshmallow with bad hair forever etched in my mind."

"Once again, it was your idea, Rodney. Even if it doesn't kill them, it's sure gonna make a mess of their attack plan."

"Just one question, sir," Ford began.

"Only one, Lieutenant?"

"How can you be certain you'll be able to release enough oil?"

One of the engineers fielded the query. "The people of Nemst have had long battles to *prevent* the blackwater from flowing into the river. Even what little escapes during the spring melt finds its ways to the hands of those who sell it in the market."

"Which reduces their profit," said another. "Each year the Nemst engineers shore up the cliffs of Black Hill, praying to Dalera that little will escape. And when it does, the Chosen..." He paused and corrected himself. "Gat and the leaders of the Citadel told us that it was the Chosen who demanded that Nemst deliver fresh water to the city, until the blackwater passes. The villagers of Nemst are embittered by this demand. There has been much talk amongst them of releasing the fortifications that hold the blackwater in place."

Rodney exchanged a glance with the Major, who tilted his head fractionally toward him, seemingly asking for one last confirmation. Upon receiving a brief nod, Sheppard crossed his arms. "Okay, folks, I think we have ourselves a plan. Now all we have to do is carry it out." He glanced at his watch. "In a little under ten hours."

CHAPTER THIRTEEN

Their arrival in Nemst was met with panic, which wasn't surprising. Over the past few hours the townspeople had weathered the Wraith ghosts and then the Darts' deadly harvest. The remaining populace was now desperate to be evacuated into the Citadel.

Rodney stepped out of the transport and directly into a throng of people shoving back and forth. *A claustrophobic's nightmare*, he instantly classified the situation. Sheppard, an engineer, and a couple of warriors had accompanied him on this bound-to-be-fun expedition, but already he was losing sight of them in the crowd.

"Save us. We beg of you!"

"Everybody calm down!" the Major shouted, rather ineffectually. A sharp whistle through his fingers produced the desired result. Rodney blinked. If Sheppard could do that, why had he instead fired his weapon when they'd showed up on this damned planet in the first place? God, but he hated questions without answers.

"We can take you to the Citadel, but we need a few of your engineers and blackwater collectors to help us mount a defense against the Wraith."

Voices rose from the crowd. "It is not safe here. We must leave at once."

"If we don't get the blackwater flowing, no one's going to be safe, in the Citadel or anywhere else!" Rodney watched the villagers hesitate. Then one stabbed a finger in the direction of his Shield.

"He is of the Chosen."

"For the forty-eighth and final time, we're not Chosen. We're..." *I don't believe I'm about to say this.* "Genes. We can use the Shields to repel the Wraith attacks, and all I need are a few people to show me the fortifications you've built against the blackwater leak."

After a moment, a man made his way to the front, with three more following him. "We will assist."

"Thank you." Another couple of people trickled out of the crowd and headed in their direction while everyone else began to push toward the transport again.

"Hey! We're going, all right?" Sheppard swore. "Just stop shoving before you trample somebody." His request went unheard as the townspeople piled into the transport. Raising a helpless shrug toward Rodney across the mass of humanity, he called, "See you later." His determined gaze refused to acknowledge the fact that 'later' was an uncertain concept at best.

"Yeah. Later."

The transport and its terrified occupants soon swallowed the Major up. Rodney followed the warriors outside, his ragtag team of eight volunteers hanging back to listen to him explain the plan.

The sounds of Darts screeching toward them punctured the night. Unable to see them, it was by auditory cues that he recognized several peeling away from their pack, presumably trying to avoid the newly established EM field generated by his and Sheppard's Shields. And not entirely successful in the attempt, as two spiraled uncontrollably toward the ground beyond a nearby hill. A few seconds later, a double explosion sounded in the distance. Probably the pilots activating their self-destruct mechanisms. Good. Two fewer life-sucking goons to worry about.

"What news have you?" one of the Nemst workers asked. "Why does the Enclave burn?"

"There's been a coup d'etat inside the Citadel," Rodney replied shortly, without taking his eyes off the worn path under his feet. The fewer times he had to recount this particular tale, the better. "The Chosen—who were not, incidentally, running things as you'd been led to believe—are also dead. That's why we're all fairly dependent on this plan to work. So if you wouldn't mind picking up the pace a little?"

The townspeople obeyed, to his surprise. The dire implications of the Chosen's fall seemed to bolster their resolve. "We will do what we must," another worker said.

The path wasn't long, fortunately. Nemst was actually situated on a plateau at the top of Black Hill. The river off to their left was running at a reasonable speed, having just exited the mountains on its way down toward the Citadel. Even in the dead of night, the twin planets rising from the east, while themselves cast in shadow, offered about the same level of illumination as a full moon on a clear night back on Earth. Helpful, that. This would be dicey enough without the additional risk of working with oil under the light of open flames. Although he'd thought to bring a flashlight, it certainly wouldn't have lasted the night.

One of the engineers pointed toward a large waterwheel. "This drives the bellows for the forge," he explained. "Our foundry makes the finest wrought iron in Dalera. It also drives the pumps to fill the barrels with blackwater and drinking water."

"Be sure to put that in your travel brochures." Rodney was growing increasingly edgy. He looked back over his shoulder and studied the snow-capped mountains, then glanced at the ground. Black Hill appeared to be an upward protrusion of shale, beneath which was a large deposit of oil. Shifting his gaze to examine the geography of the river, he worked through the situation aloud. "So when the water is high, it floods this area and cascades down the cliff to join the main body of the river. Then there's a series of short rapids before it widens and splits into the North and South Channels that surround the Citadel. Right?"

Of course it was right, and the general nodding of the others confirmed it. His primary concern was the amount of oil that would be required to pull this off. And the risk of toxic fumes blowing off unlit crude oil on the South Channel, directly into the Citadel. All right, two primary concerns.

In his borderline manic state, the entire situation was beginning to feel disturbingly Monty Pythonesque. In fact, there were three primary concerns. The wind had to pick up in order for the oil ignited on the North Channel to blow *away* from the Citadel.

When he finished explaining the plan, one of the engineers reassured him. "This time of year, the spring floods create an embankment at the entrance to South Channel, which is always silted and slow flowing. The largest volume of water flows along the North Channel, so most of the blackwater will also flow there."

"All right. That's good. That's a start. Second, we need enough oil — blackwater — to sustain the fire."

"I believe this will be likely." The engineer drew his chapped lips into a thin line. "In ages past, barbarians like Gat who controlled the city dug tunnels deep into the rock to collect blackwater to fuel their forges. The tunnels have caused the cliff to fracture in places. If a crack widens too far, the river is poisoned with the blackwater that spills out. Repairing the leaks has been constant and difficult work for many years. If we were to break through one of the patches, it is likely that a section of the cliff face will collapse."

"And there's a lot of blackwater behind it? And by a lot, I mean — well, a *lot*?" At the engineer's nod, Rodney exhaled. Coming close didn't count with this kind of thing. If they broke into the cliff face, there would be no way to seal it back up again. Still, with the added control provided by the weirs and dam, he'd definitely rather deal with the possibility of too much oil than too little.

"And if the blackwater runs dry as a result?" another man demanded. "We will have no way to support ourselves when all this is over."

A biting remark was on the tip of Rodney's tongue, prompting him to point out that post-attack revenue would be an issue only if they survived the Wraith culling in the first place. In a stroke of diplomacy that felt inherently atypical, he chose another line of thought. "You've got the lake. What's it called? Quickweed? There's little doubt that it's proof of a vast oil field in this area. Trust me, on my world, people would sell their own mothers for that land. After Black Hill is breached and a few years of floods wash the area clean, the Citadel's blackwater problem will probably go away, while you can still go on collecting the stuff via shallow wells and those pumps you're using to supply the city with water."

With every step across Black Hill, his ever-expanding mental checklist of things that could possibly go wrong was, Rodney reasoned, the result of basic paranoia, nothing more. It was a perfectly natural response to impending doom. After the past few months, he was getting accustomed to it. There was no cause for panic here. Really.

God, I hope this works.

The villagers moved with admirable efficiency, hitching a rope to a pulley system anchored at the top of the cliff. While the rest manned the ropes, two engineers rappelled down the escarpment in search of a suitable patch to exploit. Rodney opened his mouth to call out instructions, but quickly realized that there was no need. Their system was low-tech, but they had a solid grasp of the mechanics. It wasn't long before they'd chiseled a number of well-placed holes in the patch, which as far as he could tell had been fashioned from some sort of bitumen, and secured strong ropes to the timber framework that held the patch in place. The pulley took up the slack in the ropes just as the two engineers scrambled back up over the top of the cliff.

A tense silence fell when the ropes grew taut. Then, before his nerves could snap, he heard the telltale crack of the timber and felt a deep rumble underfoot. Rodney's initial rush of elation was swiftly replaced by a sense of dread. This was a serious rumble.

He had a number of utterly justified phobias, but heights wasn't one of them. Moving closer to the cliff's edge, he glanced over. "Oh, *damn*... Get back!" But it was too late. The ground beneath his feet abruptly collapsed, and he fell backward into the darkness.

"Well, we're here now, all right? So if you'd quit griping, we can save —" John was highly tempted to say 'your asses,' but checked his frustration and, offering his most winning smile, finished, "All of you."

"You say that now!" someone screamed. "But my husband is dead because the Chosen did not come."

It was the same story everywhere they'd been. Every village — and there were dozens of them — had suffered from the Darts. When John managed to calm people down enough to tell him exactly when the attacks had taken place, the pattern became chillingly clear. The Wraith had spent the last months testing the Daleran defenses. Sure, some of the Darts had gone down when Kesun transported into a village and an EM field suddenly activated. But John would bet good money that, by now, the Wraith had gotten the timing pretty much figured out. The second an EM field had activated over a village, it meant that Kesun had transported in.

During previous cullings, the Chosen had worked in groups, with at least one remaining behind in each village while the other evacuated everyone to the Citadel. With only Kesun evacuating villages this time around, the Wraith had figured out that they had at least ten, maybe fifteen minutes to cull a village after the first group was evacuated. In turn, Kesun, and now John, had learned that there was no point in going back to a village a second time, because, by then, almost everyone had been taken. And that had, naturally, reinforced the Wraith tactic of waiting until the first group had gone, then descending on the remaining villagers like a pack of sharks.

Worse, in the last few hours, the Wraith had discovered that the Citadel was now serving up a free buffet.

Well, not quite free. More Darts fell out of the sky every time Ford, Ushat, and Yann managed to locate more Genes and get them established with Shields in the Stations. Problem was, John had no idea of the range of each Shield's EM field. And he had a sinking feeling that the Wraith *did* and were finding safe flight corridors between what amounted to unconnected islands of protection.

Kesun's words came back to him in full measure. The burden of responsibility, the burden of choice. Who lived and who died. Maybe it wasn't quite that direct, because one of the great many things John didn't know was which village the Wraith would target next. But in the end, it came down to knowing that anyone he couldn't cram inside one of the transports was just not going to be there when he came back.

The first time, a woman had actually thrown her baby across the heads of the crowds and into the transport, while others thrust their children forward even while he was trying to close the doors. And the longer he delayed, the longer it would take him to get to other villages to save more.

He'd seen the look in that mother's eyes before; too many times, too many places. All he could do was shut off his emotions and save those he could. Someone, at least, had caught the baby. The mother had not been there when he'd come back. It was then that he'd figured out the Wraith's strategy and began formulating a defensive plan.

The first part involved sending Genes in pairs to the villages. Similar to when he and Rodney had transported into Nemst, one Gene stayed in the village to maintain EM coverage, while several return trips were made to the Citadel. They wouldn't have time to wait for stragglers, but instead of evacuating villages at random, he'd begun with those closest to the Citadel. As the night wore on, that would hopefully give more people time to arrive from distant settlements to the outlying transports.

He wondered how Rodney was faring. The plan sounded straightforward enough, but John knew better than most how plans could go south in a hurry.

Someone grasped Rodney's shoulder with dislocating force, and yanked him back onto solid ground—which was a relative term. One step ahead of the shifting earth, he clambered across to the stable part of the hill, the engineers scattered around him.

That had been entirely too close for his liking. He nodded his thanks to the guy who'd saved him, a huge bear of a man who introduced himself as Artos. The others gave a few weak, nervous chuckles.

From their vantage point, Rodney couldn't see the oil cascading into the river, though he could hear a voluminous rush of liquid. What he *could* see was the point at which the river bifurcated into channels. He waited, knowing that it would take several minutes before the oil came into view.

The twin planets rising in the night sky reflected a harsh alien light on the surface of the water. He looked out across the hill and found the northern side of the Citadel cast in the same eerie hue. It was attractive, in an oddly stark way. He'd never been much for subtle shades, in anything.

Rodney's momentary illusion of peace was obliterated when a squadron of Darts silhouetted themselves against the faces of the planets. An instinctive flare of dread dissipated as his fingers brushed the Shield fastened to his belt. He and the engineers were under the EM field—they were safe. The same couldn't be said of the Darts' targets. The menacing craft dived low, a series of beams sweeping across the fields.

Dealing with the Darts was a new experience, it occurred to him. Various Marines had recounted the Wraith attack on the Athosian settlement. Teyla had also described the way the blinding light emanated from the Darts to harvest any human in their path. The details had been noted in Rodney's mind, duly but with unavoidable detachment. Now, as he watched the beams play across the land, the immediacy of it all gripped him with a cold hand. People were being harvested out there, right under his gaze, and the only thing that stood between the rest of the Daleran population and a similar fate was his plan.

A shout of triumph from the engineers tore his focus away. Rodney looked down at the river and noticed that the light reflecting off its surface had changed. The agitated froth that had previously been a constant had vanished beneath the weight of the oil, and the water now reflected a dark rainbow in the night-light. As ordered, there was a gigantic oil slick heading for the Citadel.

There had to be something unhealthy about the euphoria he felt at having caused a colossal oil spill. At least out here he wouldn't have Greenpeace knocking on his door.

The oil flowed quickly down to the point where the river

diverged. The immense shadow cast by the Citadel blocked his view of the South Channel. Fine, but why wasn't he seeing the North Channel darken with oil? There'd been plenty of time for it to flow to that point. "What's going on?" he called toward the engineers. "Where's the blackwater?"

The guy who'd saved him squinted into the distance, and his face slumped in defeat. "Look," he said, pointing to the channel entrance. "The way is blocked."

"No, that can't be. It *can't*!" Rodney peered down at the mouth of North Channel. It was obstructed by debris, which forced most of the water and virtually all of the oil to divert south.

Of course. Because the cosmos so obviously enjoyed taunting him.

Aiden wasn't thrilled with the idea of leaving Lisera alone in one of the old Chosen's homes. Well, okay, it wasn't exactly like she was alone. A couple of warriors and some of the walking wounded who'd been in the mob would be there to look out for her.

The Station, a tall building the size of a medium hotel, had been ransacked during the rioting, but what remained of the interior offered evidence enough of what it must have been like. The burned and shattered vestiges of luxury made him think of the grand staircase of the *Titanic*, once designed to sit far above steerage but now resting at the bottom of the ocean just the same. He could see why the commoners resented the Chosen. They had sure lived well. But then Yann reminded him that the Chosen hadn't actually lived here for several generations. Instead, one of the city's chiefs had taken over. "Supposedly because the Chosen ordered them to do so," Yann growled. "Fools that we all were, we took the barbarians at their word."

"Didn't anyone think to say something to Kesun?"

"Yes. But it is only now that I understand his reply, that we must all return to the ways of Dalera. I thought he was giving his blessing for such actions. In fact, he was stating the only truth that matters."

This Station was becoming a makeshift hospital as well. The lady they'd met in the markets, the one Lisera called an apothecary, had taken refuge there when the warriors kicked everyone out of Sanctuary Hall to make room for incoming evacuees. Aiden had left Lisera with most of the supplies they'd recovered, to help the apothecary treat the injured as best she could. Apparently the local equivalent of doctors were hard to come by, although word had gone out for any healers to make their way there.

"I don't think it was wise to leave Lisera to be cared for only by warriors and merchants," Yann said as they walked. "I should have stayed with her."

Great. Aiden felt so much better. Not that he would have been all that comfortable with Yann staying behind, either. Lousy choices all around. "Yeah, well, we need you to round up the rest of your rebel pals and make sure they're protected."

Yann spun around to face him. "Less than twenty of those that I knew partook of the potion before Balzar's men wrested it from them."

That made Aiden pause. "I thought Ushat took care of Balzar?"

"Ushat and his warriors killed only to defend themselves and the Chosen. Gat and many of the chiefs were killed, but Balzar is a coward. He would have run and hidden in the sewers."

"So the dozen Genes we found hiding inside the transports near the bridges are probably all we're going to find." The men had thrown away their recently acquired Shields, and it had taken some convincing to get eight of them to go with the warriors to the Stations that the Major had identified, and for the others to accept new Shields and help in the evacuation of villages. They'd become a little more cooperative once it was apparent that the panic in the streets was beginning to settle down. Word was spreading that the Atlanteans had a plan that could save everyone. Instead of killing each other, the mobs patrolling the streets began to focus their aggression on making sure that the pilots of downed Darts didn't live long enough to become a problem.

Being with Yann, who carried a Shield, meant that Aiden wasn't getting spooked out by the usual Wraith tactics. Still, while moving around the Citadel between the transports and the Stations, they'd stumbled across several desiccated bodies. Not every Wraith was being dispatched. Just as troubling, not everyone in the Citadel was setting aside their differences. There was a lot of deep-seated animosity in this place, generations' worth of resentment that, having been ignited, weren't about to be extinguished by a common cause. Teyla was right. When people lost everything and everyone they'd ever cared for, long-term planning didn't enter into the picture. For many, the short-term goal wasn't survival but reprisal.

Aiden thought about the de facto government that had developed in this place, and wondered what would replace it if the society survived. Political leadership, in any of its forms, had never really wowed him. He'd found the military's clear and unequivocal chain of command an easier structure to accept. You did as you were told, and you expected those under you to do as you told them. That was the underlying code that made everything work and guaranteed that others would be watching your six just as you watched theirs.

"Look out!" Ushat shouted, knocking Aiden out of the path of an airborne axe flying from the shadows of an alleyway.

The axe's owner was a guy who smelled like the cell that Aiden and Teyla had recently inhabited. Suddenly, he, Yann, Ushat, and the two warriors with them were surrounded by a mob of about fifteen Daleran men. Surrounding *them* was a bunch of women who looked like refugees from the Salem witch trials, egging them on. "Kill the Chosen for failing to protect us! Butcher their warriors. Behead them all!"

Rodney cursed as he slipped over yet one more jagged piece of prehistoric shale. According to Artos or Amos or whatever his name was, a multitude of tiny animals lay trapped within the layers of the ancient marine bed. Fossils. He was talking about fossils to Viking engineers. "You do realize that blackwater — oil — is composed entirely of countless billions of small animals that perished here several million years ago?"

"You mean, even before the time of the Ancestors?"

Before he snapped an 'of course', Rodney realized that it was not inconceivable that the Ancients had actually inhabited the planet for millions of years. He settled on a curt "Probably," and concentrated on finding a path through the rock while trying not to slice his ankles open any more than he already had.

The point where the river divided came into view, and Artos paused. "There."

There indeed. What the man meant to convey with that word, Rodney surmised, was that they were once again screwed.

The wreckage of two Darts, probably the ones they'd heard earlier, had plowed into the cliff overlooking the entrance to the North Channel. The impact and ensuing self-destruct sequence had collapsed most of the cliff face into the waterway. And wasn't that just one more reason to hate those soulless creatures with the heat of a supernova?

Artos's gaze flitted back and forth between Rodney and the North Channel. "It is not completely impassable," he said, hesitant. "Perhaps the blackwater will still light."

"Now is a singularly bad time to try relying on optimism." There was some water getting past, true, but it was mostly at depth. Only a thin layer of oil trickled over the top. "The blackwater layer needs to be several millimeters thick to even ignite, let alone give us the sustained burn that we'll need." Recognizing belatedly that a millimeter was a foreign concept to these people, Rodney held up his thumb and forefinger at an approximate distance to explain.

The group of engineers traded despondent glances. It was evident to all that they couldn't possibly clear enough of the wreckage from the channel in time to do any good. Even if they could, the momentum of the river was firmly on the southern side now, and it wouldn't be easily or rapidly diverted. Time to shift gears once again. Trouble was, Rodney was running out of gears.

"This is getting a little old," Aiden muttered. The first few times they'd been confronted by mobs, he'd managed to scatter them by taking a page from the Major's book and firing a short round from his P-90 into the ground or over their heads. But this gang wasn't backing down.

Behind him, Ushat blew a couple of short notes on his horn. While Aiden would have given a lot for a working radio, the horns had proved to be surprisingly efficient, using a set of calls that the Major had described as a simplified Morse Code.

The present signal was one Aiden now recognized as 'under attack'. The response was immediate. They were only half a block from what had become their adopted Command Center, the City Hall-type place with all the maps. About twenty warriors appeared at one end of the alley. A batch of Teyla's new 'recruits', mostly fishermen, builders and blacksmiths whom she was helping prepare for the ambush, appeared from the other end. Before the attackers had a chance to vanish back into the sewers, Teyla signaled the rookies to pounce on them with well-placed nets. Two who tried to escape down a narrow alley were brought down by bolas.

"Wow." Aiden grinned, lowered his weapon and smiled approvingly at Teyla and the recruits. "Nice work."

"They have learned to wait until given the order to strike." Ushat looked impressed as well. "That is strong work for untrained warriors."

Yann leveled a hard stare on him. "Unlike the 'trained' warriors, those of us who live outside the Citadel have been fighting the Wraith for weeks now."

Well, there went that team-spirit moment. Aiden opened his mouth to head off the coming argument, but was interrupted by another warning call from the nearby Station. The sound abruptly halted.

Yann's expression darkened. "Lisera!"

Wordlessly, they charged toward the building.

Arriving only minutes after the aborted signal, they found the place had been plunged even deeper into chaos than before. The bodies of the apothecary and the three warriors were strewn across the floor, hacked into pieces. Lisera's terrified screams sounded from above, and Aiden felt a momentary surge of relief. The screams told him that she was still alive.

With surprising agility given the amount of armor he'd taken to wearing, Yann bounded up the stairs. Teyla was right on his heels. Ushat turned to his men with a grim command. "Search the building for those who have done this." Receiving a chest-thumping salute in acknowledgement, he followed Aiden up the steps.

When they neared the top, Yann showed no sign of slowing down. "Hold it!" Aiden hissed. The merchant's eyes dropped to Aiden's weapon, which he'd already brought to bear. For once, Yann actually listened and came to a halt, his features conflicted as Lisera's hysterical screams continued. Those weren't screams of pain, though, but rather —

Teyla must have recognized it at the same moment, because she ran ahead of Aiden. Rounding the corner into the apartment, he saw Balzar and a trio of seriously ugly brutes. They'd pinned Lisera to the bed, leaving no question as to their intent.

Before Aiden could stop him, Yann went for Balzar at full speed and laid him out with an NFL-caliber tackle. The other three dropped Lisera and spun toward their new adversaries. "Stop!" Aiden yelled, not surprised when they ignored him and picked up their axes. A warning round from his P-90 went into the ceiling, but that only served to incite them further. The Marine didn't hesitate before putting two bullets in each man's chest, felling them almost like dominoes.

He hated having to do that, but there wasn't time to reflect on how bad the situation was, because Balzar was clearly getting the better of Yann. Ushat took care of it with the blunt end of his halberd, stepping into the motion with enough force to cripple the chief. Literally. Aiden knew the sound of breaking bones.

Scrambling to cover herself, Lisera's breaths were coming in short, frantic gasps. Teyla gathered the tattered clothes and knelt beside the distraught girl, handing over her own jacket as well.

From the floor, Balzar jabbed a meaty finger at Yann's Shield and spewed a string of words at him that could only have been curses. Yann glanced at Lisera to confirm that she was all right, then kicked at Balzar's ribs, eliciting a howl.

"What have you done with the rest of the Gene potion?" demanded the merchant.

"You lied!" Balzar roared, spitting blood. "The potion does not work. I threw it to the rats."

The loss hit Aiden with a gut-wrenching sense of despair. As he watched Lisera tremble in Teyla's soothing embrace, he had to clamp down hard on the temptation to put a bullet in Balzar's head. Twelve Genes. That was all he and Yann had been able to find. The Major had talked a good story in front of the engineers, but Aiden had seen the look in his eyes. They'd barely have enough Genes to protect the Citadel. And unless McKay's half-assed plan worked, the Wraith would be climbing over the eastern wall in a matter of hours.

CHAPTER FOURTEEN

"There's got to be a way to divert it." Rodney stood with his hands on his hips, watching the oil slurp uselessly at the protrusions of rock and bits of Wraith Dart, before it veered off down the South Channel. "We don't need to force the entire volume of water north, just the oil on the surface."

The engineers nodded agreeably, which, while a pleasant change to some of his fellow scientists on Atlantis, wasn't exactly contributing to a solution. He racked his brain. What they needed was a boom, some kind of floating barrier. More than one, preferably. If they could haul something like that across the entrance to the South Channel, it would force the oil to flow north while allowing the majority of the water to continue south.

This was an industrial town. There had to be something lying around that they could co-opt. A series of boats or barges would be ideal, but he'd be willing to settle for anything that floated while staying partially submerged, was rigid but flexible, and could extend across the width of the channel. Oh, and something that was at least as thick as, say, his thigh.

How could that possibly be too much to ask?

He started scanning the area for a suitable item. Artos frowned. "What do you seek?"

Good question. Vindication? Some kind of payment on his karmic debt? Not that he believed in that sort of thing. "We need to stretch something across the river that'll divert the blackwater. Are there barges on the river anywhere?"

Comprehension was swift, but the engineer's shoulders slumped. "There were once wooden rafts used in cleaning the bridges and weirs of blackwater, but they have fallen into disrepair."

Another sign of the times. Still, it gave Rodney an idea. "What about wooden poles?" He drummed his fingers against one of the nearby pine-looking trees. "Didn't I see a stack of these near the foundry? All we have to do is fasten them together end to end. Short metal hooks and eyes would do. The current will force the whole structure to curve, which will close up the gaps between the logs."

"There are logs here." One of the Nemst engineers pointed to what looked like a long, open work shed. "Cut and being readied for the building of houses."

A warrior growled in contempt. "You people of Nemst. You know it violates Dalera's laws to cut trees from this place."

"And is it not also Dalera's law that the warriors are to patrol outside the Citadel?"

"Whoa, whoa!" Mediator was one of the few roles in which Rodney did not excel. "You want to stand here and argue or help me save your enchanting little civilization? Generations of your kind haven't been terribly successful in resolving that dispute, but if you think you can pull it off in a couple of hours, then by all means, go for it."

The practical-minded engineer broke the tension. "We will need to take one end of such a contraption to the far side of the South Channel, to the shores of the Citadel. How can this be done?"

No boats, apparently. Directing a tight but tolerant smile at the belligerent warrior, Rodney replied. "Someone will have to swim it across."

"Who among you can swim?" demanded the warrior.

Every man there shook his head. *Oh, crap.* Rodney's smile faltered, and he stared across the oil-covered waterway. Didn't that just figure. Swallowing back a new rush of apprehension, he reluctantly raised his hand.

"I swear on Dalera's name that I had no knowledge of this." Ushat stood stoically at attention before John.

"You mean you were close to Kesun all these years and you never once touched his Shield?" There was something a little weird about the way he'd worded that. Maybe that was why the warrior frowned in confusion. "Not even tempted? Y'know, just a little tap, just to see?"

Ushat responded with a look that plainly questioned John's sanity. "It is against our laws."

"The Shields were sacred, Major," Teyla explained. At least he supposed Teyla thought she was explaining, but it seemed kind of hard to believe. Still, at this point none of them needed to be reminded of the power of faith.

"The only reason he caught it, sir," Ford added, "was because Balzar was going psycho, shouting and screaming at Yann that we were all dead anyway, so why not have a little…" The Lieutenant's voice trailed off.

John got the picture. He was just relieved to know that Lisera was okay. Positioning her in the Station had seemed like a good idea, and it still was, but maybe it was time they moved their entire Command Center into the same building. Protected from the Darts, it would offer them their best vantage point during the coming assault, and it could, with well-placed warriors, be readily defended from roaming mobs.

"Balzar withdrew the inactive Shield from his pocket," Teyla continued, "and threw it at Yann."

"Who ducked," Ford finished with a broad grin. "It was just a natural reflex that Ushat caught it. And that's when it started glowing."

Looking at the warrior, John could sympathize. He remembered exactly how he'd felt when he'd sat in that screwball chair in Antarctica. Except he'd understood that it was a random gene. Ushat's entire belief structure had already undergone a severe pounding in the last few days, but this latest incident took a left turn into the bizarre.

For once, the bizarre was a good thing. Every minute John spent playing General was another minute that he couldn't be operating the transport. Currently they had only six people, himself included, to help evacuate villages. It was also fast becoming obvious that they needed a lot more than eight Genes in the Stations to deter the Darts from all sections of the Citadel. The damned Wraith seemed to almost enjoy playing aerial dodgem in order to make their culling runs across the city. Come morning, or when the Wraith attacks took a sharp upturn, presumably signaling the arrival of the hive ship, he'd have to order the villages abandoned and all Genes to man the Stations and perimeter of the Citadel. That would force the Wraith to cull only the outlying villages, or to attack the fortified walls on foot. Or both. Either way, an awful lot of people were going to die.

"This could explain why some Darts were crashing in the Citadel even after Yann's rebel Genes ditched their Shields," ventured Ford.

"People were ransacking the supplies of Shields when the Enclave was destroyed," Teyla added. "Then many people do indeed possess the gene."

That was when the penny dropped. John took a good look at Ushat. He could have been Lisera's big brother. The familial connection to Kesun, who probably had been in his fifties, was now obvious. It seemed Kesun had been doing a little gene therapy of his own. He must have realized years earlier that the Chosen were a dying breed. Caught between an entrenched set of religious laws and a genuine desire to help his people, Kesun had depended on his absolute faith in Dalera, and taken the same path that the Ancient had forged ten thousand years earlier. He'd no doubt been waiting for the elderly Chosen to die off before reintroducing the ritual of touching the Shields. Then Ushat, Lisera, and who knew how many others could be revealed as long-lost descendants. It must have sorely tested Kesun's faith when the Wraith turned up fifty years ahead of schedule.

In a perverse way, the team's arrival from Atlantis really had been the answer to Kesun's prayers, because their mere existence had substantiated the man's belief in what he'd done. Unfortunately, it had also triggered a revolution. Faith in divine guidance versus free will. John wondered how many times Kesun had flipped the proverbial coin before deciding to take control of his people's fate, relying on faith as his guide.

John caught Teyla's eye. He wasn't entirely certain what was going through her mind, but he suspected that her thoughts and his were running along the same lines. "You know," he said to

Ushat. "This confirms that Kesun was right. Everyone, beginning with the warriors and their family members, needs to touch
the Shields to find out if they have the gene."

"Why begin with the warriors?" Yann's face took on a dubi-
ous look. He was obviously worried that a new form of impe-
rialism could grow in place of the old regime. Tough to blame
him.

Not about to explain that Kesun had doubtless been smart
enough to sow his wild oats close to home, John replied,
"Because they'll take orders, which saves you and Lieutenant
Ford from having to persuade Genes to run evacuation missions
to the villages."

"Do not feel the need to be circumspect on my account, Major,"
Ushat said with a sad smile. "The mirror tells me much."

That acknowledgment surprised John. But then, Ushat was
no fool. Having seen Kesun's likeness in himself, he'd clearly
figured out where the additional Genes had come from. Now he
was doing his best to assimilate that knowledge into his long-
held beliefs.

Before Yann could come up with another objection, John
pointed to the map and added, "Ford, Teyla, get the word out
that every man, woman and child in the Citadel needs to be
tested. Anyone with the active gene should transport here so
that we can slot them into the grid, and maximize the distribution of the EM fields. Lieutenant Ford will be in charge of des-
ignating who goes where." He picked up his P-90 and headed
for the transport, glancing over his shoulder at Yann and Ushat.
"Meanwhile, you two pair up and assist with evacuating villages."

His own faith, such as it was, still lay in Rodney's plan,
because even if Kesun really had salted away a few Gene offspring, by morning the Wraith would be grounded, and pounding their frustrated claws at the gates. Without the oil fire, given
what the engineers had said about the state of the eastern wall,
it wouldn't take long for everything to hit the fan.

At least this time he was up to his eyeballs in something other than human effluent. Instead of methane and other less than pleasant organic waste molecules, Rodney was instead breathing in doubtless lethal quantities of considerably more volatile organic compounds, like benzene — a known human carcinogen — toluene, xylene, hexane, and...and...hell, he couldn't remember the entire list, which meant his faculties were already being affected. That he was pushing the tree stump ahead of him with splinter-coated fingers, staying upwind of the worst of the oil, was beside the point. The chances of finding a decent oil-stripping detergent in this hellhole that didn't scour off most of his skin with caustic compounds were remote to nonexistent. How any rational person could classify crude oil as 'sweet' or 'light' like some vintage wine was beyond him.

In formulating this aspect of the plan, Rodney had assumed that the prevailing wind would help push him across the channel. However, he hadn't banked on how effective the boom would be. The current, fed by the force of the oil, was instead pushing the entire kit and caboodle downstream until it was now almost parallel to the shore that he'd stepped from. There was absolutely no way he would be able to swim the end of the boom across the channel.

Rodney glanced back at the shore. The men were chopping down more trees — breaking more of Dalera's damned laws — in order to extend the boom. The very fact that he could see them working meant the shadow cast by the Citadel was retreating. The twin planets were almost directly overhead, from which he concluded that they had perhaps six hours until dawn.

The crunch of gravel underfoot amplified Rodney's complete and utter failure. He staggered up the beach, dropping the end of the boom in the thick black goo that covered absolutely everything. While he'd made more than his fair share of errors when it came to dealing with people, he'd never failed at actually *doing* anything in his life. This was a maddeningly inopportune moment for a first time.

Teyla's words to Lisera, that releasing her and Lieutenant Ford had been the only way to save the Dalerans, had not been entirely true. And the hollowness of that assurance had greatly disturbed Teyla. Yet as she had stood atop the wreckage of the Dart and called the mob to set aside their arguments and work together, her appeal had not been directed exclusively at the crowd. She wondered if her team had realized this. They *were* her team, above all else. Despite their differences, they shared a common goal, and their foundation of common experiences grew with each day that dawned.

Her emergence as a leader of those Dalerans who would fight the Wraith face to face had first been met with uncertainty. She was not their blessed goddess, Dalera, and she was neither of the Chosen nor one of Dalera's warriors. Acceptance had come quickly, though, for the two warriors whom she had disarmed in the Sanctuary Hall had requested to be assigned to her and given her the title of Atlantean warrior.

With these men's assistance, Teyla had quickly discovered that the Dalerans' skills with nets and bolas were not limited to warriors and hunters. One-on-one, few could match the fighting skills of a Wraith. But the nets were an effective way to disable the Wraith long enough to kill the creatures with axes.

As the night wore on and their ranks had been swelled by more and more arrivals, the large square at the base of Lisera's Station, which had become their new Command Center, filled with the sounds of clanking steel. In their shops, blacksmiths were working overtime to fashion or adjust chest armor, while their apprentices sat without rest at grinding wheels, sharpening axes and other blades. Women brought pots of soup and jugs of weak ale to everyone, or sat around fires braiding nets and fashioning bolas. Every so often, someone would break into song: haunting melodies and sad love songs, including ballads that tolf of Dalera, who had been cast aside by the Ancestors for loving a man.

Amid all of it, there was a sense of renewed hope, for the Shields had been passed around and word was spreading fast. More and more Genes were being discovered each hour. Perhaps they would be enough.

Before long, though, the mood began to shift. In a gathering of this type, any information, good or bad, diffused quickly. Teyla could sense the tone of this news before it reached her. "What is it?" she asked one of the two warriors who now stayed faithfully by her side.

"Reports from the northwest wall," the young man replied. "The lookouts there have seen the blackwater flowing downstream in unimaginable amounts."

"That is what we wished to happen." She was already anticipating the fall of the 'other shoe,' as the Major might have said.

The warrior bowed his head. "The blackwater flows down the wrong channel."

Really, there was no excuse for not having seen the solution sooner. It had to have been all the xylene fumes. Or maybe the toluene.

"Almost there," came the reassuring voice of the warrior.

"We had better damn well be," Rodney growled. They'd half-dragged and half-floated the entire boom contraption upstream past the truly obnoxious cascade of oil, which fortunately had the grace to spurt out far enough for them to walk between it and the base of the cliff. Supposedly the water across the shallowest part of the river, a short rapid, had only been waist deep. Because of the spring melt, it had turned out to be chest deep but between them, they'd managed to get the boom across the river, then down the northern bank to where the channels divided.

Rodney released his end of the oil-slicked timber pole, flexed his aching shoulders, and looked out. The men began walking the other end of the boom across the now shallow neck of the North Channel to the beach on the outside of the Citadel's walls. Then they carried it a few meters south along the embankment to the point that Rodney had been trying to reach an hour earlier. Once the men had tied off their end, the current should grab the end that Rodney held, and push it at an angle across the entrance to the other side of the South Channel, just like shutting a gate. Unless his luck changed drastically, though, there was a chance that the chain of logs was too flexible and would need help. The men waiting on the southern shore couldn't swim out to retrieve his end if it didn't quite reach. Rodney glanced up at the planets. They had maybe five hours until dawn.

He had to do this. It wasn't about self-absolution or self-survival. Well, okay, maybe that was a part of it, because if this failed the chances of him—any of them—surviving... On second thought, what good would come from knowing the odds? Forget it. This was about the fact that the arrogance he'd carried around with him most of his life really wasn't based on some deep-seated insecurity. He was *right*, dammit! And the sheer frustration that resulted from people's inability to see that he *was* right tended to aggravate the small but persistent kernel of doubt that had dogged him ever since his father had made very certain he understood the depths of his worthlessness.

"If he'd just told me that he'd never wanted me to have a dog in the first place—"

"What?"

"Cats are better, anyway. Here, take this." Rodney handed the engineer—Artos? Amos? Whatever—his backpack, which was somehow still marginally free of oil. "Meet me on the other side."

However unwittingly, he'd made some sort of emotional investment in these people, and he'd be damned if he was going to write them off just because the odds against them were so low that they no longer factored into the equation. That had never stopped Sam Carter. "If you could see me now, Colonel," he muttered, and with a grim smile, grabbed his end of the boom and stepped out with into the river of oil.

CHAPTER FIFTEEN

"So far," Ford reported to John, "more than a hundred Genes, including a lot of women and children, have turned up at the Command Center."

Over a hundred, huh? Either Kesun had been a busy guy, or alternatively—and given the ages of some of those testing positive, this seemed more likely—some of the other Chosen had also been busy over the generations. Regardless, the gene was considerably more common here than on Earth. "That's... great," John replied distractedly, staring at the hive of activity along the eastern wall. Or, rather, where the wall used to be.

"I've been implementing the plan," Ford added. "We've been sending pairs of Genes into villages. When one of them returns with the first transport full of evacuees, the second Gene hands his Shield to a warrior for a couple of seconds to blink it on and off. In the first two villages, the Darts started thinking they had the run of the place, and we took down a bunch of them. The Wraith can't tell when or where the fields are going to activate, or for how long, and it's confusing the hell out of them. For the moment, at least, they've backed off entirely." Grinning with obvious enthusiasm, he added, "That means they have to assault the Citadel on foot."

"Yeah, we got 'em exactly where we want them."

The tone of his voice must have alerted Ford, whose smile faded. "Sir? You don't think they'll strike the eastern wall?"

"Oh, that's exactly where they'll attack. Take a look down there."

Peering through the smoky haze from hundreds of workmen's torches, Ford said, "I can't..." His voice trailed off, and he sucked his breath in. "I can see the channel!"

"Yep. What we have, Lieutenant, is a mile long wide open access to the Citadel. And there are two more sections of the wall at least as bad as this."

Ford's eyes widened in alarm. "What happened?"

"Another classic case of Murphy's Law." John kicked at a loose stone, irritated with himself for not having checked the wall earlier. He could not recall seeing any major breaches when he'd flown over the Citadel, but then it had been difficult to distinguish between the jumbled black rock of the buildings and the surrounding fortifications. Although he had anticipated some damage, it was not until seeing it from ground level that he had understood the extent.

The Lieutenant offered a weak facsimile of his previous grin. "Guess it's not just the Marines they warn about that law, huh, sir?"

"Murphy was an Air Force captain."

"Really?"

"I kid you not." John gestured toward the scene below. "In terms of the Citadel, this is kind of the wrong side of the tracks. The area's been neglected for years, probably centuries. The Dalerans have been looting the fortifications for building materials. That's why Kesun gave an order for the engineers and warriors to rebuild this wall, which isn't something we can finish in the—" He glanced at his watch to check the countdown. "Two hours we have left until dawn. So unless our resident genius pulls off a minor miracle, we're in trouble."

The stuff was surprisingly good. It even had a slight... Oh, fantastic. Of course. It would have to be lemon essence. Rodney glared at the clay jar of shampoo. Maybe his allergies to citrus fruits didn't extent to alien citrus. Lemongrass, perhaps?

"Those who collected the blackwater and pitch developed the soapwater generations ago," Artos explained. Rodney was almost sure his name was Artos. "Some say that it is Wraith-craft." Even in the darkness Rodney caught his cautious look.

"I can't imagine that there's anything too complex or forbidden about producing a decent quality shampoo. There are only a few basic ingredients required—" He could have elaborated further, but decided that rinsing his hair for the third time would be more productive.

The river at Nemst could not, by even the most charitable description, be called warm. In fact it was turning him into a soprano, but he'd suffer through it in order to be oil-free. In a few hours he'd be standing very close to a rather large fire, and being covered in oil at that point would not be advisable. The boom contraption had of course worked brilliantly. By now, the team they'd left on the Citadel side of the river should have gotten word to the rest of the city's engineers. They still had to deal with the oil that had been misdirected down the South Channel, but he'd already sent word for the East Bridge weir to be raised, allowing water to flow through the submerged tunnels while retaining the oil. The cold westerly winds would blow the fumes around the southeastern end of the Citadel, not across it.

He'd considered allowing the oil in the South Channel to flow down to the point where the two waterways rejoined, to build up against the dam with the oil that was now pouring down the North Channel. However, in an oddly strategic line of thought that betrayed Sheppard's growing influence on him, he recalled a previously mentioned theory about the Wraith regrouping and attacking from a different direction. Keeping some oil in reserve in the South Channel wouldn't hurt for the moment.

As he climbed out of the river, he felt something slip against his chilled skin. The Shield! The cord had come loose. Spurred by a sense of dread, he lunged after it, chattering, "Please, please, please…"

Too late. The Shield had vanished in an instant, sliding under the dark surface. He splashed around for a few seconds, trying vainly to propel it back into view, but the visibility and the current made such an effort hopeless.

This was beyond bad. This was going to throw a king-sized wrench into the proceedings. Without a protective EM field, they were Dart fodder.

He scrambled back onto the shore and grabbed the clothes that Artos had procured for him. "We need to get back to the transport *now*," he said curtly, struggling into a pair of pants that was three sizes too big while attempting to shuffle in the right direction.

The engineer looked puzzled until his gaze fell upon the broken cord that hung limply around Rodney's neck. He paled and called to the others to follow.

Dressing while walking at a rapid clip was not a skill Rodney had ever had an opportunity to perfect, but he was faring better than he would have expected. As they hurried into the town square, heading for the transport, something flitted through his peripheral vision. One of the men behind them screamed, prompting him to whirl around.

Despite the fact that he couldn't see them, he was immediately certain that there was a Wraith nearby. Maybe he couldn't sense them the way Teyla could, but the damned things were distinctly unsettling even when not visible.

Something swooped over their heads, and somewhere behind them a second cry pierced the air, then was abruptly cut off. Rodney turned back to look. The last thing he saw before being jerked off his feet was a shimmering beam, like liquid plastic bathed in a weird, blue light, racing toward him.

John was helping Ford maneuver another block onto a shorter section of the wall when a series of notes blew from a distant horn. The notes were repeated as the message was passed down the line. Spontaneous cheers erupted from the workmen below. One of the engineers ran up to John and, grinning through a now filthy face, slapped his shoulder. "North Bridge reports a great wave of blackwater flowing swiftly down North Channel!"

Why the Wraith were even planning a ground assault if they knew that their weapons were useless had been just one more unknown to add to the ever-growing list of things that had bugged John — until he'd seen the condition of the eastern wall. Scrubbing a trickle of sweat from his eyes, he nodded. For the first time that night, he believed that they might really have a crack at making this work. "Tell your men to keep rebuilding the wall, and make sure they blanket the entire slope with sand, stones, anything that will retard the fire. And keep evacuating this part of the Citadel." Most of the flames and smoke would blow east, but the shape of the Citadel's structures would create pockets of still air. While there was little in the way of flammables to carry the fire into the city, he didn't want to take any chances.

"Why keep repairing the wall now that we know the oil's coming?" asked Ford.

"Given the fact that they've had weeks to check the place out, the Wraith must have known that they could just walk into the Citadel once they crossed the Channel." He pulled his jacket back on. Even away from the wind, the night air was cold.

Nodding, Ford said, "I got it. You want the Wraith to think the Dalerans are trying to rebuild the wall before they hit." His grin turned into a grimace. "McKay'll hold this over our heads for weeks. We'll never hear the end of it."

That triggered a query in John's mind, and he scanned the area. "Yeah, where is Rodney? If the oil has reached North Bridge, he should have been back from Nemst by now."

"Maybe he's at the Command Center." Ford also pulled on his jacket and cap.

This whole situation contained far too many 'maybes' for John's taste. He snatched up his P-90. "C'mon. McKay wouldn't have wasted any time treating us to a full color commentary."

They jogged along the alleys and into the now-deserted Sanctuary Hall that serviced this side of the city. Instead of the usual clutter, a wide path stretched from the transport to the entrance in order to facilitate the ongoing evacuations from outlying villages. John had ordered any incoming evacuees to move into safer sections of the city. If the Wraith breached the eastern wall, he didn't want them supplied with a marketplace full of defenseless MREs.

Using the lights on their P-90s to show the way, they failed to notice a bunch of goons lurking in the shadows until it was too late.

"Wraithcraft!" cried half a dozen voices. "Kill them. Their evil lamps will surely bring the Wraith upon us!"

John could see Ford roll his eyes through the dim light. In a truly bizarre way, this situation was starting to feel almost routine. Unfortunately, that didn't make it any less deadly.

Instead of his P-90, it was the transport doors opening that managed to scatter their attackers. Yann and Ushat stepped out ahead of a bunch of refugees. "What's it like out there?" John said, taking the two men aside.

"While there is much desperation, there is also much hope," replied the warrior. "With each new group we pass around several of the Shields. Always, there is at least one among them who is a Gene." He looked past John's shoulder to a teenage kid who was lingering near the entrance of the transport and gestured for the boy to join them. "This is Peryn. He comes from a village near Quickweed Lake. He will go with Yann to help transport the others from nearby villages, while I —"

"Will come with Ford and me to find McKay." John nodded for Yann to leave with the boy.

Ushat's eyes narrowed. "He has not yet returned from Nemst?"

Behind the warrior, the transport doors closed. "No."

"You have not heard from the bugler who was —?"

Ushat was interrupted by an arriving warrior. "Word from Nemst. The Gene who was with them, the one called McKay." He glanced at John, who was already feeling the clench in his gut. "His Shield was lost in the river. Wraithlight came and took all as they ran for the transport."

The clench locked tight and twisted mercilessly.

"The bugler survived," Ford blurted. "Maybe McKay —"

"The bugler's signal cut off mid-tone." Ushat turned to the warrior. "Call North Bridge and ask what they have seen of Black Hill."

John went to follow them outside when the transport lights came on again. The doors folded back and Teyla stepped out. "The first platoons of warriors and recruit fighters are ready to take their place at the eastern wall," she reported. Even in the darkness of the Hall, she must have sensed the tension, because she added, "What is it?"

"McKay's missing," he said shortly, heading outside to the sounds of the distant horn. He might not have understood the notes, but to his ears, they sounded bad.

Ushat turned to him and grasped his arm. "I am sorry for your loss, my friend. Wraithlight crosses Nemst and Black Hill unchecked."

Everything inside of John demanded that he go back to Nemst and check for himself, but if the Wraith had taken Rodney, going anywhere wasn't going to achieve a damned thing. He looked up at the stars, but they offered no insight, no visual cues to the undoubted presence of the hive ships. *Damn you, McKay, for getting yourself taken.* The stars began to wink out in that last darkness before the dawn.

"Major, it is time for us to leave."

John heard the sadness in Teyla's voice, as subtle as the gentle grasp of her fingers on his arm. He couldn't see her eyes, and there didn't seem to be a hell of a lot he could say, so he opted for reaffirming the next phase of the plan. "Yann and I will transport to the village near Quickweed Lake the moment we set fire to the river. There's enough oil here to keep the flames going for hours." He turned to head back down to the wall. "McKay did a good job."

Teyla's words followed him. "He did indeed, Major Sheppard."

Early morning mist blanketed the landscape. In the distance, Aiden could see the mountain peaks, lit by the sun still beyond his view, periodically appearing and disappearing behind fast-moving clouds. Although the air on the ground was still, the upper winds were blowing directly from the mountains.

Aiden wished the sun would slow down. The oil had reached the dam at the far end of the Citadel, which meant the entire South Channel was now flooded with the stuff. But it wasn't thick enough yet to overflow the eastern bank. Still, the low mist had some definite visibility benefits. No one could see the water until practically on top of it. That meant that the attacking Wraith wouldn't be able to spot the oil until it was too late.

Movement caught his attention from the treeline, a few miles out. It looked like the entire forest was in motion. A gust of wind blew the distant mist aside, and gasps of horror erupted all around him.

Too well trained to succumb to unwanted emotions, like dread, Aiden nevertheless silently agreed with the reaction. He gripped his weapon, knowing it would be next to useless. At best, he could maybe slow down a few of the enemy before the nets were employed. And the Wraith lined up in the distance didn't look like they would be slowed down by much.

Sheppard appeared beside him, scanning the field with a practiced gaze. "Lieutenant." His voice was cool, professional.

At the start of the Atlantis expedition, Aiden had mostly seen the laid-back side of the Major, which had borne out Colonel Sumner's initial impressions of the man. It hadn't taken long for the combat-veteran side to make itself known, from that first rescue mission to the Wraith world up through the recent Genii assault. It was that side that Aiden found himself addressing now. "There's got to be a couple of thousand of them out there, sir."

"I guess we're going to have ourselves a bigger barbeque than I expected."

The distant mist cleared again, and this time, it stayed clear. Aiden offered a feeble grin. "This is about the point when I start hoping for the wizard guy, Gandalf, to show up. Preferably with an artillery unit in tow."

"I'd go with you on the artillery, but given a choice, I'd rather have McKay be the one riding in on a white horse."

"I wouldn't put it past him, sir. You know what they say about pennies."

"Or Loonies." The bleak smile that crossed the Major's face was one Aiden had seen before. Almost without exception, officers who'd lost people under their command acted as though they'd lost a piece of themselves.

Maybe he hadn't always seen eye to eye with the scientist, but McKay had been part of Aiden's team. To a Marine, that meant more than anything. But there wasn't time to dwell on loss. They all had to focus on the battle to come.

Down on the wall, one of the engineers was motioning frantically. If he was aiming to convince the Wraith that they were desperate, it was overkill. Men and women, even kids, had spent the night building piles of black rocks against one another, but they'd hardly raised the structure above chest level.

Using his binoculars to check out what the engineer was signaling, Aiden scanned the forest. The nightmare army had begun to advance. Behind the first ranks, more Wraith appeared carrying what looked like—

"Fording bridges," muttered the Major. "I was hoping they'd use logs. Assuming those aren't made of flammable material, we'll have to ignite the oil before they breach the channel."

A series of notes from a horn, this time from the east, sounded. "The signal comes from the dam," explained the warrior with them. "They shut the sluice gates, forcing the water level in the channel to rise. Blackwater has begun to flow into the eastern fields."

"How long before it spreads?" Aiden asked him.

One of the nearby men replied, "The fields have been sown with a grain that grows in water from the spring floods. Depending on the speed of the flow, the oil should cover the fields in perhaps two to three hours."

The Major lifted his binoculars. Aiden had already noted that the attacking force had split into three broad columns. Planning their assault on multiple fronts was undoubtedly the time-tested method of triggering panic amongst the population of the Citadel. "At the rate the Wraith are moving, it'll take them at least an hour to get here."

As predicted, it took just over an hour for the first of the attacking force to arrive. The mist hadn't quite burned off the low-lying eastern fields, possibly because some of them were still partially flooded with water. Rice paddies, by the look of them. From what John could tell, no Wraith remained in the forest beyond.

"Give the order," he told the warrior with the horn. "Get everyone who doesn't have chest armor to fall back behind the first group with nets." It was a simple enough strategy, and one John had reminded them all, whether they needed to hear it or not. The Wraith weren't out to kill or injure them. They wanted their food alive and healthy. That probably wouldn't prevent them from feeding on the run — unless they were obliged to stop and figure out how to peel off the body armor.

On that score, he'd reluctantly agreed to allow a couple of Wraith bridges to ford the channel before setting the oil alight. If the enemy had been human, John would have never succumbed to the demands for revenge, but the Dalerans would not take no for an answer. They wanted, needed to confront the Wraith directly. It wasn't his place to deny them that. Besides, in all likelihood such a confrontation would better prepare them to stand their ground in the planned ambush to follow.

A warning note from the horns signaled everyone up and down the wall. John didn't need it because he could see for himself. "Crap."

The Wraith weren't going to risk floating the bridges across the narrow channel. They had stopped at the riverbank, and were now lifting the broad planks of what appeared to be a light-weight composite material, until they stood vertical.

"They're going to drop them all at once!" Aiden declared.

On second thought, maybe that wasn't such a bad thing. "The oil has a low ignition temperature," John said. "And it's thick enough to sustain a continuous blaze."

"How come you know this sort of stuff, sir?"

"I tried one of their oil lamps. And I've seen one or two oil fires before." Turning to the warrior with them, John said, "Give the order: everyone except the torchbearers to fall back as far as the first buildings. The moment the bridges are lowered, drop the torches, then get the hell out of there."

The sound echoed up and down the wall. Some of the Wraith, stonily silent on the far side of the channel until now, began pointing to the water. Others further back were lifting their feet and examining them.

The familiar tension heightened John's senses. He could feel their uncertainty. On one level, it didn't matter whether the Wraith realized what was going on and chose to withdraw before the oil was ignited. They were an enemy that, at least for the moment, couldn't be defeated outright. His entire strategy, like that of Dalera, was purely defensive. The idea was to make capturing their prey so unpleasant that they gave up and went elsewhere. But it was that 'elsewhere' that had John hoping they would indeed attack. The more Wraith died here, this morning, on this rock, the fewer could continue culling on some other planet.

During the momentary pause, John gave the order to drop the torches. As luck would have it, the horns blew at almost the exact moment as the bridges began falling into place. Then came a roar like the afterburner of a jet engine. A blast of heat followed in its wake. The horns transmitted the second 'fall back' signal along the wall. A blanket of black smoke began to billow toward them, then lifted high enough for the wind to send it up back across the eastern fields. Within minutes, the thick, choking smoke had obliterated their view.

John decided in that moment that fighting blind was actually worse than flying blind. When flying blind, he at least had instruments for reference.

Despite the overwhelming heat, a reasonable number of Wraith were managing to cross the bridges, but disoriented by smoke and batting at themselves to put out the flames, they were surprisingly easy quarry for the nets. Well, something was going right for them. John didn't dare count on things staying that way.

Along with Ford and a large contingent of warriors and Daleran fighters, John made his way through the increasingly dense smoke to the transport in the Sanctuary Hall. Pleased to see that the Hall was still empty, he ignored the sounds of heavy axes and shouts of victory coming from the direction of the wall. Their biggest test was yet to come.

"Hurry!" Yann called, running in ahead of a contingent of fighters. "To the transport."

Another series of notes erupted from the horn. Before leaving, Ushat had sorted the combatants into two groups. The best runners and most skilled net throwers would now join him and Teyla's group preparing the ambush outside the Citadel off

North Bridge. Those better armed and armored for close combat would remain here to defend against any further Wraith capable of making it across the eastern wall.

Yann piled into the transport behind Ford. It quickly filled with sweating bodies, along with the sound of clanking swords against metal breastplates, panting, and complaints from some that they had not yet managed to personally vanquish a Wraith. The fighters' demeanor was a far cry from that of the special-forces troops with whom John had often worked back on Earth. Those men had been skillful and silent. These, not so much. Fortunately, that was exactly the effect they were going for in order to lure the Wraith into the trap.

"Don't worry," John told them when the doors closed. "You'll get your chance soon enough."

The transport opened inside the now-familiar Sanctuary Hall where they'd first arrived. John stepped out, with Ford, two buglers and five warriors behind him. "Take everyone else and report to Teyla and Ushat," he ordered Yann.

A few of the Dalerans looked at him suspiciously. "You are not coming?" Yann said.

"After I see what the Wraith are doing."

Many of them remained uncertain. John was the last person to quibble about people blindly accepting orders. "We've been lucky so far; everything's gone according to plan," he called. "That's not necessarily going to keep happening, which is why it's important for you to follow my instructions. If the Wraith fall back due east, we'll need to get everyone inside the Citadel pronto, because they're likely to regroup before attacking from a different direction."

Pointing outside, he added, "Next to the Enclave, this is the highest point in the Citadel. It ought to take the first group of Wraith around forty-five minutes to make its way north to where Teyla and Ushat have set up the ambush. It'll take you about thirty minutes to reach them from the village behind. Buglers have been sent to every Station around the Citadel to signal any change in movement, but right now, I need to eyeball what's going on." He smiled grimly. "Save me a Wraith."

"If you see Lisera," Yann called to Ford, "tell her my thoughts are with her." He stabbed at the panel and the transport doors closed.

Outside, tendrils of oily smoke were blowing up the eastern side of the Citadel. It was already higher than the uppermost level of the Station. "Oh, man," Ford groaned. "The westerly wind's dying down."

"No, I don't think so." John studied the clouds. Heading east at about fifteen knots, he estimated. "The heat's creating upward vortices." Still, that wasn't going to help him see any better. "The view should be better from the top of Black Hill."

Ford shot him a knowing look. "Maybe we could scout around for McKay while we're there."

Except that he'd also given his word to Teyla, Yann, and Ushat. He'd split the difference. Twenty minutes looking around Black Hill, and then he'd double-time it from the transport to the ambush site, which should still get him there well ahead of the Wraith. "Okay, let's go check out Black Hill."

CHAPTER SIXTEEN

When the mist parted, the echoes of a thousand feet reverberating through the ground resolved itself into a dreaded truth. From her post in one of the trees, Teyla bit back a gasp. Never before had she seen such a vast horde of Wraith.

The sense of loathing and terror that rippled through those perched with her in the branches was as tangible as the chill bite of the morning air. And yet, the mere fact that the Wraith had been forced to march on the Citadel gave Teyla a measure of satisfaction that she had never before known.

Many stories from her childhood, and the drawings in the caves where her people had taken refuge, all spoke of the same thing. The Wraith came in their great ships, shredded the lives of generation after generation, and there was little anyone could do but run and hope that enough would survive to go on. But in her heart, Teyla had never accepted that this was truly the destiny of her people. Somewhere, somehow, the Wraith could be defeated.

The rebirth of Atlantis had kindled that hope until it had become something more. Now, it was a belief. True, the people of Earth were not the Ancestors. Her confidence had been tarnished by moments of disillusionment, even anger, at the newcomers' arrogance. Nevertheless, that arrogance also gave them something that had been driven from her people when the Ancestors had departed—the will to stand and fight, and not to run and hide in the face of overwhelming odds.

Now, on Dalera, the Wraith had been brought to ground. Now, she too would stand and fight.

Gasps of fear quickly turned into shrill cries to abandon their position.

"No!" Teyla shouted. "Alone, you cannot hope to flee the scourge of the Wraith. Do not let their numbers daunt you. This plan will work, but only if we stand together!"

"And if the blackwater fails to burn as you say?" shouted one.

"Then the Wraith will not come our way. You may choose to tremble among the leaves while I will return to the Citadel to fight for the lives of your loved ones."

On the ground, people paused in their preparations of the nets, and began to climb the trees to better see for themselves. "You have but a few hours to complete the traps," she called down to them. "And you will see more when they approach closer."

There was little response. Teyla grabbed the thick rope attached to the branch and swiftly lowered herself to the forest floor. "Here." She grasped one end of a large net. "I will take this." Several tense seconds passed until a boy of about thirteen clasped the other end and began hauling it up a nearby tree. His movements galvanized everyone back into action.

Climbing to a low branch, Teyla loosely fastened her corner of the net with a slipknot, then looked around. Throughout the forest, large nets were being lifted to the lower boughs, while others were buried beneath fallen leaves, and spring-loaded traps set in place.

Movement and a glint of steel told her that Ushat and his men were returning from checking the ambush line. Good. The warrior had been gone for some time and the only other Gene was some distance away. The sight of the glowing Shield around Ushat's neck brought more mutters of relief from those working on the ground.

Teyla swung down from the branch to land lightly on her feet. "You have seen?"

Ushat smiled grimly. "Many hundreds of our people are returning to the villages on the far side of Quickweed Lake. When the Genes with them hand their Shields to those who are not Genes, the Wraith will see a great feast awaiting them." He looked around and nodded his approval. "Once the Wraith learn that their passage through this forest is fraught with danger, crossing the Lake will appear their best course."

"That is what we hope," Teyla replied.

From above them, a cry went up. "It burns. The river burns — and the Wraith with them!"

This time, Teyla made no move to stop the Dalerans climbing the trees to witness for themselves. Indeed, she immediately pulled herself aloft and stared across the eastern fields. The sight was mesmerizing and more than satisfying. The entire eastern portion of South Channel was a blazing inferno. Lines of fiery serpents began to appear through the far fields, where the oil had flowed along irrigation channels. From this distance it was not possible to make out individuals, but she could see many smaller flames moving about, like the wicks of a hundred candles. Having stumbled into the oil, some of the Wraith had been set ablaze. The gruesome creatures had extraordinary regenerative properties, but it was doubtful if those caught in the fields of oil could survive such a sustained conflagration. The three vast columns of Wraith began to fall back.

Cries of joy traveled across the treetops, and Teyla felt a measure of relief. The battle to come would not be easy, but the people of Dalera were now empowered by the sight before them.

Ushat touched her arm. She took his Shield from him, and he signaled the warrior below to blow the trumpet. Reply calls from the Citadel told them that the EM fields close to North Bridge and the western end of the wall had also been disabled. Just before the roiling black smoke obscured her vision, she noticed the nearest column of Wraith headed in their direction.

"They come!" cried a lookout. At the speed the Wraith were moving, the first waves would soon be upon them — far sooner than Teyla had planned.

Awareness came in the form of a pounding headache, and hands grabbing at his shoulder, dragging him along. Then someone else was lifting his legs. A low moan sounded, and it took him a moment to realize that it had originated from him. He wasn't sure what felt worse: the throbbing pain behind his eyes, or the gelatinous sensation of nausea. The explosive noise of a

P-90 was like a dagger through his brain. Before he could stop himself, he threw up.

Someone, or more specifically someone who sounded like Ford, cursed and unceremoniously dropped him. Another report from the P-90, and then everything abruptly went quiet.

"Damn it, Rodney, rise and shine."

"Careful, sir. He's probably gonna throw up again."

"Only if you keep making such blindingly astute observations, Lieutenant." Rodney slowly sat up, but Sheppard wasted no time in dragging him further into the inn. "Whoa, whoa! Could I have half a second to get oriented here?"

"Not until I'm sure that Wraith is dead," Sheppard replied with a distinct absence of sympathy.

Rodney looked around. What were they doing inside the inn? The last thing he remembered was being shoved off the path and headfirst into the outside wall by — "Artos?"

The two officers exchanged a glance. Ford explained. "All we saw was you on the ground outside the entrance of the inn, and a Wraith heading straight for you. There was nobody else around."

A sharp pang of remorse caught Rodney unprepared. He wasn't even completely sure of the man's name, but he knew with wrenching clarity that Artos had saved his life — again.

The events of this unending night and of the days that had come before it crashed down on him in full force, and he squeezed his eyes shut. He'd had occasions to fear for his life before, but coming to Atlantis had forced him to contemplate his own mortality in a way that he'd never even considered back on Earth. Out here they'd faced death head-on and repeatedly. By now he should have become habituated to it, but he hadn't. He doubted that he ever would.

When he opened his eyes again, Sheppard was watching him with something that Rodney was surprised to see involved a measure of concern. "Take it easy," warned the Major. "If hitting the wall of the inn was what knocked you out, you might have a concussion." He crouched and activated the light on his P-90 to examine Rodney's pupils.

With a hiss of pain, Rodney batted away the torch. "The nausea's more likely related to my having ingested several barrels of not-so light crude oil than a concussion," he informed them snappishly. "Quit hovering. I'll be fine." Maybe if he repeated it a few more times, he'd start to believe it himself. *I'll be fine. No problems here. Certainly not traumatized in the slightest.*

The door to the inn banged open and two of Ushat's warriors walked in. Rodney winced when he noticed their dripping axes. "The creature is dead—of that we made certain," announced one of the men.

Standing up hadn't been the most intelligent move, but it was a far cry from being dragged around the place. "What's happening?" Rodney demanded.

"I think he was the pilot of a Dart that crashed when we turned up," Ford supplied. "He didn't look too good even before we shot him."

"Thank you, Lieutenant. I meant the situation with the oil." Now that he was on his feet, he actually felt considerably better. Squinting against the daylight filtering in through the windows, Rodney stared at Sheppard, waiting for a reply.

The Major changed the clip of his weapon and then slapped his hand against the panel by the transport doors. "Worked just fine. Ford, take McKay back to the Command Center."

"Hey! Hang on a minute. What's the big hurry?"

The doors opened, and the Major stepped in, turned around and smiled at him. "I have an ambush to attend. Ford will bring you up to speed."

"Wait!" Rodney took a step toward him. "What about the oil? Has anyone checked it now that it's daylight? If the rate of flow diminishes significantly, we may have to consider blowing out the lower section of the cliff face."

"Take Ford, the bugler, and warriors with you." Sheppard pulled a spare Shield out of his pack and tossed it to Rodney. "I understand you lost the last one."

"Sir?" Ford called, moving to stop him. "Wouldn't it be better if I—"

Reaching to the panel on the inside of the transport, Sheppard replied, "What is it with this place? Can't anyone accept orders without a philosophical debate?"

"After your good influence, can you possibly be surprised?" Rodney quipped, but the doors had already closed.

CHAPTER SEVENTEEN

"Stay here," John ordered.

"We wish to fight!" declared Peryn. He led a contingent of around two dozen kids, mostly blacksmith's apprentices but some as young as nine or ten who'd arrived in the transport just ahead of John. Between them, they'd cobbled together an eclectic collection of old axes, broken swords and chest armor made from battered metal plates.

"I need you here to help protect the village," John replied, running to the entrance of the inn. When the kids followed him outside, he turned to face the oldest. "Okay, Peryn, here's the deal. I don't know for sure if we'll be able to force all of the Wraith into Quickweed Lake. If it turns out that we can't, we're only going to be able to hold them off for so long before we have to fall back here. When that happens, we'll need you to help operate the transport to the Citadel."

Fingering the Shield around his neck, Peryn's eyes narrowed, but he nodded. "I understand."

John wasn't entirely convinced that he did, but there was no time for a discussion. He needed to catch up with Teyla, Ushat and Yann's group in the forest.

Adjusting his stride to a long, easy gait, he decided that at least it made a nice change from jogging around the piers on Atlantis—until he heard the sounds of distant fighting. What the hell? The Wraith shouldn't have arrived that fast, unless... He swallowed a rush of dread and increased his pace. *Unless the western flank of the Wraith forces double-timed it. Once again—crap.*

A rocky outcrop blocked his direct path. On the far side, he could hear what sounded like heavy hand-to-hand combat. Turning north, he ran for several hundred yards toward a large clearing. The path veered east again just as he reached it. Good thing, too. Partially obscured by smoke, Quickweed Lake really did look like an open meadow.

Reaching the scene of the battle, John paused. The forest was a mass of clanking steel and bodies engaged in a form of combat not seen on Earth for half a millennium — unless he counted Middle Earth and battles against Sauron. Even with a trained eye, it was hard to get a handle on exactly what was happening. Sunlight glinted off steel pikes and axes as the Dalerans hacked into the writhing nets suspended from the trees. All around, as far as John could see, nets were descending from the branches onto the advancing Wraith. But considerably more Wraith were getting through and attacking the Dalerans without mercy. They weren't taking captives; they were feeding.

John raised his weapon when he sighted a masked Wraith leaning over someone. The guy's breastplate had been torn off, and the Wraith lifted a hand to bury it in his victim's chest. Carefully taking aim, John sent a short burst into the stringy-haired head.

Something abruptly pushed him aside, simultaneously wrenching the P-90 from his grasp. He was slammed back into a tree, but recovered in time to parry the incoming elbow, knocking the mask from a super-size Wraith with tangled gray dreadlocks. Its lips parted to display an orthodontist's nightmare. Barely dodging a second punch to his head and a third to his hip, it came as no surprise to John that the thing was employing the same fighting technique as Teyla.

Acting on instinct, he lunged out to recover his weapon. Blow after blow came swift and heavy, and he was reminded of Teyla's warning. He had to conserve his strength. There were a dozen more Wraith where this one came from, all anxious to literally take his life.

Without warning, he was yanked backward by his vest and thrown to the ground, where the stock of his P-90 dug into his ribs. A hand descending toward his chest was interrupted when a nearby explosion knocked his attacker off its feet. A rain of Wraith chunks and armor followed. Mortally wounded, the things were blowing themselves — and their Daleran attackers—to pieces. Which meant that winning the fight against them could prove to be just as fatal as losing.

John barely had time to look up before another Wraith was on him. He ducked the armor-covered hand swinging toward his head and brought the gun up to block the next set of flashing claws. If they got out of this, he owed Teyla an apology and a promise never to avoid a sparring session again, masculine pride be damned.

The business end of an axe head suddenly appeared from *inside* the chest of his opponent, damaging the self-destruct mechanism. More enraged than shocked, the Wraith twisted around to face its new adversary. John caught a brief flash of Yann's determined face before a second blade swung from a new direction, taking the Wraith's head clean off.

Behind the collapsing Wraith, John saw Ushat. He opened his mouth to say thanks, but somewhere to his left, another small explosion was followed by a third, and then a fourth. Shifting his grip on his P-90, John reached for the knife strapped to his belt. The force of the next explosion hit him in the back, and sent him flying—directly into the path of a snarling Wraith.

"I'm just saying that we'll need to make the holes bigger."

Rodney tossed a haughty look in Ford's direction. "I'm well aware that altering the shape of C-4 will somewhat reduce its explosive potential, Lieutenant. I've forgotten more about blowing things up than you'll ever know. And since I don't normally forget anything of crucial importance—"

"Okay, okay!" Ford replied in exasperation.

It still struck Rodney as remarkable how linear most members of the military were in their thinking. Slap a block of C-4 on something, shove a J-2 cap in it, and bang. Yet, placed properly, even with the slightly reduced explosive potential that came as a result of flattening out the C-4, the damage effected could be significantly greater when using the explosive in exactly the right location—like the deep fractures of the shale cliff. "My entire reasoning for placing it here," Rodney explained with what he thought was an undue degree of patience, "is to avoid igniting the oil."

"I thought you had no idea how long the oil would flow?"

"Precisely. Which is why I want a radio controlled detonation. The lookouts on West Bridge can observe Black Hill. If the oil flow declines significantly, it will be impossible for the fire to sustain itself. The lookouts can signal us. We come back here, I hand you my Shield, we wait for our Wraith friends to notice, and…kaboom."

A blur of motion caught Teyla's eye, and she swung around with her fighting staves. This time, she was fortunate, for the attacking Wraith was badly burned and did not appear to be regenerating as it should. And yet that very fact seemed to feed its desperation.

Teyla had been pacing herself, accepting each blow that she could not deflect, and retaliating in moves that were as familiar to her as breathing. Still, the battle was not going well. There were simply too many Wraith entering the forest. Either she had underestimated their numbers, or the villages across Quickweed Lake were not providing sufficient enticement for the remainder of their adversary's forces to head in that direction.

All of the nets had now been used, and while countless Wraith lay dead, many Dalerans had also fallen. The increasing number of nearby explosions left the defenders with no choice. They would have to fall back to the transport village, escape into the Citadel and ignite the remainder of North Channel — but not until she vanquished the creature before her.

Eyes blazing, a foul stench coming from the burned flesh across its mouth, her opponent abruptly changed tactics and lunged at her — only to be jerked off balance by Major Sheppard, who had been thrown against it by the force of a nearby explosion. He recovered in time to grasp a fistful of the Wraith's remaining locks of hair and dispatch the creature with a knife.

"Fall back!" Sheppard yelled. "Fall back to the transport!"

The horn blew. The answering call did not respond for several seconds. When it came, it was weak, as if the bugler were injured. As well he might be. The defending Daleran forces were stretched thinly across the ground between Quickweed Lake and

North Bridge. There was no way to say for certain how many had succumbed.

A gust of wind through the trees brushed away the smoke, and it seemed to Teyla that the forest moved with a seething carpet of Wraith. Behind her, Major Sheppard uttered a low curse. She glanced around. The fight had somehow driven the defenders back to where the edges of the lake curved south. Their path to the village was now cut off.

"Give the signal," Ushat told the bugler. "Order the Genes at the transport not to wait for us."

"What?" Yann demanded, looking around at the exhausted and bloodied combatants with them. "You would sacrifice us?"

"No," Major Sheppard replied even as he ran along the edge of the lake. "He's trying not to sacrifice everyone else. Besides, we're not done for yet."

"And you shall not be," came a voice from behind a stand of trees. A tall boy with fair hair and cheeks still bearing the pink flush of youth led a group of children out to meet them.

"Peryn!" Sheppard's voice was filled with surprise, and frustration. "I'm pretty sure I told you to wait in the village."

"Then who would lead you to the villages on the far side of Quickweed Lake?" The youth looked northwest, across the stretch of strange green and yellow growth that carpeted the black tarpit.

"Madness!" spat Yann.

The Wraith had spied their group, and, almost as one, turned in their direction. "Or death," Teyla declared, pointing to the advancing foe.

Peryn's expression reminded Teyla of the look she sometimes saw in Major Sheppard's eyes. "Follow me," the youth vowed, "and I shall lead you to safety."

The other children quickly cast aside their weapons, removed their armor and ran light-footed onto the lake. The older boy glanced back at the adults. "Caution. Tread in *my* steps, and my steps alone."

Without hesitation, Teyla followed him. The ground was soft beneath her feet, but it did not give much. She heard Major Sheppard behind her.

Ushat's voice came from the shore. "What of the other children? Will they not fall into the slow death of black mud?"

Teyla glanced back. Like Yann and the other men, the guardsman had not moved, but instead eyed the children suspiciously.

"Follow my path alone," Peryn replied, and increased his pace, moving surefooted across the strange, spongy ground.

"I would sooner die a quick death at the hands of the Wraith than flounder in the bowels of Quickweed," declared one man.

Glancing past his shoulder, Teyla answered, "Then you shall soon have your wish." She turned her attention to her feet.

Yann, Ushat and the bugler joined them on their path across the strange-smelling place. The remaining three took a moment longer before they, too, decided that a sure death was less attractive than a possible one after all.

"Some of this stuff is solid," observed the Major. "How can you tell?"

"The color of the weeds," Teyla realized, catching up with Peryn.

The boy shot her a surprisingly adult grin. "Only those of us who live by Quickweed Lake know its secrets." The grin faded and he added, "Do not think you know the way, for the weed changes color as the sun moves west, tricking the foolhardy into paths that lead to a slow death."

"I understand. But what of the others?" Teyla glanced around at the children, all of whom were running lightly across different sections of the lake's surface.

"That's why they stripped off their armor. To lighten themselves." The Major glanced back at the Wraith.

Teyla followed his gaze. "They hesitate."

"Just as you planned, many Wraith have died or are still dying at the hands of Quickweed." Peryn paused so that the others could catch up.

"How is it that you know this?"

He snorted and pointed to the turgid gray veil smothering much of the southeastern edge of the tarpit. "We cut across part of the lake to join you. The smoke cleared in sections, and we saw."

"So the plan worked," Sheppard said. "There were just more of 'em coming our way than we'd banked on."

"And now they come after us," called one of the men. "Look!"

Behind them, the Wraith stepped cautiously out onto the lichen-covered tar. The children closest to them began to scream, but Teyla could see that their cries were for show, enticing the Wraith to an easy meal.

"We must hurry." Peryn motioned them forward, encouraging them.

"Next time I give you an order, Peryn," Major Sheppard said, "feel free to disobey me."

Teyla smiled. The youth had indeed the instincts of a warrior, and a leader. It pleased her to see that he was one of the Genes.

"You have done a great duty, young one." Ushat voiced his approval. Another series of sounds traveled from the Citadel. "A warning," he said. "They are about to set that section of the channel aflame."

"Wraith must've reached them." Sheppard squinted in the direction of the Citadel. "That means we're about to get hit with a blanket of smoke."

It was then that Teyla realized the sun was well past its zenith. "And soon, the Citadel will cast its shadow across us," she observed.

"Then we must indeed make haste." Peryn again picked up his pace.

The Major cast a worried glance at the sky, then shot her a doubtful look. "Why would the Wraith continue with the ground assault? They must know by now that—"

A panicked cry came from behind. One of the men had taken a wrong step and had fallen into a softer section of the lake. Behind him, the Wraith had foregone their fears and were bearing down upon them at great speed.

"Leave him!" squealed a second man. "The Wraith come."

Sheppard turned back, and Teyla remembered his words: *leave no one behind.*

Yann and Ushat also ran back to assist. "It is Dalera's will that all must be saved, with favor to none," Ushat barked. "Help him!"

One of the terrified men ignored him, and darted ahead of Peryn, intent on reaching the forest on the far shore.

By the time they had helped the first man back onto the path, the leading Wraith were in trouble. The children danced around them, just out of reach, goading the Wraith to catch them. Enraged, many continued in their attempt to lunge through the sticky black tar. Others, realizing their folly, began to make their way back. Teyla suspected it was too late.

The man who had gone ahead was nowhere to be seen. "He fell," called one of the children. "Over there." She pointed to a large patch of emerald green, slurping around like a living thing. Of the man, there was no sign.

"Watch your footing, now," warned Peryn. "This is the most dangerous section of Quickweed."

All of the children gathered together to form a line between the adults. Teyla did not look back as the enraged cries of the Wraith continued. Then a different sound came from the Citadel. Although they could not see through the trees to the base of the fortress, they could see a vast line of flames shooting upward.

"The weir at North Bridge has been lowered," Yann said. "Allowing the flames to travel upstream."

Peryn said nothing, but continued to drive the pace. Teyla watched his gaze darting from side to side, seeking the correct path. The shore was close, but the smoke from the new blaze was already rushing toward them. "Perhaps if the path becomes too difficult to see, we should wait and tread more slowly," she suggested.

"No." Peryn shook his head. "You do not understand. This part of the Lake cannot sustain the weight of even a child for more than a few minutes. We must keep moving, or we will sink."

Ushat cursed. "Too late!"

Turning back, Teyla saw the big warrior up to his knees in tar. Then a thick pillar of smoke hit, and he was lost from view.

"You left Major Sheppard and Teyla behind?" Aiden stared in disbelief at the bloody-faced Gene. The man had been with the last group to escape the failed ambush at Quickweed Lake.

"We had no choice. The order was given. I was barely able to close the transport doors against the Wraith. They were swarming in..." His face crumpled. "My brother fell just moments earlier, defending the entrance of the inn to give the last of us time to escape. Do you not think I would have gone back for him had I believed there was any hope?" His words were filled with bitter remorse, and he pushed aside Lisera's sympathetic hand.

Aiden glanced at McKay, but the scientist had already moved to stand by the chart table. Several of the town's engineers had transferred most of the maps and supplies into the Station where Lisera was ensconced. The once palatial living chambers had been turned into a new and more readily defensible Command Center. As the highest point in the city now that the Enclave had been destroyed, it also allowed them occasional glances through the wall of smoke blanketing the entire length of North Channel.

This, the largest room on the second level, was currently occupied by about twenty people, mostly engineers, blacksmiths, and upper level bureaucrats who had a good knowledge of the Citadel's layout, plus a few whose wounds were being tended by Lisera.

"What about the villages on the northwestern shore of the Lake?" Aiden demanded. He knew he was grasping at straws, but he was not ready to accept the fact that the rest of his team, and Ushat and Yann, had succumbed to the Wraith during the failed ambush.

The Gene shook his head. "The last anyone saw of them, your friends had their backs to Quickweed, and the Wraith were advancing on them."

A roll of bandages fell to the floor, and Lisera burst into tears. Aiden picked it up for her. Biting back a sob, she accepted it. "Please, Aiden, you must not die, too."

"I don't intend to. But I'm not staying here while the rest of my team is out there."

Swinging around to face the men, McKay asked, "Exactly how solid is the tar?" He shook his head and corrected himself. "The surface of Quickweed Lake?"

The Gene whom Lisera had been tending replied, "Those of us who harvest the pitch from the Lake know where to tread. While most of Quickweed is deadly and will consume a person before he even has a chance to cry out, many places will support the weight of a man. Finding a path across is all but impossible. Still," he mused, "the children who grow up in the villages know its secrets. They often traverse the Lake to collect special plants to trade with the apothecaries."

The scientist's eyes met Aiden's. Swallowing once, Aiden nodded determinedly. McKay had managed to survive a culling. Teyla and the Major were two of the most resourceful people he'd ever known.

McKay snatched up his pack while Aiden checked his weapon. "Where are you going?" Lisera pleaded when they made for the door.

"To find our…friends," McKay replied. He seemed almost surprised at the unfamiliar use of the last word.

"Quickweed Lake will not easily give up her secrets!" called someone as they ran down the stairs.

"Then we might be gone for a while," Aiden shot back.

"Take off your armor and get rid of your weapons." John carefully retraced his steps toward Ushat's voice.

"Leave me," the warrior replied gruffly. He had already sunk to his chest.

"No one gets left behind!" Yann snapped in response.

John could hear the anxiety in the merchant's voice. The smoke cleared momentarily, but more was coming. "Take the children ashore," he ordered Peryn. "We'll follow."

Distress was clearly written on the kid's face. "You will not be able to find the path."

"Yes, we will." Teyla pointed to the indentations left in the soft tar. "Now go." She ran across to the warrior, tugging her pack off as she went.

The thing of it was, Ushat was right. The warrior was sinking faster than John could have imagined. By the time they were in a position to help, Ushat was up to his neck.

"No!" Yann cried in denial. Moving around, desperate to save the man who had turned from adversary to friend, he stepped out into the tar, but the bugler and the guy they'd rescued earlier restrained him.

Teyla had pulled a rope from her pack, but it was too late.

"Thank you for saving my people, Major John Sheppard of Atlantis." Ushat smiled, then closed his eyes and slipped beneath the black.

In the split-second he could afford to spend on sorrow, John thought, *I hope to God that turns out to be true.*

"*No!*" Yann screamed again, lunging toward the bubbles that erupted from the pool.

Teyla grasped his arm. "Honor his death by living!"

After a moment, the blinding anguish began to clear from his eyes, and the merchant nodded dumbly. She quickly turned to retrace their steps.

More coils of smoke reached across them. John was not immune to the shock of losing Ushat, but Teyla was right. The smoke was approaching thick and fast now. So was the afternoon shadow cast by the Citadel.

"This way." Peryn appeared from within the smoke, and waved them on.

Apparently taking the other children ashore hadn't necessarily implied staying there. "Why do I even bother trying to tell you what to do?" John called. But he was having his own problems. Every step, his foot sank deeper, and each time, it was harder to withdraw.

"Close now," shouted the children, lined up along the shore.

John looked up, and saw the shapes of trees through the smoke. That was a mistake, because his next step plunged him into the tar pit.

"This doesn't look good," McKay declared when they ran out of the inn of the second village they'd checked. "Major?" he called into the choking black smoke. "Would you do us the favor of letting us know that you're not dead yet?"

"Will you keep your voice down?" Aiden barked. "If there are any Wraith around—"

"They'll be as blind as we are." McKay coughed. "God, this stuff is noxious!"

Aiden rubbed his eyes against the oily smoke. He hated to admit it, but their only chance of locating the Major and Teyla was to make as much noise as possible. "Call them," he said to the bugler who'd volunteered to accompany them.

The sound had barely finished when a kid of about nine, partially covered in black goop, ran up the slope. Passing an odd contraption that consisted of a frame, buckets half filled with tar, ropes and pulley blocks, he called, "This way. Help us!" His young features were twisted in fear.

"Oh, that's nice," McKay grumbled, bringing up the rear. "Oil *and* children."

Ignoring him, Aiden ran after the boy. His relief at seeing Teyla was momentary because she and a bunch of guys, including Yann, were pulling on a thick rope. A short distance away, obscured by smoke, was a figure buried up to his waist. "Major!" Aiden handed his weapon to McKay and ran down to help them.

Face pinched in concentration, eyes reddening in the smoke, McKay declared, "That's not going to get him anywhere." Removing his pack, he instructed Yann to toss Sheppard a second rope, and then disappeared for a few moments. When he came back, he was carrying something in his hand. McKay then looped the other ends of the rope into some sort of weird configuration involving pulley blocks and a couple of tree trunks.

"Nice of you to join us, Rodney," called the Major, his arms straining on the ropes as he fought the pull of the lake. "What do you call this? Rescue by Rube Goldberg?"

"If the first word is 'rescue,' does it matter what the other words are?"

One thing Aiden would say about the scientist: his ideas generally worked. The Major was almost completely free of the tar when one of the ropes snapped. The pulley block flung back and struck Sheppard in the temple. He fell forward in a boneless heap, landing through some stroke of luck on the shore.

"Crap!" Cursing, Aiden scrambled toward him. Of all the people in Dalera, this was the one they could least afford to have knocked out cold.

"Oh, of course he would have to go one better than me," Rodney declared when they hauled the Major up, not quite covering a note of worry in his voice. "Tarred *and* concussed."

"Save it." Aiden lifted his CO's pack and weapon. Yann and a second tar-coated man pulled the unconscious Sheppard's arms across their shoulders and hurried up the slope to the village. This was going to be close. The smoke was getting thicker, they were currently leaderless, and any minute now, the Wraith retreating from the near side of the Citadel's wall would be on them.

CHAPTER EIGHTEEN

As a child, Teyla had been told never to run off into the mists that often settled over Athos at dawn. Dangers are always greater when unseen, her father had said. It was that warning that whispered at the back of her mind she plunged through the billowing smoke toward the inn.

The series of coughs originating a short distance behind her identified Dr McKay's position. The scientist struggled to keep up with the group, but was lagging behind Yann and the other man supporting Major Sheppard. Ford, by contrast, was moving as if vision was unnecessary, staying close on the heels of the children guiding them.

"Are we…sure this is the right way?" McKay wheezed.

It disturbed Teyla that she was no longer certain of that. Her sense of direction had diminished greatly in a very short time. Ahead of her, Peryn's head bobbed in the haze. "We know," he called back. "This is our home."

A sudden change in the wind cleared the smoke for a moment, long enough for them to make out a squad of Wraith heading toward them. Teyla glanced back to urge McKay to hurry, but it was unnecessary. The scientist's face had gone slack with dread, and his pace abruptly quickened. "On second thought, how about faster," he suggested, coming abreast of Teyla. "Or possibly *much* faster!"

Lowering his weapon, one Wraith let out a guttural yell as he stared them down. McKay clutched at one of the many Shields he'd located and fastened around his belt, nearly tripping in the process. "Suddenly I'm feeling a lot more affection for Dalera and her bright ideas," he panted.

By the time they reached the inn, the trio of Wraith had closed the distance between them to mere steps. "Open the transport!" Ford shouted to McKay, but Peryn was closer and darted forward, slapping his hand down on the panel. To his credit, McKay managed to look irked without breaking stride as the group clambered into the transport.

"The doors may not close fast enough." Yann eyed the approaching Wraith with trepidation. Ford fired his P-90 at the same moment that Teyla pressed the trigger of hers, knocking the lead Wraith back a step or two. Fearful of ricochets inside the transport, they were forced to cease firing when the doors began to slide shut, leaving the Wraith enough time to lunge forward and thrust an arm into the narrowing gap.

Shouts of surprise and terror intermingled for an instant before the arm fell to the floor, severed by the unyielding doors. The appendage twitched for a few seconds before going still. The brief silence that followed was broken by a disgusted sound from McKay. "If this were Earth, someone would be filing a lawsuit over that hazard. I suppose there could have been worse ways for us to discover that these doors aren't fitted with any kind of safety recoil mechanism."

"Are you complaining? It just saved your life." Turning to the men supporting his commander's weight, Ford froze. "Oh, *damn* it!"

"Not the turn of phrase I would have used, Lieutenant, but—"

"Can it, doc! The Major's not breathing."

The transport doors folded open as McKay jerked toward him in shock. "And you've only just now noticed this?" he yelled. "What the hell kind of medical training did they give you?"

"Battlefield triage!" the Marine shouted back. "This look like any battlefield you've ever seen?"

Understanding that McKay's reaction was born of panic rather than true anger, Teyla used a gentle hand to pull him out of the way of the others. The two Daleran men lifted Sheppard's body out of the transport and laid him on the floor of the Sanctuary Hall. Ford crouched down to check the Major's pulse. "Still steady," he reported, studying the man's color, which even Teyla could see was unhealthy under the smears of black on his face. "His airway's blocked by tar—who knows how much he inhaled when he fell. We have to either clear it or — "

His hesitation told her that he didn't like the alternative. "Or what?" McKay demanded. "Did that battlefield medical training include instructions on performing a tracheotomy?"

"Yeah, it did, but it's not like I've actually done one!" Ford's voice rose in volume as he repeatedly clenched and unclenched a fist. "If I have to do it, we should get him to the Command Center first. I left most of our medical supplies there, including the instruments that I need to make the incision."

McKay flinched at the word 'incision' but charged ahead. "Forget about the 'ifs' and make a decision, Lieutenant, because as we stand here and debate, the Major is losing brain cells and he is dying. I know he's been there before, but this time it'll stick."

With a flash of resolve that seemed motivated by both irritation and fear, Ford turned his back on McKay and reached down to tilt Sheppard's head back. "I think the tar's hardened into a solid piece blocking both his nose and mouth. Teyla, if I can get this stuff off, be ready to start breathing for him."

Remembering the resuscitation techniques that Dr Beckett had taught her, she nodded once and knelt by the Major's head. Ford grasped the thick black gunk and ripped it free, exposing abraded skin and lips with an alarmingly blue tint. Teyla bent forward and breathed into her friend's still form.

Upon the second breath, Sheppard gave a choking gasp, and she and Ford rolled him onto his side to expel some lingering oil. The gagging subsided, but he did not fully wake.

As relief washed over her, Teyla heard one of the children cry out, and she shot to her feet — only to see their bugler pierced by the blade of a rebel assailant. Another man who had been with them since before Quickweed Lake was quickly felled, and a gang of nine soon surrounded their group. The one she presumed was their leader held a long knife at the struggling child's neck.

She burned, both with fury toward those responsible and with rage toward herself for being unable to protect the others. The bugler had stayed faithfully beside them for so long, unarmed throughout much of this madness, and in letting their guard down, they had failed him.

The gang's intent was clear as they bound her wrists and did likewise to Ford, McKay and Yann. They looked her up and down, openly appraising. Their leers did not frighten her. With or without the use of her hands she would quite swiftly take away their ability to procreate. Glancing around, she noticed that several of the children, including Peryn, had slipped away into the murky darkness of the Sanctuary Hall. They at least would be safe for a time.

A muted groan from the floor signaled the beginnings of Major Sheppard's return to consciousness. As pleased as she was to hear it, the timing was unfortunate. One of the gang delivered a merciless kick to the side of his head, and her team-mate went limp again.

Under his breath, Ford uttered a word Teyla suspected was a particularly foul epithet. "Oh, *that's* what he needed to round out his day," McKay muttered.

"What purpose do your actions serve?" Yann demanded of the gang's leader. "We all battle the Wraith now. Kill us and there will be fewer left to stand against them!"

"We don't plan to kill *all* of you." The leader, a man whose brutish demeanor reminded Teyla of Balzar, turned a knowing sneer on her. "Only the ones we have no use for." He all but slung the whimpering child aside, and she landed in a sprawled heap at Dr McKay's feet.

"This one is known to me." Another rebel spoke up, giving Yann a hard jab in the shoulder. "You are the one who became Chosen. These are the visitors who bring the *genetherapy*!"

"We reject the name Chosen," Yann said, defiant. "We are Genes."

His protest was lost amid a sudden flurry of arguments between gang members. Clearly they wanted to be a part of this new elite, the Genes, but none agreed on how to achieve that aim.

"You can provide this *genetherapy*." The leader stopped in front of McKay, assessing him. "We have no need of the others."

"I'd rethink that if I were you." McKay stood rigidly straight, his features conveying an odd mix of apprehension and exasperation. "The only person who can administer the *genetherapy* is this man here—" He indicated Ford with a jerk of his chin. "—and the only person who can get it for you is the one you just brain-damaged."

Unmoved, the leader stepped back over Sheppard's sprawled body, apparently to position himself for a wider swing, and raised the long handle of his axe. Smirking at McKay, he adjusted his grip on the weapon. "So you are not needed after all?"

Eyes widening in alarm, McKay's gaze followed the motion of the axe, but his voice was more impatient than fearful as he replied, "Oh, for crying out loud, would you just slow down for one damn—"

A pack of children appeared from within the darkest recesses of the hall, shrieking, "The Wraith come! We beg your protection!"

Teyla recognized the children, and the look in their eyes. She'd seen that same contrived expression of terror when they had enticed the Wraith into Quickweed Lake.

The thugs hesitated, their glances darting back and forth between the deepening shadows of the Sanctuary Hall. "They hide in the darkness," one girl whimpered, clutching at the first meaty hand within reach.

It was a masterful ploy, Teyla acknowledged. The sunlight was growing fainter in the windows, and the smoke still hung in the air, creating many potential places for danger to lurk unseen. But although she trusted the children, she was not assured that their cries might not have some truth to them.

A piercing scream broke the tension, as a Wraith arm sprang out of the shadows and snatched one of the children out of sight. The scream became a horrific plea for mercy that quickly faded into the oily blackness.

That was enough to convince the thugs, who fled the Hall with frantic shouts. "And now you've changed your minds yet *again*?" McKay yelled over them, his voice pitched high. He jumped when a figure emerged from the shadow where the child had disappeared. "Holy—"

The figure coalesced into Peryn, the taken child perched on his shoulders. Both grubby faces were lit by victorious grins, and the smaller child held a lifeless Wraith arm like a prize.

Yann gave a throaty chuckle. "Well done!" he congratulated the children, who scampered out of the darkness to help free the adults.

Her bonds untied, Teyla offered an approving smile, admiring the skills garnered by the young of this world. She could not mask her amusement at Dr McKay's face as he slumped in sheer relief. The girl who'd been thrown to the floor now patted his hand reassuringly.

The moment of levity passed, and Teyla joined Ford at the Major's side.

"Still breathing okay," Ford judged. "But that second blow to the head couldn't have done him any good. We should get him back to the Command Center."

Yann bent to lift the unconscious man again, and this time McKay stepped in to assist. Teyla enlisted the children to help her collect their packs and weapons, and they made their way outside to the road. Her eyes were constantly in motion. They had been ambushed once. She would not allow such a thing to occur a second time.

On the road, they passed groups of people clustered together, protecting themselves as best they could. The illumination provided by the flames from the burning North Channel was only minimal, and the oily smoke further hampered their vision. There were few warriors in evidence until they were almost to the base of the Command Center Station, where a large number of Dalerans were concentrated. From within the throng, the two warriors who had become Teyla's personal guards noticed the group's approach and hurried toward her.

"Thank Dalera," one greeted. "We believed you to be lost when we became separated."

"I am pleased to see you well," Teyla replied.

One of the men looked over her shoulder. "Where is Ushat?"

Teyla felt the pain of loss anew. She held the man's eyes and said, "Ushat fell bravely, as a true warrior of Dalera."

His eyes showed his grief, but he lifted his chin and nodded once.

"We have much to do still. Can you organize the other warriors? They are needed to protect the refugees entering the Sanctuary Hall. Now that night falls and the transports are no longer necessary to evacuate outlying villages, we should move as many people as possible inside for their security."

"What of the Wraith? Have they not fallen back from the Northern Wall?" the other asked, pointing in the direction of the flames. "We lowered the weir as ordered. The entire Northern Channel is now ablaze."

"You have done very well," she assured them.

McKay, however, was less gracious. "In an ideal world, sure, but I think we've demonstrated conclusively that this is anything but. What's to stop the Wraith from changing gears and attacking from the south?"

While it was normal for the Wraith to attack with ferocity, Teyla had never before heard of them continuing a cull in the face of such resistance. Reluctantly conceding Dr McKay's point, she said, "Your people are not yet safe. Go now and protect them."

The warriors exchanged a glance, then thumped their breastplates in acknowledgement and departed.

"Would it have been too much to ask that they help out a little before dashing off?" McKay grumbled, struggling to stay upright as he and Yann muscled Sheppard up the steps.

At the first landing, they were met by Lisera, who had rushed down from the upper level with as much haste as her leg would allow. "Yann!" Flying past Ford, she clung to the young merchant's arm. "I feared you dead." The girl pulled Yann forward, leaving the majority of Sheppard's weight to fall on McKay. The scientist yelped a warning, and Ford moved immediately to his aid, sparing a bewildered glance for Lisera's sudden change in affections.

Rather than express gratitude for the assistance, McKay commented, "Lost your admirer, did you?"

The Lieutenant smirked. "At least I had one."

There was an empty bed in the corner of the first level, onto which they maneuvered the Major. Yann sent one of the children off to find a healer. Teyla was deeply concerned to see no sign of awareness from her team leader. They had need of his guidance, and she found his stillness troubling.

"I wish I could tell how serious his concussion is." Ford made an abortive attempt at pacing beside the bed. "He needs Beckett and Atlantis, not this."

"And how do you suggest we accomplish that?" McKay snapped, carefully rearranging the chain of Shields around his belt. "Considering he's the only one who can actually fly the jumper in space?"

"You were awfully hot to prove you could fly it when we came in."

But as it was apparent to all that since there was no way to reach the jumper, the debate was meaningless.

Through cracked and smoke-clouded windowpanes, Teyla could see that darkness had now completely fallen on the city. In the distance, beyond the walls of the Citadel, she imagined that she could see the glow of flames. The Wraith appeared to be setting the abandoned villages and the fields ablaze. As on other planets, here, too, the Wraith were determined to ensure that any humans who survived their culling were robbed of even a modest ability to restore their world.

With nightfall had come an uneasy quiet. Inside the room they occupied, warriors and the city's engineers continued to discuss strategies in low tones, allowing the soft moans of the wounded and the whispered reassurances of their caregivers to be heard. It was a scene that the Athosian had never witnessed before. In her experience, battles with the Wraith were swift and decisive. This strange state that was neither victory nor defeat was most unusual. Though it was better than constant terror, Teyla found herself hoping that it would not last long.

Rodney snapped out of his light doze when someone rushed in, calling a halt to the few moments of rest they'd managed to grab. Typical.

"I bring news," called the warrior, his gaze sweeping over the room. "Where is the one called Major Sheppard?"

"Indisposed, unfortunately." Rodney stood from his singularly uncomfortable seat on a wooden chest by the door. All the halfway decent chairs had been taken upstairs, where most of the wounded were. "Why? What's gone wrong now?"

"Before night fell, the Wraith could be seen massing in the forest on the far side of South Channel," the man announced, catching his breath.

"Just as they did before their initial attack on the East Wall." Teyla's puzzlement was evident. Rodney shared it.

From a purely theoretical point of view, he had understood that the Wraith might regroup and attack from the south. Fortunately, he'd had the foresight to leave the oil in the South Channel in the first place. Still— "That makes no sense. They've seen the oil. They have to realize we'll light it. What the hell are they planning?" It was a rhetorical question, and the others treated it as such, but he would have appreciated an answer. It was all very well for him to come up with his standard brilliant solution, but that solution was predicated on comprehending the problem first. And with no clear idea of the Wraith's plan, there was no way to predict what that problem would be. *Think, damn it.*

A glance toward the bed told him that Sheppard's condition was unchanged. In a brief departure from rational thought, Rodney felt a flicker of envy toward his teammate. What he wouldn't give for just a few minutes of actual sleep. "I can't tell you how grateful I am for all your help here," he told the Major under his breath.

"We need intel on their movements," Ford said, moving out of Lisera's way as she stepped in to remove Sheppard's oil-slicked boots. "We're blind without it. And the only way to acquire that is to transport into the nearest village, take a look around, and report back."

Teyla nodded. "I agree."

"How nice for you." Rodney squeezed his eyes shut, forcing back a burgeoning tension headache. "Has it occurred to you that the Wraith have almost certainly figured out the trick with the Shields by now? If I were them, and I was amassing an assault force, I'd immediately put a guard on the village transports to pick off the first Gene who sticks his head out."

"So we'll take a bunch of warriors, transport into one of the villages further out, and walk in."

"And how many is 'a bunch' when you have no idea of the size of the opposing force?"

"Which brings us back to why we need the intel!" Ford stalked across the room, visibly frustrated. "Staying back here out of their reach might seem safer, McKay, but if we don't do something, pretty soon there won't be any place out of their reach."

"You are missing my point!" Rodney bristled at the Lieutenant's insinuation. His instincts toward self-preservation were unmatched, but this was about common sense and staying alive long enough to accomplish something of value. "They could cross the river and build up their forces and equipment to scale the wall under the cover of darkness. We need to ignite the oil that's already there. And sooner is preferable to later."

Both Teyla and Ford turned inquisitive glances toward him. "When did you start looking at the tactical big picture?" the Lieutenant wanted to know.

"When our resident field commander went down for the count and left us in a thoroughly untenable situation. Do your best to keep up." A bothersome side effect of looking at the big picture was that Rodney immediately saw the big obstacle as well. He was reasonably certain that there was an insufficient volume of oil in the South Channel to maintain the sustained conflagration that appeared necessary to dissuade the Wraith. That left only one solution. "We'll also have to adjust the boom to increase the flow of oil."

"Won't that allow the fire to jump upstream?" Yann asked, obviously nervous about the prospect.

Behind him, some of the children ducked closer, drawn in by the conversation. Lisera made a vain attempt to guide them away, which only added to Rodney's increasing exasperation. He needed to pace without these small hindrances cluttering up the floor. "If anything, reducing the oil flow in North Channel will reduce the risk of the flames jumping past the West Bridge and igniting Black Hill."

"Hold on a minute." Ford wiped sweaty, oil-streaked hands on his pants. "Lighting that first quadrant was one thing; it's contained by the raised weirs and bridges. But if we do this in the South Channel and the Wraith react the same way they did the first time, by diverting west —"

"I'm aware of the ramifications," Rodney snapped.

"There won't be anything to stop the fire from spreading all the way to Black Hill," Ford persisted. "The smoke will cover the entire Citadel."

"Don't stop there, Lieutenant. If you're going to insist on stating the obvious, go all the way with it." The difference between himself and most people, Rodney reasoned, was that his own imagination was limitless to a fault. "Should we be unable to control the spread of the fire, with an oil source this rich, the resulting underground blaze could last for years, if not centuries. Fumes and smoke would make the Citadel and probably the surrounding area completely uninhabitable. It's a worst-case scenario. I'll state that on the record. Now you tell me what other choice we have."

Ford spoke up as Liserà finally managed to shoo the children away. "We should at least evacuate everyone who can't fight or operate a Shield." He turned to address a nearby warrior. "Get everyone from the Sanctuary Halls and bring them to the highest areas that are still accessible, around here and near the Enclave. As much as is possible, they'll be protected from the smoke — and the Wraith if they get through."

The warrior glanced at Rodney, who nodded absently, and left to comply. The man disappeared through the door at almost the same moment that someone passed him to enter.

"The healer comes," Lisera said, moving aside and quietly dissolving the argument for the time being.

A stooped man with greying hair and long beard approached

and took a seat beside Sheppard. "He was struck in the head?" asked the healer, studying his new patient.

"Twice," confirmed Ford. "And he was deprived of air for a couple of minutes."

While Lisera instructed two nearby women to fetch soap-water and vegetable oil, the healer checked the Major's pupils and studied the impressive bruises forming on either side of his head. "I do not believe the blows have caused his brain to swell," he said at last. Rodney wished he could have some confidence in that assertion.

The commotion around him seemed to rouse Sheppard. He stirred minutely, his eyes sliding half-open before closing again.

"Wake, son," coaxed the healer, patting a tar-coated shoulder. Ford and Teyla crowded in, as did Peryn. Rodney hung back, partially to avoid overwhelming the battered Major, but mostly out of a dislike for dense huddles of people.

Sheppard managed to open his eyes fully, but they were bright and unfocused. "Welcome back, sir," Ford smiled. "You freaked us out a little back there."

There was a faint response, but it was hardly more than a groan. The Lieutenant's grin faltered. "You remember what's going on, right? And who you are, and all that?"

The ensuing pause was unnerving enough to them all that Rodney broke in. "For the love of God, Major, just give us something to demonstrate that your brains aren't running out your ears."

After another beat of silence, the reply came, weak but unequivocal. "Shut up, Rodney."

Ford smirked. "He remembers, all right."

The healer lifted a gnarled hand. Sheppard's eyes followed the motion, but with a sluggish delay. Seemingly satisfied with that result, the healer withdrew a small bottle from a pouch at his belt and helped the Major to drink its contents before easing his head back to the pillow. "Rest now," he said kindly.

Sheppard looked inclined to obey, but momentarily fixed a disoriented gaze on Ford. "We safe?" he murmured.

Ford's flinch most likely went unnoticed by his CO. "We're

on it, sir."

The swiftness with which Sheppard sank back into oblivion bothered Rodney. "What was in that stuff you just gave him?"

"The potion will allow him to sleep through the night," the old man replied, returning the bottle to his pouch.

"What?" Rodney snapped at him. "You gave him something to sleep at a time like this? We need him awake and alert—"

"You are of the Chosen." The healer stood and stared at Rodney from beneath a pair of fuzzy white eyebrows. "It rests with you to decide what must be done. But I warn you that forcing him to wake now will only confuse him and delay healing. If you seek his counsel, then you must wait until morning."

While he had never been much of a champion of the medical profession, Rodney wasn't about to grant a glorified witch doctor the same deference Carson Beckett had earned. "And you're convinced that's prudent based on a five-second exam and some hand-waving?"

"Dr McKay," Teyla said, her tone carrying a familiar admonition.

"Not this time, Teyla." He watched the healer step back with a slight bow, unruffled. The old man's composure only heightened Rodney's anxiety. "I'm willing to respect their ways up to a point, but the Major could have intracranial bleeding for all that guy knows. Not to mention the fact that we could do with a little tactical advice here!"

"Athosian healers have developed many treatments without the benefit of sophisticated equipment," she countered, her features carved in stone. "These people did manage to survive for many generations without our assistance."

"Noted, but I'll once again point out that current conditions make it improbable that they'll survive for many generations *more* without our assistance."

"I must take my leave," the old man announced. "There are many who are more gravely injured than this Chosen, and Dalera has commanded that all should be treated equally."

"Guys," Ford said quietly, flicking his gaze toward the foot of the bed. Lisera had returned, flanked by two older women holding buckets and cloths.

"It does not serve Major Sheppard well to remain covered in oil," said one of the women hesitantly, her discomfort surely caused by the tension humming between the team members. "With your permission?"

After a moment, Rodney realized that she was looking to him for a go-ahead. "Sure, yeah. Just, ah, understand that our people aren't too fond of being unclothed in front of others, all right?"

The women looked at him oddly, while Lisera blushed a little and ducked her head. Rodney made a mental note to mock Sheppard later for sleeping through his sponge bath.

Now he just had to ensure that he'd get that chance. "Anyone have any information on the status of the North Channel?" Rodney asked the room in general, turning back to the problem at hand.

"Word comes from West Bridge that the oil is flowing as strongly as ever," one of the townspeople answered promptly. "It continues to feed the flames."

The unqualified success of his previous plan gave him far less satisfaction than it had earlier, since major modifications were now required. "All right. We need to flow more oil into the South Channel. I need—" Rodney snapped his fingers repeatedly, trying to recall the name of the engineer, but then he remembered that the man was dead. That memory gave him pause. Artos had saved his life. "The men who walked the boom across the channel," he said in a subdued voice. Clearing his throat of something that seemed to have caught there, he added, "They'll have to lengthen it."

"I will locate them and set them to work," Yann determined.

"What, while I wait here and babysit the Major? I'm sure it won't shock you to learn that my trust doesn't run that deep. I'm going out to supervise. This is too important."

"Go ahead," Ford said, folding his arms across his P-90. "I'm going out to do some recon on the Wraith positions. Like it or not, we can't do without intel."

"Have it your way," Rodney retorted, tired of arguing. The Lieutenant appeared fixated on his role of playing commando.

So be it. "Take that previously mentioned contingent of guards, and do me the favor of remembering my dissent if you should happen to get yourself killed."

"Four men only. Any more and we risk being heard."

"I will accompany Lieutenant Ford." Teyla checked the clip of her P-90. "We will also need a Gene to operate the transport."

"I can go," Peryn chimed in, stepping away from where he'd been hovering near Lisera.

"No," Ford started to say, but Rodney cut him off with a wave.

"Take him. He's quicker and more maneuverable than just about everyone else around here." The idea of sending someone who was hardly more than a child off to face the Wraith struck a dark chord in his mind, but again, options were limited. Besides, if the Wraith broke through into the Citadel, it was only a matter of time before they were all dead. "Do what you have to do, and we'll meet back here."

Checking his collection of Shields one more time, Rodney picked up his weapon and spared another glance toward Sheppard. *We'll meet back here,* he repeated to himself.

The two groups made their way downstairs and out into the streets. The glow from the fire along the entire North Channel was marginally reassuring, but the desperate expressions of the evacuees inside the dimly lit Sanctuary Hall was not. Eyes peered out of bloody, dust-covered faces. It felt to Rodney as if they were claiming pieces of him, or the desired outcome, for themselves. He swallowed and cringed. He didn't want to be here. In fact, he just wanted to lie down and sleep. This wasn't his job; it was the Major's. But the faces urged him on, pushing him from behind, crowding him until he was almost relieved to escape into the transport.

That's when he noticed the gaggle of children trailing in his wake. "When did I become the Pied Piper?" His recollection of the outcome of that particular Grimms' tale was that things had not ended well for the children. At Yann's blank look, Rodney rolled his eyes. "Go back," he told the kids, attempting to brush them off. "Seriously, get lost! You can't help me, and you're better off in the Station."

"We'd rather go," one little girl informed him almost cheerfully. It was the same child that had been carelessly tossed against him by Balzar's clone.

"I'm sorry, did I miss the part where I asked what you'd rather do?"

"Give it up, Doc," Ford called from inside the transport. "They've bailed us out more than once already."

"Some days it doesn't pay to get out of bed," Rodney sighed. Looking up at his teammates preparing to depart, he could only offer a feeble, "Good luck."

"To you as well," Teyla replied.

The doors closed on them, and Rodney jerked away from the little girl, who'd somehow taken an interest in his fingers. "The moment any one of you asks me for chocolate, I'm calling the whole thing off."

Teyla must have picked up on Aiden's misgivings, because when Peryn closed the doors of the transport, she turned to him and said, "Dr McKay is worried for Major Sheppard."

"Yeah, me too."

"Have you given thought to how we will proceed if he does not regain consciousness?"

Aiden's mouth abruptly went dry. Among other things, it'd mean relying on McKay to pilot the jumper. Great. Now they were bound to have transportation issues. Still, the immediate problem was of more importance.

"Where do you wish us to go?" Peryn was staring at the map mounted inside the transport.

"We should take a look around the area south of where the Wraith are amassing their forces." Aiden indicated a light about five miles out on the southern side of the Citadel.

"We must not let our arrival alert them." Teyla pointed out. To Peryn, she said, "As soon as you select the destination, hand me your Shield."

The four warriors—two of them trainees—who had vol-

unteered to accompany them readied their axes. Holding the
Shield over Teyla's palm in one hand, Peryn pressed the lights
that Aiden had selected. The moment the doors began to unfold,
he released the Shield, which was a bad move. The doors continued to fold back, revealing an inn full of Wraith with their
stunners trained on them.

Aiden instantly fired a round into the leading Wraith's chest,
but then something knocked him off his feet, and everything
went black.

CHAPTER NINETEEN

The transports near the bridges differed from their more common counterparts. Instead of being located in an inn or one of the Sanctuary Halls, each opened directly into the street leading to the bridge itself. "It is for the purpose of moving goods," Yann explained when Rodney expressed surprise at their destination. "This way, carts may enter the Citadel from the bridges and be transported into the Sanctuary Halls to unload."

Recalling something of that nature in the initial briefing, Rodney's interest was quickly diverted to the sight through the closed portcullis of the West Bridge. Flames crawling up into the night sky cast an orange glow over the entire North Wall. Although the wind had dropped with the fall of night, the hot air generated by the blaze and the sheer cliff face leading up to the Enclave seemed to propel most of the oil-laden smoke away. The force of the heat surprised him — it felt like a physical presence. Despite nearly burning his hand on the heavy iron of the portcullis, he would, if pressed, have admitted to a certain fascination. People who battled massive forest fires and oil blazes spoke of fire as a living entity. Watching the way the flames curled and danced across the waters of North Channel, he was beginning to understand the analogy.

Glancing west, Rodney was pleased to note that the oil was flowing at a satisfactory pace.

"It is good that you survived." Turning, he met the grim faces of the men who had dragged the boom across the channel the previous evening. The warrior added, "We heard that the Wraith culled all those who had remained behind."

The unspoken question hung between them like an embarrassing smell. "Yes, well, the Shield fell off when I was in the river." Rodney saw no reason to elaborate on exactly when that unfortunate event had occurred.

A hand clasped his shoulder and he was reluctantly drawn into a display of male bonding that involved embraces and back thumping. Moving past the moment as quickly as possible, he explained what needed to be done, adding, "Once again, we're a little pressed for time. And we'll need rope, lots of rope."

The men, supported by a gaggle of chattering children, led the way to a subterranean passage, claiming it allowed access outside the Citadel near where the end of the boom was secured.

"Are there many more of these tunnels?" Rodney asked, stooping to pass through the low entrance.

"Thousands," the lead man, another of the engineers, replied. "They provide access for workers to service the sewers and the pumps that supply the Citadel with water."

Given the sophistication of their weirs, it made sense that a place this big would have a decent wastewater system. Except of course that it wasn't exactly operating as designed. Aside from the fact that Gat's crew had evidently used part of the system to stash their food, there was the little matter of raw effluent in the streets. "And how much service actually gets performed?" Rodney's breath hitched as the septic smell hit him again. At street level, the oil fire had actually masked the stench for a while, but down here it was another story.

"To allow the home of Dalera to fall into such a state is unconscionable," Yann spat.

The engineers rounded on him. "There were too few of us to more than maintain the water supply coming into the city."

"I do not blame you," Yann elaborated. "This is but further proof that the barbarians failed in their leadership. When this culling is passed, never again shall those who blaspheme against Dalera be allowed into our city, except to take temporary refuge from the Wraith."

Apparently speaking ill of the dead wasn't a concern around here. All Rodney could think was that he'd be damned before he got involved in sorting out this world's plumbing issues.

"The sewerage should be the least of our worries," grumbled another engineer, clutching a torch to light the increasingly claustrophobic passages. "The blackwater has discouraged the

Wraith, but it has also made its way into every pump in the city. For the foreseeable future, freshwater will have to be brought in from Nemst."

Yet another shortcoming in Dalera's design, to Rodney's way of thinking. If the water intakes had only been placed at different levels in the Channels, the 'blackwater' problem would have been entirely avoided. Of course, it was probable that Dalera had never envisioned this particular situation. "Assuming that there will be a foreseeable future," he muttered, sidestepping a putrid mess that, he was certain, had passed through someone's intestines.

The engineer's complaints continued. Too tired to voice any kind of objection, Rodney concentrated on watching his step, but after a while the droning conversation had a soporific effect. He began to wonder if he was sleepwalking through a particularly tedious nightmare involving children and alimentary canals.

"Agh!" The engineer kicked out at a rat-sized animal. With a flash of green fur, the creature scuttled down a side tunnel.

One of the children, whom Rodney conceded had been unnaturally quiet during this particular part of their excursion, bent low to follow.

"What are you doing?" Rodney snapped, repulsed by the frothy muck splashing onto his boots.

"This way," the engineer said, getting down on all fours in the sludge and following her.

"What? Are you kidding me?" He could already feel himself hyperventilating. Not a pleasant thought, because it meant that he was inhaling even more of the rank air than previously.

"The passage is short, and leads directly outside."

The wound on Rodney's arm began to ache. He'd forgotten about it during his immersion in the oil, but now every injury he'd sustained, from the goose egg-sized lump on his head to the splinters in his fingers, throbbed unmercifully. Hell, in the last week he'd fallen into a waste tank and swum through a river of oil. What were a few rat droppings, a little stagnant…water…and a very, very tight black hole?

Reluctantly crouching on all fours, he pretended to ignore

the slimy sensation beneath his hands, squeezed his eyes shut, thought of wide-open meadows, and followed. Spurred on by the brush of a breeze against his cheek, he increased his pace, as much as that was possible when crawling. Of course, nobody had considered warning him that the tunnel came to an end at least two feet above ground level, a fact that resulted in him tumbling down a sand dune and into a shallow pool of sludge.

The children, naturally, found this highly entertaining. Rodney was slightly mollified by the fact that Yann followed suit, and arrived in the mess face-down.

By the time Rodney had managed to scrub off the worst of the filth in the questionably cleaner sand, the engineers had fastened the thick rope to the end of the boom and were easing it out into the channel. He suffered a moment's panic because, unlike polypropylene, the fibrous braid was not entirely buoyant. However, it was soon apparent that, while the rope sunk beneath the oil, it floated on the water. This proved to be ideal, and within a surprisingly short space of time they had ascertained the exact amount they needed to adjust the length of the rope and, hence, the shape of the boom, in order to control the volume of oil flowing down both channels.

While all of that was gratifying, it also meant that he had endured these past hours for absolutely no reason. He could have been lying down in a nice warm bed someplace, sleeping. Preferably after a hot meal. Which reminded him that he wasn't entirely certain when he'd last eaten, and that his blood sugar was unquestionably approaching dangerously low levels.

While the engineers and warriors worked out a system of signals with the buglers, Rodney made himself moderately comfortable on the oily beach and reached into his pocket for a powerbar. He'd chewed through almost the entire thing before he realized that the children were clustered around him, staring at him. Okay, he couldn't state with unqualified certainty that they were all staring, because half of them were in shadow, but he could feel their eyes boring into him — or maybe it was the powerbar.

"What?" he demanded around a mouthful. "Am I the only

one who thought to bring some food?"

Their gazes remained fixed and a little hollow. Comprehension, when it finally came, hit him hard and turned the food to stone in his stomach. Not one of the children had an ounce of fat anywhere on them. Images of the squalid conditions in the Citadel, the bodies discarded like garbage, assaulted him.

Rodney's initial indignation about the Daleran culture had been largely theoretical. But that recollection, and the expression on the children's faces, now drove home an unexpected insight. His own childhood, while less than ideal, had at least come with parents, food and a roof over his head. "You shouldn't be here," he said quietly, without the annoyance of his earlier brush-off. "I mean, you're *kids* — you should be in bed. Where are your parents?"

The children traded tentative, sorrowful glances that sliced into his soul. He never should have asked. None of them had parents, or beds. Their village had surely been destroyed by now.

"Who's going to look after you?" A delayed realization had him backpedaling almost before the words were out of his mouth. "I'm not volunteering, mind you. I just..."

"Peryn is a Gene," ventured the little girl, the quiet one. "He has promised to look out for us."

Well, that was something, even if it was depressingly little. And it wouldn't matter much if they didn't hold off the Wraith. Every muscle in his body was begging to lie down on the beach and sleep, but Rodney pushed himself up and nodded toward Yann and one of the engineers. Together with the children and the buglers, they trudged back up the passageway.

Even before they emerged from the tunnel, they could hear the sounds of utter pandemonium. A street battle had gotten underway in their absence. The incipient panic, which Rodney had been keeping just barely contained since landing this role in *Survivor Dalera,* instantly escalated to an entirely new level.

The townspeople, along with many of the warriors who had been *their* enemy just twenty-four hours previously, were engaged in vicious hand-to-hand combat with the Wraith. How the hell had the creatures managed to get inside the Citadel? And why were so many people fighting? "Aren't they supposed to have evacuated to higher ground?" he called to Yann. And right at that moment, he didn't care much that his voice had cracked.

"They have no choice!" Yann declared. "*We* have no choice. We fight and die, or we cower and die!" He ran into the throng, battleaxe in hand, apparently determined to slog it out until the bitter end. Noble of him, to be sure, but not exactly what Rodney had in mind.

Swept up in the crowd, he dodged and ducked, weaving his way through axe-wielding men and warriors alike. Even a few women, their faces contorted with rage, were getting the drop on the Wraith swarming out of the transport near the West Bridge—a fact that answered his earlier question and chilled him to the core.

Forgetting the weapon strapped to his hip, Rodney desperately tried to work his way against the crowd, but he was forced along with the throng. He stumbled and was elbowed aside, landing heavily against a set of steps. The pounding in his skull double-timed it, setting up a jarring cadence that seemed out of synch with the throbbing wound on his arm. Then he lifted his head and realized that the fall had actually managed to pull him out of the mass of humanity. Scrambling up a few more steps to see above the chaos, he turned—and saw inside the opening doors of the transport. While Wraith poured out, into the gingery light cast by the burning river, he caught a glimpse of a familiar blond head: Peryn. The boy's face was bruised and bloodied, and he looked like a rag doll in the grip of a Wraith.

The idea that he'd predicted the Wraith's tactics so accurately was more than a little disturbing to Rodney. Ford and Teyla would have done everything in their power to protect Peryn, which made the boy's capture a near-certain sign that they both were now dead.

By the look of things, the Wraith's fury at having been thwarted had overwhelmed their interest in taking prisoners. They were storming up and out of the transport in a bloody rampage. While most were intent on moving uphill in the direction of the now burned out Enclave, one group had veered toward West Bridge. Once in Wraith hands, the weir would likely be lowered, allowing the fire to spread upstream. This was no longer a culling; it was annihilation.

Sickened by the carnage and frozen with despair, Rodney thought again of his teammates. Ford and Teyla had thrown themselves into defending these people and had paid the price for it. By now Major Sheppard probably was also dead, thanks to that quack healer. When the Marines came looking for them, the Wraith would obliterate the jumpers the moment they came through the 'gate.

Rodney was completely, utterly alone. Alone, and about to become Wraithmeat.

It seemed so incredibly wasteful that he should die like this. There was so much he had yet to contribute to the galaxy, either this one or his own. All his work, all the half-finished theories, cut short by this insanity.

Something grabbed his ankle, and pulled him off his feet. He looked up into the grotesque mask of a huge Wraith. Closing his eyes, he whispered, "I'm sorry, Elizabeth."

Waking to a foul smell, Aiden battled the telltale after-effects of being hit with a Wraith stunner. Which was kind of weird. He hadn't been expecting to wake at all, or at least not in any sort of condition that didn't come with retirement benefits.

"Lieutenant Ford."

Determinedly pushing aside the grating pins and needles sensation, Aiden looked around in the darkness. "Teyla? What happened? Where are we?" He tried to move, but realized he was wrapped in some sort of bandages, or netting maybe, which partially covered his mouth.

A sense of revulsion stronger than anything he'd ever experienced hit him like a physical blow. He was wrapped in a Wraith cocoon.

"Here, to your left. I believe we are still inside the inn of the village into which we transported."

Anger, all of it directed squarely at himself, quickly replaced Aiden's loathing. "Where's everyone else?" He tried moving his face up and down to dislodge the stuff.

There was silence for a moment, then Teyla replied, "I believe that Peryn at least is still alive."

The sticky bonds were more elastic than he'd first thought, and he managed to get his nose and mouth clear. Maybe the Wraith that had wrapped him hadn't been focused on the job. There was a lot going on, after all. "How do you know?" He tried shifting his hands around to tear through the binding. Not so easy. But then, he conceded that the Wraith had had at least ten thousand years to perfect their methods of storing food supplies.

"I was not rendered entirely unconscious by their stunners."

Possibly it was the darkness, or his own sense of failure in carrying out what should have been a straightforward reconnaissance mission, but Aiden was sure that he could hear self-recrimination in Teyla's voice. McKay's parting shot now hit him, and he said, "You think they used Peryn to transport into the Citadel?" So why were he and Teyla still in one piece? Twisting his hands around, he was determined to get free. No way was he letting his mission turn into a complete snafu.

"Yes, but not immediately. I am not entirely certain of what occurred, but I sensed...confusion. I believe that the Wraith were uncertain which of us was responsible for operating the transport."

"So they kept us alive just in case." The residual stickiness that had plagued Aiden's senses was clearing, and he could make out a pallid shape in the direction of Teyla's voice. She was only a few feet away. "What about—?" He didn't need to finish the sentence. The stark light cast by the overhead planets shone through the open windows of the inn. He spotted four desiccated bodies, slumped against one wall. Their chest armor had been ripped off and tossed in a separate pile — which Teyla, or the cocooned shape of Teyla, was currently up against.

Rocking back and forth in an attempt to loosen the rubbery netting, Aiden bumped into her.

"Do not waste your energy, Lieutenant. You will not escape the bindings so easily."

"Well, I'm not just going to lie here and wait for more Wraith to turn up," he retorted. "Unless you can pull another one of those Houdini tricks of yours."

"If you will hold still," she said with a touch of exasperation, "I have located a shard of metal. But I can only grasp it with my mouth."

Several minutes passed while he felt Teyla squirming beside him, and then abruptly, he felt a hole in the netting large enough to stick his hand through. That gave him sufficient leverage to tear away more of the binding until he could reach his knife and cut away the rest.

Once Teyla was free, Aiden searched the inn for their packs and weapons. He barely glanced at the dead men on the floor, but his teammate seemed to be taking an unhealthy interest in them. Although two of them were the warriors who had stuck with Teyla from the start, it wasn't like the Athosian to be morbid, so he said, "It's not your fault that they're dead. It could just as easily have been you and me lying there."

"That is what disturbs me. Why did they let us live, and instead feed on these men?"

"You said it yourself." Aiden found his P-90 and checked the weapon. He'd fired several rounds into the nearest Wraith before being hit with the stunner. "They must have thought that we would be more useful to them alive, at least for now. Major Sheppard said that when he was held captive by the Wraith, they tried to pull something from his mind."

Teyla rounded on her heel and stared at him. "What did you say?"

Not sure what button he'd just pressed, Aiden shrugged. "Some sort of interrogation, I guess. Although I can't say I believe in the mind reading thing, that queen or caretaker or whatever she was sure did something to the Major on the hive ship. The guys who captured us were probably ordered to keep us on ice until someone up the chain of command could get here."

"And leave us unguarded?"

"Hey, I'm not the Wraith expert around here. That's your department." He glanced through the window and up at the sky. "All I do know is that we've got about six hours until dawn. And since we're not going to be able to get back into the Citadel without Peryn, I say we carry out the original mission, and then find some other way back inside."

Teyla's eyes dropped. "Perhaps not."

Following the direction of her gaze, Aiden swore. Outside, dozens, maybe hundreds of Wraith were making a beeline for the inn. "Is there a back way out of this place?" Before he'd even gotten the words out of his mouth, a light from behind signaled the returning transport.

Nowhere to run, nowhere to hide. Outside, the crunch of boots grew louder. Beside him, Teyla lifted her P-90 and readied her aim at the opening transport doors. This time, he doubted that the Wraith would bother to gift-wrap them before feeding.

CHAPTER TWENTY

The Wraith's head rolled off its shoulders. Rodney blinked, staring in fascination. Then the torso collapsed on him and something gushed out over his face and eyes. Unable to cry out in revulsion, simply because the sheer weight of the thing had driven all the air from his lungs, he discovered a reserve of strength that he hadn't believed possible and shoved the creature off himself.

"Oh…*God*!" The stench of whatever passed for blood was, as incredible as it seemed, actually worse than anything he had so far encountered.

Before he could even begin to get his bearings, his shoulder was more or less wrenched from its socket by someone hauling him further up the stairs. Multiple someones, more accurately. Not content with extending the length of his arm by several inches, a bunch of other hands began pushing at his legs, urging him to climb higher and yelling something that sounded like, "This way!"

Suddenly he found himself standing on a balcony or porch, surrounded by the children, Yann, and the engineer who had returned with them. Everyone was jabbering at once, asking him inane questions about what they could do next.

How the hell was he supposed to know? While they stood there, another gang of Wraith poured up and out of the transport. Most were swarming uphill; however, a group broke off and headed around the fountain in the center of the square and toward the bridge. The Dalerans had somehow managed to defend the entrance to the bridge, but at this rate, it was only a matter of time before they were overrun.

The blood from the felled Wraith dripped into Rodney's eyes. Yelling in frustration and disgust, he rubbed the heels of his hands across his face, trying to wipe the stuff away. "Precisely how am I supposed to magically ascertain what to do when I can't even see? Hasn't anyone got any water in this place?"

A bubble of stunned silence seemed to encapsulate the group. Then the little girl tugged at his shirt. He looked down at her and snapped, "What?"

"The wells are all dry. Now there is only blackwater."

And that, combined with the children's expressions, their trust and faith in him, suddenly pulled Rodney from his funk. They needed him; *everyone* needed him. Maybe Ford and Teyla were dead, but the Major might only have a headache. And what about Atlantis? Zelenka simply wasn't capable of looking after things as well as Rodney. Okay, so maybe Zelenka was capable, but it would give the Czech scientist entirely too much satisfaction to know that Rodney had been unable to solve what amounted to a relatively straightforward problem. He peered at the transport. "Am I imagining things, or is that set slightly downhill from the square?"

"The transport was built as such so that barrels and carts could readily be moved from the bridge and inside."

"Of course it was." His mind already taking two steps at a time, Rodney turned to the engineer. "Where's the mechanism that controls the water supply to that fountain?"

"There, in the pump-house by the bridge." The man pointed to a huge metal door set in the wall on the far side of the square, directly opposite the transport. "All major water pumps are located by the channels."

Where else would you have a water pump? Perfect. Just perfect. All they had to do was negotiate a path through a horde of incoming Wraith hell-bent on capturing the bridge. No problem. Swallowing back his fear, he began to ask if there was another way to the pump-house, but Yann had already divined his intention. "You mean to burn the transport!"

"Yes, of course, but destroying one transport would only force the Wraith to divert their invasion to elsewhere in the Citadel. The idea is to get the oil into the transport *before* igniting it. Which means waiting until the doors open..." His words trailed off as the implications of that planned action hit home.

The Wraith had control of the transports only because they had Peryn. Rescuing the kid was out of the question; there was no way anyone, including the indomitable and surprisingly quick-witted Major, could pull that off. In order to save the Citadel, they — *he* — would have to incinerate the boy along with the arriving Wraith.

Rodney's throat tightened and his hands knotted into involuntary fists. The children were staring at him, as if they could read his thoughts. He wanted to say something, to explain that this was just how it had to be, but the engineer had turned to run down the steps.

"There is a passage beneath us," the man said over his shoulder, his eyes taking in Yann.

More tunnels. Wonderful. But at least this one was short and almost tall enough for Rodney to stand without damaging yet more vertebrae.

On the way, they stopped at a primitive pipe system, and the engineer turned a series of cocks and handles. "This will prevent the blackwater that is pumped into the fountain from draining through the outlets. Instead, it will quickly overflow onto the square."

"And down toward the transport? You're sure about that?" Rodney demanded.

Bobbing his head as he trotted along, the engineer replied, "It has nowhere else to flow, except perhaps the storage houses behind."

"Which contain what exactly? The last thing we need is a Pyrrhic victory."

"Blackpowder," Yann replied.

"Oh, well, that's just *great*!" Rodney stumbled to a halt. "You didn't think to mention that sooner?" Saved from the Wraith only to have their entire civilization destroyed by the resulting firestorm. Then again— "How much blackpowder?"

"Only a few barrels. And all of the nearby structures are stone," Yann said, urging Rodney to keep moving. "It is one law that no one disobeys, for all understand the damage just one measure of blackpowder can do."

The tunnel abruptly opened out into a room that, while large, was crammed with hand-operated machinery. Rodney could tell at a glance what the oversized gears, chains and pulleys controlled. "The portcullis and weir," the engineer provided unnecessarily, leading them up a set of steps to ground level.

Which naturally made the building a prime target. Once the portcullis was open, the Wraith had free entry into the Citadel. Was it his imagination, or were those Wraith claws he could hear pounding at the gates?

The thick, iron doors burst open wide, but before he could feel more than an additional spike in his permanently elevated sense of incipient panic, several trainee warriors staggered inside, along with a dozen injured combatants. The noise of the battle outside wasn't exactly offering Rodney inspiration. Ignoring the new arrivals, he demanded, "The pumps?"

"You can observe from up there." The engineer pointed to an area at the top of another set of steps. Presumably they led to one of the Stations that serviced the mechanism attached to the portcullis. Leaving Yann and the children to deal with wounded, Rodney ran up the rough stairs and stared out through a wide gap in the stonework.

Although he was separated from the blazing channel by a thick wall, the heat was nevertheless rolling across the square in waves. The air between him and the battle on the streets below seemed to jump and dance in the sienna light. Apparently the engineer hadn't needed to do much to get the pumps operational. From the fountain in the center of the courtyard gushed a massive volume of oil. Seconds later, a nearby bugler blew a series of notes.

Rodney fingered his weapon. By the light of the outside fire, he could clearly see the transport doors. He'd heard about what Sheppard had done to — or perhaps for — Colonel Sumner. Maybe when he got back to Atlantis he should actually learn to shoot the gun at something more than a paper target. Not that he particularly wanted to use a gun at all, but there were some circumstances in which he conceded that it could prove necessary. Of course, whether he'd actually be capable of putting a bullet through a child's head—

"Buglers are spreading the word," Yann announced, joining him. "Everyone who can do so will evacuate the area around the transport and storehouses, while the warriors will stay and fight until the last."

Wincing, Rodney nodded. Whatever antiquated system the Dalerans employed to keep the pumps operational was now working overtime. Oil spilled from the small pond at the base of the fountain and onto the ground. While the first few rivulets were diverted by bodies, the direction of flow was definitely toward the transport—which had just opened to reveal yet more incoming Wraith. He could hear the quaver in Yann's voice as the man said, "I do not know for how long the warriors will be able to hold them."

Rodney glanced back at Yann, and noticed that he was carrying a warrior's bola. In the square, attackers and defenders alike were slipping and skidding through the oil. Using his field glasses, Rodney noted that many of the Wraith had a somewhat singed look. Eyes flashing in the light of the Channel fire, they now diverted their efforts from merely random havoc, destruction, and a clear desire to break into the pump-house to getting well clear of the cascading oil. They had obviously intuited what was coming.

The doors of the transport closed before any oil could flow inside, which Rodney counted as a good thing. The next group of inbound Wraith wouldn't have a clue what was waiting for them. Moments later, the entire area around the low-lying transport began filling with oil.

Yann pulled a metallic stick from his pocket. With a thin-lipped grin at Rodney, he said, "Wraithcraft." The object, not unlike that which Rodney had seen Teyla and several Athosians use, sent a spidery red beam at the bola's balls. The wadding immediately ignited. Yann waited until both balls were burning well before swinging the weapon slowly around his head.

The thumps on the iron doors below increased, and the children clambered up the steps. This time, their cries were genuine. Rodney had no idea why they were running to him. He couldn't offer them any protection, and even if this did work, there was no guarantee that the Wraith now swarming across the square wouldn't overrun them.

"Get back!" Yann yelled at the children. "Hide your faces behind the walls. When the blackpowder blows, it may well destroy this part of the bridge."

Teyla did not hesitate. Even so, Lieutenant Ford proved somewhat faster in firing his weapon at the solitary Wraith emerging from the transport and into the inn.

Seemingly oblivious to its wounds, the Wraith released his grip on Peryn and charged them. Although Teyla could not make out her teammate's words, she understood the Lieutenant's intent. Quickly circling the Wraith, she darted into the transport, ducking low to avoid the hail of bullets now punching through their attacker's head.

Face bleeding from a deep slice along his cheek, Peryn pulled himself to his feet and lunged at the panel inside the transport. Teyla cried out to wait, but Lieutenant Ford was on her heels, shouting for Peryn to close the doors. A quick glance out, and she saw the wounded Wraith harshly knocked aside by those now storming into the inn. Before she could direct him to do otherwise, Peryn stabbed at the light on the panel, and the doors opened to the sight of a tremendous battle — and a gush of blackwater.

"That won't happen," Rodney declared confidently. "A blast through the air is a woefully inefficient coupling mechanism against heavy stonework — *Now*!" he yelled at Yann. Across the square, several lights indicated that the transport was opening. Calling downstairs, he added, "Stop pumping and close off the valves!"

The heavy bola flew from Yann's grasp, a pinwheel of flame arcing across the heads of the combatants. Rodney noticed that the transport doors folded back — to reveal only three people, two of whom were knocked off their feet by the flood of oil. The flaming bola landed with a gut-punching *whoomp* in the oil-filled fountain. The last thing that he saw before fire engulfed the transport was the surprised look on Teyla's face.

"*No!*" The cry ripped uselessly from his throat and spilled out into the searing wave of heat. Something grabbed him by the jacket and roughly jerked him to the floor, a fraction of a second before a massive explosion sent a shudder through the stone bridge and spattered them with chunks of debris.

Jerking himself free of the children's hands, Rodney grasped the edge of the window and peered out. It took several minutes before the smoke cleared enough to see the substantial crater where the transport and adjoining storehouse had once been.

The pain in Rodney's throat, and indeed all of his many injuries, evaporated in the face of this new reality. He'd blown things up before. He was incredibly good at blowing things up. That there might have been people in those things — buildings, aircraft and whatever else the Air Force had seen fit to destroy — could be dismissed because they had been The Enemy. That's the way it was in war. Things got broken, and blown up, and casualties resulted.

But not your...friends. You didn't blow up your friends. *Well done, McKay.*

His breath hitched and his eyes stung and there seemed to be a great deal of moisture on his cheeks. The sound of someone sobbing seemed unreasonably loud in the silence. Rodney was only grateful that it wasn't coming from him, but from one of the children. What little consolation he could draw from the situation was that being blown up had provided a more humane death than being trapped inside a room of burning oil.

Yann grasped his shoulder. "The Wraith may have captured more Genes and entered the Citadel through other transports."

Swallowing, Rodney nodded. "We need to get back to the Command Center and assess the situation." Which, loosely translated, meant that he hoped the Major was finally awake. Between the clouds of smoke, he noticed, the sky was definitely getting lighter.

CHAPTER TWENTY-ONE

Lisera was drying Major Sheppard's feet with a soft cloth when she felt him move.

"Cut it out," he mumbled, batting away the object that Dr McKay had gruffly informed her was a pen flashlight. The Major's face expressed his displeasure and pain.

"Didn't know you were awake." His face expressing extreme relief, McKay pulled the flashlight aside. "How's the head?"

Only half listening to the conversation between the visitors from Atlantis, Lisera sat back. While their arrival had altered her life in wondrous ways, the world was still fraught with dangers and death. Those with her in the Station now protected her from the likes of Balzar, but only because their survival depended on her newfound abilities. She felt their resentment and began to understand why the Chosen had retreated to the Enclave.

She glanced at Yann, who was quietly talking in the corner to the other children from Quickweed Lake, trying to console them over the death of Peryn.

When learning earlier of the failed ambush at the Lake, Lisera had been surprised to find herself grieving for the young merchant. While they now called themselves Genes, like her, Yann was nonetheless the blessed of Dalera, chosen to protect her people. Even Aiden had not been of such status. Had he not gone against the wishes of Dr McKay, Peryn would not have been captured and the attack at North Bridge would never have resulted. Although she could not find it in her heart to like Dr McKay, she did not blame him for the deaths of Peryn, Aiden, and Teyla. As a Gene, she knew now that choices had to be made, often painful ones. In order to save the Citadel, Dr McKay could not have acted any differently.

"...most likely as a result of that concoction served up by the local Juju man," McKay was saying. "Fortunately, you have a particularly thick skull. However, the general consensus is that you also have a concussion."

"I'll be fine. Out of curiosity, what the hell hit me?" The Major eased himself upright, wincing with each movement.

Looking discomfited, Dr McKay replied, "How was I to know that whoever makes the ropes around here has lousy quality control? Anyway, as I said before, you're heavier than you look. Combined with the sucking potential of that tar, I suppose it was—"

"Sucking potential?" Major Sheppard paused in his movements and regarded Dr McKay.

The scientist's expression flattened and he replied, "In your current state, I didn't want to confuse you with big words like 'viscosity'."

"What do you mean, my current state?" The covering on Major Sheppard's body slipped low, and, realizing he was naked beneath, he grabbed the edges. "What the...?" In an effort to clear his eyes, he opened and closed them several times.

Lisera stood and placed a cloth with warm soapwater into the Major's hands. "Here, use this to wash the oil from your eyes."

Now that the Major was awake, Yann, trailed by the children, came to join them.

"Oil?" The Major sat back and brought the cloth to his face.

"We used vegetable oil to remove the tar," she explained. "But I fear your fine uniform is no longer useable." She glanced at the pile of blackened clothes on the floor.

"This is all adorably domestic." Dr McKay crossed his arms and glared at her. "But we've got a few pressing issues to discuss, so if you will excuse us—"

"Hold up, Rodney. How long have I been out?"

Under Major Sheppard's gaze, Lisera replied, "It is dawn. You have slept through the night."

"Okay." Still attempting to focus, he asked Dr McKay, "What's happening?"

"The Wraith mounted an assault from the south. Fortunately," Dr McKay added with an expression Lisera had grown to dislike, "I had the foresight to maintain a reserve of oil in the eastern end of South Channel for just such an eventuality. We upped the volume and set it alight."

"You mean the Wraith are still hanging around? Haven't they already taken hundreds of people from the outlying villages?"

"Several thousand, including the far-flung barbarian towns," Yann corrected. "I have spoken to many Genes. They tell of villages empty of life, some destroyed before the arrival of the transport."

Behind him, the children nodded in sage agreement. None shed tears, for the horrors they had witnessed had withered their capacity to do so.

"Since when have those been operating again?" McKay snapped at Yann. "Didn't we definitively establish that using the transports outside of the Citadel while the Wraith are attacking is a huge mistake?"

A knowing smile crossed Yann's face. "Not if each transport is filled with armed warriors, and the Gene within does *not* release his Shield before establishing the area is safe."

"This is hardly a suitable time to get cocky!"

Lisera did not wish to speak out of turn, but with a pacifying gesture toward both men, she attempted to redirect the conversation. "Yann and Dr McKay heroically defended against a Wraith invasion at North Bridge."

Looking momentarily pleased with himself, Dr McKay said, "Yes, I suppose it was rather heroic, wasn't it?" But the pride fell from his voice even as he spoke, and his eyes were masked by sorrow.

Major Sheppard's gaze quickly took in the room. "Where are Ford and Teyla?"

Swallowing once, Dr McKay avoided the Major's piercing look. "If the Lieutenant hadn't been obstinate enough to ignore my warning about ill-conceived reconnaissance missions —"

"McKay! Where *are* they?"

When Dr McKay explained what had transpired during the evening, the Major was silent for a long moment, his expression revealing little. Although his gaze was laden with repressed grief, his only reply was, "After all that, the Wraith are *still* attacking?" He placed the cloth on a side table, and went to toss back the cover, but paused.

As a Chosen — this new term, Gene, did not seem fitting — Lisera was now a leader of her people, and she was curious. "The teaching windows tell us that — "

Dr McKay waved his hand dismissively. "Parables for the illiterate. The Ancient texts explained that the length of the sieges varied, depending on how many generations passed between culls." He shared a look with Major Sheppard; a secret, perhaps, one that Lisera could not divine.

A gentle touch on her arm drew her attention to Yann. "Perhaps it would be best if you take the young ones to the top of the Station where they may find something to eat."

The children were also beginning to crowd around the bed. Although she would have preferred to stay, Lisera sensed the Major's unease and recalled Dr McKay's earlier comment about clothing. She decided to accept Yann's counsel and gestured to the young ones, guiding them out of the room. There was much still for these Chosen to do, and many things still uncertain.

Having learned the hard way once or twice that a spare uniform could come in handy, John was satisfied that his practice of stashing one in his pack had once again paid off. He leaned down to secure his not-quite-ruined leg holster and immediately reconsidered the motion as a rush of nausea sideswiped him. Whether it was from the knock on the head or the figurative sucker punch of what he'd just learned, he didn't know, and wasn't sure he wanted to.

They were your people, under your command. Not just your friends but your responsibility as well. And this time, there was no question of maybe. McKay and Yann had seen the transport explode.

He'd be able to function, even if he couldn't remember the last time he'd felt this lousy. Someone had bandaged his head and he'd fumbled through the medical pack until he found some Tylenol but he would have sold his soul for an ice pack. Even so, he recognized that he ought to be grateful for escaping asphyxiation.

Teyla and Ford… He swallowed, trying to control the churning in his stomach. He'd deal with their loss in his own way, the only way he knew. Burying grief wasn't terribly beneficial to one's mental health, but it would get him through the day. It always had before.

Right now, he had to concern himself with those who were still alive. Atlantis would be sending the cavalry by nightfall, and he didn't want Markham and Stackhouse's teams having to contend with a Wraith armada.

What the hell was driving the Wraith to mount a ground assault on a highly defensible Citadel, when they'd already culled thousands? Sure, maybe they had woken early and were a little on the hungry side, but from what he'd seen thus far in the Pegasus Galaxy, few people had the capacity to fight back. And any who did got themselves annihilated. By inflicting too many casualties on the Wraith, the Dalerans were just asking for one of those hive ships to start firing on the Citadel. The network of Shields might knock out most weapons, but not all. Something else was going on here. "Rodney, I need more to go on. Explain to me the exact sequence of the Wraith attacks."

When the scientist had finished, John's first instinct was to lay into him for failing to see the obvious, but the look of grief and desperation in McKay's eyes stopped him. The man wasn't a military tactician. Still, John was too frayed to keep the edge out of his voice when he said, "It didn't occur to you that the Wraith might have *lured* you into releasing more oil into South Channel and igniting it?"

"What are you talking about? Why…" Rodney's voice trailed off and his eyes opened wide with comprehension. "Of course! Damn it!" Balling his fists in frustration, he ranted, "I was working through all this earlier and wanted to ask you about why they'd fall for the same trap twice. Then that voodoo-looking healer insisted on knocking you out, and—just…*Damn* it!"

Looking confused, Yann asked, "Why would the Wraith wish to do such a thing?"

"To force the population of the Citadel to evacuate," John

replied, walking across to the chart table. Each step sent a stabbing pain through the top of his head. Hoping no one would notice that he needed the support in order to keep standing, he placed his hands on the edge of the table and examined the large animal hide map. The smell of the thing normally wouldn't have bothered him, but at the moment there weren't really any sensations that didn't bother him.

"Evacuate where?" Yann moved to join him. The merchant's face fell the moment the words were out of his mouth. "Into the unprotected villages! But then why have the Wraith themselves not set fire to the oil that is flowing from Black Hill?"

"As I have explained repeatedly to any number of engineers," Rodney retorted impatiently, "this particular brand of crude oil needs to be several millimeters thick in order to ignite. Only by backing it up against a raised weir did we have sufficient volume to make that work. Having said that, once ignited, by lowering the weirs, the flames traveled upstream faster than the oil could move down. The converse also applies. Backing up the oil flow again behind raised weirs and dams will starve the fires downstream and extinguish them."

"Okay, maybe we should start doing just that." John combed through the maps, trying to find a more detailed plan of the Enclave. "You said the Wraith only invaded the Citadel via the transport at North Bridge?"

His forehead creasing in thought, Rodney replied, "I had assumed that they wanted to open the portcullis protecting the bridge, but in fact they wanted to lower the weir, which would have allowed the fire to spread all the way up to Black Hill."

Yann looked doubtful. "While it is true that some of the Wraith attempted to capture the bridge, most made for the Enclave."

Which confirmed what John was beginning to suspect. The Wraith wanted to flush people out of the Citadel, but having captured a Gene, they'd also been trying to get to the Enclave. Maybe Kesun hadn't been lying about only the Chosen being able to enter the Enclave — the true Enclave, not the temple that was now a burned-out hulk.

Rodney's fingers traced sight lines across the map of the

Citadel. Abruptly they stopped. "Oh, you have *got* to be kidding me…" He snatched up the map and brandished it front of John's face. "I can't believe I didn't see it before. The distribution of the Chosen's homes, the Stations, isn't random. They form a power grid!"

Despite the medication, John was starting to wonder if it was physiologically possible for his head to explode. "I think we were starting to get that, Rodney, thanks."

"Yes, but what you didn't get, and I didn't understand until now because the Ancient writings — Dalera's writings, presumably — weren't as explicit as they should have been, was that when every one of these Stations has a Gene in residence, the grid itself acts as a gigantic capacitor."

"To power what? The Shields?"

"No, no, no, no, no!" Oddly, Rodney's jerky dance of barely-contained enthusiasm wasn't visibly different from his mid-panic attack look. "A weapon!"

"That is why so many at North Bridge fought the Wraith," Yann said, turning to Rodney. "Although the Chosen had lost the respect of many, with the return of the Wraith and your arrival from Atlantis, all realized that Dalera's sacred weapon is not a myth. It must be protected at all costs."

Warriors and city officials were now crowding around the table, talking about the weapon. Naturally, no one had ever seen it because it was inside the Enclave, but all of them were convinced it existed.

"Why *is* it that nobody thinks to mention little details like this earlier?" Rodney's face had turned an entertaining puce, but then it shifted, chameleon-like, to a shade that John recognized as ecstatic pink. "That's it! My God, that's incredible!" declared his teammate. "Dalera didn't have a ZPM, so she figured out how to power a weapon via this grid!"

"Okay," John said, attempting to keep himself from swaying. "That's good. But it doesn't explain why the Wraith are trying to get to it — assuming that's their intention. They can't use it."

"Peryn probably could have," Rodney said, his voice contemplative. "He was a natural Gene carrier."

This still wasn't adding up. "So the Wraith figured on what? Grabbing themselves what would have to be a relatively low-tech weapon dependent on someone with the ATA gene to operate?"

"And thus I remind you that the Wraith have apparently succeeded in constructing—what was the last count? Sixty, I believe?—hive ships doubtless powered by something similar to a ZPM. Sadly, they weren't born yesterday. Given their level of technology, they could conceivably reverse-engineer any weapon. Or at least, they must think that they can. With an ATA gene bearer held prisoner—"

He didn't have to explain further. Turning to Yann, John asked, "Have all of the outlying villages now been evacuated?"

"Yes. And amongst the refugees more and more Genes are being discovered. They are now returning to the villages so that they may use the Shields in such a way that it confuses the Wraith."

Okay. That was something to work with. "Order all of the Genes to get back here, immediately. If McKay is right—"

"Of course I'm right!"

"—we need to get every one of the Stations manned to slot into this weapon's grid. Equally importantly, if just one Gene is captured by a Wraith, we could be in serious trouble."

Yann's eyes widened, and he turned and began issuing orders to the warriors.

"We have to get to the Enclave," Rodney declared, snatching up his pack. "Although the temple or whatever it was has been destroyed, despite what I said to Lisera earlier, the teaching windows in Sanctuary Hall might offer a clue as to the exact location of this weapon." He strode determinedly to the door, speaking as he went.

"Just hang on a minute." John pulled on his own pack and picked up his P-90, pleased to see that it had been cleaned and loaded. Ford must have... *Damn*. Quickly heading off that thought before it could lead somewhere he wasn't prepared to go, he followed McKay out and down the stairs. "What exactly are you proposing?" He paused when they reached the bottom of

the steps. Affixing a contemplative look on his face would hopefully mask the fact that he could barely see through the hammering
in his skull. Christ, but concussions sucked. "Wouldn't it be
better if we go straight to the Enclave?"

"And spend hours sifting through charcoal? The teaching
windows are our best option." He shot a narrow-eyed look at
John. "You should wait here."

"Who, me?" John smiled and swallowed back the almost
overwhelming need to throw up. "Just a little headache. All I
need is some fresh air."

Outside, the light was dim, the air hazy and anything but
fresh. Regretting the action almost before he took it, John set as
brisk a pace as he could manage. Although most of the smoke
was blowing away from the Citadel, that wouldn't last long if
the Wraith decided to take matters into their own hands and
light a few incendiary weapons over Black Hill.

Swept off her feet, Teyla had managed to catch sight of two
things simultaneously. One had been the face of Dr McKay, who
appeared to have been shouting at someone, and the other had
been a wall of flames screaming toward them atop the wave of
oil.

Peryn's reflexes had fortunately remained sharp, and he'd
slapped his hand down on a button before the doors were fully
open. A wall of heat had struck, but the doors had kept the fire
itself at bay.

"They'll need reinforcements!" Aiden declared instantly, trying, and failing, to stand in the swirling blackwater. "We need to
get back to the Command Center and find a bugler."

The transport opened into the remains of a building that had
recently been ravaged by fire. Weapon poised, Teyla stepped out
and looked around. The structure was too large to have been the
Sanctuary Hall, and the little she could see through the smoking
ruins indicated that they were still inside the Citadel. She turned
to Peryn. "Where have you taken us?"

Before he could respond, a tremendous, ground-shaking
explosion erupted from somewhere nearby. It was immediately

followed by a massive pall of gray smoke. Glass shards crunching underfoot, Teyla ran with Ford across to where a wall had stood until recently, and looked out.

"On second thought, maybe reinforcements won't be necessary," the Lieutenant offered when the worst of the smoke cleared.

It appeared that the transport they had most recently used at North Bridge was gone, along with a nearby building. Although she could not be certain from this angle, it seemed that the majority of the Wraith had been killed by the explosion. As she and Ford watched, the remaining Wraith were overrun by warriors and Dalerans arriving from adjacent streets.

Teyla noticed that Peryn had not followed her and Ford, but instead was still standing in the transport, staring at the residue of blackwater pooling at his feet. Returning to him, she said, "Peryn? What is it?"

He glanced up once, and in the light given off by the oil fire, she saw that his youthful face was pale and wracked with guilt. Quickly averting his gaze, he whispered, "I tried to fight them."

Understanding his dilemma, Teyla took Peryn's chin in her hand and lifted his face until their eyes met. "There is no shame in being captured."

"They were so strong!" Peryn's voice fractured, and he tried to stem his tears. "The Wraith... It was like he was inside my head, forcing me."

"Hey, it's not your fault, okay?" Lieutenant Ford clasped a hand on his shoulder. "You couldn't help what they did to you."

"I...I did not let them see this." Peryn wiped his eyes and pointed to a recess in the inside wall of the transport.

Teyla bent to look. "This is the panel the Major discovered soon after we arrived."

Ford walked back outside into the ruins and looked around. "This must be the Enclave. Or at least it *was* the Enclave. Not much left, now."

"Why did you bring us here, Peryn?" Teyla asked, following

the Lieutenant. The smell of burned remains was strong. While familiar to her, it was an odor that had, until recently, had been exclusively associated with the Wraith. Such a waste, that Dalerans should fight among each other.

"In my head…" The boy followed them, sniffing noisily. "I don't know. This place seemed important to them somehow, and they made it feel like it was important to me. That's how they tried to get me to come here."

His words disturbed Teyla in ways that she could not fully articulate, perhaps because they seemed connected to her ability to sense the Wraith. "Then you did well to conceal the fact."

Nodding in agreement, Lieutenant Ford moved out ahead of them. "Maybe we should take a look around before we report back."

During the walk to the Sanctuary Hall, John did in fact begin to feel better. The sight of crowded refugees filling the streets also helped, because their presence was a testimony to how many had been saved. Once inside, though, he began to realize that not everyone was quite so pleased. The place was filled not only with villagers but inhabitants of the Citadel, anxious to escape the worst excesses of those who roamed the lower levels of the city, pillaging and killing. The end of the Wraith siege wouldn't be the end of the Dalerans' battle.

An unexpected wave of regret struck John. Ushat would have made the Dalerans a decent leader — not just because he was a Gene, but also because he'd been an honorable man. His loss had left a vacuum in any potential leadership for these people. Worse, the muttered conversations made it clear that many viewed the ambush and overall defensive strategy as a failure. It sounded like a hell of a lot of more people had also been lost during the battle at North Bridge.

John recognized the deep lethargy that so easily infected the battle-weary. It was tough to avoid even when trained, and these people weren't. Few had had anything resembling sleep for days. He doubted the food situation was much better. While there were all those storage rooms that Gat had been filling, it would take time and organizational skills to properly distribute their contents. And although the Darts were no longer a constant threat, the unknown, unpredictable presence of the Wraith brought an air of uncertainty that permeated everything with a stench as perceptible as the oil fires.

"Why do you sit cowering in darkness?"

Yann's raised voice reverberated through John's head. He hadn't even noticed the merchant following them. It seemed that wherever they went, they attracted a train of guards. And was that a bunch of kids trying to hide behind their ever-present bugler?

"It matters not whether you transgressed in the past," Yann was saying to the crowds. "It matters not that you might once have blasphemed. For in these last days we have proven to the Wraith that we can stand together as one under Dalera's rule. And we have shown them that we cannot be vanquished."

Despite a clear lack of caffeine, Rodney was all but bouncing from foot to foot, drawing on his apparently endless reserve of spring-coiled energy. Just standing next to the scientist made John feel dizzy. Maybe Rodney was right. He should probably be lying down someplace. Fine — once they found the weapon, he'd take a seat and let the thing take care of their problems.

"When this is over," Yann continued, "we shall be as one, forged by the fires of battle — "

"C'mon, c'mon, c'mon!" Rodney said under his breath. "Save the hackneyed rhetoric for the polling booth."

"Polling booth?" John gave him a quizzical glance.

Rodney shrugged. "I took the opportunity to explain the basic principles of democracy."

"What opportunity was that?"

"When you were passed out." He peered into John's face, and appeared dissatisfied by what he saw. "Speaking of which, you really don't look good."

"Not trying to win a beauty pageant. Can we move on?"

Yann had stopped talking, and a few halfhearted cheers bounced off the walls.

"Don't let the somewhat pedestrian response bother you,"

Rodney assured Yann. "Once they get the hang of the idea—"

A sharp set of bugle notes interrupted him. Several women cried out in terror, and everyone began speaking at once.

"What?" John demanded.

Yann paled. "One of the scouting parties has not returned. It is feared that the Wraith have captured another Gene."

The words were barely out of his mouth when a brilliant ball of light burst overhead, and the entire Hall rattled and shook. Several teaching windows shattered and rained glass down onto the terrified refugees. John was busy fighting off the blinding jolt of pain that coursed through his already fragile brain as the compression wave from the explosion hit. For half a second, he wondered if he'd met up with a stun grenade.

"Holy crap!" declared Rodney, who had also been knocked to the floor beside him. "What was that?"

Surprised that he could actually hear anything at all, John replied, "I think the Wraith just got fed up with playing Capture the Flag. Really big hive ships mean—"

"Really big guns."

A second explosion rocked the Sanctuary Hall, and one of the walls cracked wide open. "Black Hill!" Terrified voices took up the cry. "Black Hill burns and the fire races toward us!"

"The Shields—" Yann called, not understanding.

"Only defend the Citadel, not Black Hill!" Rodney's eyes were huge with terror when he glanced over John's shoulder. "At the risk of sounding like a broken record, we're screwed."

Looking back at the transport, John saw its activation lights begin to glow. Realization hit him in that moment: with the Enclave and North Bridge transports unserviceable, Sanctuary Hall was the most likely disembarkation point for the Wraith to mount a second invasion.

Here we go again.

Well, if his time was up, he was damn sure going to go out with all his ammunition expended.

Straining to focus through the haze and the ache throbbing behind his eyes, he raised his weapon as the transport doors folded back.

CHAPTER TWENTY-TWO

Several hours exploring the Enclave had revealed nothing except the degree of hatred the Daleran rebels had had for the Chosen. So much anger directed—indeed, misdirected—against something other than the Wraith bothered Teyla deeply.

Walking back to the transport with her, Lieutenant Ford seemed pensive and withdrawn. When she inquired as to what disturbed him so much, he replied, "A second team will be coming through the 'gate tonight, and we still have no way of warning them. Dammit!" He kicked at the remains of what had once been a fine floor mosaic. A few tiny tiles skittered across the ground. The color of the ceramic reminded Teyla of something.

Back inside the transport, she crouched before the recessed panel. In all, there were three buttons, one of which was a bright aquamarine. "Peryn, which of these did you use to bring us here?"

He stepped inside and pointed to the navy button. Teyla recalled that the Major had used the yellow button to reveal the panel displaying the Citadel's transport map.

"What is it?" Lieutenant Ford asked.

Examining the transport map again, Teyla realized that no light existed to represent the transport room where they were currently standing. Pointing to the third, aquamarine button, she said, "I believe we should attempt to see what this reveals."

"You sure?" The Lieutenant's voice betrayed his uncertainty. "We could end up in another Wraith ambush."

"I do not believe so. Peryn?"

Ford shrugged, but readied his weapon in preparation. The boy's touch revealed a new wall panel—which folded back to expose a second, previously unseen map of the Citadel. The lights indicated that a secondary transport system existed, one that had been kept hidden from all but the Chosen.

Lowering his P-90, Lieutenant Ford ran his finger around the sequence of lights. "The Stations!" he declared.

"I believe you are correct."

"Y'know, I'd wondered about that. Didn't make a whole lot of sense that the Chosen had to walk all the way to a Sanctuary Hall just to operate a transport, especially in the middle of a Wraith attack."

"Two lights exist here in the Enclave, side by side," Teyla observed. "This would indicate that an additional transport must exit nearby."

"Or on different levels?"

"Perhaps." She nodded when Peryn looked at her for permission. When the boy touched the second light, the transport doors folded shut, and immediately opened into a small room. Teyla lifted her weapon at the same instant as Lieutenant Ford. Two Wraith Queens stared at them.

Rodney wasn't confident that he'd be able to hit anything with his gun, but under the current circumstances — namely, another occurrence of all-but-certain death — it seemed prudent to make an attempt. He scrambled to withdraw the sidearm from its holster and bring it to bear on the transport.

When the doors opened, it took him a moment to comprehend just what he was seeing. Ford stepped out of the transport with his P-90 aimed, Teyla following behind with Peryn. As they stood in the Sanctuary Hall, whole and unhurt and defying all bounds of logic, Rodney felt his knees give just a bit before he locked them. Likewise, if his eyes were suddenly stinging, it had to be a consequence of the remaining smoke. This changed... well, it changed *everything*.

The motion of the doors galvanized him into action. "Don't let them shut!" he shouted, darting forward. "The next time it shows up, it could be full of Wraith."

Instantly understanding, Peryn ducked back to the panel and halted the mechanism. Ford and Teyla barely had time to step away before the children swarmed past and mobbed Peryn, their shouts of joy mingling together.

"Good to see you on your feet again, Major." Ford approached his commanding officer with a broad grin and a hand extended.

Sheppard shook it firmly and clapped the Lieutenant on the back, his weapon forgotten at his side. "Not half as good as it is to see the two of you." His voice was rough, and Rodney imagined he could see a telltale brightness in the other man's eyes. Then again, the Major had been pretty glassy-eyed for a while now.

"Gotta say, though, sir, you're not looking so great."

"Everybody's a critic." Sheppard deflected the comment. "Let's have a sit rep, Lieutenant."

"Starting with how you managed to escape the explosion at North Bridge," Rodney put in, still trying to recover his composure.

"Yeah, that was close. We're lucky Peryn's quick on the trigger, or we wouldn't have transported out in time. It was bizarre. Somehow all the oil backed up through the fountains or something..." Ford seemed to have picked up Rodney's discomfort, because he pulled back with a suspicious glare. "You were actually *trying* to drown us in oil, weren't you?"

"Surely you can understand that we might have had more reason to expect the Wraith to be in that transport rather than you." A rapid shift in emotional states seemed to be an obligatory part of battlefield operations. Falling back onto his natural defensiveness, then, seemed the most prudent course of action to Rodney.

"Peryn then took us into what remains of the Enclave," Teyla continued. "It appears that there are two separate systems of transports, one of which was kept secret from all but the Chosen. When we used this hidden transport, we found…something of great interest."

"It looks sorta like some weird Ancient technology, sir," Ford broke in.

Rodney felt his face go slack. Defensiveness immediately shifted into aggression. "Again with the information that should have been presented earlier." Striding toward the transport, he was soon caught up in a throng of refugees, swarming around him in desperation. Hands grabbed at him, causing him to wonder if they were purposely trying to drive him into additional therapy.

"We must leave!" one cried. "The rivers burn. All around the Citadel is fire!"

The thick black smoke seemed to bear that statement out. It blocked much of the sunlight outside and began to roll into the Sanctuary Hall through the smashed windows.

"The Wraith are *everywhere*!" another voice wailed. "There is no place safe."

"The safest thing you can do right now is stay put!" Sheppard called back. "Or at least it will be once I take a look at this device." He reached out to grip a warrior's arm. "All of you need to stay here and fight off any Wraith that come through the transport."

The trainee warriors shared looks of disbelief and dismay. "You would leave us now, when we are most in need?" one demanded. Murmurs of "typical Chosen" reached Rodney's ears.

"I'm not running," Sheppard protested. "Dalera's weapon is our best hope of beating the Wraith, and I'm telling you I can make it work."

You hope, Rodney didn't add. There were a lot of uncertainties built into that assertion, not the least of which was the hope that they had been able to get sufficient Genes to man the Stations.

The Hall tumbled into bedlam. Refugees began to push and shove, frantic to pack into the transport. Beside Rodney, people were starting to crush against the children, trying to force them out. Someone was going to get trampled very soon if this wasn't stopped. Peryn and Yann were yelling at everyone to calm down, but it was useless. Sheppard glanced over at Teyla and tapped his P-90. She nodded, resigned, and he fired a short burst over the crowd's heads into the far wall. The Major's features immediately twisted into a grimace. Obviously he hadn't considered the effect of the gun's loud report on a concussion. The desired effect was achieved, however, as the shouting halted.

"The room's not big enough for all these people to cram in," Ford said. "And I don't think it would be such a great idea, anyway, given what else we found in there."

"Would you care to elaborate on that statement, Lieutenant?" Rodney snapped.

Ford glanced around. "I don't think so. Let's just say you're going to have to see it to believe it."

"We will transport everyone to the upper level of the Enclave." Teyla raised her voice for all to hear, and once again Rodney understood why she was the leader of her people. "You will be safe there. I will stay with you."

"So will I," put in Peryn.

"Major Sheppard will operate Dalera's Weapon, and the Wraith *will* fall. Do not abandon your resolve now, after so much has been sacrificed for your survival."

"She speaks true." Yann stepped next to Teyla. "I will return in the transport, and I will not leave it until all of you have a place in the Enclave. The Genes have risked their lives this past day transporting you and your families from the outlying villages. Remember that, and know that as one of that number, I will not betray your trust."

Their assurances calmed everyone down enough for the doors to close, and Rodney had to admit that it sounded good. He understood with agonizing clarity that nowhere in the Citadel would be safe. But these people had lived all their lives with a perception of the Enclave as a fortress of strength, always protected. That, if nothing else, had to give them some comfort.

A new thought occurred to him, and he began to comprehend just what had been at stake when the Chosen had made the awful choice to leave villagers to the Wraith rather than risk being captured themselves. It hadn't been an act of cowardice or superiority, but instead the only way of protecting the Enclave, and by extension the heart of their defensive system and their weapon. It was yet one more apology he might have made for his earlier assumptions, but, as with so much about this situation, it would come far too late.

The first group of refugees poured out of the transport and

into the gutted ruins. Through crumbling walls and broken windowpanes, a ring of fire and black smoke was visible around the Citadel. Although in places the smoke wasn't terribly high, corresponding to the level of oil in that quadrant, the conflagration at Black Hill was immense and almost mesmeric. Due to the elevation of the plateau where the Enclave temple had once stood, the air was much clearer, but Rodney knew that wouldn't last for long. A dark smudge in the sky caught his gaze, and he tried not to think too hard about the possibility that it was a group of Darts amassing for some kind of coordinated run.

"Getting rid of the Wraith isn't going to solve the oil problem," Ford commented, stepping out of the transport and over a blackened beam.

Would he never learn? "Thank you for once again illuminating the patently obvious, Lieutenant. One problem at a time if you don't mind."

The Marine ignored him and turned to Sheppard. "Knock 'em dead, sir."

"That's the plan," replied the Major. "See you back here when it's over."

The transport had finally emptied, leaving only Rodney along with Sheppard, Teyla and the children. The little girl who'd seemingly been tailing Rodney for hours had somehow managed to attach one small, sticky hand to his. He didn't bother trying to extricate himself before pressing the button that Teyla indicated. The doors shut and re-opened again — and never in his life had he been so taken aback. He fumbled for his weapon, but the child clinging to him joined in the chorus of terrified screams and welded herself to his legs.

"It is all right," Teyla declared, exiting the transport ahead of Sheppard. "They cannot harm you." She smiled reassuringly at the children and walked across to the transparent stasis chambers embedded in one wall. "I believe they are in a form of hibernation."

Extracating himself from the cluster of limbs, Rodney joined Teyla and Sheppard staring with a mixture of repugnance and fascination at the naked Wraith curled into fetal positions. Not-

ing the framework surrounding the Wraith's heads, and recalling the little he'd gleaned about Dalera's experiments, he
immediately assessed the situation. "Oh…my. Oh, wow! This
is amazing. Do you realize what this is?" But there was little
time to admire Dalera's handiwork. If his theory was correct,
the power grid would only work if all of the Genes maintained
their positions — and with choking, oily smoke rolling in, that
wouldn't be for long, assuming that they were all manned in the
first place.

"The reason why the Wraith are hell bent on breaking into
the Citadel?" Sheppard made no effort to disguise his shock. "I
thought you said this was a weapon?"

The children were wandering around the room with their
mouths agape. "Don't touch anything." Rodney pulled off his
pack, lowered it to the ground, and scanned what looked to be a
patchwork of consoles made up from several different types of
technology. While some of it was decidedly Ancient in origin,
much was unfamiliar to him. "Dalera experimented with a neural interface for a weapon. I had assumed it was something like
the weapons chair. Apparently not."

Sheppard turned to him. "Didn't you say that it was unsuccessful?"

"In her colleagues' opinion, yes, but I'm wondering if her
banishment really was due to her choice in husbands, or — "

"The nature of her experiments." Sheppard turned his attention back to the Queens.

Nodding curtly, Rodney added, "Once exiled, Dalera wouldn't
have had access to much in the way of technology. Instead, she
cobbled together whatever she could find — including control
panels from… I don't know." He examined the consoles again.
"Wraith ships, perhaps."

"They don't look ten thousand years old." Sheppard studied
the Wraith uncertainly. "And they're kind of small — younger
than the last Queen I met. I gotta say, the whole eyes-open thing
is a little on the freaky side."

"Being in stasis," Rodney muttered, searching for a familiar point of reference, "theoretically they should age, but at a

vastly decelerated rate." Rubbing his forehead in frustration, he snapped, "I'm never going to be able to get this operational. I can't even use my instruments to create an interface... Wait. Here's something."

He flipped open a panel similar to the one that Kesun had used to display charts of the planet's land mass. Instead of maps, though, the information offered a tantalizing insight into the weapon's plan. It vindicated his theory that the Stations were vital hubs in a kind of circuit board that powered a weapon, in addition to providing a defensive strategy. It also indicated something that looked like —

Realization hit Rodney with almost painful force. That was why her colleagues had dismissed the experiments as a failure. But Dalera had continued with them nonetheless. "That's why the Wraith are attacking!" He turned to Sheppard. "What role do queen bees play a hive?"

"They make lots of baby bees?"

"Yes, of course, Major, but more importantly they control the activity of every bee in the hive." Now that Rodney understood what was going on, it was hard to keep his words from tumbling over each other. "These weren't Queens when they were placed in these chambers. They were larvae, babies, whatever you call these things when they're young. Dalera incorporated them as a biological component to a weapons' system, but —"

"In the years hence, they grew into adults." Teyla turned to face him, a less than thrilled expression on her face.

"The determination of the Wraith attack and their unwillingness to bomb this Citadel would indicate that their offensive is considerably more than a mere culling. Instead of mounting the intended defense, these two —" Rodney rapped a knuckle against the hood of one of the stasis chambers. "—are most likely using the Wraith equivalent of pheromones to *drive* the attack, but in such a way that will ensure their retrieval."

"Well, there's one solution to that." The Major stepped back, raised his weapon and, cringing against the anticipated shock, aimed it at the stasis chambers.

"Would you just hold on a moment?" Rodney shouted. "Not

every solution comes at the end of a gun." He felt a momentary twinge of guilt when Sheppard winced. The Major really did not look good. And unless he found a solution to this further problem that the vaunted Dalera had failed to foresee, none of them would fare too well when the Wraith burst in here to rescue their Queens-in-waiting.

"Move back!" Aiden ordered, ushering people away from the entrance of the transport. "We need the space to get everyone in the next group out of the transport as quickly as possible."

The Dalerans were reluctant to shift their positions near the doors. Parents grasped children, terrified of losing them in the crowd, while many of the elderly stared at their surroundings with tears in their eyes. In the distance, a squadron of Darts had set up a holding pattern, obviously hovering just outside the edge of the Shields' influence. They were like vultures, waiting to strike as soon as the Dalerans were forced to evacuate the Citadel.

Aiden turned to pose a question to Yann, Peryn having returned in the transport for the next group, but it was answered by the wails of the villagers.

"The sacred Enclave is destroyed," sobbed a woman near his elbow. "Our last sanctuary offers nothing but false hope."

"Surely we are lost now," cried another. "Who could have done this?"

"Who is responsible for burning the Enclave?"

Aiden stared at them. They'd wanted to save these people, from oppression and from the Wraith, but had they ever had a chance at saving them from themselves?

"This was but one building, the temple," Yann reminded them as he went back inside the transport to retrieve the next lot. "The heart of the Enclave, Dalera's weapon, remains untouched. With the help of all the Genes, you will be protected."

The transport doors closed, and Aiden's thoughts turned to Lisera, still at her post in the Station. The smoke was most likely closing in—

Hearing a noise nearby, he spun around, bringing his P-90 to bear. A short distance away, the remains of a fountain toppled to one side, and an area about the size of a manhole opened up. Elsewhere, timbers creaked and glass shifted as more holes began opening up. People scuttled away, screaming, "Wraith! The Wraith are here!" And this time, they weren't jumping at shadows.

It was the childish giggle that alerted Rodney. It was so unexpected that he glanced around. The children were huddled together in the shadows on the other side of the room, about as far from the Wraith as anyone could possibly get. He didn't much blame them. So what did they find so hilarious?

"It feels funny," the little girl supplied.

Even in the darkness, Rodney could see that she had inserted her hand in something. "I thought I told you not to touch anything!" he admonished, striding across to them. But when he saw what she was touching, instead of batting her hand away, for a brief, insane moment he considered adopting the child. "Major!"

The children parted to let Sheppard through. He immediately placed his hand against the same rubbery control device that normally existed on an Ancient chair. Nothing happened. Before Rodney could so instruct him, the Major stepped into the stasis chamber and leaned back.

The resulting hum sounded almost like a sigh, as if the system were somehow grateful to have been awakened. A blue glow lit the entire room, eliciting gasps of wonder from the children. The little girl who had previously appropriated Rodney's hand seemed oblivious to their rapidly approaching doom. "It is very beautiful."

Rodney didn't see anything particularly beautiful about a piece of technology. All it had done so far was turn itself on. If the blasted thing performed as he hoped, then he'd consider viewing it more poetically. "Major, think about where we are in the solar system," he instructed. "*Rapidly*."

"How would I know the first thing about where we are in this solar system?"

Even as he spoke, however, an image appeared overhead. Rather than a diagram of space, it was instead a map of the planet. The murmurs, punctuated by several 'oohs' and 'ahs' from the kids, grew louder. Rodney was fairly amazed himself, and unlike them, he'd seen this kind of thing before.

Two large blips appeared on the projected image. Wraith hive ships, almost certainly. Thousands of smaller blips winked into existence — Darts, no doubt — and buzzed around the larger blips like gnats.

"I'm thinking about shooting them down," Sheppard said in a hopeful voice. Silence stretched as everyone watched the projection for any change.

"Nothing's happening." Rodney felt his pulse accelerate. "Maybe it's the concussion — maybe you bashed in whatever neurological centers this thing taps into."

"Or maybe I've used up my allocated brain power for the day," Sheppard shot back.

"Major, your propensity for snarking at inopportune moments—"

"Rodney, unless you want to try this yourself, shut the hell up."

They'd found the weapon and activated it. Surely that would be enough. Wouldn't it? How much more could Dalera ask of them? *Come on, come on...* "The interface!" he blurted, and scrambled around the console for a piece of curved ceramic that he'd seen earlier. Snatching it up and thrusting it into Sheppard's free hand, he ordered, "Put it on!"

Sheppard turned the ceramic over. It was identical to the skull caps worn by the Wraith. His gaze slid from his teammate to the Queens, then back to Rodney. He didn't need to voice his concern. This contraption could very well link his mind in some way to the Wraith. But as usual, they were out of options. Jamming the thing on his head, he said, "This is Wraith tech, right? I'm gonna try something a little different."

Choking back his panicked impatience, Rodney watched as the scene playing over Sheppard's head changed to a three-dimensional map of the Citadel and surrounding countryside.

Behind them, the transport doors opened and a wild-eyed

Peryn staggered to the entrance, but did not step out. "The Wraith have invaded the Enclave. Lieutenant Ford…ordered me to tell you."

Teyla ran to him and caught him in her arms before he fell to the floor.

"Don't let that transport recycle or we're all dead!" Rodney directed his order at Teyla, but then his eyes fell to the Shield on Peryn's belt. It had stopped glowing. Swinging around, Rodney saw that Sheppard's had also ceased to glow. Desperately, he grabbed his own methodically accumulated collection of Shields. "No, no, no no! This can't be happening!" Every one of the Shields had turned black.

"Wraithlight! Wraithlight!" people screamed.

"What the…?" Aiden looked up and saw hundreds of Darts crossing what he had thought of as the no-fly zone. Glancing at the Gene beside him, he noticed that the man's Shield had gone black. The momentary surge of panic that hit Aiden was brief, but it was just long enough to allow the Wraith he'd been pumping bullets into to reach him. Next thing he knew, he was on the ground and the Wraith was standing over him with its hand upraised.

For the second time in less than ten minutes, Rodney felt his knees give way. He clasped the edge of the console, swallowing against his suddenly dry mouth. This time they were dead, no question about it. The little girl squealed and ran into the transport, trying to hide behind Peryn. Several of the other children followed—until Teyla slowly stood and walked toward him, her eyes fastened to a point over Sheppard's head.

Rodney turned and looked up at the hologram. The images of dozens of frighteningly familiar lights shot out of multiple locations around the Enclave.

The expected impact of the hand on Aiden's chest never came. Abruptly the Wraith vanished in a liquid blue beam.

Around him, the sounds of the battle ceased and everything went strangely quiet. He picked himself up, grabbed his weapon, which had been knocked out of his hand, and looked around the Enclave. The Wraith were gone. He staggered across to the upended fountain where most of the creatures had been pouring out, and looked down. All he could see was the remains of plumbing. There was no sign of the Wraith anywhere. The Major had done... Aiden wasn't entirely certain what he'd done, but he turned to the group with a yell of triumph. "It's Dalera's weapon. Major Sheppard is using it to attack the Wraith!"

Just at that moment, the transport doors opened and a second group came rushing out. But then they paused and, along with the first bunch of refugees who had been fighting off the Wraith, looked skyward.

Yann stepped out behind them and came across to Aiden. Like everyone who stood amid the ruins of the once elegant temple, the Gene watched in awe as the watery blue beams streaked across the sky, cutting through the squadrons of Wraith Darts — which began falling from the sky. Even through the thickening black smoke of the oil fires, they caught sight of balls of fire where the craft hit the ground.

"How can this be?" breathed a villager. "Who does this?"

"We do!" Yann shouted, jabbing a victorious fist into the air. "Our brothers and sisters hold the power of Dalera's Weapon now. By joining together we have made ourselves worthy of her glory and driven the Wraith from our world!"

Cheers swept through the crowd. The warriors congratulated each other and mingled with the townspeople, reveling in the moment. Yann slapped Aiden on the back, nearly knocking him off his feet in the process. For the first time since Aiden had set foot on the planet, he heard the sound of Daleran laughter.

"Finally," he said under his breath. Finally, these people believed they had a future.

In the weapon room, the din of celebrating young voices was piercing. Rodney cringed, sure that the noise wasn't doing the Major's headache any favors. "All right, enough already," he snapped, locking his fear back up behind a familiar veneer of annoyance. "Imminent doom averted and all that. Next."

His relief was so strong it hurt, and the best way to conceal that was to move briskly on to the next problem. They'd won the battle, but the unchecked oil fire was likely to make the Citadel and nearby countryside—possibly even the entire planet—unfit for life. Nor was there any guarantee that the hive ships wouldn't wait around and send in more Darts as soon as evacuations began. Yet another unanswerable question he'd inevitably be required to answer.

Rodney opened his mouth to instruct the Major to explore any other functions the device might have—and stopped mid-thought when the activation lights died out. Whether through the departure of one of the Genes or through some malfunction in the device, the grid had failed. He resisted the urge to kick something—could they not get a break for *once*?

Without a word, Sheppard dropped his hand and opened his eyes. At the same time a distant explosion made itself known. Even from inside the room, they could feel a tremor. Rodney stared at Sheppard. "What did you do?"

Sheppard merely returned his gaze. "What's the one way you can extinguish an oil fire?"

Another wave of relief washed over him, and once again Rodney was surprised and impressed by the pilot's resourcefulness. "Nice work."

"A guy's gotta make himself useful."

Oddly enough, Sheppard's shield turned aquamarine. Rodney glanced down at his own and noted that they had begun to glow. Of course. He should have realized sooner. "The Shields went temporarily inactive because the device doesn't allow you to defend and attack simultaneously."

"That's how it works on the *Enterprise*, so it seemed worth a try." Stepping out of the chamber, Sheppard stumbled, listing to one side. Rodney instinctively reached out to steady him. "It's okay. I'm good." The Major tried to smile, but seemed to recognize that he wasn't fooling anyone.

For Sheppard's sake, the sooner they got back to Atlantis, the better. Unfortunately, there was still the minor matter of the hive ships in orbit around the planet.

Rodney took one last look around before stepping into the transport. The Wraith that had been swept up in the reconfigured beams had to have been transported somewhere. And then there was the issue of leaving two Wraith Queens behind —

— which was suddenly was no longer an issue. Features tightened against the pain, Sheppard was standing at the door of the transport, unleashing a hail of bullets into the stasis chambers.

When the clip was finally empty, Rodney batted away at the cordite-smelling smoke. "Was that really wise?"

Turning back toward him, Sheppard said simply, "Yes." The grim look on the Major's face told Rodney a great deal more. It had also answered his question of whether the device had brought him into contact with the minds of the immature Queens.

Swallowing again, this time against a momentary surge of nausea, Rodney nodded to Peryn, signaling it was time to leave.

Somewhere between the weapon room and Nemst, they'd managed to lose most of their entourage, while acquiring Ford and Teyla. John wasn't entirely certain what they were doing in the village. Something about Teyla needing to be outside the influence of the Shielded Citadel to sense whether or not the Wraith had departed. It sounded like it would have made sense had his brain not been fairly scrambled.

When the doors to the transport opened, it was to a scene of devastation. The roof of the inn had collapsed, and they could see outside to the sky, now more or less free of the ubiquitous oily smoke. A large group of people, mostly men that John recognized as residents of Nemst, were surveying the area and looking mighty unhappy. He didn't recall suggesting that anyone could safely leave the Citadel, but then, just staying upright was enough of a challenge for him at the moment. Having extra eyes and weapons around the place was probably a good idea in case they ran into any Wraith he hadn't managed to scoop up with Dalera's nifty anti-Wraith beam.

"The Wraith," Teyla stated, her voice edged with a familiar bitterness. "They have retaliated by destroying much of the town."

Rodney opened his mouth to correct that misconception, but seemed to think better of it. Which was fortunate. Concussed or not, John knew the makings of a lynch mob when he saw one, and he'd already had a taste of Daleran 'gratitude'.

They climbed over more wreckage until they were standing in what had once been the inn's entrance. "This is the way of the Wraith. Even when they are able to cull most of a population, they destroy much that remains behind." The Athosian was directing her speech to the citizens of Nemst. Her stance and the quick look she sent John told him exactly what he needed to know. The Wraith had left. Even in his admittedly addled state, he understood what the Athosian was now trying to achieve.

Outside the inn they found a sight familiar to John. The men with them reacted with astonishment and anger. One of them released a cry of despair. "The wheel! The waterwheel that has stood for countless generations — it's gone!"

Someone else began talking about the forge, and all too soon, the murmurs began turning to blame. "The Wraith destroyed our village because of the blackwater."

"Why should we have to bear this burden alone?"

"Who will rebuild our beautiful forge?"

Beautiful forge? John ran an unsteady hand across his eyes. He was about to snap out a reply, but Yann beat him to it. "Thank Dalera that you still live to see and speak of such things. When the Wraith have departed, we will rebuild." He strode out purposefully behind Ford as they made their way across the splintered wreckage to the impressive crater that had replaced most of the hill.

The bitter complaints and recriminations dropped to muttered whispers. Yeah, there was no getting around it. This place was going to face some serious social and political fallout.

"I do not believe Major Sheppard is well," Teyla said softly.

"Try telling him that." Aiden used his binoculars to look out across the Citadel. When one of the blue beams had targeted a squadron of Darts heading west toward Nemst, Aiden hadn't been entirely certain what to expect. But the Major had apparently taken a page out of Red Adair's book. By using the beam to remove their Wraith pilots at just the right moment, the uncontrolled Darts had plunged into Black Hill. The massive explosion had starved the raging oil fire of oxygen just long enough for the flames to be extinguished. True, a few of the Darts had overshot their mark and crashed into Nemst, but when the bulk of the hill had collapsed its center, it had cut off the flow of oil. With nothing to feed it, the fire around the Citadel also was rapidly dying down. Although the resultant haze would provide a spectacular sunset, the strong afternoon west wind had blown the worst of the smoke away.

Teyla sighed. "Were I in his position, I would be much the same." Aiden met her eyes, and she added, "As would you."

Shrugging, he replied, "As long as we don't have to go one-on-one with any Wraith who might have been left behind, he should be okay, but we really need to get him back to Atlantis."

"The Wraith departed soon after the Major unleashed the weapon. None remain. Of that I am now certain."

"And that's a perfect end to a perfect day." McKay turned back from the edge of the cliff, where everyone else was gathered, and strode across to the two of them. It hadn't taken the scientist long to regain his typical bluster. "The oil flow has stopped, all right. Which of course was the desired outcome, but only if the Wraith don't come back."

"No!" came the forceful voice of one of the Nemst townsfolk. The guy marched up to the Major and waved a threatening finger under his nose. "It is your fault that our magnificent town is in ruins. You will not now bring the full force of the Wraith down upon us—"

"And steal our livelihood," another injected.

"—by destroying what little remains of Black Hill!" finished the first man.

McKay gestured in the direction of the men. "As I was about to explain."

Aiden moved the same instant as Teyla. Letting the Dalerans think that the Wraith had blown up Nemst seemed the wisest course of action. The Major was in no shape to be fielding an argument.

"Do you deny that releasing the blackwater onto the river defended the Citadel against the Wraith?" Yann yelled back just as loudly.

"The Citadel, yes. But what of our home?"

"It was the will of Dalera that the Citadel be your place of refuge during a Wraith culling," Teyla began. "Never in all my travels have I seen a world untouched by the Wraith. They destroy what humans have built in order to stop us from finding ways to defeat them. What you call Wraithcraft— " She paused and shook her head.

"What you call Wraithcraft," McKay continued, "interferes with the operation of the Shields. But in and of itself, it isn't bad. For the most part, it isn't even designed by the Wraith, but they'd prefer you to remain ignorant of it in order to prevent you from developing a functioning civilization."

"Dalera offers a truly fortunate defense," Teyla interjected. "For as long as you work together and use the Shields, you will always have the power to fend off the worst Wraith depravations."

"Then the Citadel must pay *us* for the blackwater you used." The man's glare moved from Teyla and Yann to McKay. "But you will not steal from us any further." He crossed his arms belligerently. "You will not destroy the cliff holding back the last of *our* blackwater."

"So," Major Sheppard replied with a weary expression. "Where would you like us to take you when the Wraith resume their attack? East wall, maybe? Or would you rather just stay here sitting on your hoard of black gold?"

The Nemst townsfolk looked unsure. "What of Dalera's Weapon?"

"The things specifically used to power it…died."

"I don't know if anyone's noticed," McKay said, staring out across the countryside. "But I can't see any sign of the Wraith. Y'know?" A confident smile crossed his face, and he eyed his collection of now dull Shields. "I think we really did make them turn tail and leave. It may not be necessary to blow up the remains of the cliff after all."

Aiden clamped his jaw shut. Just once, couldn't the scientist get with the program and see what was happening around him? Another few minutes and the townspeople might have been forced to concede that to survive the Wraith in the long term, they had to follow Dalera's plan to protect the Citadel. And that meant working together and being willing to employ every resource they had, including their oil. Sure, it was great that they wouldn't have to use it now, but right at this moment, that wasn't the point.

Teyla, too, pursed her lips, while Sheppard just shot McKay an incredulous look. "Thank you, Rodney."

The scientist's supercilious smirk faded into uncertainty. "Well, isn't that a good thing?"

"Yes," Teyla replied, her biting tone leaving no room for doubt. "Truly wonderful."

"What do you think?" The Major turned to Teyla. "Are they likely to be hanging around?" He'd obviously abandoned the attempt to get the townsfolk to consider anything other than themselves.

The golden light from the afternoon sun failed to take the edge off Teyla's tightly drawn features. Still glaring at McKay, she replied, "The Wraith do not linger when they are finished, but travel swiftly to the next world. I believe Dalera will be safe once more — until the next culling generations from now."

"You know," McKay said. "I stood on this same spot the night before last, watching the Wraith Darts zooming around like they owned the place."

"Which they did," Teyla reminded him.

"Oh, I don't know." McKay seemed suddenly aware of the resentful Nemst townsfolk. "While you were all safe and snug inside the Citadel, your engineers didn't hesitate to put their lives on the line implementing my plan."

"And where are those men now?" snapped the guy who'd been doing all the complaining. "One of them was my cousin, and he has not returned." His eyes narrowed and turned cunning. "Why is it that you alone survived?"

McKay took a step back. "Hey! That's not true. What about the rest of the team who readjusted the length of boom across the channel? They're still around... Aren't they?"

"Indeed they are," Yann interceded. "Your cousin assists in the rebuilding of the East wall. Come, I will take you to him."

"What need do we have of this wall now that the Wraith have left? We need the men back here, to rebuild Nemst!"

"And who will provide the necessary payment for this rebuilding?"

The argument continued on the walk to the inn, and Aiden let out a soft sigh.

McKay waited until the Dalerans were out of earshot before saying, "Although those crashed Darts successfully collapsed most of the hill, the bottom of the cliff where Ford and I inserted the C-4 is still intact. I set the charges to go off remotely, but unless I detonate it soon, the flow won't nearly be sufficient to sustain the blaze."

"I do not think it will be necessary," Teyla said.

"Seriously? You really, truly don't think the Wraith will be coming back?"

"No," Teyla replied in a barely civil voice. "I no longer sense their nearness."

Visibly slumping in relief, McKay let out a long sigh. "Okay. Do you realize I haven't eaten since — ?"

"McKay!"

The scientist appeared taken back by the edge in the Major's voice. "What?"

"Maybe you hadn't noticed, but the good citizens of Dalera don't appear to be tossing flowers at us, thanking us for saving their collective butts from the Wraith."

Scratching his chin, McKay replied. "Yes, I had noticed some reticence in their attitude. I mean, the nerve of that guy, blaming me for surviving the death of…" His voice trailed off and he swallowed. "Maybe you're right. Maybe we should quietly make our exit stage left."

With a shake of her head, Teyla turned and walked ahead of them.

CHAPTER TWENTY-THREE

The dark, cold place inside of Teyla had vanished as if it had never existed. Although she had not been able to sense the Wraith when they had first arrived on this world, she had nevertheless felt a vague disquiet that had also now vanished. Perhaps that was due to Major Sheppard's killing the young Queens.

Now, with the certain departure of the Wraith would come even more recriminations. In the minds of the Dalerans, the Wraith attacked only when people strayed from Dalera's laws. First they came in small numbers, to test the faith of Dalera's followers. They had not attacked in full measure until strangers using Wraithcraft had arrived; strangers who did not worship Dalera, nor were they truly of Atlantis. Indeed, strangers who had decried the Daleran beliefs and worked to change them. Then and only then had the Wraith plundered what the Dalerans would nostalgically call their once peaceful world.

Such cynicism had been foreign to Teyla until recently, but she now recognized that what set the Dalerans apart from other planets in the Pegasus Galaxy was their isolation. With no knowledge of the Wraith cullings elsewhere, they would most likely fall back on their beliefs.

Teyla had indicated to the Nemst townspeople that they should return to the Citadel first. It took longer than expected for the transport to recycle, and she was considering the wisdom of waiting, when the lights warned that someone was returning.

The doors folded back to reveal Lisera, Yann, and several Shield-bearing warriors. Peryn, who was now wearing a warrior's uniform, was also with them. The look of unhappiness on all of their faces was clear.

"Our people owe you a debt of gratitude that we are unable to pay," Yann said, stepping out of the transport.

"See?" McKay tossed a smug smile in Teyla's direction.

"Rodney." Major Sheppard's eyebrows lowered warningly. "Let the man finish."

Yann averted his eyes for an instant, then turned back to them. "Nevertheless I would suggest it is best that you depart Dalera and not return."

"Excuse me?" McKay demanded. He turned around and raised his hands in the air. "This is the thanks we get for— Ow!" The scientist's left leg buckled. He shot an accusing stare at Major Sheppard and limped around in a circle, favoring his left foot. "What the hell was that for?"

Ignoring him, Yann continued, "We were hard pressed to prevent many of the Nemst villagers, and indeed many from other villages, from returning here to punish you for bringing the curse of the Wraith upon us."

"*We* brought the curse?" McKay was indignant. "Of all the insane—"

"Dr McKay," Teyla warned him, "My boot is far heavier than Major Sheppard's. And unlike the Major, I do not hold my blows."

"We should not delay," Yann continued, gesturing for them to step into the transport. "While the warriors have sworn fealty to me as the first Gene, several hundred Genes are now known. We believe the number may eventually exceed a thousand."

"That's good," Major Sheppard replied. "It means that you should be able to make a real attempt at implementing Dalera's long-term plan."

"Without the need to resort to Wraithcraft," Yann added. "However, the people of Nemst are determined in their resolve. They need find only one Gene to operate the transport in order to locate you." He shook his head in shame. "Such thanks you do not deserve, but their voices are loud. I doubt we can quell them if you remain."

Resting on the crutches that Dr Beckett had given her, Lisera offered Ford a smile that was no longer shy, or innocent. Teyla considered it more an expression of regality. An uneasy coldness touched her heart. Only the knowledge that so many Genes had been discovered tempered her fear that the Daleran society would once more be plunged back into the inequity that had driven both Dr McKay and Yann to act as they had.

"Hey, Lisera," said Lieutenant Ford, moving closer. "You're really getting the hang of those things. About the plaster—"

"The healer told me that he has used a similar method to set the bones of broken limbs. He assures me that the white rock can be removed with ease, when the time is right." Lisera offered a wider smile to Yann, who came and stood by her side in an undeniably possessive manner.

"That's…great," Ford replied uncertainly.

Major Sheppard was talking quietly to Peryn, thanking him for his assistance and courage, and congratulating him on his newfound status as one of Dalera's warriors. A Gene whom Teyla did not recognize touched the screen on the transport. Moments later, the doors opened to a familiar inn and the brisk smell of the ocean. This village, at least, had been left standing. That fact might yet give trouble to Yann, if there were others who thought as the townspeople of Nemst did and became resentful that the merchant had not suffered the same loss as they.

Lisera addressed them all. "I shall be forever grateful for having been privileged to see Atlantis. It is my hope that one day the Ancestors, including Dalera, will return there and take up their rightful position. Until that time comes, we—" She glanced around at the other Genes. "We will endeavor to lead our people as Dalera wished."

McKay's face hardened. He opened his mouth to speak, but Teyla's warning look was sufficient. Curling his lips in distaste, he pulled the brace of Shields from around his neck, muttering something about Zelenka's hypotheses having been proven useless anyway, and thrust the devices into Peryn's hand before stalking out of the transport.

An uncomfortable silence followed, until Major Sheppard also removed his Shield and handed it to the young warrior. "Okay, well… Good luck."

Touching his cap in farewell, Ford smiled at Lisera. "I kept my promise, right?"

"You did, Aiden Ford. And I shall never forget you. None of us will, for we intend to rebuild that which has been destroyed, and inscribe all of your names as great warriors from a world that is no longer legendary, but real."

"Cool," the Lieutenant replied. He then joined Teyla and the Major, waiting near the bar.

The transport doors closed. Teyla glanced at Major Sheppard, who stared longingly at a barrel in the corner. "Just wondering how well one of those barrels of beer would travel, and wondering if we could hide it." He shot them a grin, but it was empty, and his face was pale and drawn.

Except for the chirping of a few night insects, coming awake now that the sun had fully set, the walk to the puddle jumper was made in silence. Immersed in his anger, Dr McKay apparently failed to notice that the Major's step was becoming less certain. Teyla exchanged a look with Lieutenant Ford, but there was little more they could do for Major Sheppard until they reached Atlantis.

Once inside the jumper, McKay slouched into his seat and shook his head. "If I wasn't living it, I wouldn't believe a single detail of this," he said as the preflight checks were completed with something less than flawless precision. "Haven't we demonstrated clearly enough, through our blatant disregard for our personal safety during the attack on *their* world, that we're on their side?"

"Do you view the situation so clearly, Doctor?" Teyla replied, feeling an immense weariness. "Without the immediate threat of the Wraith, and without the stability they once had, there will be many 'sides' among these people."

The look McKay gave her in return was unexpected. It was not the haughty expression to which she had become accustomed, but a more subdued one. "You're assuming that I'm utterly incapable of recognizing my own misjudgments," he said, his tone cool. "I'm well aware of the role I played in this madness."

Surprised, she met his gaze and discovered a reflection of her own conflicted thoughts. "Much has happened that we did not foresee," she said finally. It was an odd sort of truce, but it would suffice for the moment.

"As rough as it'll be to have to start over, the Dalerans kinda have a second chance to set things up right," Lieutenant Ford offered from his place beside her. She envied his optimistic outlook. "Don't you think, Major?"

Sheppard's response was listless. "Let's go home."

The team's final view of the Citadel was markedly different from its first. Then, there had been unabashed awe at its powerful stature. Now, the ruins of the Enclave, harshly lit by the rising twin planets, were visible from above. So too was all other evidence of the devastation brought by the Wraith and the Dalerans themselves. As the edifice became smaller in the windscreen, however, the areas of damage became less noticeable.

"They'll rebuild," Ford asserted, and Teyla wondered if he was trying to convince his teammates or himself.

"You want to know what drives me up the wall?" Dr McKay began, apparently dissatisfied with the silence that had fallen. "None of this had to happen. Granted, the Wraith attack was pretty much inevitable, but so much of the petty infighting was just unbelievably destructive and completely useless to anyone's cause."

The scientist's latest tirade was little more than ambient noise to Teyla. If it helped his peace of mind to be speaking continuously, then so be it. She watched the sky around them darken from blue to black as the jumper climbed through the atmosphere. Before long, the Stargate came into view, and she realized that this strange, difficult journey was at last nearing its end.

"...not the best strategy ever devised. When confronted by the potential salvation of your civilization, try to lock it up in a cell. I recognize that most Earth cultures can't point any fingers when it comes to acknowledging the greater good, but—"

"Rodney?" The interruption came from the pilot's seat, cutting through McKay's diatribe despite its low volume.

"What?"

Sheppard's voice was strained. "You have the controls."

McKay blinked in confusion, which turned instantly to shock as the Major slumped over in his seat, all color drained from his features.

"*Shit.*"

Teyla sprang from her chair, as did Ford. Together they eased their team leader's motionless form out of the seat and down to the floor of the jumper. McKay's eyes were wide as he took in the control panel in front of him. "Uh, okay. No sweat. These things read your mind, and my mind's at least as well structured as his."

"That's not a great sign, passing out like that," Ford said, worriedly checking the Major's pulse. "Dial the 'gate!"

"Backseat driving is not appreciated right now." Nevertheless, McKay tapped out the correct sequence on the DHD, and the Stargate came to life in the windscreen. "Atlantis, this is Jumper One."

"Good to hear from you, Jumper One. You're significantly overdue to check in. We were getting ready to send the contingency team after you."

"Yes, well, we're on our way home now." McKay winced. "And as much as I hate being predictable, we need a medical team standing by."

Grodin's voice was quickly replaced by Dr Weir's. "Rodney, am I talking to you instead of the Major because he's once again the reason for the medical team?"

"Excellent deduction. It was a slight variation on the irresistible force, immovable object problem. Head injury — or more accurately, two head injuries, about twenty-four hours ago. He was functioning adequately earlier, but he just collapsed."

"So *you're* navigating the jumper?"

"I can't tell you how much your confidence inspires me, Elizabeth. All the same, I think I'm going to need my undivided attention for this, so how about we chat when we're both on the same side of the wormhole?"

"Understood. Good luck."

Lieutenant Ford sat cross-legged on the deck beside his commanding officer. "I think the Major's okay for now." He raised his voice. "Hey, McKay—whatever you do, make sure the drive pods are retracted, all right?"

"If I were the superstitious type, I would make you very sorry for that comment, Lieutenant." Their course was slow, but McKay's hand betrayed a slight tremor. "You two might want to grab hold of something. Purely as a precaution. I'm not certain that we're straight and level, given that this is space and all and I have *no* idea which way is supposed to be 'up'."

"You'll be fine. Just calm down."

"That's very easy for you to say. The 'gate looks a lot bigger when someone else is trying to thread this needle!" The rippling pool grew until it filled the windscreen, and their new pilot's anxiety level appeared to spike. "Don't crash, don't crash, don't crash," he repeated in a low voice, his forehead dotted with sweat.

Teyla looked over at Ford, who was attempting and failing to mask a smirk. She opened her mouth to ask him what he found amusing, but the event horizon swallowed them up.

When the jumper was once again intact and hovering in the 'gateroom, McKay sagged back in his seat. "Oh, thank God." Within seconds, he had recovered his usual supercilious bearing and even offered an indifferent salute to Dr Weir, standing at the railing, as they rose into the jumper bay. "Make sure to tell Sheppard just how well I did that, for the record. No more of these baby-step lessons."

"It was the autopilot, Doc." When the scientist turned to glare at him, Ford grinned. "It takes over at a specified distance in front of the 'gate, remember?"

It was difficult to tell whether McKay's expression of disbelief was directed at the Lieutenant or at himself for having forgotten. Ford appeared to be enjoying the other man's uncharacteristic speechlessness. "Seriously, it'll park itself and everything."

"I don't need it to park itself for me. I think I can find an empty spot in the bay all by myself, thank you." To prove his point, McKay made a show of locating the manual control and guiding the jumper toward the landing platform.

"Do they test you on parallel parking on Canadian driver's

tests?" Ford prodded.

"I hardly think that Americans can point any fingers regarding driving ability."

The craft seemed not quite level to Teyla, but the others were too occupied with their discussion to heed her uncertain "Doctor — ?"

Then there was a scrape of metal against metal, and she instinctively bent low to shield the Major's body as they lurched.

"Damn it!" McKay clumsily maneuvered the jumper into place and settled it on the deck. "There's no conceivable way I'm ever going to hear the end of this, is there?"

Ford rolled his eyes. "Only you could bottom out a jumper."

"Hey, without me you'd still be on the other side of the 'gate, so I don't think a little gratitude is too much to ask."

Upon lowering the hatch, they were greeted first by Dr Beckett, who bustled in to examine Major Sheppard. Dr Weir followed in his wake. Atlantis's leader regarded the team: one unconscious, another in foul-smelling peasant's garb, and the remaining two grimy and battered. "I'm guessing this is going to take a while to explain."

"That's a good bet, ma'am," Ford replied. "Doc, is the Major going to be all right?"

"Aye, but he'll not be happy for a while." Beckett motioned to a pair of medics waiting nearby with a gurney. "I'll want to see the rest of you in the infirmary as well. Shower first if you like, but take longer than half an hour and I'll send out search parties."

His mild threat was met by a trio of unenthusiastic nods. Dr Weir studied their faces and frowned slightly. "We'll debrief later, when Major Sheppard's able to participate. Just tell me this: did we do what we set out to do?"

Teyla was unsure how to answer. It was Dr McKay who spoke up, already halfway turned toward the door. Though she couldn't see his face, his voice was tinged with defeat. "That depends on your point of view."

He was out on one of the more out-of-the-way balconies,

looking with unseeing eyes at the tiny whitecaps below, when someone finally took the trouble to track him down. "Hey," came the simple greeting from behind him.

Rodney turned his head halfway toward the doors, but continued to lean forward on the railing, absorbing the chill of the brisk wind. "How'd you know to look for me here?"

Sheppard held up a life sign detector. "Figured you'd be the little dot that wanted to be as far as possible from the other little dots."

"Remind me to lock those up when not being used for official purposes." But he didn't object when the Major ambled over to stand next to him at the railing. "Carson finally sprang you loose?"

"On the condition that I take a few days off from doing anything, quote, 'bloody foolish.' I'm taking that to mean that I get a temporary reprieve from my regular dose of Athosian-style ass-kicking. How is it that you managed to avoid a concussion, anyway?"

"Obviously there's someone in this galaxy with a harder head than you."

"Okay," Sheppard commented slowly. "That's new. The typical McKay brand of humor isn't self-deprecating. Usually it's... well, deprecating everyone else."

Rodney heard the other man's puzzlement immediately. "I'm a man of many talents, Major."

An uncomfortable silence reigned for a few moments as they both stared out into the water. "Lousy mission."

"Noticed that, did you?"

Sheppard cursed under his breath. "For Christ's sake, Rodney, if you're pissed, get pissed. Don't just keep sulking indefinitely. Yell about it for a while and be glad someone's actually willing to listen. You weren't the only one who had the week from hell, all right?"

There was an unfamiliar current in that tone, and Rodney glanced over. A stay in the infirmary had returned the Major's color and bearing to normal, but something dark still lingered behind his eyes. A fresh wave of self-loathing rolled through

Rodney as he realized that Sheppard had been forced to make a number of exceptionally ugly choices during the mission, a burden that until now had gone unnoticed by at least one of his teammates. *And once again we see that the world—any world—does not revolve around Rodney McKay.*

He decided to offer an olive branch in the form of the confession Sheppard had apparently come here to draw out. What the hell—maybe it *would* help in some immeasurable way. "Look down there." Rodney waved a hand at a pier that had taken a pounding in the recently passed storm. "We did everything we could think of, and we just barely made it through. We tried to change things for the better on Dalera, and it all went to hell anyway and will probably revert back to business as usual before long. It's hard to keep from wondering if there really *is* any good we can do out here. Maybe the universe is just going to do what it wants to do, no matter how much we run around and wring our hands."

Fatalism rang loudly in that declaration, but Sheppard seemed unmoved. "I don't believe that, and neither do you."

"Oh, I don't?"

"No. If that were true, you would have wanted to leave the Dalerans to sleep in the bed they made right from the start. You sure wouldn't have busted your butt to defend the Citadel the way you did. It undeniably sucks that it got so bad, but a lot of people are still alive on that planet because of what we did. A lot. Don't trivialize that."

It was a reasonable statement, but for once, Rodney knew he needed more than reason to get past whatever this was. "This from the guy who flipped a coin to decide whether or not to go to another galaxy? The guy who's proved to be utterly indispensable on this expedition, but who wouldn't even be here if not for a piece of metal that fell face-up? You're part of what's screwing up my outlook, damn it."

The resulting laugh caught him off-guard. "*I'm* an accessory to your existential crisis?" Sheppard shook his head, ignoring Rodney's withering glare. "This I have to clear up, just for the record. Okay, yes, I flipped a coin. But I left out the part where

I didn't like the result and flipped it again."

There was a pause while Rodney studied his face, gauging his honesty. "You're serious?"

"Yeah. If we were supposed to go hands-off on everything and expect to be led by the nose through life, what good would it be to have a gigantic brain like yours?"

Rodney's mouth closed with an audible click. "Oh. Well... okay. That's something." It wasn't much, and he was pretty sure they both knew it, but it might keep them going, which was about all he could ask. Any port in a storm, and all that. "I was so sure we could fix things somehow. This is kind of a first, running into something I couldn't fix. Well, maybe not the very first. There was that time when Major...um, Colonel Carter—"

Abruptly he straightened. "Listen, don't think I don't appreciate this. I just... Sometimes I'm not entirely sure what it is we're doing here." The only thing Rodney despised more than not knowing something was admitting it in public. He watched Sheppard for his reaction, already primed to revert to full-on sarcasm at the first sign of danger.

The Major's gaze didn't change. "The best we can." After a moment, he tipped his head toward the door. "Come on. Dr Weir wants to do the debriefing, and since I'm temporarily grounded and have nothing better to do..."

Rodney turned to follow him without a second thought, realizing with a considerable degree of surprise that there were those on this expedition who were worthy of being followed. In a way, he'd envied the Dalerans their faith, as faith of any kind had never come easy to him. In this place, though, it often seemed like faith in each other was all they had to sustain them. Maybe that counted for something, too.

A typical post-mission debriefing lasted approximately an hour and a half. A debriefing with Atlantis's prime team averaged about two hours. This one took nearly four.

Elizabeth listened with amazement to the account of the uprising and the Wraith attack. She noted that the team members traded control of the narrative back and forth, sensing each other's strengths and viewpoints. If this was how they compiled an after-action report, she had little doubt that their off-world capabilities were becoming similarly integrated. Good for them. To look at them a few months ago, four exceedingly different personalities, she wouldn't have believed it.

"Well, I'd like to thank Rodney for his commendable performance on your return trip," she began. "Most people don't have such stressful first solo spaceflights."

Lieutenant Ford snorted. "The Major could've done better even *with* the concussion."

Unexpectedly, Rodney didn't offer a biting retort, only a bored and vaguely morose look. John, however, stepped in. "Obviously not, since I was too busy taking a header into the controls," he pointed out wryly. "We got home, so no whining. But McKay, don't think this'll get you out of your next lesson. I can put up with a lot, but dinged fenders—"

That got the anticipated reaction. "Spare me," Rodney shot back. "There's not a scratch on your beloved ride. I told you they're practically indestructible."

"Jumpers aside," Elizabeth said, redirecting the conversation, "does anybody see a circumstance in which returning to Dalera would be beneficial to us or them?"

Heads shook around the table. "I would've liked to have taken a look inside one of the downed Darts. Some weren't wrecked that badly," John said.

"More importantly," Rodney said, "that Wraith-specific beam. I've got some ideas about that."

"But we'd be running a pretty big risk to go back," John cut him off gently. "If any of the Genes got it in their heads to mess with us, all they'd have to do is park themselves next to the jumper with a Shield, and we'd be grounded. The Ancients put the 'gate in orbit for a reason. If we leave the Dalerans alone, maybe they'll manage to get back on track as far as Dalera's original plan is concerned."

A derisive chuckle emanated from Rodney's side of the table. "Who's laying odds?"

Elizabeth turned toward him. "Not feeling optimistic?"

"Einstein said that the definition of insanity is doing the same thing over and over and expecting a different result."

"We don't know that they'll revert completely back to their old system," she pointed out. "From what you've said, I think they have a reasonable chance of adapting their mindset. Yann in particular seems to have evolved a fairly balanced attitude about the whole system."

"He's only one man."

"We were only four." Teyla's lyrical voice broke into the exchange. "And yet we helped mount the defense that saved Dalera from utter destruction."

Elizabeth exchanged an approving glance with the Athosian woman. At that moment the similarities between them, as the leaders of their respective peoples, seemed especially apparent. "We didn't come to Atlantis simply to find a ZPM and a few gadgets," she stated. "Our mission is much broader than that. We were tasked to learn all we can, from the Ancients and from whomever else we may find along the way. I suspect that this past week has fulfilled our mandate better than you think."

There was a pause before John offered, "Well, firmly in the category of 'good to know on one level and really *not* good on another,' we've got some firsthand evidence of what will and won't kill a Wraith. We also saw enough of the hive ships' destructive capabilities to know that we really don't want to meet one in a dark alley."

Rodney continued to study the table top until he suddenly jumped in his seat and glared at John. Elizabeth suspected that his shin had come into contact with the Major's boot. "I suppose there are avenues to be explored on the topic of electromagnetic field theory and that Wraith beam," mumbled the scientist.

"You mean the Illudium PU-36 Explosive Space Modulator?" Ford put in with a grin.

The expression on Rodney's face was priceless, caught somewhere between annoyance and utter bewilderment. He turned to John for help, but the military commander was already chuckling.

"Marvin the Martian. Ford, I just might reinstate your naming rights for that one."

Hiding her own smile, Elizabeth asked, "Any mission-related information to add, Lieutenant?"

Ford blinked. "Uh, no, ma'am. Just thinking about how Lisera will do. You know, with her new responsibilities and all."

"The Aiden Ford Fan Club loses its only member." Rodney affected a grave mien. "Truly a dark day."

"At least I came back through the 'gate wearing my own clothes."

Elizabeth shook her head and made a shooing motion with her hand. "Get out of here. Take the rest of the day to decompress a little. Rodney, since I know 'decompress' means 'go to the lab' in your mind, check out what Dr Gaul's working on. He said earlier that he'd found something on the long-range sensors. A satellite of some kind, at a unique point between a planet and its sun where the gravitational force does something interesting — ?"

"A Lagrange Point? Really?" Some of the spark returning to his eyes, Rodney stood up from the table. "If you'll excuse me."

The others drifted toward the doors as well, until only John and Elizabeth remained. By unspoken agreement, they moved to stand at the edge of the room, where the 'gate was just visible behind the partitions. "Your cold must be on the way out," he observed.

"It seems to be gone. Strange kind of bug, according to Carson. Different from Earth, but in some ways much the same." She crossed her arms and leaned back against one of the panels. "I think we should talk more seriously about accelerating the gene therapy program on Atlantis. Not only is there the obvious efficiency benefit from having more people who are capable of interacting with the city, but..." She didn't want to compare their expedition to the class struggle on Dalera, but it lurked in the back of her mind.

"Yeah. Anything that might remove an artificial barrier between people sounds like a good idea to me."

Grateful that he seemed to understand, she smiled. "So, for future reference, do you see a circumstance where offering the gene therapy to a culture might be beneficial?"

"Theoretically, sure. The Athosians could certainly have handled it, if it had offered them a viable defense against the Wraith. And it would have worked for the Dalerans if we'd had a little more intel on what was really going on."

"Fair enough. Rodney will be all right, don't you think?"

"I do," John replied gamely. "He got his world pretty well rocked, but he's nothing if not resilient." He glanced out at the control room, where two technicians were testing a console damaged in the storm. "We all are."

"I won't argue with that." Elizabeth cocked an eyebrow. "Out of curiosity, do you have any idea what's interesting about a Lagrange Point?"

"Not really, but I have a feeling it won't be long before I'm forced to find out."

ABOUT THE AUTHORS

Sonny Whitelaw

With a degree in geomorphology and anthropology, Sonny Whitelaw decided that a career in academia wouldn't be as much fun as running a dive charter yacht and adventure tourism business in the South Pacific. Photojournalism came as a natural extension to her travels, and Sonny's work has been featured in numerous international publications, including National Geographic.

Sonny is also the author of *Stargate SG-1: City of the Gods*, *The Rhesus Factor*, a contemporary eco-thriller, and *Ark Ship*, a sci-fi drama. She currently resides in Brisbane with her two children.

For more information, visit www.sonnywhitelaw.com

Elizabeth Christensen

Although currently a resident of central Ohio, Elizabeth Christensen still considers Novi, Michigan, to be her hometown. A civilian engineer with the U.S. Air Force, she works on propulsion and aircraft subsystems projects at Wright-Patterson Air Force Base. She received two aerospace engineering degrees and witnessed five seasons of stellar football from the University of Michigan. When not dodging Nerf balls thrown by her co-workers, she shares pilot-in-command time in a Grumman Tiger airplane with her husband. This is her first novel.

For more information, visit www.elizabethchristensen.com

STARGÅTE
SG·1™

STARGATE
ATLÅNTIS™

**Original novels based on
the hit TV shows,
STARGATE SG-1 and
STARGATE ATLANTIS**

AVAILABLE NOW

**For more information, visit
www.stargatenovels.com**

What you don't know can kill you

STARGATE
ATLANTIS

RELIQUARY

Martha Wells

Based on the hit television series created by
Brad Wright and Robert C. Cooper

Series number: SGA-2

STARGATE ATLANTIS: RELIQUARY

by Martha Wells
Price: £6.99 (UK), $7.99 (US)
ISBN: 0-9547343-7-8

While exploring the unused sections of the Ancient city of Atlantis, Major John Sheppard and Dr. Rodney McKay stumble on a recording device that reveals a mysterious new Stargate address. Believing that the address may lead them to a vast repository of Ancient knowledge, the team embarks on a mission to this uncharted world.

There they discover a ruined city, full of whispered secrets and dark shadows. As tempers fray and trust breaks down, the team uncovers the truth at the heart of the city. A truth that spells their destruction.

With half their people compromised, it falls to Major John Sheppard and Dr. Rodney McKay to risk everything in a deadly game of bluff with the enemy. To fail would mean the fall of Atlantis itself – and, for Sheppard, the annihilation of his very humanity…

Order your copy directly from the publisher today by going to www.stargatenovels.com or send a cheque or money order (currency: GB Pounds) made payable to "Fandemonium" to: Stargate Novels, Fandemonium Books, PO Box 795A, Surbiton KT5 8YB, United Kingdom.

Price
UK orders: £8.30 (£6.99 + £1.31 P&P)
Rest of the World orders: £9.70 (£6.99 + £2.71 P&P).

Or check your local bookshop – available on special order if they are out of stock (quote the ISBN number listed above).

STARGATE ATLANTIS: RISING

by **Sally Malcolm**
Price: £6.99 (UK), $7.99 (US)
ISBN: 0-9547343-5-1

Following the discovery of an Ancient outpost buried deep in the Antarctic ice sheet, Stargate Command sends a

Series number: SGA-1

new team of explorers through the Stargate to the distant Pegasus galaxy.

Emerging in an abandoned Ancient city, the team quickly confirms that they have found the Lost City of Atlantis. But, submerged beneath the sea on an alien planet, the city is in danger of catastrophic flooding unless it is raised to the surface. Things go from bad to worse when the team must confront a new enemy known as the Wraith who are bent on destroying Atlantis.

Stargate Atlantis is the exciting new spin-off of the hit TV show, Stargate SG-1. Based on the script of the pilot episode, Rising is a must-read for all fans and includes deleted scenes and dialog not seen on TV – with photos from the pilot episode.

Series number: SG1-6

SIREN SONG

by Holly Scott and Jaimie Duncan
Price: £6.99
ISBN: 0-9547343-6-X

Bounty-hunter, Aris Boch, once more has his sights on SG-1. But this time Boch isn't interested in trading them for cash. He needs the unique talents of Dr. Daniel Jackson – and he'll do anything to get them.

Taken to Boch's ravaged home-world, Atropos, Colonel Jack O'Neill and his team are handed over to insane Goa'uld, Sebek. Obsessed with opening a mysterious sub-terranean vault, Sebek demands that Jackson translate the arcane writing on the doors. When Jackson refuses, the Goa'uld resorts to devastating measures to ensure his cooperation.

With the vault exerting a malign influence on all who draw near, Sebek compels Jackson and O'Neill toward a horror that threatens both their sanity and their lives. Meanwhile, Carter and Teal'c struggle to persuade the starving people of Atropos to risk everything they have to save SG-1 – and free their desolate world of the Goa'uld, forever.

Order your copy directly from the publisher today by going to www.stargatenovels.com or send a cheque or money order (currency: GB Pounds) made payable to "Fandemonium" to: Stargate Novels, Fandemonium Books, PO Box 795A, Surbiton KT5 8YB, United Kingdom.

Price
UK orders: £8.30 (£6.99 + £1.31 P&P)
South Africa, Australia and New Zealand orders:
£9.70 (£6.99 + £2.71 P&P). Not available outside these territories.

Or check your local bookshop – available on special order if they are out of stock (quote the ISBN number listed above).

THE COST OF HONOR

Part two of two parts

by Sally Malcolm
Price: £6.99
ISBN: 0-9547343-4-3

In the action-packed sequel to *A Matter of Honor*, SG-1 embark on a desperate mission to save SG-10 from the edge of a black hole. But the price of heroism may be more than they can pay...

Returning to Stargate Command, Colonel Jack O'Neill and his team find more has changed in their absence than they had expected. Nonetheless, O'Neill is determined to face the consequences of their unauthorized activities, only to discover the penalty is far worse than anything he could have imagined.

With the fate of Colonel O'Neill and Major Samantha Carter unknown, and the very survival of the SGC threatened, Dr. Daniel Jackson and Teal'c mount a rescue mission to free their team-mates and reclaim the SGC. Yet returning to the Kinahhi homeworld, they learn a startling truth about its ancient foe. And uncover a horrifying secret...

Order your copy directly from the publisher today by going to www.stargatenovels.com or send a cheque or money order (currency: GB Pounds) made payable to "Fandemonium" to: Stargate Novels, Fandemonium Books, PO Box 795A, Surbiton KT5 8YB, United Kingdom.

<u>Price</u>
UK orders: £8.30 (£6.99 + £1.31 P&P)
South Africa, Australia and New Zealand orders:
£9.70 (£6.99 + £2.71 P&P). Not available outside these territories.

Or check your local bookshop – available on special order if they are out of stock (quote the ISBN number listed above).

The team is stranded on a doomed world

STARGATE SG·1

CITY OF THE GODS

Sonny Whitelaw

Based on the hit television series developed by
Brad Wright and Jonathan Glassner

Series number: SG1-4

CITY OF THE GODS

by Sonny Whitelaw
Price: £5.99
ISBN: 0-9547343-3-5

When a Crystal Skull is discovered beneath the Pyramid of the Sun in Mexico, it ignites a cataclysmic chain of events that maroons SG-1 on a dying world.

Xalótcan is a brutal society, steeped in death and sacrifice, where the bloody gods of the Aztecs demand tribute from a fearful and superstitious population. But that's the least of Colonel Jack O'Neill's problems. With Xalótcan on the brink of catastrophe, Dr. Daniel Jackson insists that O'Neill must fulfil an ancient prophesy and lead its people to salvation. But with the world tearing itself apart, can anyone survive?

As fear and despair plunge Xalótcan into chaos, SG-1 find themselves with ringside seats at the end of the world…

• Special section: Excerpts from Dr. Daniel Jackson's mission journal.

Order your copy directly from the publisher today by going to www.stargatenovels.com or send a cheque or money order (currency: GB Pounds) made payable to "Fandemonium" to: **Stargate Novels, Fandemonium Books, PO Box 795A, Surbiton KT5 8YB, United Kingdom.**

<u>Price</u>
UK orders: £7.30 (£5.99 + £1.31 P&P)
South Africa, Australia and New Zealand orders:
£8.70 (£5.99 + £2.71 P&P). Not available outside these territories.

Or check your local bookshop – available on special order if they are out of stock (quote the ISBN number listed above).

A MATTER OF HONOR

Part one of two parts

by Sally Malcolm
Price: £5.99
ISBN: 0-9547343-2-7

Five years after Major Henry Boyd and his team, SG-10, were trapped on the edge of a black hole, Colonel Jack O'Neill discovers a device that could bring them home.

But it's owned by the Kinahhi, an advanced and paranoid people, besieged by a ruthless foe. Unwilling to share the technology, the Kinahhi are pursuing their own agenda in the negotiations with Earth's diplomatic delegation. Maneuvering through a maze of tyranny, terrorism and deceit, Dr. Daniel Jackson, Major Samantha Carter and Teal'c unravel a startling truth – a revelation that throws the team into chaos and forces O'Neill to face a nightmare he is determined to forget.

Resolved to rescue Boyd, O'Neill marches back into the hell he swore never to revisit. Only this time, he's taking SG-1 with him…

Order your copy directly from the publisher today by going to www.stargatenovels.com or send a cheque or money order (currency: GB Pounds) made payable to "Fandemonium" to: Stargate Novels, Fandemonium Books, PO Box 795A, Surbiton KT5 8YB, United Kingdom.

<u>Price</u>
UK orders: £7.30 (£5.99 + £1.31 P&P)
South Africa, Australia and New Zealand orders:
£8.70 (£5.99 + £2.71 P&P). Not available outside these territories.

Or check your local bookshop – available on special order if they are out of stock (quote the ISBN number listed above).

SACRIFICE MOON

By Julie Fortune
Price: £5.99
ISBN: 0-9547343-1-9

Series number: SG1-2

Sacrifice Moon follows the newly commissioned SG-1 on their first mission through the Stargate.

Their destination is Chalcis, a peaceful society at the heart of the Helos Confederacy of planets. But Chalcis harbors a dark secret, one that pitches SG-1 into a world of bloody chaos, betrayal and madness. Battling to escape the living nightmare, Dr. Daniel Jackson and Captain Samantha Carter soon begin to realize that more than their lives are at stake. They are fighting for their very souls.

But while Col Jack O'Neill and Teal'c struggle to keep the team together, Daniel is hatching a desperate plan that will test SG-1's fledgling bonds of trust and friendship to the limit...

Order your copy directly from the publisher today by going to www.stargatenovels.com or send a cheque or money order (currency: GB Pounds) made payable to "Fandemonium" to: **Stargate Novels, Fandemonium Books, PO Box 795A, Surbiton KT5 8YB, United Kingdom.**

<u>Price</u>
UK orders: £7.30 (£5.99 + £1.31 P&P)
South Africa, Australia and New Zealand orders:
£8.70 (£5.99 + £2.71 P&P). Not available outside these territories.

Or check your local bookshop – available on special order if they are out of stock (quote the ISBN number listed above).